RUDYARD KIPLING

K I M

Rudyard Kipling's KIM is the tale of an Irish boy raised as an Indian in imperial India. It is the story of his coming of age in a world of high adventure, mystic quests, and hidden games of espionage played out between the Russians and the British in the mountain passages of Asia. It is a book that has enthralled generations of readers both by the exuberance of its storytelling and its vital and unforgettable portrait of the India of bazaars and sacred rivers, holy men and rogues, ancient custom and colonial society.

EVERYMAN,
I WILL GO WITH THEE,
AND BE THY GUIDE,
IN THY MOST NEED
TO GO BY THY SIDE

RUDYARD KIPLING

KIM

WITH AN INTRODUCTION
BY JOHN BAYLEY

EVERYMAN'S LIBRARY
Alfred A. Knopf   New York   London   Toronto

203

THIS IS A BORZOI BOOK
PUBLISHED BY ALFRED A. KNOPF

First published 1901
First included in Everyman's Library, 1995
Copyright by The National Trust for Places of Natural Beauty and
Historic Interest
Introduction, Bibliography and Chronology Copyright © 1995
by Everyman's Library
Typography by Peter B. Willberg
Fifth printing (US)

US website: www.randomhouse.com/everymans

ISBN: 978-0-679-44360-5 (US)
978-1-85715-203-6 (UK)

A CIP catalogue reference for this book is available from the
British Library

Book design by Barbara de Wilde and Carol Devine Carson

Typeset in the UK by AccComputing, North Barrow, Somerset

Printed and bound in Germany by GGP Media GmbH, Pössneck

KIM

INTRODUCTION

Kim was first published in 1901, the year before Kipling and his wife settled at Batemans, the house in Sussex where they were to live until his death in 1936. So in a sense *Kim* represented not only the crowning achievement of the Indian experience that had meant so much to him, but also a final farewell to the East. He had left India for the last time twelve years before. His tales and poems from India – notably *Plain Tales from the Hills*, and *Barrack Room Ballads* – had made him a literary celebrity when he arrived back in London, and he was determined to capitalize on this, and to extend the range of his writing to English and American subjects. In 1892 he married Caroline Balestier, an American girl, and lived for the next four years near her parents' home in Vermont. But Indian experiences from his early life continued to fuel his creative energy, and it was here that he wrote *The Jungle Book*, published in 1894, and here too that the picaresque Indian novel that was to become *Kim* first began to take shape.

It took him the longest time to write of any of his books. And its origins as a story of India go right back to the early days in Lahore, when Kipling worked as an apprentice journalist on *The Civil and Military Gazette*, and lived with his mother and father in their big bungalow outside the city. Although he had been born in India, Kipling had spent his childhood and schooldays in England (he was at school at Westward Ho! which he describes in *Stalky and Co*) and he returned to work on the Lahore paper when he was not yet seventeen. He was an immensely precocious young man; and it was not long before he was writing marvellously vivid and detailed sketches of Indian city life with titles like 'The City of Dreadful Night', 'The Gate of a Hundred Sorrows', and 'On the City Wall'. Interestingly, there is a stark and almost surrealist quality about these early visions of the teeming multisocial life of India, which is for the most part absent when Kipling looks back on the India he had once known, in the more mellow and retrospective panorama of *Kim*. There is a parellel here with the young Dickens, whose first impressions of London life in *Sketches by Boz* have little of the lovable or roguish picturesque of the scenes and characters in his later novels, but are in most cases harsh and squalid, as well as bitterly knowing.

Most of Kipling's early sketches were published in collections such as *Life's Handicap* and *Plain Tales from the Hills*; but while still in India he formed the intention of writing a much more ambitious work, which would have been based on the raffish characters and odd misfits whom we encounter in the opium dens, doss houses, and prostitutes' houses of the earlier stories. This large-scale novel of Anglo-Indian low life would certainly have been highly original, for the time and place, and would have been based on the precedents of Balzac and Zola, writers whom the youthful Kipling greatly admired. The influence of de Maupassant is also highly visible throughout the early tales, giving them their terse vividness and their not altogether convincing flavour of expert local knowledge and world-weary cynicism. Kipling was not yet twenty after all, and very far from being world-weary: in fact he took, and always continued to take, a huge delight in everything he saw, as well as a consuming social and technical interest.

This novel was to have been called *Mother Maturin*, a rambling account of a broken-down old Irish lodging-house keeper and her patrons, purporting to be written by one of them, an alcoholic and opium addict called Jellaludin Macintosh. He was to be portrayed as a drifter with one foot in the grave, who is still intensely proud of his Scottish ancestry, and the academic credentials that he claims ('I was once a Fellow of the College'). There were indeed then a surprising number of such drop-outs in the big cities of India, forerunners of the hippies and drug-users who frequent the Far East in our own time. Kipling encountered many of them, and encouraged their reminiscences, the fruit of which appears in that brief but masterful fantasy, 'The Man Who Would Be King', the tale he was later to write about two tramps who founded a kind of native empire, somewhere behind Afghanistan.

Kipling was fascinated by such misfits and drop-outs, though it is to be doubted if he ever met any who were still in good enough shape to have the ambition of becoming native kings. But no doubt some were still resourceful enough, and many were Irish, like Mother Maturin herself. Kipling was always delighted by Irish people and admired them; as he admired soldiers like Private (sometimes Sergeant) Mulvaney, of the *Soldiers Three* tales, a kindly, eloquent, and ultimately rather tragic figure, the backbone of the British army and intensely proud of his regiment, in which he was frequently punished and reduced in rank for fits of drunkenness or insubordination. Kim's father was to be such a man; and there was already a hint of the subject matter of *Kim*, although Kipling at this stage seems to have been more intrigued by the European flotsam and jetsam among India's teeming millions, than he was interested by the more complex world of Indian culture and society.

At any rate *Mother Maturin*, though some of it was written, was never completed or published. Kipling's father seems to have been partly responsible for discouraging his son about the project, and Kipling was always intensely filial, devoted to his parents, and keen to enlist their help with his work. J. Lockwood Kipling was himself very much a scholar and man of learning, curator of the Lahore museum and an expert on Buddhism and on Indian art and sculpture. It was no doubt his influence and knowledge that makes Buddhism bulk so large in the world of *Kim*, although as a historical fact it never took root in the plains of India, where the gods and beliefs of Hinduism remained the norm.

As a man with a highly respectable and respected place in Anglo-Indian society, Kipling *père* may have felt that his brilliant son's interest in low life was not quite the thing. If so, he showed percipience; for the slow-maturing masterpiece of *Kim* was clearly to be a much more remarkable and considerable achievement, coming as it did to crown his son's literary reputation; whereas a youthfully raffish picaresque novel of Anglo-Indian low life would hardly have given that career an auspicious beginning. Kipling was always very conscious of the need to make the right sort of sensation with his work at the right time; and he was conscious, too, of his own weakness in long-range narrative and plotting, a weakness that the superb assurance of *Kim* sets aside, although it is still visible there.

Kipling's mother pointed this out to him as he strove to complete the novel while living at his parents' retirement home in Wiltshire; and she teased him gently about his difficulties where novel plotting was concerned. He always took her advice in good part and profited from it, for she was well known as one of the wittiest and most intelligent women in Anglo-India: there is no doubt a good deal of her in the brilliantly sharp-tongued Mrs Hauksbee of *Plain Tales from the Hills*, as well as in the masterful and strong-willed old Hindu lady, or Sahiba, who befriends Kim.

So this was the background of Kipling's only undoubted masterpiece in the novel form – what of its purpose and method? Something is revealed by the title Kipling originally thought of – 'Kim of the Rishti' – that is, Kim of the Irish, or the Irish regiment. It was more important at first, perhaps, that Kim was a child of the regiment than that he had become to all intents and purposes a little Hindu boy. There were many novels of the time, and later, which featured fantasies of picturesque natives or wild men who turn out to be English or European, even English aristocrats, as in the case of Tarzan or of that famous best-seller *The Sheikh*. *Kim* in one sense is not so far away, for the popular style of archetype has always exercised great attraction in any widely read literary work.

It seems, however, that as he worked with a slowness rare for him on his long considered project, Kipling became increasingly absorbed by the contrast he found he had set up – almost accidentally. It was not a simple matter of East is East and West is West, on the theme of which he had written poems and stories when he was a young man. Rather it was something more like the opposite. *Kim* is one of the very few texts of the time – perhaps the only one – to suggest in copious if indirect detail that all the world's separate races do the same thing in their own way, and have the same kinds of degree of enlightenment or non-enlightenment. All exercise the same kinds of understanding, and our understanding will reveal their essential similarity.

About the same time he was wrestling with the latter part of the story of *Kim*, Kipling wrote a poem called 'Jobson's Amen', which makes the same kind of point with a greater and more obvious degree of irony. Jobson is a son of Empire, a humble worker in the governmental projects of improvement in agriculture and engineering, but he does not despise the races he works among; rather he has himself become one of them, in terms of an essential awareness.

> 'Blessed be the English and all their ways and works.
> Cursed be the Infidels, Hereticks, and Turks!'
> 'Amen,' quo' Jobson, 'but where I used to lie
> Was neither Candle, Bell nor Book to curse my brethren by ...

The English the English the English are best: but – Jobson has toiled in Africa, Asia, India, and he doesn't intend to go home.

> 'Amen,' quo' Jobson, 'but where I mean to die
> Is neither rule nor calliper to judge the matter by:

> But Himalaya heavenward-heading, sheer and vast, sheer and vast,
> In a million summits bedding on the last world's past –
> A certain sacred mountain where the scented cedars climb,
> And – the feet of my Beloved hurrying back through Time!'

Kipling's feeling for the sacred mountains of India had always been of a near mystic sort – one of his most memorable stories from *The Jungle Book* is 'The Miracle of Purun Bhagat', which tells of a very high-ranking and Europeanized Indian official, who abandons fame and office to end his days as a hermit in the high hills.

To a degree remarkable at that time, Kipling gave no precedence to the faith of his own class and country – rather the opposite. 'Lispeth' of *Plain Tales from the Hills*, the proto-type of 'the Woman of Shamlegh' in *Kim*, finally rejects missionary endeavour and the Christian message.

> Look, you have cast out Love! What Gods are these
> You bid me please?
> The Three in One, the One in Three? No so!
> To my own Gods I go.
> It may be they shall give me greater ease
> Than your cold Christ and tangled Trinities.

Kipling was well aware of the European crisis of faith in his own time, of the sort he had found in writers like Hardy, or more flamboyantly in such a poet as Swinburne; but by the time he wrote *Kim* this crisis no longer seemed to him to matter very greatly. Not only are all the creeds of *Kim* a matter for the individual, or for the kind of society that holds them, but they have no force beside and without the power of human love, the deep instinct which drives the lama unknowingly, as much as it does Kim and his other benefactors. This is attested in the last words of the novel, when the lama feels that he has found his sacred River of the Arrow, and that his quest is ended.

> He crossed his hands on his lap and smiled, as a man may who has won salvation for himself and his beloved.

Clearly Kipling does not actually believe in the lama's mystic river, and in his quest, however much he may respect the impulses behind it; but he did very much believe in, and understand very deeply, the lama's feelings for Kim himself. While he was writing the novel, at the end of his time in America, he lost his own first-born and dearly loved daughter Josephine in an influenza epidemic, in which he himself also nearly died; and the references in his work to this 'Best Beloved' are always very moving. The spirit of his child, come back through time, appears in the later stories, as well as in the poems in *Puck of Pook's Hill*, even in the last line of 'Jobson's Amen'. There is no doubt that there is in *Kim* a mature experience of love, and of loss as well; for the lama's anguish when he sees his *chela* taken from him by the two chaplains and the soldiers, and thinks they may never meet again, is one of the most moving moments in the novel.

> His God is as his Fates assign –
> His prayer is all the world's – and mine.

But apart from these high matters there is of course in *Kim* a less regenerate Kipling who revels in the Great Game – the business of spying and being spied upon, across the huge and shadowy border between the southern conquests of the old Tsarist empire and the sprawling territories of British India. This was then a very real business; and indeed it could be said to have led indirectly to the nemesis of the Soviet empire, when Russia invaded Afghanistan, that disputed territory between the imperialist powers for a hundred and fifty years. But Kipling does not really do this spy theme justice, in terms of its potential as a subject; not does he even try to. He was no John Buchan or Ian Fleming; and he had no knack for the extended thriller. The foreign agents and spies in *Kim* are mere puppets, and the plot deals with them in a distinctly perfunctory way. It is plain that Kiping's heart is not in this part of the story, although elsewhere in his work he takes the themes of ancient and modern warfare, and competitive violence and revenge, very seriously indeed, exploring them with a passion that led, both in his time and our own, to his rejection as a great writer by the orthodox liberal establishment.

But even that establishment has had to make an exception for *Kim*. In it Kipling's love of Indian life shines through the rather flimsy outlines of the story, and recurs again and again in the detail of the folk he describes, and the vivid impression of colloquial speech with which he endows them. What remains most in the reader's mind perhaps, and appears more marked if he returns later to Kipling's strange masterpiece, is the way in which the business of living – intrigue, passion, desire; the wish and ambition to be someone in the world's complex affairs – are contrasted with the counter-urge towards peace, freedom, detachment; death, it may be, rather than life. The lama of course gives the proper Buddhist view of the dilemma – being bound upon the Wheel of Things, and the possibility of Nirvana – but what matters much more is the power with which the book conveys these things in its own literary and imaginative terms. Kipling's vision of India seems to make the contrast between detachment and tranquillity on the one hand, and frenzied pullulating activity on the other, seem as natural as the Indian weather, the heat and the rains.

... he looked upon the trees and the broad fields, with the thatched huts hidden among crops – looked with strange eyes unable to take up the size and proportion and use of things – stared for a still half-hour. All that while he felt, though he could not put it into words, that his soul was out of gear with its surroundings – a cog-wheel unconnected with any machinery, just like the idle cog-wheel of a cheap Beheea sugar-crusher laid by in a corner. The breezes fanned

over him, the parrots shrieked at him, the noises of the populated
house behind – squabbles, orders, and reproofs – hit on dead ears.

'I am Kim. I am Kim. And what is Kim?' His soul repeated it
again and again.

Kim at the end of the book has admittedly been very ill, after
the exhaustion of bringing the lama home from the high hills,
and having his adventure with the two foreign spies; but his
vision of things here seems entirely and quite naturally
consonant with the whole tenor of the book. There is nothing
strained or mystical about it. It is just the way things are, and
are bound to be in India; and presently Kim regains his
ordinary daily sense of fitting into a meaningful and coherent
world, in which he has his own place among the teeming
millions, whose eyes are bright with their own individual
purposes.

Entirely typical of Kipling too, and just right in its context,
is his implicit comparison of man and his mental processes to
one of man's own machines – the 'cheap Beheea sugar-crusher'
– which conveys both the triviality of human activity in the
vast perspective revealed by the experience of India, and
Kipling's own mania for significant detail. It is worth contrasting in its turn a passage such as this with the much more
emphatic and self-important symbolism of E. M. Forster's *A
Passage to India*: the echo of the Marabar caves, and Mrs
Moore's vision of emptiness as she returns to Bombay, and the
unexpected death that awaits her. Forster makes the point at
length, and with his own spell of convincing eloquence, and
yet it is all there in *Kim*, as a practical reality, not to be
bothered about too much by men and women who have their
own work to get on with.

For this is the point on which Kipling does lay emphasis –
emphasis of his own kind. There is always work to be done,
and the fact that it is ultimately and totally without purpose is
neither here nor there. The Great Game must go on; the
masses must be fed, cared for, and allocated their own certain
and definite place in the scheme of things. The lama does not
have any monopoly of wisdom, or even a claim to wisdom any
greater than that of Strickland the policeman or Mahbub Ali
the horse-dealer. Not only are all bound up on the Wheel of

Things, which is the lama's and the Buddhist way of putting it, but all are answerable in the here and now to the requirements of what Kipling in 'If' called 'the unforgiving minute'. 'One instant's toil to thee denied/Stands all eternity's offence' is for Kipling a truth as important as may be the infinite cycles of birth and death, or the attainment of Nirvana.

So work is the thing, even in a universe of infinite size and apparent meaninglessness. We are told at the beginning that little Kim 'did nothing with an immense success', which is fine for a child but not for an adolescent, who must be set to work. Work is itself both an aspect and the reward of curiosity, the *sine qua non* of worldly happiness. When Colonel Creighton enlists Kim in the secret service he tells him 'in three days thou wilt go with me to Lucknow, seeing and hearing new things all the while.'

If work is salvation for the individual, and particularly, in this context, for those who toil in the full reality of the Indian phenomenon, as Kipling presents it, work is also the bringer and guarantor of virtue. One of the most striking things about *Kim* is how effortlessly and without any fuss at all Kipling seems to establish the related but contrasting *goodness* of Kim and the lama. Truly good characters in fiction are rare, as has often been pointed out: the novelist finds it far easier, as well as more rewarding, to explore and analyse evil, weakness and duplicity. Kipling shows no sign of being particularly interested in the virtues of the lama, or of Kim, but he keeps them steadily in view, enlarging them as the action proceeds and their quality and meaning become clearer to the reader. The lama has a very just idea of Kim's character – 'thoughtful, wise and courteous, but something of a small imp' – and Kim understands the lama and his 'holiness', though without knowing or caring that he does so.

That said, it has not infrequently been implied by critics hostile to Kipling and his world that *Kim* gives an inherently sentimental view not only of India but of human nature and human affairs generally. As regards India, the best reply to that seems to be the comment of the venerable and delightful Indian author Nirad Chaudhuri, who said that *Kim* 'is the very best picture of India by an English author'. The more deep-lying charge, of seeing the world in general in *Kim* through a pair of rose-coloured spectacles, is more difficult to assess, and so to answer. Does it mean that Kipling leaves out the more brutal factual aspects of life and death, procreation or excretion? (One of Chaudhuri's own severest criticisms of his fellow countrymen is their insanitary toilet habits.) If so, the same charge would apply equally to every nineteenth-century novelist, from Dickens to Henry James. The point of course is what, in this direction, can be implied, suggested and inferred; and here Kipling is as realistic as any of his peers. India is not only a magical but also a terrifying place, where a human being may be alive in the morning and dead by nightfall: and when that truth in the book is understood, as it is in Kipling's other stories of India, all else follows. It is true that Kim, like Mahbub Ali and the Sahiba and all the rest of them, is given, as it were, temporary leave from the hazards of real existence: no story could function if that were not the case in some degree. True, too, that Kim is, as Angus Wilson put it, 'flirtatious with all and sundry', without being even in his adolescence a fully sexual being. But that too is taken care of by the way in which the Woman of Shamlegh (a unique and Kiplingesque mixture of a games mistress with the Wife of Bath) yearns for him sexually; while the Sahiba watches over him with all the sexual jealousy of a lover and protector.

Kipling in fact – to quote again the words of Angus Wilson in his excellent study *The Strange Ride of Rudyard Kipling* – successfully contrived in *Kim* 'to create a world that is real and ideal at one and the same time.' It is both a fairy story and an accurate and highly detailed picture of a complex and colourful society. (Again we should not forget Kipling's early and profound debt to the French realists Balzac and Zola, nor the fact that both have been cogently reassessed by modern critics as fantasists and romantics on a fabulous scale.) There is no barrier in Kipling's world between the factual and the marvellous. Rather the two are aspects of each other, and Kim's endless wish for further sights and journeys, like Sinbad's in *The Arabian Nights*, shows how the two can be one and the same.

The 'insatiable curiosity' that gets the Elephant's Child into trouble in *Just So Stories*, also preserves him in that charming fable, and makes him what he is. That curiosity is the driving force in all Kipling's work; and, oddly enough, it is much rarer among writers – even great writers – than their readers might assume. Writers more often stake out their own patch, the area in which they are at home, and in which they feel a full creative and authorial confidence. And indeed readers in one sense rather prefer this. They like to feel at home with a writer, and to know how they stand in relation to his work. We certainly cannot do this with Kipling. Unlike most novelists he is all over the place. A comparison of any such writer with such a giant as Shakespeare is obviously beside the point; and indeed there are many ways in which Kipling is totally un-Shakespearian. He is assertive at all times, even preacherly: wanting always to buttonhole the reader and give him the facts of the case, and what he should think about it as a result. His convictions and prejudices are all on the surface; and he can be frenetic, almost hysterical, in the way he airs and propounds them.

But, having said that, there is usually another and a deeper side to his desire to tell us what he thinks, and to impose his own views. As with D. H. Lawrence, with whom he has a surprising amount in common as a writer of genius, there is a spirit in his work which bids us, as Lawrence himself put it, 'to trust the tale rather than the teller'. Kipling was perfectly conscious of that spirit, and claimed to defer to it in all matters that concerned art. He called it his 'Daemon'. Without this strange power, as he remarks in a poem, a writer like himself is 'even as other men'. The Daemon's ways are mysterious; and a writer can only do his best work by putting himself passively under its influence and at its disposal. Sometimes, so present is the personality of Kipling in all his work, the reader might be forgiven for thinking that this Daemon is remarkably like Kipling himself, is indeed indistinguishable from him. Kipling was no dramatist, and in this sense he is wholly unlike Shakespeare, or even unlike the poet Browning, whom he had so passionately admired when he was young, and whose influence can be seen in many of his dialogue and monologue poems.

And yet the presence of another and less intrusive person than himself is certainly there in all his best work – quietly contradicting, or quietly suggesting a rather different point of view. It is in the silence that we can feel behind the speech of the lama in *Kim*, giving the lie in the end to all human effort, as to all those unregenerate impulses that are so evident in Kipling: impulses towards self-assurance, confidence in mission and in race, aggression, repression, revenge. All these more obviously demonic factors drove Kipling on, as a man among men; and yet he was right to suggest that his own 'Daemon' – and the difference in spelling is clearly not accidental – was not in this sense demonic, but very much the opposite.

The writer, like a child, asks questions, asserts, and pretends to knowledge. The Daemon, like an ideal adult, knows, tolerates and understands. That seems in the end to be the relation between the contrasting sides of Kipling's genius, and it is of course very evident in all the relationships in *Kim*. Kim's destiny, and his quest, are very different from the lama's: and yet the pair of them not only live harmoniously together but share a deep affection and understanding. It is an ideal paradigm of the child–adult relation. Kim represents the happy and harmonious side of Kipling's nature, but of course there was a very different side, and a very different story of childhood. If Kim's is an ideal world of childhood, or rather one that represented, as Angus Wilson said, the real and the ideal together, then the opposite side of the coin is that earlier dark and powerful tale 'Baa Baa, Black Sheep'. It tells the story of what happened to Kipling himself as a child when his parents sent him and his sister home – the usual thing in the Anglo-Indian society of those days – to be educated and looked after in England. Kipling's mother and father had bad luck in their choice of a home and a foster-parent, although there is some evidence that Kipling himself did not have so dreadful a time as the boy Punch does in the story. Its most poignant aspect is not so much the injuries and injustice inflicted on the child, or that he feels to be inflicted, as the sheer horror of deprivation: loss of parents, loss of home, above all loss of his childhood India – the paradise withdrawn from him at the age of six or seven.

It is that paradise which is recaptured in *Kim*. The reader who wishes to understand Kipling, and the contrasting sides of his genius, can hardly do better for a start than to read *Kim*, in conjunction with 'Baa Baa, Black Sheep', and two of the earlier Indian stories: 'The Strange Ride of Morrowbie Jukes', and 'At the End of the Passage'. Both are nightmares, illustrative of loneliness, fear, and the horror of great desolation; and both tell a tale of India that is not in *Kim*. Kipling knew both sides of the matter; and either he or his Daemon was abundantly capable of showing them to us. These works can be read again and again; and all have the power of great art to sustain and console us, even at their most harrowing.

Of all comparatively recent writers – and it is worth remembering that although he was of an earlier generation, he died at a later date than D. H. Lawrence – Kipling may be the one who makes the present day reader most wonder at the sheer *otherness* of the past, while in the same moment contriving to make that past seem as alive as the present.

Foreignness and familiarity meet on unique terms in his books, as do so many other contrasts: reticence with vulgarity, a fanatic earnestness with a relaxed and engaging humour; joy with woe. And as Blake wrote:

> Joy and woe are woven fine,
> A clothing for the soul divine;
> And when this we truly know,
> Safely through the world we go.

That verse seems oddly right for Kim and for his journey; and it would be an amusing exercise in comparative wisdom to reflect what the lama would make of it. *Kim* has its own secret inside, like all of Kipling's works, and even what might be called its secret jokes. 'Little Friend of all the World', for example, may strike the reader at first as sentimental. But it is intended to be, like all the flowery phraseology of Oriental language. Kim, we should remember, is a Little Friend of all the World in the same sense that for the police Sahib who knows the language, and knows how to turn a compliment, the elderly Hindu Sahiba is a 'Moon of Paradise', a 'Disturber of

Integrity', and 'Dispenser of Delights'. Kipling always enjoyed a joke, and for preference quite an obscure one.

It remains for me to comment on the, at that time, unparalleled brilliance of Kipling's descriptions in *Kim* of the East, and Eastern scenery. A vision of the Gangetic plain and of the Grand Trunk Road, with the myriad flocks of green parrots screeching past into mango and bamboo plantations, is likely to remain with the reader as abidingly as Kipling's account of the Himalayas, a world of mountains and vistas so huge that 'one day's march carried them no further, it seemed, than a dreamer's clogged pace bears him in a nightmare'. Today those Himalayas are climbed and tramped over in all seasons by cosmopolitan parties fully equipped with the latest technical devices, but in Kipling's time the great mountains were still truly mysterious, their summits unclimbed and their slopes and valleys not yet surveyed. Kipling had seen them and walked a little way among them, and the vision remained with him.

He is equally good on the urban sprawl of Lucknow, Umballa or Lahore, and the Indian world of the train. As he observes in the first chapter, everyone in that teeming world necessarily lived, despite religion and the caste system, on the closest possible terms with everyone else. The great gun Zam-Zammah is a microcosm of the unending layers of Indian history, Moslem following Hindu, and the English the Mogul conquerors; while the immense and complex social fabric of India remains unchanged. Little Chota Lal, one of Kim's urchin acquaintance, scrambling up Zam-Zammah 'in his gilt-embroidered cap', is used as social illustration. 'His father was worth perhaps half a million sterling, but India is the only truly democratic country in the world.' Those telling social observations, jauntily and as it were negligently thrown off, are typical of Kipling's method, a method that was to make him admired by the serious-minded practitioners of the new science of Sociology – men like Durkheim and Weber – when they came to read him.

The whole feel and atmosphere of *Kim* depends on this fact that everyone talks to everyone else, forming one gigantic and involuntary family. The same point is glanced at again in the fourth chapter, when the lama and Kim have been adopted by the redoubtable old Sahiba, who travels the Grand Trunk Road with her motley mixed entourage. 'The old lady had retreated behind her curtains, but mixed most freely in the talk, her servants arguing with and contradicting her as servants do throughout the East.' It is these extended glimpses of Indian life and society which give such a durable and endless fascination to Kipling's book. Indeed, some of its readers and critics have been reminded of Chaucer's *Canterbury Tales*, whose vanished medieval world bears no small resemblance to the Indian world of *Kim* – a world which has also vanished or is vanishing today.

Beside these things, as I have said, the 'story' of *Kim* exists only to keep the wonderful and colourful tapestry in motion. However much the military experts, like Creighton Sahib, are reputed to know of India, their activities are stuck, so to speak, on the outside, and they are only ciphers compared to the book's true realities. Even so, those activities provide moments of such sheer descriptive audacity and brilliance that the reader's breath is taken away. After Kim has discomfited the two sinister foreigners, and purloined their precious booty of maps, codes and secret surveys, he finds himself reluctantly compelled to get rid of all their expensive gear; and this he does by pitching it over the edge of a Himalaya, into the bottomless drop of what is known ironically by the inhabitants as 'Shamlegh midden', where no human foot has trod. The passage is full of Kiplingesque *schadenfreude*, superbly suited to the child in Kim.

A thousand feet below lay a long, lazy, round-shouldered bank of mist, as yet untouched by the morning sun. A thousand feet below that was a hundred-year-old pine-forest. He could see the green tops looking like a bed of moss when a wind-eddy thinned the cloud.

'No! I don't think any one will go after *you*!'

The wheeling basket vomited its contents as it dropped. The theodolite hit a jutting cliff-ledge and exploded like a shell; the books, inkstands, paint-boxes, compasses, and rulers showed for a few seconds like a swarm of bees. Then they vanished; and, though Kim, hanging half out of the window, strained his young ears, never a sound came up from the gulf.

'Five hundred – a thousand rupees could not buy them,' he thought sorrowfully.

After the marvellous bravura passage of visual and evocative description, Kim's own little rueful reflection is entirely typical of the charm of the book, and of Kipling's magic in it. This writer, or his Daemon, wrote it well.

John Bayley

JOHN BAYLEY is former Thomas Warton Professor of English Literature at the University of Oxford. He is the author of *Tolstoy and the Novel* and books about Hardy, Shakespeare and Housman.

SELECT BIBLIOGRAPHY

———

RUDYARD KIPLING, *Plain Tales from the Hills*, Macmillan, 1888.

——*Life's Handicap*, Macmillan, 1891.

——*Something of Myself*, Macmillan, 1937.

BAYLEY, JOHN, 'The False Structure', *English Literature in Transition*, Athlone Press, 1986.

CARRINGTON, CHARLES, *Rudyard Kipling: His Life and Work*, Macmillan, 1955; 3rd edition 1978. The official biography – and the best.

CORNELL, LOUIS L., *Kipling in India*, Macmillan and St Martin's Press, 1966.

DOBREE, BONAMY, *Rudyard Kipling: Realist and Fabulist*, Oxford University Press, 1967.

RUTHERFORD, ANDREW, ed., *Kipling's Mind and Art* (critical essays), Oliver & Boyd, 1964.

SANDISON, ALAN, *The Wheel of an Empire*, Macmillan, 1967.

TOMPKINS, J. M. S., *The Art of Rudyard Kipling*, Methuen, 1959.

WILSON, ANGUS, *The Strange Ride of Rudyard Kipling*, Secker & Warburg, 1977.

WOODRUFF, PHILIP, *The Men Who Ruled India*, Jonathan Cape, Part 1, 1953; Part 2, 1954.

A Note on the Text: This text of *Kim* is taken from the definitive Sussex Edition of 1937–9, including all Kipling's own revisions.

CHRONOLOGY

DATE	AUTHOR'S LIFE	LITERARY CONTEXT
1865	Birth of Rudyard Kipling (30 December) to John Lockwood Kipling and Alice Kipling (*née* Macdonald) in Bombay, where his father is Professor of Architectural Sculpture at the Jeejeebhoy School of Art.	Dickens: *Our Mutual Friend*. Carroll: *Alice's Adventures in Wonderland*. Arnold: *Essays in Criticism* (1st series). Chatterji: *Durgeśanandini*.
1868	Kipling accompanies his mother to England. Birth of his sister Alice Macdonald Kipling ('Trix') in London. Return to Bombay.	Dostoevsky: *The Idiot*. Morris: *The Earthly Paradise* (to 1870). Browning: *The Ring and the Book*. Collins: *The Moonstone*. Harte: *The Luck of the Roaring Camp and Other Sketches*.
1869		Tolstoy: *War and Peace*. Zola: *Thérèse Raquin*. Verne: *Journey Round the World in Eighty Days*. Gilbert: *Bab Ballads*.
1871	The Kiplings visit England again, returning to Bombay without their children, who are left in the care of Captain and Mrs Holloway at Southsea. Kipling later described their home as 'The House of Desolation'. Christmas visits to The Grange in Fulham, home of his Aunt Georgie and her husband the Pre-Raphaelite painter Edward Burne-Jones (William Morris and his family were also regular guests) were among the few high spots of these early years in England.	George Eliot: *Middlemarch* (to 1872). Ruskin: *Fors Clavigera* (to 1878). Carroll: *Through the Looking-Glass*. Macdonald: *At the Back of the North Wind*. Abdullah Bilgrami: *The Romance of Amir-Hamzah*.
1872		Turgenev: 'Spring Torrents'. Zola: *La Curée*. Macdonald: *The Princess and the Goblin*.
1873–4		

End of American Civil War. Assassination of Lincoln. Lord John Russell becomes British Prime Minister, following death of Palmerston. Rebellion in Jamaica brutally suppressed. Colonial Laws Validity Act: colonial legislatures ennabled to pass their own laws provided that these do not contravene statutes of Westminster Parliament.

Disraeli forms Conservative ministry (February). Abyssinian campaign. Flogging abolished as punishment in the British army. First annual Trades Union Congress held in Manchester. Gladstone Prime Minister (December).

Suez Canal opens. Red River Rebellion in Canada. Disestablishment of Irish Church.

Paris Commune. End of Franco-Prussian War. Kaiser Wilhelm I of Prussia proclaimed German Emperor at Versailles. Abolition of purchase of army commissions. Trade Unions legalized in Britain. Royal Albert Hall opened. Meeting of Stanley and Livingstone at Ujiji. Darwin: *The Descent of Man.*

Vote by Secret Ballot at Parliamentary elections imposed by law. Murder of Earl of Mayo, Indian Viceroy. Disraeli's Crystal Palace speech exalting the Crown as focus of the new imperialism.

Ashanti war (Gold Coast).

DATE	AUTHOR'S LIFE	LITERARY CONTEXT
1875	Kipling's father appointed Principal of the Mayo College of Art in Lahore, and Curator of the Lahore Museum.	Trollope: *The Way We Live Now*. Eliot: *Daniel Deronda* (to 1876).
1876		Twain: *Tom Sawyer*.
1877	Kipling's mother in England. Spends summer with the children in Epping and then takes lodgings in London.	Tolstoy: *Anna Karenina*. Zola: *L'Assommoir*. Flaubert: *Trois Contes*.
1878	Kipling enters the United Services College at Westward Ho! in north Devon. Cormell Price, the headmaster, encourages his enthusiasm for literature. Kipling's father arrives in England (the first time his son has seen him since 1871): they go to Paris where John Lockwood Kipling is in charge of the Indian exhibit at the Paris Exhibition.	Hardy: *The Return of the Native*. Henry James: 'Daisy Miller'.
1879		Stevenson: *Travels with a Donkey*. Meredith: *The Egoist*.
1880	Kipling meets and falls in love with Florence Garrard.	Dostoevsky: *The Brothers Karamazov*. Maupassant: 'Boule de suif'. Henty: *The Young Buglers*.
1881	Edits United Services College's *Chronicle*. *Schoolboy Lyrics* privately printed in Lahore.	James: *The Portrait of a Lady*; *Washington Square*. Harris: *Uncle Remus*.
1882	Leaves school. Sails for India, joining parents in Lahore. Works on the *Civil and Military Gazette* (*CMG*) as assistant to the Editor.	Twain: *The Prince and the Pauper*. Leslie Stephen begins compiling and editing the *Dictionary of National Biography*.
1883	Kipling's mother collects Trix from England. Kipling's first visit to Simla, where he spends many annual leaves during his time in India. Family are reunited in Lahore for Christmas.	Maupassant: *Une Vie*; *Clair de lune*. Stevenson: *Treasure Island*. James: *The Siege of London* (stories). Henty: *Under Drake's Flag*. Olive Schreiner: *Story of an African Farm*.

CHRONOLOGY

Lord Carnavon holds conversations in London over a possible South African federation. Disraeli (PM since 1874) buys Britain shares in the Suez Canal. Public Health Act in Britain. Prince of Wales visits India. *Trial by Jury*: first of the Gilbert and Sullivan operas produced by D'Oyley Carte (to 1896). Telephone invented by Alexander Graham Bell.

Queen Victoria proclaimed Empress of India in Delhi. Annexation of the Transvaal. Gaika campaign: Kaffirs in Transkei suppressed. Stanley completes 1000 day trek across Africa from Dar es Salaam to the mouth of the Congo river.

Congress of Berlin over Eastern Question. Second Afghan War (to 1881). Paris World Exhibition.

Zulu War.

Liberals win majority in General Election: Gladstone becomes Prime Minister. Transvaal Boers declare Republic; First Boer War begins. Lord Roberts's march from Kabul to the relief of Kandahar; defeat of Ayub Khan.

British force defeated by Boers at Majuba Hill. Convention of Pretoria: British recognize independent Boer Republic of Transvaal, with Kruger as President. Amir favourable to British installed in Afghanistan. Tsar Alexander II assassinated in Russia. Opening of Natural History Museum in South Kensington. Second Irish Land Act.

Murder of Irish Secretary and Under-Secretary in Phoenix Park, Dublin. Britain occupies Egypt and the Sudan. Married Women's Property Act.

Liberal Viceroy Lord Ripon attempts to place British and Indian magistrates on equal terms. Anglo-Egyptian force defeated in the Sudan by followers of El-Mahdi.

DATE	AUTHOR'S LIFE	LITERARY CONTEXT
1884	Writes series of special reports on 'The Viceroy at Patiala' – his first major piece of work for the *CMG*. Engagement to Florence Garrard broken off. A volume of verse parodies by Kipling and his sister published as *Echoes*.	Twain: *Huckleberry Finn*. Maupassant: *Miss Harriet*. Huysmans: *A Rebours*. Henty: *With Clive in India*. Nazir Ahmad: *The Repentance of Nussooh* (in translation).
1885	Kipling special correspondent for *CMG* at meeting of new Viceroy of India and Amir of Afghanistan in Rawalpindi. Walking tour in Himalayas. *Quartette* published – the work of all four Kiplings.	Maupassant: *Bel-Ami*. Zola: *Germinal*. Stevenson: *A Child's Garden of Verses*. Pinero: *The Magistrate*. Meredith: *Diana of the Crossways*.
1886	Joins Masonic Lodge 'Hope and Perseverance', no. 782, in Lahore. *Departmental Ditties*.	Stevenson: *Dr Jekyll and Mr Hyde*; *Kidnapped*. James: *The Bostonians*. Haggard: *King Solomon's Mines*. Frances Hodgson Burnett: *Little Lord Fauntleroy*.
1887	Transfers to work on *The Pioneer* in Allahabad.	Haggard: *She*. Maupassant: *Mont-Oriol*; *Le Horla*. Chekhov: 'The Kiss'.
1888	*Plain Tales from the Hills*. Takes on extra responsibility of writing for *The Week's News*, a new publication sponsored by *The Pioneer*.	Hardy: *Wessex Tales*. Wilde: *The Happy Prince and Other Tales*. Morris: *A Dream of John Ball*. Chekhov: 'The Steppe'.
1888–9	*Soldiers Three, The Story of the Gadsbys, In Black and White, Under the Deodars, The Phantom Rickshaw, Wee Willie Winkie* published in the Indian Railway Library series.	
1889	Leaves India, travelling to San Francisco via Hong Kong and Japan with friends. Crosses the United States alone, writing the articles later collected in *From Sea to Sea*. Falls in love with Caroline Taylor. Sails to England. Makes successful London literary début: stories and verses appear in *Macmillan's* and *St James's Gazette*. Retains A. P. Watt as his agent.	Twain: *A Connecticut Yankee at King Arthur's Court*. Jerome: *Three Men in a Boat*. Stevenson: *The Master of Ballantrae*. Tolstoy: *The Kreutzer Sonata*. Chekhov: 'A Dreary Story'. Tennyson: 'Crossing the Bar' (last poem).

CHRONOLOGY

Third Reform Bill: uniform male suffrage in rural and urban areas. General Gordon arrives in Khartoum. 'Scramble for Africa' beginning; Berlin Conference on West Africa. Lord Dufferin Viceroy of India. Fabian Society founded. Society of Authors founded.

Khartoum falls to the Mahdi: death of Gordon. Salisbury forms Conservative ministry. First Indian National Congress. Third Burma War.

Upper Burma annexed; long period of guerrilla warfare follows. Gladstone Prime Minister for the third time; resigns on the defeat of his first Home Rule Bill for Ireland. Salisbury Prime Minister (to 1892). Colonial and Indian Exhibition in London.

Queen Victoria's Golden Jubilee. 'Bloody Sunday': clashes between police and demonstrators in Trafalgar Square. First Colonial Conference of imperial prime ministers is held in London. Britain annexes Zululand. Match girls' strike in London. Cecil Rhodes obtains monopoly of mining rights in Matabeleland. First exhibition of Arts and Crafts Guild. Wilhelm II becomes Kaiser.

London dock strike. Rhodes's British South Africa Company receives royal charter. Eiffel Tower built.

DATE	AUTHOR'S LIFE	LITERARY CONTEXT
1890	Indian Railway Library stories republished in England. Suffers breakdown. Engagement to Caroline Taylor broken off. Travels to Italy. Kipling the subject of a leading article in *The Times*. His parents visit England (May–September). First meeting with Caroline Balestier, sister of his American friend Wolcott. Novel, *The Light That Failed*, published.	Ibsen: *Hedda Gabler.* James: *The Tragic Muse.* Wilde: *The Picture of Dorian Gray.* Maupassant: *L'Inutile Beauté.*
1891	Revised edition of *The Light That Failed*. Travels to New York. *Life's Handicap* (stories). Embarks on world tour, taking in South Africa, Australia, New Zealand and (for the last time) India. Returns to England in December on hearing of the death of Wolcott Balestier.	Morris: *News from Nowhere.* Hardy: *Tess of the d'Urbervilles.* Gissing: *New Grub Street.*
1892	Marries Caroline Balestier ('Carrie') in January (the bride is given away by Henry James). Round-the-world honeymoon tour cut short by collapse of the Oriental Banking Company and the loss of Kipling's savings. The couple take up residence in Brattleboro, Vermont, on the Balestier family estate. Daughter Josephine born in December. *The Naulahka* (novel, written with Wolcott Balestier); *Barrack-Room Ballads.*	Conan Doyle: *The Adventures of Sherlock Holmes.* Gissing: *Born in Exile.* Wilde: *Lady Windermere's Fan.* James: *The Lesson of the Master* (stories). G. & W. Grossmith: *The Diary of a Nobody.* Whitman: *Leaves of Grass* (3rd ed.). Chekhov: 'Ward No. 6'. Zola: *Le Débâcle.*
1893	*Many Inventions* (stories). Kiplings move into a house designed and built for them north of Brattleboro.	James: *The Real Thing* (stories). Pinero: *The Second Mrs Tanqueray.*
1894	Trip to England. *The Jungle Book.* Makes speech at Westward Ho! Returns to Vermont.	Conan Doyle: *Memoirs of Sherlock Holmes.* Twain: *Pudd'nhead Wilson.* Shaw: *Arms and the Man.* Hope: *The Prisoner of Zenda.*

CHRONOLOGY

Fall of Bismarck. Parnell resigns as Irish Nationalist leader. Rhodes becomes Prime Minister of Cape Colony. British South Africa Company founds city of Salisbury in Basutoland. Treaties with Belgium, France, Germany and Portugal define and extend British interests throughout the African continent. Stanley: *In Darkest Africa*. Morris founds Kelmscott Press.

Education Act abolishes fees for elementary schooling in England and Wales.

Indian Councils Act. Resignation of Salisbury: Gladstone Prime Minister for fourth and last time.

Gladstone's second Irish Home Rule Bill rejected by Lords. Independent Labour Party founded, led by James Keir Hardie. Rising in Matabeleland against British South Africa Company.

Gladstone resigns, having split the Liberals over Home Rule. Dreyfus affair. Nicholas II becomes Tsar. *The Yellow Book* founded (to 1897). First Promenade Concert at Queen's Hall, London.

DATE	AUTHOR'S LIFE	LITERARY CONTEXT
1895	In Washington, DC (February). In England (July–August). *Out of India* (non-fiction); *The Second Jungle Book.*	Crane: *The Red Badge of Courage.* Hardy: *Jude the Obscure.* Wells: *The Time Machine.* Wilde: *The Importance of Being Earnest*; *An Ideal Husband.* James: *Terminations* (stories).
1896	Birth of second daughter, Elsie, in February. Quarrel with brother-in-law Beatty Balestier results in court case; Kiplings leave Brattleboro and return to England, settling at Maidencombe in Devon. *The Seven Seas* (verse).	Housman: *A Shropshire Lad.* Wells: *The Island of Doctor Moreau.* Conrad: *An Outcast of the Islands.* James: *Embarrassments* (stories). Stevenson: *Weir of Hermiston.* Beerbohm: *The Works of Max Beerbohm.* Chekhov: 'My Life'.
1897	Moves to London, then to Rottingdean in Sussex, where the Burne-Joneses are neighbours. Birth of son, John, in August. *Captains Courageous* (novel).	Conrad: *The Nigger of the 'Narcissus'.* Wells: *The Invisible Man.*
1898	Takes family to Cape Town for the first of many winters. Meets Sir Alfred Milner and Cecil Rhodes, who becomes a close friend. Visits Rhodesia. With Channel fleet on manoeuvres. *The Day's Work* (stories); *The Fleet in Being* (history).	James: 'The Turn of the Screw'; 'In the Cage'. Wells: *The War of the Worlds.* Hardy: *Wessex Poems.* Bridges: *Poetical Works* (to 1905).
1899	Ill-fated trip to the United States. Kipling nearly dies from pneumonia in New York. Death of Josephine in March. Family return to England. Kipling never again visits America. *Stalky & Co.* Writes 'The White Man's Burden'.	Yeats: *The Wind among the Reeds.* Chekhov: 'The Lady with the Little Dog'.
1900	Visits South Africa (January–April); works on staff of the army newspaper, *The Friend*, during the Boer War. Witnesses minor action at Karee Siding.	Conrad: *Lord Jim.* Freud: *The Interpretation of Dreams.* Dreiser: *Sister Carrie.*
1901	In South Africa during the early part of the year – the visit becomes an annual ritual until 1908. *Kim.*	Mann: *Buddenbrooks.*

CHRONOLOGY

DATE	AUTHOR'S LIFE	LITERARY CONTEXT
1902	*Just So Stories.* Moves to Batemans at Burwash in Sussex, the family home for the rest of Kipling's life.	James: *The Wings of the Dove.* Conrad: *Heart of Darkness.* Bennett: *Anna of the Five Towns.* Conan Doyle: *The Hound of the Baskervilles.* Masefield: *Salt-Water Ballads.*
1903	*The Five Nations* (verse).	Conrad: *Typhoon.* Butler: *The Way of All Flesh.* Shaw: *Man and Superman.* London: *The Call of the Wild.* Childers: *The Riddle of the Sands.* Ahmad: *The Bride's Mirror* (in translation).
1904	*Traffics and Discoveries* (stories).	Conrad: *Nostromo.* James: *The Golden Bowl.* Chekhov: *The Cherry Orchard.* Tolstoy: *Hadji Murad.* Barrie: *Peter Pan.* Chesterton: *The Napoleon of Notting Hill.*
1905		Wells: *Kipps.* Granville-Barker: *The Voysey Inheritance.* Wharton: *The House of Mirth.*
1906	*Puck of Pook's Hill.*	Galsworthy: *The Man of Property* (1st vol. of *The Forsyte Saga*). Sinclair: *The Jungle.*
1907	Awarded Nobel Prize for Literature. Receives honorary degrees from Durham and Oxford Universities. Tour of Canada.	Conrad: *The Secret Agent.* Gosse: *Father and Son.* Belloc: *Cautionary Tales.* Synge: *The Playboy of the Western World.*
1908	Honorary degree from Cambridge. Motor tour through north of England. *Letters to the Family.*	Forster: *A Room with a View.* Bennett: *The Old Wives' Tale.*
1909	*Actions and Reactions; Abaft the Funnel* (two collections of stories).	Wells: *Tono-Bungay; Ann Veronica.* Galsworthy: *Strife.* Gide: *La Porte étroite.*
1910	*Rewards and Fairies.* Death of Kipling's mother.	Wells: *The History of Mr Polly.* Forster: *Howards End.* Bennett: *Clayhanger.*

CHRONOLOGY

Salisbury retires; Balfour becomes Prime Minister. Peace Treaty of Vereeniging ends Boer War. Emmeline Pankhurst founds Women's Social and Political Union.

Resignation of Joseph Chamberlain from the Cabinet to campaign against free trade and in favour of special trading concessions for British colonies. Anglo-French *Entente Cordiale.*

Liberals win landslide victory in General Election. Russo-Japanese War (to 1905).

Bengal partition: unrest in India. Curzon resigns as Viceroy over reorganization of Indian army. Balfour resigns over tariff reform. First Russian Revolution.

Anglo-Russian Entente. Parliamentary Labour Party founded. Launch of *HMS Dreadnought*, first modern battleship.

Second Hague Conference. Triple Entente between Britain, France and Russia.

Asquith becomes Prime Minister. Suffragette protests in London. Austria annexes Bosnia and Herzegovina. Formation of Muslim League in India.

Lloyd George introduces People's Budget. Morley-Minto constitutional reforms in India. Blériot flies across the Channel.

Death of Edward VII. Liberals narrowly re-elected. Union of South Africa, with dominion status, established.

DATE	AUTHOR'S LIFE	LITERARY CONTEXT
1911	Death of Kipling's father. *A History of England* (with C. R. L. Fletcher). Tours of France and Ireland.	Brooke: *Poems.* Pound: *Canzoni.* Mansfield: *In a German Pension.* Chesterton: *The Innocence of Father Brown.* Beerbohm: *Zuleika Dobson.*
1912	Motor tour in west of England. *Songs from Books.*	Mann: *Death in Venice.* *Georgian Poetry*, ed. Edward Marsh, 5 vols (to 1922). Tagore: *Gitanjali: Song Offering.*
1913	Voyage to Egypt and up the Nile. Kipling's play, *The Harbour Watch*, produced.	Proust: *A la Recherche du temps perdu* (to 1927). Lawrence: *Sons and Lovers.* Alain-Fournier: *Le Grand Meaulnes.* Wharton: *The Custom of the Country.* Cather: *O Pioneers!*
1914	Speech on Ulster at Tunbridge Wells. Secures commission in Irish Guards for his son John from Lord Roberts.	Joyce: *Dubliners.* Lawrence: *The Prussian Officer* (stories). Hardy: *Satires of Circumstance.* Yeats: *Responsibilities.* Burroughs: *Tarzan of the Apes.*
1915	Invited to visit the French Army in the field. John Kipling reported wounded and missing on his first day in action during the battle of Loos (27 September). His body is never found. Kipling suffers attack of gastritis: onset of permanent illness. *France at War, The Fringes of the Fleet, The New Army in Training* (war pamphlets).	Lawrence: *The Rainbow.* Conrad: *Victory.* Ford: *The Good Soldier.* Buchan: *The Thirty-Nine Steps.* Maugham: *Of Human Bondage.* Muhammad Iqbal: *The Secrets of the Self.*
1916	*Sea Warfare.*	Joyce: *A Portrait of the Artist as a Young Man.* Shaw: *Pygmalian.* Tr. Constance Garnett: *The Tales of Tchehov* (to 1922).
1917	Becomes member of the Imperial War Graves Commission. Visits Italian front. *A Diversity of Creatures* (stories).	T. S. Eliot: *Prufrock and Other Observations.* Yeats: *The Wild Swans at Coole.* Barrie: *Dear Brutus.*

CHRONOLOGY

DATE	AUTHOR'S LIFE	LITERARY CONTEXT
1918	*The Eyes of Asia* (collection of imaginary letters from Indian soldiers on the Western front). 'Kipling's Message' (speech).	Strachey: *Eminent Victorians.* Cather: *My Antonia.*
1919	*The Years Between* (verse).	Shaw: *Heartbreak House.* Beerbohm: *Seven Men.* Maugham: *The Moon and Sixpence.* Wodehouse: *My Man Jeeves.* Tagore: *The Home and the World.*
1920	Honorary degree from Edinburgh University. Visits French battlefields, including Chalkpit Wood, where his son had gone missing. *Letters of Travel.*	Mansfield: *Bliss and Other Stories.* Lawrence: *Women in Love.* Fitzgerald: *This Side of Paradise.* Sinclair Lewis: *Main Street.*
1921	Visits Algiers. Honorary degrees from the Sorbonne and the University of Strasbourg.	Huxley: *Crome Yellow.*
1922	Tour to Gibraltar and Spain. Visit to French cemeteries; hears King George's address in Boulogne. In London nursing home for examination: has abdominal operation.	Eliot: *The Waste Land.* Joyce: *Ulysses.* Woolf: *Jacob's Room.* Mansfield: *The Garden Party and Other Stories.* Lawrence: *England, My England* (stories). Hašek: *The Good Soldier Švejk.* Ahmed Ali: *Ocean of Night.*
1923	Rectorial address at St Andrews. *The Irish Guards in the Great War; Land and Sea Tales.*	Huxley: *Antic Hay.*
1924	Daughter Elsie marries Captain George Bambridge.	Forster: *A Passage to India.* Ford: *Parade's End* (to 1928). Shaw: *St Joan.* O'Casey: *Juno and the Paycock.* Mann: *The Magic Mountain.* Tagore: *Gora.*
1925	Motor tours through France and west of England. Seriously ill with pneumonia.	Woolf: *Mrs Dalloway.* Fitzgerald: *The Great Gatsby.* Dreiser: *An American Tragedy.* Hemingway: *In Our Time.* Kafka: *The Trial.* Gide: *Les Faux-Monnayeurs.*

HISTORICAL EVENTS

Women over 30 gain the vote. Armistice.

Versailles Peace Conference. Punjab riots. Government of India Act.

Formation of League of Nations. Prohibition in US. Government of Ireland Act: Home Rule for North and South, with two separate Parliaments.

First All-India Parliament opens in Delhi. Southern Ireland becomes free state, with dominion status.

Civil war in Ireland. Coalition falls and Bonar Law forms Conservative ministry. Mussolini forms Fascist government in Italy. USSR established. Stalin becomes General Secretary of the Communist Party Central Committee.

Baldwin becomes Prime Minister. Hitler's coup in Munich fails. Writes *Mein Kampf*. German financial crisis.

Death of Lenin. Resignation of Baldwin. Ramsay MacDonald forms minority government (first Labour government) January–November. Baldwin returns to office after Conservative election victory.

Treaty of Locarno.

DATE	AUTHOR'S LIFE	LITERARY CONTEXT
1926	*Debits and Credits* (stories).	Kafka: *The Castle.* O'Casey: *The Plough and the Stars.* T. E. Lawrence: *The Seven Pillars of Wisdom.* Milne: *Winnie-the-Pooh.*
1927	Voyage to Brazil (January–April). Attends the opening of Indian War Memorial in France.	Woolf: *To the Lighthouse.* Hemingway: *Men Without Women.*
1928	Kipling a pallbearer at funeral of Thomas Hardy. *A Book of Words.*	Waugh: *Decline and Fall.* Lawrence: *Lady Chatterley's Lover*; *The Woman Who Rode Away* (stories). Sassoon: *Memoirs of a Fox-Hunting Man.*
1929	Visits war graves in Egypt and Palestine.	Remarque: *All Quiet on the Western Front.* Graves: *Goodbye to All That.* Hemingway: *A Farewell to Arms.* J. Cowper Powys: *Wolf Solent.*
1930	Voyage to the West Indies. Attends dedication of monument to the missing at Dud Corner, Loos. *Thy Servant a Dog.*	Hardy: *Collected Poems.* Lawrence: *The Virgin and the Gipsy*; *Love Among the Haystacks* (stories). Sassoon: *Memoirs of an Infantry Officer.* Pritchett: *The Spanish Virgin and Other Stories.* Walpole: *The Herries Chronicle* (to 1933).
1931	In nursing home for examination: doctors decide against an operation.	Woolf: *The Waves.* Owen, *Poems*, ed. Blunden. Prem Chand: *Deliverance.*
1932	Tour of the Midlands in new Rolls Royce. Kipling made honorary Fellow of Magdalene College, Cambridge. *Limits and Renewals* (stories).	Waugh: *Black Mischief.* Huxley: *Brave New World.* Faulkner: *Light in August.* Iqbal: *Javid-Nama.*
1933	Duodenal ulcer diagnosed. Kipling elected to Institut de France. *Souvenirs de France.*	Hemingway: *Winner Take Nothing.* Coward: *Private Lives*; *Design for Living.* J. Cowper Powys: *A Glastonbury Romance.*
1935	Begins his autobiography.	Eliot: *Murder in the Cathedral.* Isherwood: *Mr Norris Changes Trains.*

CHRONOLOGY

HISTORICAL EVENTS

General Strike in Britain. Germany admitted to League of Nations. First television demonstrated.

Lindberg flies the Atlantic.

Hoover becomes US President. Full suffrage for women in Britain. Viceroy (Lord Irwin) promises India dominion status, which fails to satisfy demands of Ghandi's Congress Party for independence. Stalin introduces first Five Year Plan in USSR. Fleming discovers penicillin.

Wall Street crash. Beginning of world depression. Ramsay MacDonald Prime Minister. First use of term *apartheid* at Kroonstad, South Africa.

Ghandi begins civil disobedience campaign in India. Opening of first of a series of Round Table Conferences on India in London (to 1933). Nazis win seats from moderates in German elections.

Delhi Pact: Ghandi suspends campaign of disobedience.

Indian National Congress outlawed; Ghandi arrested. Oswald Mosley founds British Union of Fascists. Unemployed marchers clash with police in London.

Hitler becomes German Chancellor. Nazi persecution of Jews begins. Churchill first warns of German rearmament. Franklin D. Roosevelt's 'New Deal' announced in the US.

Second Government of India Act: proposes a federation with eleven provincial assemblies having considerable autonomy (operative from 1937); Burma, Aden and Kuwait no longer under Viceroy's authority. Italy invades Abyssinia. Baldwin Prime Minister after MacDonald's retirement.

DATE	AUTHOR'S LIFE	LITERARY CONTEXT
1936	Kipling is taken ill in London and dies in Middlesex hospital (18 January).	Auden: *Look, Stranger!* Sassoon: *Sherston's Progress.* Orwell: *Keep the Aspidistra Flying.* Faulkner: *Absalom, Absalom!* Prem Chand: *Godan.*
1937	*Something of Myself* published posthumously.	Steinbeck: *Of Mice and Men.* Hemingway: *To Have and Have Not.* Orwell: *The Road to Wigan Pier.* Woolf: *The Years.* Karen Blixen: *Out of Africa.*

HISTORICAL EVENTS

Spanish civil war begins. Death of George V. Abdication crisis. Jarrow march.

Japanese invade China. Baldwin retires; Neville Chamberlain becomes Prime Minister. Eire becomes a sovereign state. Bombing of Guernica.

Rudyard Kipling
KIM

Chapter 1

O ye who tread the Narrow Way
By Tophet-flare to Judgment Day,
Be gentle when 'the heathen' pray
To Buddha at Kamakura!
            Buddha at Kamakura.

HE sat, in defiance of municipal orders, astride the gun
Zam-Zammah on her brick platform opposite the old
Ajaib-Gher – the Wonder House, as the natives call the
Lahore Museum. Who hold Zam-Zammah, that 'fire-
breathing dragon', hold the Punjab, for the great green-
bronze piece is always first of the conqueror's loot.

There was some justification for Kim – he had kicked Lala
Dinanath's boy off the trunnions – since the English held the
Punjab and Kim was English. Though he was burned black as
any native; though he spoke the vernacular by preference, and
his mother-tongue in a clipped uncertain sing-song; though
he consorted on terms of perfect equality with the small boys
of the bazar; Kim was white – a poor white of the very
poorest. The half-caste woman who looked after him (she
smoked opium, and pretended to keep a second-hand furni-
ture shop by the square where the cheap cabs wait) told the
missionaries that she was Kim's mother's sister; but his
mother had been nurse-maid in a Colonel's family and had
married Kimball O'Hara, a young colour-sergeant of the
Mavericks, an Irish regiment. He afterwards took a post on
the Sind, Punjab, and Delhi Railway, and his Regiment went
home without him. The wife died of cholera in Ferozepore,
and O'Hara fell to drink and loafing up and down the line
with the keen-eyed three-year-old baby. Societies and chaplains, anxious for the child, tried to catch him, but O'Hara
drifted away, till he came across the woman who took opium
and learned the taste from her, and died as poor whites die in

3

India. His estate at death consisted of three papers – one he called his '*ne varietur*' because those words were written below his signature thereon, and another his 'clearance-certificate'. The third was Kim's birth-certificate. Those things, he was used to say, in his glorious opium-hours, would yet make little Kimball a man. On no account was Kim to part with them, for they belonged to a great piece of magic – such magic as men practised over yonder behind the Museum, in the big blue-and-white Jadoo-Gher – the Magic House, as we name the Masonic Lodge. It would, he said, all come right some day, and Kim's horn would be exalted between pillars – monstrous pillars – of beauty and strength. The Colonel himself, riding on a horse, at the head of the finest Regiment in the world, would attend to Kim – little Kim that should have been better off than his father. Nine hundred first-class devils, whose God was a Red Bull on a green field, would attend to Kim, if they had not forgotten O'Hara – poor O'Hara that was gang-foreman on the Ferozepore line. Then he would weep bitterly in the broken rush chair on the veranda. So it came about after his death that the woman sewed parchment, paper, and birth-certificate into a leather amulet-case which she strung round Kim's neck.

'And some day,' she said, confusedly remembering O'Hara's prophecies, 'there will come for you a great Red Bull on a green field, and the Colonel riding on his tall horse, yes, and' – dropping into English – 'nine hundred devils.'

'Ah,' said Kim, 'I shall remember. A Red Bull and a Colonel on a horse will come, but first, my father said, will come the two men making ready the ground for these matters. That is how my father said they always did; and it is always so when men work magic.'

If the woman had sent Kim up to the local Jadoo-Gher with those papers, he would, of course, have been taken over by the Provincial Lodge, and sent to the Masonic Orphanage in the Hills; but what she had heard of magic she distrusted. Kim, too, held views of his own. As he reached the years of indiscretion, he learned to avoid missionaries and white men of serious aspect who asked who he was, and what he did. For Kim did nothing with an immense success. True, he knew the wonderful walled city of Lahore from the Delhi Gate to the outer Fort Ditch; was hand in glove with men who led lives stranger than anything Haroun al Raschid dreamed of; and he lived in a life wild as that of the Arabian Nights, but missionaries and secretaries of charitable societies could not see the beauty of it. His nickname through the wards was 'Little Friend of all the World'; and very often, being lithe and inconspicuous, he executed commissions by night on the crowded housetops for sleek and shiny young men of fashion. It was intrigue, of course – he knew that much, as he had known all evil since he could speak, – but what he loved was the game for its own sake – the stealthy prowl through the dark gullies and lanes, the crawl up a water-pipe, the sights and sounds of the women's world on the flat roofs, and the headlong flight from housetop to housetop under cover of the hot dark. Then there were holy men, ash-smeared *fakir*s by their brick shrines under the trees at the riverside, with whom he was quite familiar – greeting them as they returned from begging-tours, and, when no one was by, eating from the same dish. The woman who looked after him insisted with tears that he should wear European clothes – trousers, a shirt, and a battered hat. Kim found it easier to slip into Hindu or Mohammedan garb when engaged on certain businesses. One of the young men of fashion – he who was found dead at the bottom of a well on the night of the earthquake – had once given him a complete suit of Hindu kit, the costume of a low-caste street boy, and Kim stored it in a secret place under some baulks in Nila Ram's timber-yard, beyond the Punjab High Court, where the fragrant deodar logs lie seasoning after they have driven down the Ravi. When there was business or frolic afoot, Kim would use his properties, returning at dawn to the veranda, all tired out from shouting at the heels of a marriage procession, or yelling at a Hindu festival. Sometimes there was food in the house, more often there was not, and then Kim went out again to eat with his native friends.

As he drummed his heels against Zam-Zammah he turned now and again from his king-of-the-castle game with little Chota Lal and Abdullah the sweetmeat-seller's son, to make a rude remark to the native policeman on guard over rows of shoes at the Museum door. The big Punjabi grinned tolerantly: he knew Kim of old. So did the water-carrier, sluicing water on the dry road from his goat-skin bag. So did Jawahir Singh, the Museum carpenter, bent over new packing-cases. So did everybody in sight except the peasants from the country, hurrying up to the Wonder House to view the things that men made in their own province and elsewhere. The Museum was given up to Indian arts and manufactures, and anybody who sought wisdom could ask the Curator to explain.

'Off! Off! Let me up!' cried Abdullah, climbing up Zam-Zammah's wheel.

'Thy father was a pastry-cook, Thy mother stole the *ghi*,' sang Kim. 'All Mussalmans fell off Zam-Zammah long ago!'

'Let *me* up!' shrilled little Chota Lal in his gilt-embroidered cap. His father was worth perhaps half a million sterling, but India is the only democratic land in the world.

'The Hindus fell off Zam-Zammah too. The Mussalmans pushed them off. Thy father was a pastry-cook −'

He stopped; for there shuffled round the corner, from the roaring Motee Bazar, such a man as Kim, who thought he knew all castes, had never seen. He was nearly six feet high, dressed in fold upon fold of dingy stuff like horse-blanketing, and not one fold of it could Kim refer to any known trade or profession. At his belt hung a long open-work iron pencase and a wooden rosary such as holy men wear. On his head was a gigantic sort of tam-o'-shanter. His face was yellow and wrinkled, like that of Fook Shing, the Chinese bootmaker in the bazar. His eyes turned up at the corners and looked like little slits of onyx.

'Who is that?' said Kim to his companions.

'Perhaps it is a man,' said Abdullah, finger in mouth, staring.

'Without doubt,' returned Kim; 'but he is no man of India that *I* have ever seen.'

'A priest, perhaps,' said Chota Lal, spying the rosary. 'See! He goes into the Wonder House!'

'Nay, nay,' said the policeman, shaking his head. 'I do not understand your talk.' The constable spoke Punjabi. 'O Friend of all the World, what does he say?'

'Send him hither,' said Kim, dropping from Zam-Zammah, flourishing his bare heels. 'He is a foreigner, and thou art a buffalo.'

The man turned helplessly and drifted towards the boys. He was old, and his woollen gaberdine still reeked of the stinking artemisia of the mountain passes.

'O Children, what is that big house?' he said in very fair Urdu.

'The Ajaib-Gher, the Wonder House!' Kim gave him no title – such as Lala or Mian. He could not divine the man's creed.

'Ah! The Wonder House! Can any enter?'

'It is written above the door – all can enter.'

'Without payment?'

'I go in and out. *I* am no banker,' laughed Kim.

'Alas! I am an old man. I did not know.' Then, fingering his rosary, he half turned to the Museum.

'What is your caste? Where is your house? Have you come far?' Kim asked.

'I came by Kulu – from beyond the Kailas – but what know you? From the Hills where' – he sighed – 'the air and water are fresh and cool.'

'Aha! Khitai [a Chinaman],' said Abdullah proudly. Fook Shing had once chased him out of his shop for spitting at the joss above the boots.

'Pahari [a hillman],' said little Chota Lal.

'Aye, child – a hillman from hills thou'lt never see. Didst hear of Bhotiyal [Tibet]? I am no Khitai, but a Bhotiya [Tibetan], since you must know – a lama – or, say, a *guru* in your tongue.'

'A *guru* from Tibet,' said Kim. 'I have not seen such a man. They be Hindus in Tibet, then?'

'We be followers of the Middle Way, living in peace in our lamasseries, and I go to see the Four Holy Places before I die. Now do you, who are children, know as much as I do who am old.' He smiled benignantly on the boys.

'Hast thou eaten?'

He fumbled in his bosom and drew forth a worn wooden begging-bowl. The boys nodded. All priests of their acquaintance begged.

'I do not wish to eat yet.' He turned his head like an old tortoise in the sunlight. 'Is it true that there are many images in the Wonder House of Lahore?' He repeated the last words as one making sure of an address.

'That is true,' said Abdullah. 'It is full of heathen *būts*. Thou also art an idolater.'

'Never mind *him*,' said Kim. 'That is the Government's house and there is no idolatry in it, but only a Sahib with a white beard. Come with me and I will show.'

'Strange priests eat boys,' whispered Chota Lal.

'And he is a stranger and a *būt-parast* [idolater],' said Abdullah, the Mohammedan.

Kim laughed. 'He is new. Run to your mothers' laps, and be safe. Come!'

Kim clicked round the self-registering turnstile; the old man followed and halted amazed. In the entrance-hall stood the larger figures of the Greco-Buddhist sculptures done, savants know how long since, by forgotten workmen whose hands were feeling, and not unskilfully, for the mysteriously transmitted Grecian touch. There were hundreds of pieces, friezes of figures in relief, fragments of statues and slabs crowded with figures that had encrusted the brick walls of the Buddhist *stupas* and *viharas* of the North Country and now, dug up and labelled, made the pride of the Museum. In open-mouthed wonder the lama turned to this and that, and finally checked in rapt attention before a large alto-relief representing a coronation or apotheosis of the Lord Buddha. The

Master was represented seated on a lotus the petals of which were so deeply undercut as to show almost detached. Round Him was an adoring hierarchy of kings, elders, and old-time Buddhas. Below were lotus-covered waters with fishes and water-birds. Two butterfly-winged *dewas* held a wreath over His head; above them another pair supported an umbrella surmounted by the jewelled headdress of the Bodhisat.

'The Lord! The Lord! It is Sakya Muni himself,' the lama half sobbed; and under his breath began the wonderful Buddhist invocation:

> To Him the Way, the Law, apart,
> Whom Maya held beneath her heart,
> Ananda's Lord, the Bodhisat.

'And He is here! The Most Excellent Law is here also. My pilgrimage is well begun. And what work! What work!'

'Yonder is the Sahib,' said Kim, and dodged sideways among the cases of the arts and manufacturers wing. A white-bearded Englishman was looking at the lama, who gravely turned and saluted him and after some fumbling drew forth a note-book and a scrap of paper.

'Yes, that is my name,' smiling at the clumsy, childish print.

'One of us who had made pilgrimage to the Holy Places – he is now Abbot of the Lung-Cho Monastery – gave it me,' stammered the lama. 'He spoke of these.' His lean hand moved tremulously round.

'Welcome, then, O lama from Tibet. Here be the images, and I am here' – he glanced at the lama's face – 'to gather knowledge. Come to my office awhile.' The old man was trembling with excitement.

The office was but a little wooden cubicle partitioned off from the sculpture-lined gallery. Kim laid himself down, his ear against a crack in the heat-split cedar door, and, following his instinct, stretched out to listen and watch.

Most of the talk was altogether above his head. The lama, haltingly at first, spoke to the Curator of his own lamassery, the Such-zen, opposite the Painted Rocks, four months' march away. The Curator brought out a huge book of photos and showed him that very place, perched on its crag, overlooking the gigantic valley of many-hued strata.

'Ay, ay!' The lama mounted a pair of horn-rimmed spectacles of Chinese work. 'Here is the little door through which we bring wood before winter. And thou – the English know of these things? He who is now Abbot of Lung-Cho told me, but I did not believe. The Lord – the Excellent One – He has honour here too? And His life is known?'

'It is all carven upon the stones. Come and see, if thou art rested.'

Out shuffled the lama to the main hall, and, the Curator beside him, went through the collection with the reverence of a devotee and the appreciative instinct of a craftsman.

Incident by incident in the beautiful story he identified on the blurred stone, puzzled here and there by the unfamiliar Greek convention, but delighted as a child at each new trove. Where the sequence failed, as in the Annunciation, the Curator supplied it from his mound of books – French and German, with photographs and reproductions.

Here was the devout Asita, the pendant of Simeon in the Christian story, holding the Holy Child on his knee while mother and father listened; and here were incidents in the legend of the cousin Devadatta. Here was the wicked woman who accused the Master of impurity, all confounded; here was the teaching in the Deer-park; the miracle that stunned the fire-worshippers; here was the Bodhisat in royal state as a prince; the miraculous birth; the death at Kusinagara, where the weak disciple fainted; while there were almost countless repetitions of the meditation under the Bodhi tree; and the adoration of the alms-bowl was everywhere. In a few minutes the Curator saw that his guest was no mere bead-telling mendicant, but a scholar of parts. And they went at it all over again, the lama taking snuff, wiping his spectacles, and talking at railway speed in a bewildering mixture of Urdu and Tibetan. He had heard of the travels of the Chinese pilgrims, Fu-Hiouen and Hwen-Tsiang, and was anxious to know if there was any translation of their record. He drew in his breath as he turned helplessly over the pages of Beal and Stanislas Julien. ' 'Tis all here. A treasure locked.' Then he composed himself reverently to listen to fragments hastily rendered into Urdu. For the first time he heard of the labours of European scholars, who by the help of these and a hundred other documents have identified the Holy Places of Buddhism. Then he was shown a mighty map, spotted and traced with yellow. The brown finger followed the Curator's pencil from point to point. Here was Kapilavastu, here the Middle Kingdom, and here Mahabodhi, the Mecca of Buddhism; and here was Kusinagara, sad place of the Holy One's death. The old man bowed his head over the sheets in silence for a while, and the Curator lit another pipe. Kim had fallen asleep. When he waked, the talk, still in spate, was more within his comprehension.

'And thus it was, O Fountain of Wisdom, that I decided to go to the Holy Places which His foot had trod – to the Birthplace, even to Kapila; then to Mahabodhi, which is Buddh Gaya – to the Monastery – to the Deer-park – to the place of His death.'

The lama lowered his voice. 'And I come here alone. For five – seven – eighteen – forty years it was in my mind that the Old Law was not well followed; being overlaid, as thou knowest, with devildom, charms, and idolatry. Even as the child outside said but now. Ay, even as the child said, with *būt-parasti*.'

'So it comes with all faiths.'

'Thinkest thou? The books of my lamassery I read, and they were dried pith; and the later ritual with which we of the Reformed Law have cumbered ourselves – that, too, had no worth to these old eyes. Even the followers of the Excellent One are at feud on feud with one another. It is all illusion. Ay, *maya*, illusion. But I have another desire' – the seamed yellow face drew within three inches of the Curator, and the long forefinger-nail tapped on the table. 'Your scholars, by these books, have followed the Blessed Feet in all their wanderings;

but there are things which they have not sought out. I know nothing – nothing do I know but I go to free myself from the Wheel of Things by a broad and open road.' He smiled with most simple triumph. 'As a pilgrim to the Holy Places I acquire merit. But there is more. Listen to a true thing. When our gracious Lord, being as yet a youth, sought a mate, men said, in His father's Court, that He was too tender for marriage. Thou knowest?'

The Curator nodded, wondering what would come next.

'So they made the triple trial of strength against all comers. And at the test of the Bow, our Lord first breaking that which they gave Him, called for such a bow as none might bend. Thou knowest?'

'It is written. I have read.'

'And, overshooting all other marks, the arrow passed far and far beyond sight. At the last it fell; and, where it touched earth, there broke out a stream which presently became a River, whose nature, by our Lord's beneficence, and that merit He acquired ere He freed himself, is that whoso bathes in it washes away all taint and speckle of sin.'

'So it is written,' said the Curator sadly.

The lama drew a long breath. 'Where is that River? Fountain of Wisdom, where fell the arrow?'

'Alas, my brother, I do not know,' said the Curator.

'Nay, if it please thee to forget – the one thing only that thou hast not told me. Surely thou must know? See, I am an old man! I ask with my head between thy feet, O Fountain of Wisdom. We *know* He drew the bow! We *know* the arrow fell! We *know* the stream gushed! Where, then, is the River? My dream told me to find it. So I came. I am here. But where is the River?'

'If I knew, think you I would not cry it aloud?'

'By it one attains freedom from the Wheel of Things,' the lama went on, unheeding. 'The River of the Arrow! Think again! Some little stream, maybe – dried in the heats? But the Holy One would never so cheat an old man.'

'I do not know. I do not know.'

The lama brought his thousand-wrinkled face once more a handsbreadth from the Englishman's. 'I see thou dost not know. Not being of the Law, the matter is hid from thee.'

'Ay – hidden – hidden.'

'We are both bound, thou and I, my brother. But I' – he rose with a sweep of the soft thick drapery – 'I go to cut myself free. Come also!'

'I am bound,' said the Curator. 'But whither goest thou?'

'First to Kashi [Benares]: where else? There I shall meet one of the pure faith in a Jain temple of that city. He also is a Seeker in secret, and from him haply I may learn. Maybe he will go with me to Buddh Gaya. Thence north and west to Kapilavastu, and there will I seek for the River. Nay, I will seek everywhere as I go – for the place is not known where the arrow fell.'

'And how wilt thou go? It is a far cry to Delhi, and farther to Benares.'

'By road and the trains. From Pathânkot, having left the Hills, I came hither in a *te-rain*. It goes swiftly. At first I was amazed to see those tall poles by the side of the road snatching up and snatching up their threads,' – he illustrated the stoop and whirl of a telegraph-pole flashing past the train. 'But later, I was cramped and desired to walk, as I am used.'

'And thou art sure of thy road?' said the Curator.

'Oh, for that one but asks a question and pays money, and the appointed persons despatch all to the appointed place. That much I knew in my lamassery from sure report,' said the lama proudly.

'And when dost thou go?' The Curator smiled at the mixture of old-world piety and modern progress that is the note of India today.

'As soon as may be. I follow the places of His life till I come to the River of the Arrow. There is, moreover, a written paper of the hours of the trains that go south.'

'And for food?' Lamas, as a rule, have good store of money somewhere about them, but the Curator wished to make sure.

'For the journey, I take up the Master's begging-bowl. Yes.

Even as He went so go I, forsaking the ease of my monastery. There was with me when I left the hills a *chela* [disciple] who begged for me as the Rule demands, but halting in Kutu awhile a fever took him and he died. I have now no *chela*, but I will take the alms-bowl and thus enable the charitable to acquire merit.' He nodded his head valiantly. Learned doctors of a lamassery do not beg, but the lama was an enthusiast in this quest.

'Be it so,' said the Curator, smiling. 'Suffer me now to acquire merit. We be craftsmen together, thou and I. Here is a new book of white English paper: here be sharpened pencils two and three – thick and thin, all good for a scribe. Now lend me thy spectacles.'

The Curator looked through them. They were heavily scratched, but the power was almost exactly that of his own pair, which he slid into the lama's hand, saying: 'Try these.'

'A feather! A very feather upon the face!' The old man turned his head delightedly and wrinkled up his nose. 'How scarcely do I feel them! How clearly do I see!'

'They be *bilaur* – crystal – and will never scratch. May they help thee to thy River, for they are thine.'

'I will take them and the pencils and the white note-book,' said the lama, 'as a sign of friendship between priest and priest – and now –' He fumbled at his belt, detached the open-work iron pencase, and laid it on the Curator's table. 'That is for a memory between thee and me – my pencase. It is something old – even as I am.'

It was a piece of ancient design, Chinese, of an iron that is not smelted these days; and the collector's heart in the Curator's bosom had gone out to it from the first. For no persuasion would the lama resume his gift.

'When I return, having found the River, I will bring thee a written picture of the Padma Samthora such as I used to make on silk at the lamassery. Yes – and of the Wheel of Life,' he chuckled, 'for we be craftsmen together, thou and I.'

The Curator would have detained him: they are few in the world who still have the secret of the conventional brush-pen

Buddhist pictures which are, as it were, half written and half drawn. But the lama strode out, head high in air, and pausing an instant before the great statue of a Bodhisat in meditation, brushed through the turnstiles.

Kim followed like a shadow. What he had overheard excited him wildly. This man was entirely new to all his experience, and he meant to investigate further, precisely as he would have investigated a new building or a strange festival in Lahore city. The lama was his trove, and he purposed to take possession. Kim's mother had been Irish too.

The old man halted by Zam-Zammah and looked round till his eye fell on Kim. The inspiration of his pilgrimage had left him for awhile, and he felt old, forlorn, and very empty.

'Do not sit under that gun,' said the policeman loftily.

'Huh! Owl!' was Kim's retort on the lama's behalf. 'Sit under that gun if it please thee. When didst thou steal the milk-woman's slippers, Dunnoo?'

That was an utterly unfounded charge sprung on the spur of the moment, but it silenced Dunnoo, who knew that Kim's clear yell could call up legions of bad bazar boys if need arose.

'And whom didst thou worship within?' said Kim affably, squatting in the shade beside the lama.

'I worshipped none, child. I bowed before the Excellent Law.'

Kim accepted this new God without emotion. He knew already a few score.

'And what dost thou do?'

'I beg. I remember now it is long since I have eaten or drunk. What is the custom of charity in this town? In silence, as we do of Tibet, or speaking aloud?'

'Those who beg in silence starve in silence,' said Kim, quoting a native proverb. The lama tried to rise, but sank back again, sighing for his disciple, dead in far-away Kulu. Kim watched – head to one side, considering and interested.

'Give me the bowl. I know the people of this city – all who are charitable. Give, and I will bring it back filled.'

Simply as a child the old man handed him the bowl.

'Rest, thou. *I* know the people.'

He trotted off to the open shop of a *kunjri*, a low-caste vegetable-seller, which lay opposite the belt-tramway line down the Motee Bazar. She knew Kim of old.

'Oho, hast thou turned *yogi* with thy begging-bowl?' she cried.

'Nay,' said Kim proudly. 'There is a new priest in the city – a man such as I have never seen.'

'Old priest – young tiger,' said the woman angrily. 'I am tired of new priests! They settle on our wares like flies. Is the father of my son a well of charity to give to all who ask?'

'No,' said Kim. 'Thy man is rather *yagi* [bad-tempered] than *yogi* [a holy man]. But this priest is new. The Sahib in the Wonder House has talked to him like a brother. O my mother, fill me this bowl. He waits.'

'That bowl indeed! That cow-bellied basket! Thou hast as much grace as the holy bull of Shiv. He has taken the best of a basket of onions already, this morn; and forsooth, I must fill thy bowl. He comes here again.'

The huge, mouse-coloured Brahmini bull of the ward was shouldering his way through the many-coloured crowd, a stolen plantain hanging out of his mouth. He headed straight for the shop, well knowing his privileges as a sacred beast, lowered his head, and puffed heavily along the line of baskets ere making his choice. Up flew Kim's hard little heel and caught him on his moist blue nose. He snorted indignantly, and walked away across the tram-rails, his hump quivering with rage.

'See! I have saved more than the bowl will cost thrice over. Now, mother, a little rice and some dried fish atop – yes, and some vegetable curry.'

A growl came out of the back of the shop, where a man lay.

'He drove away the bull,' said the woman in an undertone. 'It is good to give to the poor.' She took the bowl and returned it full of hot rice.

'But my *yogi* is not a cow,' said Kim gravely, making a hole with his fingers in the top of the mound. 'A little curry is good, and a fried cake, and a morsel of conserve would please him, I think.'

'It is a hole as big as thy head,' said the woman fretfully. But she filled it, none the less, with good, steaming vegetable curry, clapped a fried cake atop, and a morsel of clarified butter on the cake, dabbed a lump of sour tamarind conserve at the side; and Kim looked at the load lovingly.

'That is good. When I am in the bazar the bull shall not come to this house. He is a bold beggar-man.'

'And thou?' laughed the woman. 'But speak well of bulls. Hast thou not told me that some day a Red Bull will come out of a field to help thee? Now hold all straight and ask for the holy man's blessing upon me. Perhaps, too, he knows a cure for my daughter's sore eyes. Ask him that also, O thou Little Friend of all the World.'

But Kim had danced off ere the end of the sentence, dodging pariah dogs and hungry acquaintances.

'Thus do we beg who know the way of it,' said he proudly to the lama, who opened his eyes at the contents of the bowl. 'Eat now and – I will eat with thee. Ohé, *bhisti*!' he called to the water-carrier, sluicing the crotons by the Museum. 'Give water here. We men are thirsty.'

'We men!' said the *bhisti*, laughing. 'Is one skinful enough for such a pair? Drink, then, in the name of the Compassionate.'

He loosed a thin stream into Kim's hands, who drank native-fashion; but the lama must needs pull out a cup from his inexhaustible upper draperies and drink ceremonially.

'*Pardesi* [a foreigner],' Kim explained, as the old man delivered in an unknown tongue what was evidently a blessing.

They ate together in great content, clearing the begging-bowl. Then the lama took snuff from a portentous wooden snuff-gourd, fingered his rosary awhile, and so dropped into the easy sleep of age, as the shadow of Zam-Zammah grew long.

Kim loafed over to the nearest tobacco-seller, a rather lively young Mohammedan woman, and begged a rank cigar of the brand that they sell to students of the Punjab University who copy English customs. Then he smoked and thought, knees to chin, under the belly of the gun, and the outcome of his thoughts was a sudden and stealthy departure in the direction of Nila Ram's timber-yard.

The lama did not wake till the evening life of the city had begun with lamp-lighting and the return of white-robed clerks and subordinates from the Government offices. He stared dizzily in all directions, but none looked at him save a Hindu urchin in a dirty turban and Isabella-coloured clothes. Suddenly he bowed his head on his knees and wailed.

'What is this?' said the boy, standing before him. 'Hast thou been robbed?'

'It is my new *chela* [disciple] that is gone away from me, and I know not where he is.'

'And what like of man was thy disciple?'

'It was a boy who came to me in place of him who died, on account of the merit which I had gained when I bowed before the Law within there.' He pointed towards the Museum. 'He came upon me to show me a road which I had lost. He led me into the Wonder House, and by his talk emboldened me to speak to the Keeper of the Images, so that I was cheered and made strong. And when I was faint with hunger he begged for me, as would a *chela* for his teacher. Suddenly was he sent. Suddenly has he gone away. It was in my mind to have taught him the Law upon the road to Benares.'

Kim stood amazed at this, because he had overheard the talk in the Museum, and knew that the old man was speaking the truth, which is a thing a native on the road seldom presents to a stranger.

'But I see now that he was but sent for a purpose. By this I know that I shall find a certain River for which I seek.'

'The River of the Arrow?' said Kim, with a superior smile.

'Is this yet another Sending?' cried the lama. 'To none have

I spoken of my search, save to the Priest of the Images. Who art thou?'

'Thy *chela*,' said Kim simply, sitting on his heels. 'I have never seen anyone like to thee in all this my life. I go with thee to Benares. And, too, I think that so old a man as thou, speaking the truth to chance-met people at dusk, is in great need of a disciple.'

'But the River – the River of the Arrow?'

'Oh, that I heard when thou wast speaking to the Englishman. I lay against the door.'

The lama sighed. 'I thought thou hadst been a guide permitted. Such things fall sometimes – but I am not worthy. Thou dost not, then, know the River?'

'Not I.' Kim laughed uneasily. 'I go to look for – for a bull – a Red Bull on a green field who shall help me.' Boylike, if an acquaintance had a scheme, Kim was quite ready with one of his own; and, boylike, he had really thought for as much as twenty minutes at a time of his father's prophecy.

'To what, child?' said the lama.

'God knows, but so my father told me. I heard thy talk in the Wonder House of all those new strange places in the Hills, and if one so old and so little – so used to truth-telling – may go out for the small matter of a river, it seemed to me that I too must go a-travelling. If it is our fate to find those things we shall find them – thou, thy River; and I, my Bull, and the Strong Pillars and some other matters that I forget.'

'It is not pillars but a Wheel from which I would be free,' said the lama.

'That is all one. Perhaps they will make me a king,' said Kim, serenely prepared for anything.

'I will teach thee other and better desires upon the road,' the lama replied in the voice of authority. 'Let us go to Benares.'

'Not by night. Thieves are abroad. Wait till the day.'

'But there is no place to sleep.' The old man was used to the order of his monastery, and though he slept on the ground, as the Rule decrees, preferred a decency in these things.

'We shall get good lodging at the Kashmir Serai,' said Kim, laughing at his perplexity. 'I have a friend there. Come!'

The hot and crowded bazars blazed with light as they made their way through the press of all the races in Upper India, and the lama mooned through it like a man in a dream. It was his first experience of a large manufacturing city, and the crowded tram-car with its continually squealing brakes frightened him. Half pushed, half towed, he arrived at the high gate of the Kashmir Serai: that huge open square over against the railway station, surrounded with arched cloisters, where the camel and horse caravans put up on their return from Central Asia. Here were all manner of Northern folk, tending tethered ponies and kneeling camels; loading and unloading bales and bundles; drawing water for the evening meal at the creaking well-windlasses; piling grass before the shrieking, wild-eyed stallions; cuffing the surly caravan dogs; paying off camel-drivers; taking on new grooms; swearing, shouting, arguing, and chaffering in the packed square. The cloisters, reached by three or four masonry steps, made a haven of refuge around this turbulent sea. Most of them were rented to traders, as we rent the arches of a viaduct; the space between pillar and pillar being bricked or boarded off into rooms, which were guarded by heavy wooden doors and cumbrous native padlocks. Locked doors showed that the owner was away, and a few rude – sometimes very rude – chalk or paint scratches told where he had gone. Thus: 'Lutuf Ullah is gone to Kurdistan.' Below, in coarse verse: 'O Allah, who sufferest lice to live on the coat of a Kabuli, why hast thou allowed this louse Lutuf to live so long?'

Kim, fending the lama between excited men and excited beasts, sidled along the cloisters to the far end, nearest the railway station, where Mahbub Ali, the horse-trader, lived when he came in from that mysterious land beyond the Passes of the North.

Kim had had many dealings with Mahbub in his little life,

– especially between his tenth and his thirteenth year – and the big burly Afghan, his beard dyed scarlet with lime (for he was elderly and did not wish his grey hairs to show), knew the boy's value as a gossip. Sometimes he would tell Kim to watch a man who had nothing whatever to do with horses: to follow him for one whole day and report every soul with whom he talked. Kim would deliver himself of his tale at evening, and Mahbub would listen without a word or gesture. It was intrigue of some kind, Kim knew; but its worth lay in saying nothing whatever to anyone except Mahbub, who gave him beautiful meals all hot from the cookshop at the head of the serai, and once as much as eight annas in money.

'He is here,' said Kim, hitting a bad-tempered camel on the nose. 'Oh, Mahbub Ali!' He halted at a dark arch and slipped behind the bewildered lama.

The horse-trader, his deep, embroidered Bokhariot belt unloosed, was lying on a pair of silk carpet saddle-bags, pulling lazily at an immense silver hookah. He turned his head very slightly at the cry; and seeing only the tall silent figure, chuckled in his deep chest.

'Allah! A lama! A Red Lama! It is far from Lahore to the Passes. What dost thou do here?'

The lama held out the begging-bowl mechanically.

'God's curse on all unbelievers!' said Mahbub. 'I do not give to a lousy Tibetan; but ask my Baltis over yonder behind the camels. They may value your blessings. Oh, horseboys, here is a countryman of yours. See if he be hungry.'

A shaven, crouching Balti, who had come down with the horses, and who was nominally some sort of degraded Buddhist, fawned upon the priest, and in thick gutturals besought the Holy One to sit at the horseboys' fire.

'Go!' said Kim, pushing him lightly, and the lama strode away, leaving Kim at the edge of the cloister.

'Go!' said Mahbub Ali, returning to his hookah. 'Little Hindu, run away. God's curse on all unbelievers! Beg from those of my tail who are of thy faith.'

'Maharaj,' whined Kim, using the Hindu form of address,

and thoroughly enjoying the situation; 'my father is dead – my mother is dead – my stomach is empty.'

'Beg from my men among the horses, I say. There must be some Hindus in my tail.'

'Oh, Mahbub Ali, but am *I* a Hindu?' said Kim in English.

The trader gave no sign of astonishment, but looked under shaggy eyebrows.

'Little Friend of all the World,' said he, 'what is this?'

'Nothing. I am now that holy man's disciple; and we go a pilgrimage together – to Benares, he says. He is quite mad, and I am tired of Lahore city. I wish new air and water.'

'But for whom dost thou work? Why come to me?' The voice was harsh with suspicion.

'To whom else should I come? I have no money. It is not good to go about without money. Thou wilt sell many horses to the officers. They are very fine horses, these new ones: I have seen them. Give me a rupee, Mahbub Ali, and when I come to my wealth I will give thee a bond and pay.'

'Um!' said Mahbub Ali, thinking swiftly. 'Thou hast never before lied to me. Call that lama – stand back in the dark.'

'Oh, our tales will agree,' said Kim, laughing.

'We go to Benares,' said the lama, as soon as he understood the drift of Mahbub Ali's questions. 'The boy and I, I go to seek for a certain River.'

'Maybe – but the boy?'

'He is my disciple. He was sent, I think, to guide me to that River. Sitting under a gun was I when he came suddenly. Such things have befallen the fortunate to whom guidance was allowed. But I remember now, he said he was of this world – a Hindu.'

'And his name?'

'That I did not ask. Is he not my disciple?'

'His country – his race – his village? Mussalman – Sikh – Hindu – Jain – low caste or high?'

'Why should I ask? There is neither high nor low in the Middle Way. If he is my *chela* – does – will – can anyone take him from me? for, look you, without him I shall not find my River.' He wagged his head solemnly.

'None shall take him from thee. Go, sit among my Baltis,' said Mahbub Ali, and the lama drifted off, soothed by the promise.

'Is he not quite mad?' said Kim, coming forward to the light again. 'Why should I lie to thee, Hajji?'

Mahbub puffed his hookah in silence. Then he began, almost whispering: 'Umballa is on the road to Benares – if indeed ye two go there.'

'Tck! Tck! I tell thee he does not know how to lie – as we two know.'

'And if thou wilt carry a message for me as far as Umballa, I will give thee money. It concerns a horse – a white stallion which I have sold to an officer upon the last time I returned from the Passes. But then – stand nearer and hold up hands as begging – the pedigree of the white stallion was not fully established, and that officer, who is now at Umballa, bade me make it clear.' (Mahbub here described the horse and the appearance of the officer.) 'So the message to that officer will be: "The pedigree of the white stallion is fully established." By this will he know that thou comest from me. He will then say "What proof hast thou?" and thou wilt answer: "Mahbub Ali has given me the proof." '

'And all for the sake of a white stallion,' said Kim, with a giggle, his eyes aflame.

'That pedigree I will give thee now – in my own fashion – and some hard words as well.' A shadow passed behind Kim, and a feeding camel. Mahbub Ali raised his voice.

'Allah! Art thou the only beggar in the city? Thy mother is dead. Thy father is dead. So is it with all of them. Well, well –' He turned as feeling on the floor beside him and tossed a flap of soft, greasy Mussalman bread to the boy. 'Go and lie down among my horseboys for to-night – thou and the lama. Tomorrow I may give thee service.'

Kim slunk away, his teeth in the bread, and, as he

expected, he found a small wad of folded tissue-paper wrapped in oilskin, with three silver rupees – enormous largesse. He smiled and thrust money and paper into his leather amulet-case. The lama, sumptuously fed by Mahbub's Baltis, was already asleep in a corner of one of the stalls. Kim lay down beside him and laughed. He knew he had rendered a service to Mahbub Ali, and not for one little minute did he believe the tale of the stallion's pedigree.

But Kim did not suspect that Mahbub Ali, known as one of the best horse-dealers in the Punjab, a wealthy and enterprising trader, whose caravans penetrated far and far into the Back of Beyond, was registered in one of the locked books of the Indian Survey Department as C25 1B. Twice or thrice yearly C25 would send in a little story, baldly told but most interesting, and generally – it was checked by the statements of R17 and M4 – quite true. It concerned all manner of out-of-the-way mountain principalities, explorers of nationalities other than English, and the gun-trade – was, in brief, a small portion of that vast mass of 'information received' on which the Indian Government acts. But, recently, five confederated Kings, who had no business to confederate, had been informed by a kindly Northern Power that there was a leakage of news from their territories into British India. So those Kings' Prime Ministers were seriously annoyed and took steps, after the Oriental fashion. They suspected, among many others, the bullying, red-bearded horse-dealer whose caravans ploughed through their fastnesses belly-deep in snow. At least, his caravan that season had been ambushed and shot at twice on the way down, when Mahbub's men accounted for three strange ruffians who might, or might not, have been hired for the job. Therefore Mahbub had avoided halting at the insalubrious city of Peshawur, and had come through without stop to Lahore, where, knowing his country-people, he anticipated curious developments.

And there was that on Mahbub Ali which he did not wish to keep an hour longer than was necessary – a wad of closely folded tissue-paper, wrapped in oilskin – an impersonal, unaddressed statement, with five microscopic pin-holes in one corner, that most scandalously betrayed the five confederated Kings, the sympathetic Northern Power, a Hindu banker in Peshawur, a firm of gun-makers in Belgium, and an important, semi-independent Mohammedan ruler to the south. This last was R17's work, which Mahbub had picked up beyond the Dora Pass and was carrying in for R17, who, owing to circumstances over which he had no control, could not leave his post of observation. Dynamite was milky and innocuous beside that report of C25; and even an Oriental, with an Oriental's views of the value of time, could see that the sooner it was in the proper hands the better. Mahbub had no particular desire to die by violence, because two or three family blood-feuds across the Border hung unfinished on his hands, and when these scores were cleared he intended to settle down as a more or less virtuous citizen. He had never passed the serai gate since his arrival two days ago, but had been ostentatious in sending telegrams to Bombay, where he banked some of his money; to Delhi, where a sub-partner of his own clan was selling horses to the agent of a Rajputana state; and to Umballa, where an Englishman was excitedly demanding the pedigree of a white stallion. The public letter-writer, who knew English, composed excellent telegrams, such as: '*Creighton, Lauel Bank, Umballa. Horse is Arabian as already advised. Sorrowful delayed pedigree which am translating.*' And later to the same address: '*Much sorrowful delay. Will forward pedigree.*' To his sub-partner at Delhi he wired: '*Lutuf Ullah. Have wired two thousand rupees your credit Luchman Narain's bank.*' This was entirely in the way of trade, but every one of those telegrams was discussed and re-discussed, by parties who conceived themselves to be interested, before they went over to the railway station in charge of a foolish Balti, who allowed all sorts of people to read them on the road.

When, in Mahbub's own picturesque language, he had muddied the wells of inquiry with the stick of precaution, Kim had dropped on him, sent from Heaven; and, being as prompt as he was unscrupulous, Mahbub Ali, used to taking all sorts of gusty chances, pressed him into service on the spot.

A wandering lama with a low-caste boy-servant might attract a moment's interest as they wandered about India, the land of pilgrims; but no one would suspect them or, what was more to the point, rob.

He called for a new light-ball to his hookah, and considered the case. If the worst came to the worst, and the boy came to harm, the paper would incriminate nobody. And he would go up to Umballa leisurely and – at a certain risk of exciting fresh suspicion – repeat his tale by word of mouth to the people concerned.

But R17's report was the kernel of the whole affair, and it would be distinctly inconvenient if that failed to come to hand. However, God was great, and Mahbub Ali felt he had done all he could for the time being. Kim was the one soul in the world who had never told him a lie. That would have been a fatal blot on Kim's character if Mahbub had not known that to others, for his own ends or Mahbub's business, Kim could lie like an Oriental.

Then Mahbub Ali rolled across the serai to the Gate of the Harpies who paint their eyes and trap the stranger, and was at some pains to call on the one girl who, he had reason to believe, was a particular friend of a smooth-faced Kashmiri pundit, who had waylaid his simple Balti in the matter of the telegrams. It was an utterly foolish thing to do; because they fell to drinking perfumed brandy against the Law of the Prophet, and Mahbub grew wonderfully drunk, and the gates of his mouth were loosened, and he pursued the Flower of Delight with the feet of intoxication till he fell flat among the cushions, where the Flower of Delight, aided by a smooth-faced Kashmiri pundit, searched him from head to foot most thoroughly.

About the same hour Kim heard soft feet in Mahbub's deserted stall. The horse-trader, curiously enough, had left his door unlocked, and his men were busy celebrating their return to India with a whole sheep of Mahbub's bounty. A sleek young gentleman from Delhi, armed with a bunch of keys which the Flower had unshackled from the senseless one's belt, went through every single box, bundle, mat, and saddle-bag in Mahbub's possession even more systematically than the Flower and the pundit were searching the owner.

'And I think,' said the Flower scornfully an hour later, one rounded elbow on the snoring carcass, 'that he is no more than a pig of an Afghan horse-dealer, with no thought except women and horses. Moreover, he may have sent it away by now – if ever there were such a thing.'

'Nay – in a matter touching Five Kings it would be next his black heart,' said the pundit. 'Was there nothing?'

The Delhi man laughed and resettled his turban as he entered. 'I searched between the soles of his slippers as the Flower searched his clothes. This is not the man but another. I leave little unseen.'

'They did not say he was the very man,' said the pundit thoughtfully. 'They said, "Look if he be the man, since our counsels are troubled."'

'That North country is full of horse-dealers as an old coat of lice. There is Sikandar Khan, Nur Ali Beg, and Farrukh Shah – all heads of *kafilas* [caravans] – who deal there,' said the Flower.

'They have not yet come in,' said the pundit. 'Thou must ensnare them later.'

'Phew!' said the Flower with deep disgust, rolling Mahbub's head from her lap. 'I earn my money. Farrukh Shah is a bear, Ali Beg a swashbuckler, and old Sikandar Khan – yaie! Go! I sleep now. This swine will not stir till dawn.'

When Mahbub woke, the Flower talked to him severely on the sin of drunkenness. Asiatics do not wink when they have outmanoeuvred an enemy, but as Mahbub Ali cleared his throat, tightened his belt, and staggered forth under the early morning stars, he came very near to it.

'What a colt's trick!' said he to himself. 'As if every girl in Peshawur did not use it! But 'twas prettily done. Now God

He knows how many more there be upon the Road who have orders to test me – perhaps with the knife. So it stands that the boy must go to Umballa – and by rail – for the writing is something urgent. I abide here, following the Flower and drinking wine as an Afghan coper should.'

He halted at the stall next but one to his own. His men lay there heavy with sleep. There was no sign of Kim or the lama.

'Up!' He stirred a sleeper. 'Whither went those who lay here last even – the lama and the boy? Is aught missing?'

'Nay,' grunted the man, 'the old madman rose at second cockcrow saying he would go to Benares, and the young one led him away.'

'The curse of Allah on all unbelievers!' said Mahbub heartily, and climbed into his own stall, growling in his beard.

But it was Kim who had wakened the lama – Kim with one eye laid against a knot-hole in the planking, who had seen the Delhi man's search through the boxes. This was no common thief that turned over letters, bills, and saddles – no mere burglar who ran a little knife sideways into the soles of Mahbub's slippers, or picked the seams of the saddle-bags so deftly. At first Kim had been minded to give the alarm – the long-drawn *cho-or – choor!* [thief! thief!] that sets the serai ablaze of nights; but he looked more carefully, and, hand on amulet, drew his own conclusions.

'It must be the pedigree of that made-up horse-lie,' said he, 'the thing that I carry to Umballa. Better that we go now. Those who search bags with knives may presently search bellies with knives. Surely there is a woman behind this. Hai! Hai!' in a whisper to the light-sleeping old man. 'Come. It is time – time to go to Benares.'

The lama rose obediently, and they passed out of the serai like shadows.

Chapter 2

And whoso will, from Pride released,
Contemning neither creed nor priest,
May feel the Soul of all the East
About him at Kamakura.
Buddha at Kamakura.

THEY entered the fort-like railway station, black in the
end of night; the electrics sizzling over the goods-yard
where they handle the heavy Northern grain-traffic.

'This is the work of devils!' said the lama, recoiling from
the hollow echoing darkness, the glimmer of rails between the
masonry platforms, and the maze of girders above. He stood
in a gigantic stone hall paved, it seemed, with the sheeted
dead – third-class passengers who had taken their tickets
overnight and were sleeping in the waiting-rooms. All hours
of the twenty-four are alike to Orientals, and their passenger
traffic is regulated accordingly.

'This is where the fire-carriages come. One stands behind
that hole' – Kim pointed to the ticket-office – 'who will give
thee a paper to take thee to Umballa.'

'But we go to Benares,' he replied petulantly.

'All one. Benares then. Quick: she comes!'

'Take thou the purse.'

The lama, not so well used to trains as he had pretended,
started as the 3.25 a.m. south-bound roared in. The sleepers
sprang to life, and the station filled with clamour and
shootings, cries of water and sweetmeat vendors, shouts of
native policemen, and shrill yells of women gathering up their
baskets, their families, and their husbands.

'It is the train – only the *te-rain*. It will not come here.
Wait!' Amazed at the lama's immense simplicity (he had
handed him a small bag full of rupees), Kim asked and paid
for a ticket to Umballa. A sleepy clerk grunted and flung out a
ticket to the next station, just six miles distant.

'Nay,' said Kim, scanning it with a grin. 'This may serve for farmers, but I live in the city of Lahore. It was cleverly done, Babu. Now give the ticket to Umballa.'

The Babu scowled and dealt the proper ticket.

'Now another to Amritzar,' said Kim, who had no notion of spending Mahbub Ali's money on anything so crude as a paid ride to Umballa. 'The price is so much. The small money in return is just so much. I know the ways of the *te-rain* ... Never did *yogi* need *chela* as thou dost,' he went on merrily to the bewildered lama. 'They would have flung thee out at Mian Mir but for me. This way! Come!' He returned the money, keeping only one anna in each rupee of the price of the Umballa ticket as his commission – the immemorial commission of Asia.

The lama jibbed at the open door of a crowded third-class carriage. 'Were it not better to walk?' said he weakly.

A burly Sikh artisan thrust forth his bearded head. 'Is he afraid? Do not be afraid. I remember the time when I was afraid of the *te-rain*. Enter! This thing is the work of the Government.'

'I do not fear,' said the lama. 'Have ye room within for two?'

'There is no room even for a mouse,' shrilled the wife of a well-to-do cultivator – a Hindu Jat from the rich Jullundur district. Our night trains are not as well looked after as the day ones, where the sexes are very strictly kept to separate carriages.

'Oh, mother of my son, we can make space,' said the blue-turbaned husband. 'Pick up the child. It is a holy man, see'st thou?'

'And my lap full of seventy times seven bundles! Why not bid him sit on my knee, Shameless? But men are ever thus!' She looked round for approval. An Amritzar courtesan near the window sniffed behind her head drapery.

'Enter! Enter!' cried a fat Hindu money-lender, his folded account-book in a cloth under his arm. With an oily smirk: 'It is well to be kind to the poor.'

'Ay, at seven per cent a month with a mortgage on the unborn calf,' said a young Dogra soldier going south on leave; and they all laughed.

'Will it travel to Benares?' said the lama.

'Assuredly. Else why should we come? Enter, or we are left,' cried Kim.

'See!' shrilled the Amritzar girl. 'He has never entered a train. Oh, see!'

'Nay, help,' said the cultivator, putting out a large brown hand and hauling him in. 'Thus is it done, father.'

'But – but – I sit on the floor. It is against the Rule to sit on a bench,' said the lama. 'Moreover, it cramps me.'

'I say,' began the money-lender, pursing his lips, 'that there is not one rule of right living which these *te-rain*s do not cause us to break. We sit, for example, side by side with all castes and peoples.'

'Yea, and with most outrageously shameless ones,' said the wife, scowling at the Amritzar girl making eyes at the young sepoy.

'I said we might have gone by cart along the road,' said the husband, 'and thus have saved some money.'

'Yes – and spent twice over what we saved on food by the way. That was talked out ten thousand times.'

'Ay, by ten thousand tongues,' grunted he.

'The Gods help us poor women if we may not speak. Oho! He is of that sort which may not look at or reply to a woman.' For the lama, constrained by his Rule, took not the faintest notice of her. 'And his disciple is like him?'

'Nay, mother,' said Kim most promptly. 'Not when the woman is well-looking and above all charitable to the hungry.'

'A beggar's answer,' said the Sikh, laughing. 'Thou hast brought it on thyself, sister!' Kim's hands were crooked in supplication.

'And whither goest thou?' said the woman, handing him the half of a cake from a greasy package.

'Even to Benares.'

'Jugglers belike?' the young soldier suggested. 'Have ye any tricks to pass the time? Why does not that yellow man answer?'

'Because,' said Kim stoutly, 'he is holy, and thinks upon matters hidden from thee.'

'That may be well. We of the Ludhiana Sikhs' – he rolled it out sonorously – 'do not trouble our heads with doctrine. We fight.'

'My sister's brother's son is *naik* [corporal] in that regiment,' said the Sikh craftsman quietly. 'There are also some Dogra companies there.' The soldier glared, for a Dogra is of other caste than a Sikh, and the banker tittered.

'They are all one to me,' said the Amritzar girl.

'That we believe,' snorted the cultivator's wife malignantly.

'Nay, but all who serve the Sirkar with weapons in their hands are, as it were, one brotherhood. There is one brotherhood of the caste, but beyond that again' – she looked round timidly – 'the bond of the *Pulton* – the Regiment – eh?'

'My brother is in a Jat regiment,' said the cultivator. 'Dogras be good men.'

'*Thy* Sikhs at least were of that opinion,' said the soldier, with a scowl at the placid old man in the corner. '*Thy* Sikhs thought so when our two companies came to help them at the Pirzai Kotal in the face of eight Afridi standards on the ridge not three months gone.'

He told the story of a Border action in which the Dogra companies of the Ludhiana Sikhs had acquitted themselves well. The Amritzar girl smiled; for she knew the tale was to win her approval.

'Alas!' said the cultivator's wife at the end. 'So their villages were burnt and their little children made homeless?'

'They had marked our dead. They paid a great payment after we of the Sikhs had schooled them. So it was. Is this Amritzar?'

'Ay, and here they cut our tickets,' said the banker, fumbling at his belt.

The lamps were paling in the dawn when the half-caste guard came round. Ticket-collecting is a slow business in the East, where people secrete their tickets in all sorts of curious places. Kim produced his and was told to get out.

'But I go to Umballa,' he protested. 'I go with this holy man.'

'Thou canst go to Jehannum for aught I care. This ticket is only to Amritzar. Out!'

Kim burst into a flood of tears, protesting that the lama was his father and his mother, that he was the prop of the lama's declining years, and that the lama would die without his care. All the carriage bade the guard be merciful – the banker was specially eloquent here – but the guard hauled Kim on to the platform. The lama blinked – he could not overtake the situation – and Kim lifted up his voice and wept outside the carriage window.

'I am very poor. My father is dead – my mother is dead. O charitable ones, if I am left here, who shall tend that old man?'

'What – what is this?' the lama repeated. 'He must go to Benares. He must come with me. He is my *chela*. If there is money to be paid –'

'Oh, be silent,' whispered Kim; 'are we Rajahs to throw away good silver when the world is so charitable?'

The Amritzar girl stepped out with her bundles, and it was on her that Kim kept his watchful eye. Ladies of that persuasion, he knew, were generous.

'A ticket – a little *tikkut* to Umballa – O Breaker of Hearts!' She laughed. 'Hast thou no charity?'

'Does the holy man come from the North?'

'From far and far in the North he comes,' cried Kim. 'From among the hills.'

'There is snow among the pine-trees in the North – in the hills there is snow. My mother was from Kulu. Get thee a ticket. Ask him for a blessing.'

'Ten thousand blessings,' shrilled Kim. 'O Holy One, a woman has given us in charity so that I can come with thee – a woman with a golden heart. I run for the *tikkut*.'

The girl looked up at the lama, who had mechanically followed Kim to the platform. He bowed his head that he might not see her, and muttered in Tibetan as she passed on with the crowd.

'Light come – light go,' said the cultivator's wife viciously.

'She has acquired merit,' returned the lama. 'Beyond doubt it was a nun.'

'There be ten thousand such nuns in Amritzar alone. Return, old man, or the *te-rain* may depart without thee,' cried the banker.

'Not only was it sufficient for the ticket, but for a little food also,' said Kim, leaping to his place. 'Now eat, Holy One. Look. Day comes!'

Golden, rose, saffron, and pink, the morning mists smoked away across the flat green levels. All the rich Punjab lay out in the splendour of the keen sun. The lama flinched a little as the telegraph-posts swung by.

'Great is the speed of the *te-rain*,' said the banker, with a patronizing grin. 'We have gone farther since Lahore than thou couldst walk in two days: at even, we shall enter Umballa.'

'And that is still far from Benares,' said the lama wearily, mumbling over the cakes that Kim offered. They all unloosed their bundles and made their morning meal. Then the banker, the cultivator, and the soldier prepared their pipes and wrapped the compartment in choking, acrid smoke, spitting and coughing and enjoying themselves. The Sikh and the cultivator's wife chewed *pan*; the lama took snuff and told his beads, while Kim, cross-legged, smiled over the comfort of a full stomach.

'What rivers have ye by Benares?' said the lama of a sudden to the carriage at large.

'We have Gunga,' returned the banker, when the little titter had subsided.

'What others?'

'What other than Gunga?'

'Nay, but in my mind was the thought of a certain River of healing.'

'That is Gunga. Who bathes in her is made clean and goes to the Gods. Thrice have I made pilgrimage to Gunga.' He looked round proudly.

'There was need,' said the young sepoy drily, and the travellers' laugh turned against the banker.

'Clean – to return again to the Gods,' the lama muttered. 'And to go forth on the round of lives anew – still tied to the Wheel.' He shook his head testily. 'But maybe there is a mistake. Who, then, made Gunga in the beginning?'

'The Gods. Of what known faith art thou?' the banker said, appalled.

'I follow the Law – the Most Excellent Law. So it was the Gods that made Gunga. What like of Gods were they?'

The carriage looked at him in amazement. It was inconceivable that anyone should be ignorant of Gunga.

'What – what is thy God?' said the money-lender at last.

'Hear!' said the lama, shifting the rosary to his hand. 'Hear: for I speak of Him now! O people of Hind, listen!'

He began in Urdu the tale of the Lord Buddha, but, borne by his own thoughts, slid into Tibetan and long-droned texts from a Chinese book of the Buddha's life. The gentle, tolerant folk looked on reverently. All India is full of holy men stammering gospels in strange tongues; shaken and consumed in the fires of their own zeal; dreamers, babblers, and visionaries: as it has been from the beginning and will continue to the end.

'Um!' said the soldier of the Ludhiana Sikhs. 'There was a Mohammedan regiment lay next to us at the Pirzai Kotal, and a priest of theirs – he was, as I remember, a *naik* – when the fit was on him, spake prophecies. But the mad all are in God's keeping. His officers overlooked much in that man.'

The lama fell back on Urdu, remembering that he was in a strange land. 'Hear the tale of the Arrow which our Lord loosed from the bow,' he said.

This was much more to their taste, and they listened

curiously while he told it. 'Now, O people of Hind, I go to seek that River. Know ye aught that may guide me, for we be all men and women in evil case.'

'There is Gunga – and Gunga alone – who washes away sin,' ran the murmur round the carriage.

'Though past question we have good Gods Jullundur-way,' said the cultivator's wife, looking out of the window. 'See how they have blessed the crops.'

'To search every river in the Punjab is no small matter,' said her husband. 'For me, a stream that leaves good silt on my land suffices, and I thank Bhumia, the God of the Homestead.' He shrugged one knotted, bronzed shoulder.

'Think you our Lord came so far North?' said the lama, turning to Kim.

'It may be,' Kim replied soothingly, as he spat red *pan*-juice on the floor.

'The last of the Great Ones,' said the Sikh with authority, 'was Sikander Julkarn [Alexander the Great]. He paved the streets of Jullundur and built a great tank near Umballa. That pavement holds to this day; and the tank is there also. I never heard of thy God.'

'Let thy hair grow long and talk Punjabi,' said the young soldier jestingly to Kim, quoting a Northern proverb. 'That is all that makes a Sikh.' But he did not say this very loud.

The lama sighed and shrank into himself, a dingy, shapeless mass. In the pauses of their talk they could hear the low droning –'*Om mane pudme hum! Om mane pudme hum!*' – and the thick click of the wooden rosary beads.

'It irks me,' he said at last. 'The speed and the clatter irk me. Moreover, my *chela*, I think that maybe we have overpassed that River.'

'Peace, peace,' said Kim. 'Was not the River near Benares? We are yet far from the place.'

'But – if our Lord came North, it may be any one of these little ones that we have run across.'

'I do not know.'

'But thou wast sent to me – wast thou sent to me? – for the

merit I had acquired over yonder at Such-zen. From beside the cannon didst thou come – bearing two faces – and two garbs.'

'Peace. One must not speak of these things here,' whispered Kim. 'There was but one of me. Think again and thou wilt remember. A boy – a Hindu boy – by the great green cannon.'

'But was there not also an Englishman with a white beard – holy among images – who himself made more sure my assurance of the River of the Arrow?'

'He – we – went to the Ajaib-Gher in Lahore to pray before the Gods there,' Kim explained to the openly listening company.

'And the Sahib of the Wonder House talked to him – yes, this is truth – as a brother. He is a very holy man, from far beyond the Hills. Rest, thou. In time we come to Umballa.'

'But my River – the River of my healing?'

'And then, if it please thee, we will go hunting for that River on foot. So that we miss nothing – not even a little rivulet in a field-side.'

'But thou hast a Search of thine own?' The lama – very pleased that he remembered so well – sat bolt upright.

'Ay,' said Kim, humouring him. The boy was entirely happy to be out chewing *pan* and seeing new people in the great good-tempered world.

'It was a bull – a Red Bull that shall come and help thee – and carry thee – whither? I have forgotten. A Red Bull on a green field, was it not?'

'Nay, it will carry me nowhere,' said Kim. 'It is but a tale I told thee.'

'What is this?' The cultivator's wife leaned forward, her bracelets clinking on her arm. 'Do ye both dream dreams? A Red Bull on a green field, that shall carry thee to the heavens – or what? Was it a vision? Did one make a prophecy? *We* have a Red Bull in our village behind Jullundur city, and he grazes by choice in the very greenest of our fields!'

'Give a woman an old wife's tale and a weaver-bird a leaf

and a thread, they will weave wonderful things,' said the Sikh. 'All holy men dream dreams, and by following holy men their disciples attain that power.'

'A Red Bull on a green field, was it?' the lama repeated. 'In a former life it may be thou hast acquired merit, and the Bull will come to reward thee.'

'Nay – nay – it was but a tale one told to me – for a jest belike. But I will seek the Bull about Umballa, and thou canst look for thy River and rest from the clatter of the train.'

'It may be that the Bull knows – that he is sent to guide us both,' said the lama, hopefully as a child. Then to the company, indicating Kim: 'This one was sent to me but yesterday. He is not, I think, of this world.'

'Beggars aplenty have I met, and holy men to boot, but never such a *yogi* nor such a disciple,' said the woman.

Her husband touched his forehead lightly with one finger and smiled. But the next time the lama would eat they took care to give him of their best.

And at last – tired, sleepy, and dusty – they reached Umballa City Station.

'We abide here upon a law-suit,' said the cultivator's wife to Kim. 'We lodge with my man's cousin's younger brother. There is room also in the courtyard for thy *yogi* and for thee. Will – will he give me a blessing?'

'O holy man! A woman with a heart of gold gives us lodging for the night. It is a kindly land, this land of the South. See how we have been helped since the dawn!'

The lama bowed his head in benediction.

'To fill my cousin's younger brother's house with wastrels –' the husband began, as he shouldered his heavy bamboo staff.

'Thy cousin's younger brother owes my father's cousin something yet on his daughter's marriage-feast,' said the woman crisply. 'Let him put their food to that account. The *yogi* will beg, I doubt not.'

'Ay, I beg for him,' said Kim, anxious only to get the lama under shelter for the night, that he might seek Mahbub Ali's

Englishman and deliver himself of the white stallion's pedigree.

'Now,' said he, when the lama had come to an anchor in the inner courtyard of a decent Hindu house behind the cantonments, 'I go away for a while – to – to buy us victual in the bazar. Do not stray abroad till I return.'

'Thou wilt return? Thou wilt surely return?' The old man caught at his wrist. 'And thou wilt return in this very same shape? Is it too late to look tonight for the River?'

'Too late and too dark. Be comforted. Think how far thou art on the road – an hundred miles from Lahore already.'

'Yea – and farther from my monastery. Alas! It is a great and terrible world.'

Kim stole out and away, as unremarkable a figure as ever carried his own and a few score thousand other folk's fate slung round his neck. Mahbub Ali's directions left him little doubt of the house in which his Englishman lived; and a groom, bringing a dog-cart home from the Club, made him quite sure. It remained only to identify his man, and Kim slipped through the garden hedge and hid in a clump of plumed grass close to the veranda. The house blazed with lights, and servants moved about tables dressed with flowers, glass, and silver. Presently forth came an Englishman, dressed in black and white, humming a tune. It was too dark to see his face, so Kim, beggar-wise, tried an old experiment.

'Protector of the Poor!'

The man backed towards the voice.

'Mahbub Ali says –'

'Hah! What says Mahbub Ali?' He made no attempt to look for the speaker, and that showed Kim that he knew.

'The pedigree of the white stallion is fully established.'

'What proof is there?' The Englishman switched at the rose-hedge in the side of the drive.

'Mahbub Ali has given me this proof.' Kim flipped the wad of folded paper into the air, and it fell in the path beside the man, who put his foot on it as a gardener came round the corner. When the servant passed he picked it up, dropped a

rupee – Kim could hear the clink – and strode into the house,
never turning round. Swiftly Kim took up the money; but for
all his training, he was Irish enough by birth to reckon silver
the least part of any game. What he desired was the visible
effect of action; so, instead of slinking away, he lay close in the
grass and wormed nearer to the house.

He saw – Indian bungalows are open through and through
– the Englishman return to a small dressing-room, in a corner
of the veranda, that was half office, littered with papers and
despatch-boxes, and sit down to study Mahbub Ali's message. His face, by the full ray of the kerosene lamp, changed
and darkened, and Kim, used as every beggar must be to
watching countenances, took good note.

'Will! Will, dear!' called a woman's voice. 'You ought to be
in the drawing-room. They'll be here in a minute.'

The man still read intently.

'Will!' said the voice, five minutes later. '*He*'s come. I can
hear the troopers in the drive.'

The man dashed out bareheaded as a big landau with four
native troopers behind it halted at the veranda, and a tall,
black-haired man, erect as an arrow, swung out, preceded by
a young officer who laughed pleasantly.

Flat on his belly lay Kim, almost touching the high wheels.
His man and the black stranger exchanged two sentences.

'Certainly, sir,' said the young officer promptly. 'Everything waits while a horse is concerned.'

'We shan't be more than twenty minutes,' said Kim's man.
'You can do the honours – keep 'em amused, and all that.'

'Tell one of the troopers to wait,' said the tall man, and they
both passed into the dressing-room together as the landau
rolled away. Kim saw their heads bent over Mahbub Ali's
message, and heard the voices – one low and deferential, the
other sharp and decisive.

'It isn't a question of weeks. It is a question of days – hours
almost,' said the elder. 'I'd been expecting it for some time,
but this' – he tapped Mahbub Ali's paper – 'clinches it.
Grogan's dining here to-night, isn't he?'

'Yes, sir, and Macklin too.'

'Very good. I'll speak to them myself. The matter will be referred to the Council, of course, but this is a case where one is justified in assuming that we take action at once. Warn the Pindi and Peshawur brigades. It will disorganize all the summer reliefs, but we can't help that. This comes of not smashing them thoroughly the first time. Eight thousand should be enough.'

'What about artillery, sir?'

'I must consult Macklin.'

'Then it means war?'

'No. Punishment. When a man is bound by the action of his predecessor –'

'But C25 may have lied.'

'He bears out the other's information. Practically, they showed their hand six months back. But Devenish would have it there was a chance of peace. Of course they used it to make themselves stronger. Send off those telegrams at once – the new code, not the old – mine and Wharton's. I don't think we need keep the ladies waiting any longer. We can settle the rest over the cigars. I thought it was coming. It's punishment – not war.'

As the trooper cantered off, Kim crawled round to the back of the house, where, going on his Lahore experiences, he judged there would be food – and information. The kitchen was crowded with excited scullions, one of whom kicked him.

'Aie,' said Kim, feigning tears. 'I came only to wash dishes in return for a bellyful.'

'All Umballa is on the same errand. Get hence. They go in now with the soup. Think you that we who serve Creighton Sahib need strange scullions to help us through a big dinner?'

'It is a very big dinner,' said Kim, looking at the plates.

'Small wonder. The guest of honour is none other than the Jang-i-Lat Sahib [the Commander-in-Chief].'

'Ho!' said Kim, with the correct guttural note of wonder. He had learned what he wanted, and when the scullion turned he was gone.

'And all that trouble,' said he to himself, thinking as usual in Hindustani, 'for a horse's pedigree! Mahbub Ali should have come to me to learn a little lying. Every time before that I have borne a message it concerned a woman. Now it is men. Better. The tall man said that they will loose a great army to punish someone – somewhere – the news goes to Pindi and Peshawur. There are also guns. Would I had crept nearer. It is big news!'

He returned to find the cultivator's cousin's younger brother discussing the family law-suit in all its bearings with the cultivator and his wife and a few friends, while the lama dozed. After the evening meal some one passed him a water-pipe; and Kim felt very much of a man as he pulled at the smooth coconut-shell, his legs spread abroad in the moon-light, his tongue clicking in remarks from time to time. His hosts were most polite; for the cultivator's wife had told them of his vision of the Red Bull, and of his probable descent from another world. Moreover, the lama was a great and venerable curiosity. The family priest, an old, tolerant Sarsut Brahmin, dropped in later, and naturally started a theological argument to impress the family. By creed, of course, they were all on their priest's side, but the lama was the guest and the novelty. His gentle kindliness, and his impressive Chinese quotations, that sounded like spells, delighted them hugely; and in this sympathetic, simple air, he expanded like the Bodhisat's own lotus, speaking of his life in the great hills of Such-zen, before, as he said, 'I rose up to seek enlightenment.'

Then it came out that in those worldly days he had been a master-hand at casting horoscopes and nativities; and the family priest led him on to describe his methods; each giving the planets names that the other could not understand, and pointing upwards as the big stars sailed across the dark. The children of the house tugged unrebuked at his rosary; and he clean forgot the Rule which forbids looking at women as he talked of enduring snows, landslips, blocked passes, the remote cliffs where men find sapphires and turquoise, and that wonderful upland road that leads at last into Great China itself.

'How thinkest thou of this one?' said the cultivator aside to the priest.

'A holy man – a holy man indeed. His Gods are not the Gods, but his feet are upon the Way,' was the answer. 'And his methods of nativities, though that is beyond thee, are wise and sure.'

'Tell me,' said Kim lazily, 'whether I find my Red Bull on a green field, as was promised me.'

'What knowledge hast thou of thy birth-hour?' the priest asked, swelling with importance.

'Between first and second cockcrow of the first night in May.'

'Of what year?'

'I do not know; but upon the hour that I cried first fell the great earthquake in Srinagar which is in Kashmir.' This Kim had from the woman who took care of him, and she again from Kimball O'Hara. The earthquake had been felt in India, and for long stood a leading date in the Punjab.

'Ai!' said a woman excitedly. This seemed to make Kim's supernatural origin more certain. 'Was not such an one's daughter born then –'

'And her mother bore her husband four sons in four years – all likely boys,' cried the cultivator's wife, sitting outside the circle in the shadow.

'None reared in the knowledge,' said the family priest, 'forget how the planets stood in their Houses upon that night.' He began to draw in the dust of the courtyard. 'At least thou hast good claim to a half of the House of the Bull. How runs thy prophecy?'

'Upon a day,' said Kim, delighted at the sensation he was creating, 'I shall be made great by means of a Red Bull on a green field, but first there will enter two men making all things ready.'

'Yes: thus ever at the opening of a vision. A thick darkness that clears slowly; anon one enters with a broom making ready the place. Then begins the Sight. Two men – thou sayest? Ay, ay. The Sun, leaving the House of the Bull, enters that of the Twins. Hence the two men of the prophecy. Let us now consider. Fetch me a twig, little one.'

He knitted his brows, scratched, smoothed out, and scratched again in the dust mysterious signs – to the wonder of all save the lama, who, with fine instinct, forbore to interfere.

At the end of half an hour, he tossed the twig from him with a grunt.

'Hm! Thus say the stars. Within three days come the two men to make all things ready. After them follows the Bull; but the sign over against him is the sign of War and armed men.'

'There was indeed a man of the Ludhiana Sikhs in the carriage from Lahore,' said the cultivator's wife hopefully.

'Tck! Armed men – many hundreds. What concern hast thou with war?' said the priest to Kim. 'Thine is a red and an angry sign of War to be loosed very soon.'

'None – none,' said the lama earnestly. 'We seek only peace and our River.'

Kim smiled, remembering what he had overheard in the dressing-room. Decidedly he was a favourite of the stars.

The priest brushed his foot over the rude horoscope. 'More than this I cannot see. In three days comes the Bull to thee, boy.'

'And my River, my River,' pleaded the lama. 'I had hoped his Bull would lead us both to the River.'

'Alas, for that wondrous River, my brother,' the priest replied. 'Such things are not common.'

Next morning, though they were pressed to stay, the lama insisted on departure. They gave Kim a large bundle of good food and nearly three annas in copper money for the needs of the road, and with many blessings watched the two go southward in the dawn.

'Pity it is that these and such as these could not be freed from the Wheel of Things,' said the lama.

'Nay, then would only evil people be left on the earth, and who would give us meat and shelter?' quoth Kim, stepping merrily under his burden.

'Yonder is a small stream. Let us look,' said the lama, and he led from the white road across the fields; walking into a very hornets' nest of pariah dogs.

Chapter 3

Yea, voice of every Soul that clung
To life that strove from rung to rung
When Devadatta's rule was young,
    The warm wind brings Kamakura.
                Buddha at Kamakura.

Behind them an angry farmer brandished a bamboo pole. He was a market-gardener, Arain by caste, growing vegetables and flowers for Umballa city, and well Kim knew the breed.

'Such an one,' said the lama, disregarding the dogs, 'is impolite to strangers, intemperate of speech and uncharitable. Be warned by his demeanour, my disciple.'

'Ho, shameless beggars!' shouted the farmer. 'Begone! Get hence!'

'We go,' the lama returned, with quiet dignity. 'We go from these unblessed fields.'

'Ah,' said Kim, sucking in his breath. 'If the next crops fail, thou canst only blame thine own tongue.'

The man shuffled uneasily in his slippers. 'The land is full of beggars,' he began, half apologetically.

'And by what sign didst thou know that we would beg from thee, O Mali?' said Kim tartly, using the name that a market-gardener least likes. 'All we sought was to look at that river beyond the field there.'

'River, forsooth!' the man snorted. 'What city do ye hail from not to know a canal-cut? It runs as straight as an arrow, and I pay for the water as though it were molten silver. There is a branch of a river beyond. But if ye need water I can give that – and milk.'

'Nay, we will go to the river,' said the lama, striding out.

'Milk and a meal,' the man stammered, as he looked at the strange tall figure. 'I – I would not draw evil upon myself –

46

or my crops. But beggars are so many in these hard days.'

'Take notice.' The lama turned to Kim. 'He was led to speak harshly by the Red Mist of anger. That clearing from his eyes, he becomes courteous and of an affable heart. May his fields be blessed! Beware not to judge men too hastily, O farmer.'

'I have met holy ones who would have cursed thee from hearthstone to byre,' said Kim to the abashed man. 'Is he not wise and holy? I am his disciple.'

He cocked his nose in the air loftily and stepped across the narrow field-borders with great dignity.

'There is no pride,' said the lama, after a pause, 'there is no pride among such as follow the Middle Way.'

'But thou hast said he was low-caste and discourteous.'

'Low-caste I did not say, for how can that be which is not? Afterwards he amended his discourtesy, and I forgot the offence. Moreover, he is as we are, bound upon the Wheel of Things; but he does not tread the way of deliverance.' He halted at a little runlet among the fields, and considered the hoof-pitted bank.

'Now, how wilt thou know thy River?' said Kim, squatting in the shade of some tall sugar-cane.

'When I find it, an enlightenment will surely be given. This, I feel, is not the place. O littlest among the waters, if only thou couldst tell me where runs my River! But be thou blessed to make the fields bear!'

'Look! Look!' Kim sprang to his side and dragged him back. A yellow-and-brown streak glided from the purple rustling stems to the bank, stretched its neck to the water, drank, and lay still – a big cobra with fixed, lidless eyes.

'I have no stick – I have no stick,' said Kim. 'I will get me one and break his back.'

'Why? He is upon the Wheel as we are – a life ascending or descending – very far from deliverance. Great evil must the soul have done that is cast into this shape.'

'I hate all snakes,' said Kim. No native training can quench the white man's horror of the Serpent.

'Let him live out his life.' The coiled thing hissed and half opened its hood. 'May thy release come soon, brother!' the lama continued placidly. 'Hast *thou* knowledge, by chance, of my River?'

'Never have I seen such a man as thou art,' Kim whispered, overwhelmed. 'Do the very snakes understand thy talk?'

'Who knows?' He passed within a foot of the cobra's poised head. It flattened itself among the dusty coils.

'Come, thou!' he called over his shoulder.

'Not I,' said Kim. 'I go round.'

'Come. He does no hurt.'

Kim hesitated for a moment. The lama backed his order by some droned Chinese quotation which Kim took for a charm. He obeyed and bounded across the rivulet, and the snake, indeed, made no sign.

'Never have I seen such a man.' Kim wiped the sweat from his forehead. 'And now, whither go we?'

'That is for thee to say. I am old, and a stranger – far from my own place. But that the *rêl*-carriage fills my head with noises of devil-drums I would go in it to Benares now ... Yet by so going we may miss the River. Let us find another river.'

Where the hard-worked soil gives three and even four crops a year – through patches of sugar-cane, tobacco, long white radishes, and nol-kol, all that day they strolled on, turning aside to every glimpse of water; rousing village dogs and sleeping villages at noonday; the lama replying to the volleyed questions with an unswerving simplicity. They sought a River – a River of miraculous healing. Had any one knowledge of such a stream? Sometimes men laughed, but more often heard the story out to the end and offered them a place in the shade, a drink of milk, and a meal. The women were always kind, and the little children as children are the world over, alternately shy and venturesome. Evening found them at rest under the village tree of a mud-walled, mud-roofed hamlet, talking to the headman as the cattle came in from the grazing-grounds and the women prepared the day's last meal. They had passed beyond the belt of market-gardens round hungry Umballa, and were among the mile-wide green of the staple crops.

He was a white-bearded and affable elder, used to entertaining strangers. He dragged out a string bedstead for the lama, set warm cooked food before him, prepared him a pipe, and, the evening ceremonies being finished in the village temple, sent for the village priest.

Kim told the older children tales of the size and beauty of Lahore, of railway travel, and such-like city things, while the men talked, slowly as their cattle chew the cud.

'I cannot fathom it,' said the headman at last to the priest. 'How readest thou this talk?' The lama, his tale told, was silently telling his beads.

'He is a Seeker,' the priest answered. 'The land is full of such. Remember him who came only last month – the *fakir* with the tortoise?'

'Ay, but that man had right and reason, for Krishna Himself appeared in a vision promising him Paradise without the burning-pyre if he journeyed to Prayag. This man seeks no God who is within my knowledge.'

'Peace, he is old: he comes from far off, and he is mad,' the smooth-shaven priest replied. 'Hear me.' He turned to the lama. 'Three *koss* [six miles] to the westward runs the great road to Calcutta.'

'But I would go to Benares – to Benares.'

'And to Benares also. It crosses all streams on this side of Hind. Now my word to thee, Holy One, is rest here till tomorrow. Then take the road' (it was the Grand Trunk Road he meant) 'and test each stream that it overpasses; for, as I understand, the virtue of thy River lies neither in one pool nor place, but throughout its length. Then, if thy Gods will, be assured that thou wilt come upon thy freedom.'

'That is well said.' The lama was much impressed by the plan. 'We will begin tomorrow, and a blessing on thee for showing old feet such a near road.' A deep, sing-song Chinese half-chant closed the sentence. Even the priest was impressed, and the headman feared an evil spell: but none could look at the lama's simple, eager face and doubt him long.

'Seest thou my *chela*?' he said, diving into his snuff-gourd with an important sniff. It was his duty to repay courtesy with courtesy.

'I see – and hear.' The headman rolled his eye where Kim was chatting to a girl in blue as she laid crackling thorns on a fire.

'He also has a Search of his own. No river, but a Bull. Yea, a Red Bull on a green field will some day raise him to honour. He is, I think, not altogether of this world. He was sent of a sudden to aid me in this search, and his name is Friend of all the World.'

The priest smiled. 'Ho, there, Friend of all the World,' he cried across the sharp-smelling smoke, 'what art thou?'

'This Holy One's disciple,' said Kim.

'He says thou art a *būt* [a spirit].'

'Can *būts* eat?' said Kim, with a twinkle. 'For I am hungry.'

'It is no jest,' cried the lama. 'A certain astrologer of that city whose name I have forgotten –'

'That is no more than the city of Umballa where we slept last night,' Kim whispered to the priest.

'Ay, Umballa was it? He cast a horoscope and declared that my *chela* should find his desire within two days. But what said he of the meaning of the stars, Friend of all the World?'

Kim cleared his throat and looked around at the village greybeards.

'The meaning of my Star is War,' he replied pompously.

Somebody laughed at the little tattered figure strutting on the brickwork plinth under the great tree. Where a native would have lain down, Kim's white blood set him upon his feet.

'Ay, War,' he answered.

'That is a sure prophecy,' rumbled a deep voice. 'For there is always war along the Border – as I know.'

It was an old, withered man, who had served the Government in the days of the Mutiny as a native officer in a newly raised cavalry regiment. The Government had given him a good holding in the village, and though the demands of his sons, now grey-bearded officers on their own account, had impoverished him, he was still a person of consequence. English officials – Deputy Commissioners even – turned aside from the main road to visit him, and on those occasions he dressed himself in the uniform of ancient days, and stood up like a ramrod.

'But this shall be a great war – a war of eight thousand.' Kim's voice shrilled across the quick-gathering crowd, astonishing himself.

'Redcoats or our own regiments?' the old man snapped, as though he were asking an equal. His tone made men respect Kim.

'Redcoats,' said Kim at a venture. 'Redcoats and guns.'

'But – but the astrologer said no word of this,' cried the lama, snuffing prodigiously in his excitement.

'But *I* know. The word has come to me, who am this Holy One's disciple. There will rise a war – a war of eight thousand redcoats. From Pindi and Peshawur they will be drawn. This is sure.'

'The boy has heard bazar-talk,' said the priest.

'But he was always by my side,' said the lama. 'How should he know? *I* did not know.'

'He will make a clever juggler when the old man is dead,' muttered the priest to the headman. 'What new trick is this?'

'A sign. Give me a sign,' thundered the old soldier suddenly. 'If there were war my sons would have told me.'

'When all is ready, thy sons, doubt not, will be told. But it is a long road from thy sons to the man in whose hands these things lie.' Kim warmed to the game, for it reminded him of experiences in the letter-carrying line, when, for the sake of a few pice, he pretended to know more than he knew. But now he was playing for larger things – the sheer excitement and the sense of power. He drew a new breath and went on.

'Old man, give *me* a sign. Do underlings order the goings of eight thousand redcoats – with guns?'

'No.' Still the old man answered as though Kim were an equal.

'Dost thou know who He is, then, that gives the order?'

'I have seen Him.'

'To know again?'

'I have known Him since he was a lieutenant in the *topkhana* [the Artillery].'

'A tall man. A tall man with black hair, walking thus?' Kim took a few paces in a stiff, wooden style.

'Ay. But that anyone may have seen.' The crowd were breathless-still through all this talk.

'That is true,' said Kim. 'But I will say more. Look now. First the great man walks thus. Then He thinks thus.' (Kim drew a forefinger over his forehead and downwards till it came to rest by the angle of the jaw.) 'Anon He twitches his fingers thus. Anon He thrusts his hat under his left armpit.' Kim illustrated the motion and stood like a stork.

The old man groaned, inarticulate with amazement; and the crowd shivered.

'So – so – so. But what does He when He is about to give an order?'

'He rubs the skin at the back of his neck – thus. Then falls one finger on the table and He makes a small sniffing noise through his nose. Then He speaks, saying: "Loose such and such a regiment. Call out such guns."'

The old man rose stiffly and saluted.

'"For"' – Kim translated into the vernacular the clinching sentences he had heard in the dressing-room at Umballa – '"For," says He, "we should have done this long ago. It is not war – it is a chastisement. Snff!"'

'Enough. I believe. I have seen Him thus in the smoke of battles. Seen and heard. It is He!'

'I saw no smoke' – Kim's voice shifted to the rapt sing-song of the wayside fortune-teller. 'I saw this in darkness. First came a man to make things clear. Then came horsemen. Then came He, standing in a ring of light. The rest followed as I have said. Old man, have I spoken truth?'

'It is He. Past all doubt it is He.'

The crowd drew a long, quavering breath, staring alternately at the old man, still at attention, and ragged Kim against the purple twilight.

'Said I not – said I not he was from the other world?' cried the lama proudly. 'He is the Friend of all the World. He is the Friend of the Stars!'

'At least it does not concern us,' a man cried. 'O thou young soothsayer, if the gift abides with thee at all seasons, I have a red-spotted cow. She may be sister to thy Bull for aught I know –'

'Or I care,' said Kim. 'My Stars do not concern themselves with thy cattle.'

'Nay, but she is very sick,' a woman struck in. 'My man is a buffalo, or he would have chosen his words better. Tell me if she recover?'

Had Kim been at all an ordinary boy, he would have carried on the play; but one does not know Lahore city, and least of all the *fakir*s by the Taksali Gate, for thirteen years without also knowing human nature.

The priest looked at him sideways, something bitterly – a dry and blighting smile.

'Is there no priest, then, in the village? I thought I had seen a great one even now,' cried Kim.

'Ay – but –' the woman began.

'But thou and thy husband hoped to get the cow cured for a handful of thanks.' The shot told: they were notoriously the closest-fisted couple in the village. 'It is not well to cheat the temples. Give a young calf to thine own priest, and, unless thy Gods are angry past recall, she will give milk within a month.'

'A master-beggar art thou,' purred the priest approvingly. 'Not the cunning of forty years could have done better. Surely thou hast made the old man rich?'

'A little flour, a little butter and a mouthful of cardamoms,' Kim retorted, flushed with the praise, but still cautious – 'does one grow rich on that? And, as thou canst see, he is mad. But it serves me while I learn the road at least.'

He knew what the *fakir*s of the Taksali Gate were like when they talked among themselves, and copied the very inflection of their lewd disciples.

'Is his Search, then, truth or a cloak to other ends? It may be treasure.'

'He is mad – many times mad. There is nothing else.'

Here the old soldier hobbled up and asked if Kim would accept his hospitality for the night. The priest recommended him to do so, but insisted that the honour of entertaining the lama belonged to the temple – at which the lama smiled guilelessly. Kim glanced from one face to the other, and drew his own conclusions.

'Where is the money?' he whispered, beckoning the old man off into the darkness.

'In my bosom. Where else?'

'Give it me. Quietly and swiftly give it me.'

'But why? Here is no ticket to buy –'

'Am I thy *chela*, or am I not? Do I not safeguard thy old feet about the ways? Give me the money and at dawn I will return it.' He slipped his hand above the lama's girdle and brought away the purse.

'Be it so – be it so.' The old man nodded his head. 'This is a great and terrible world. I never knew there were so many men alive in it.'

Next morning the priest was in a very bad temper, but the lama was quite happy; and Kim had enjoyed a most interesting evening with the old man, who brought out his cavalry sabre and, balancing it on his dry knees, told tales of the Mutiny and young captains thirty years in their graves, till Kim dropped off to sleep.

'Certainly the air of this country is good,' said the lama. 'I sleep lightly, as do all old men; but last night I slept unwaking till broad day. Even now I am heavy.'

'Drink a draught of hot milk,' said Kim, who had carried not a few such remedies to opium-smokers of his acquaintance. 'It is time to take the Road again.'

'The long Road that overpasses all the rivers of Hind,' said the lama gaily. 'Let us go. But how thinkest thou, *chela*, to recompense these people, and especially the priest, for their great kindness? Truly they are *būt-parast*, but in other lives, maybe, they will receive enlightenment. A rupee to the temple? The thing within is no more than stone and red paint, but the heart of man we must acknowledge when and where it is good.'

'Holy One, hast thou ever taken the Road alone?' Kim looked up sharply, like the Indian crows so busy about the fields.

'Surely, child: from Kulu to Pathânkot – from Kulu, where my first *chela* died. When men were kind to us we made offerings, and all men were well-disposed throughout all the Hills.'

'It is otherwise in Hind,' said Kim drily. 'Their Gods are many-armed and malignant. Let them alone.'

'I would set thee on thy road for a little, Friend of all the World – thou and thy yellow man.' The old soldier ambled up the village street, all shadowy in the dawn, on a gaunt, scissor-hocked pony. 'Last night broke up the fountains of remembrance in my so-dried heart, and it was as a blessing to me. Truly there is war abroad in the air. I smell it. See! I have brought my sword.'

He sat long-legged on the little beast, with the big sword at his side – hand dropped on the pommel – staring fiercely over the flat lands towards the North. 'Tell me again how He showed in thy vision. Come up and sit behind me. The beast will carry two.'

'I am this Holy One's disciple,' said Kim, as they cleared the village-gate. The villagers seemed almost sorry to be rid of them, but the priest's farewell was cold and distant. He had wasted some opium on a man who carried no money.

'That is well spoken. I am not much used to holy men, but respect is always good. There is no respect in these days – not even when a Commissioner Sahib comes to see me. But why should one whose Star leads him to war follow a holy man?'

'But he *is* a holy man,' said Kim earnestly. 'In truth, and in

talk and in act, holy. He is not like the others. I have never
seen such an one. We be not fortune-tellers, or jugglers, or
beggars.'

'*Thou* art not. That I can see. But I do not know that other.
He marches well, though.'

The first freshness of the day carried the lama forward with
long, easy, camel-like strides. He was deep in meditation,
mechanically clicking his rosary.

They followed the rutted and worn country road that
wound across the flat between the great dark-green mango-
groves, the line of the snow-capped Himalayas faint to the
eastward. All India was at work in the fields, to the creaking of
well-wheels, the shouting of ploughmen behind their cattle,
and the clamour of the crows. Even the pony felt the good
influence and almost broke into a trot as Kim laid a hand on
the stirrup-leather.

'It repents me that I did not give a rupee to the shrine,' said
the lama on the last bead of his eighty-one.

The old soldier growled in his beard, so that the lama for
the first time was aware of him.

'Seekest thou the River also?' said he, turning.

'The day is new,' was the reply. 'What need of a river save
to water at before sundown? I come to show thee a short lane
to the Big Road.'

'That is a courtesy to be remembered, O man of good will.
But why the sword?'

The old soldier looked as abashed as a child interrupted in
his game of make-believe.

'The sword,' he said, fumbling it. 'Oh, that was a fancy of
mine – an old man's fancy. Truly the police orders are that no
man must bear weapons throughout Hind, but' – he cheered
up and slapped the hilt – 'all the constabeels hereabout know
me.'

'It is not a good fancy,' said the lama. 'What profit to kill
men?'

'Very little – as I know; but if evil men were not now and

then slain it would not be a good world for weaponless dreamers. I do not speak without knowledge who have seen the land from Delhi south awash with blood.'

'What madness was that, then?'

'The Gods, who sent it for a plague, alone know. A madness ate into all the Army, and they turned against their officers. That was the first evil, but not past remedy if they had then held their hands. But they chose to kill the Sahibs' wives and children. Then came the Sahibs from over the sea and called them to most strict account.'

'Some such rumour, I believe, reached me once long ago. They called it the Black Year, as I remember.'

'What manner of life hast thou led, not to know The Year? A rumour indeed! All earth knew, and trembled!'

'Our earth never shook but once – upon the day that the Excellent One received Enlightenment.'

'Umph! I saw Delhi shake at least; and Delhi is the navel of the world.'

'So they turned against women and children? That was a bad deed, for which the punishment cannot be avoided.'

'Many strove to do so, but with very small profit. I was then in a regiment of cavalry. It broke. Of six hundred and eighty sabres stood fast to their salt – how many, think you? Three. Of whom I was one.'

'The greater merit.'

'Merit! We did not consider it merit in those days. My people, my friends, my brothers fell from me. They said: "The time of the English is accomplished. Let each strike out a little holding for himself." But I had talked with the men of Sobraon, of Chilianwallah, of Moodkee and Ferozeshah. I said: "Abide a little and the wind turns. There is no blessing in this work." In those days I rode seventy miles with an English Memsahib and her babe on my saddle-bow. (Wow! That was a horse fit for a man!) I placed them in safety, and back came I to my officer – the one that was not killed of our five. "Give me work," said I, "for I am an outcast among my own kind, and my cousin's blood is wet on my sabre." "Be content," said he. "There is great work forward. When this madness is over there is a recompense." '

'Ay, there is a recompense when the madness is over, surely?' the lama muttered half to himself.

'They did not hang medals in those days on all who by accident had heard a gun fired. No! In nineteen pitched battles was I; in six-and-forty skirmishes of horse; and in small affairs without number. Nine wounds I bear; a medal and four clasps and the medal of an Order, for my captains, who are now generals, remembered me when the Kaisar-i-Hind had accomplished fifty years of her reign, and all the land rejoiced. They said: "Give him the Order of Berittish India." I carry it upon my neck now. I have also my *jaghir* [holding] from the hands of the State – a free gift to me and mine. The men of the old days – they are now Commissioners – come riding to me through the crops – high upon horses so that all the village sees – and we talk out the old skirmishes, one dead man's name leading to another.'

'And after?' said the lama.

'Oh, afterwards they go away, but not before my village has seen.'

'And at the last what wilt thou do?'

'At the last I shall die.'

'And after?'

'Let the Gods order it. I have never pestered Them with prayers. I do not think They will pester me. Look you, I have noticed in my long life that those who eternally break in upon Those Above with complaints and reports and bellowings and weepings are presently sent for in haste, as our Colonel used to send for slack-jawed down-country men who talked too much. No, I have never wearied the Gods. They will remember this, and give me a quiet place where I can drive my lance in the shade, and wait to welcome my sons: I have no less than three – Rissaldar-majors all – in the regiments.'

'And they likewise, bound upon the Wheel, go forth from life to life – from despair to despair,' said the lama below his breath, 'hot, uneasy, snatching.'

'Ay,' the old soldier chuckled. 'Three Rissaldar-majors in three regiments. Gamblers a little, but so am I. They must be well mounted; and one cannot take the horses as in the old days one took women. Well, well, my holding can pay for all. How thinkest thou? It is a well-watered strip, but my men cheat me. I do not know how to ask save at the lance's point. Ugh! I grow angry and I curse them, and they feign penitence, but behind my back I know they call me a toothless old ape.'

'Hast thou never desired any other thing?'

'Yes – yes – a thousand times! A straight back and a close-clinging knee once more; a quick wrist and a keen eye; and the marrow that makes a man. Oh, the old days – the good days of my strength!'

'That strength is weakness.'

'It has turned so; but fifty years since I could have proved it otherwise,' the old soldier retorted, driving his stirrup-edge into the pony's lean flank.

'But I know a River of great healing.'

'I have drank Gunga-water to the edge of dropsy. All she gave me was a flux, and no sort of strength.'

'It is not Gunga. The River that I know washes from all taint of sin. Ascending the far bank one is assured of Freedom. I do not know thy life, but thy face is the face of the honourable and courteous. Thou hast clung to thy Way, rendering fidelity when it was hard to give, in that Black Year of which I now remember other tales. Enter now upon the Middle Way which is the path to Freedom. Hear the Most Excellent Law, and do not follow dreams.'

'Speak, then, old man,' the soldier smiled, half saluting. 'We be all babblers at our age.'

The lama squatted under the shade of a mango, whose shadow played checkerwise over his face; the soldier sat stiffly on the pony; and Kim, making sure that there were no snakes, lay down in the crotch of the twisted roots.

There was a drowsy buzz of small life in hot sunshine, a cooing of doves, and a sleepy drone of well-wheels across the fields. Slowly and impressively the lama began. At the end of ten minutes the old soldier slid from his pony, to hear better as he said, and sat with the reins round his wrist. The lama's voice faltered – the periods lengthened. Kim was busy watching a grey squirrel. When the little scolding bunch of fur, close pressed to the branch, disappeared, preacher and audience were fast asleep, the old officer's strong-cut head pillowed on his arm, the lama's thrown back against the tree-bole, where it showed like yellow ivory. A naked child toddled up, stared, and, moved by some quick impulse of reverence, made a solemn little obeisance before the lama – only the child was so short and fat that it toppled over sideways, and Kim laughed at the sprawling, chubby legs. The child, scared and indignant, yelled aloud.

'Hai! Hai!' said the soldier, leaping to his feet. 'What is it? What orders? ... It is ... a child! I dreamed it was an alarm. Little one – little one – do not cry. Have I slept? That was discourteous indeed!'

'I fear! I am afraid!' roared the child.

'What is it to fear? Two old men and a boy? How wilt thou ever make a soldier, Princeling?'

The lama had waked too, but, taking no direct notice of the child, clicked his rosary.

'What is that?' said the child, stopping a yell midway. 'I have never seen such things. Give them me.'

'Aha,' said the lama, smiling, and trailing a loop of it on the grass:

> This is a handful of cardamoms,
> This is a lump of *ghi*:
> This is millet and chillies and rice,
> A supper for thee and me!

The child shrieked with joy, and snatched at the dark, glancing beads.

'Oho!' said the old soldier. 'Whence hadst thou that song, despiser of this world?'

'I learned it in Pathânkot – sitting on a doorstep,' said the lama shyly. 'It is good to be kind to babes.'

'As I remember, before the sleep came on us, thou hadst told me that marriage and bearing were darkeners of the true light, stumbling-blocks upon the Way. Do children drop from Heaven in thy country? Is it the Way to sing them songs?'

'No man is all perfect,' said the lama gravely, recoiling the rosary. 'Run now to thy mother, little one.'

'Hear him!' said the soldier to Kim. 'He is ashamed for that he has made a child happy. There was a very good house-holder lost in thee, my brother. Hai, child!' He threw it a pice. 'Sweetmeats are always sweet.' And as the little figure capered away into the sunshine: 'They grow up and become men. Holy One, I grieve that I slept in the midst of thy preaching. Forgive me.'

'We be two old men,' said the lama. 'The fault is mine. I listened to thy talk of the world and its madness, and one fault led to the next.'

'Hear him! What harm do thy Gods suffer from play with a babe? And that song was very well sung. Let us go on and I will sing thee the song of Nikal Seyn before Delhi – the old song.'

And they fared out from the gloom of the mango tope, the old man's high, shrill voice ringing across the field, as wail by long-drawn wail he unfolded the story of Nikal Seyn [Nicholson] – the song that men sing in the Punjab to this day. Kim was delighted, and the lama listened with deep interest.

'*Ahi! Nikal Seyn is dead – he died before Delhi! Lances of the North, take vengeance for Nikal Seyn.*' He quavered it out to the end, marking the trills with the flat of his sword on the pony's rump.

'And now we come to the Big Road,' said he, after receiving the compliments of Kim; for the lama was markedly silent. 'It is long since I have ridden this way, but thy boy's talk stirred me. See, Holy One – the Great Road which is the backbone of all Hind. For the most part it is shaded, as here, with four lines of trees; the middle road – all hard – takes the quick traffic. In the days before rail-carriages the Sahibs travelled up and down here in hundreds. Now there are only country-carts and such like. Left and right is the rougher road for the heavy carts – grain and cotton and timber, fodder, lime and hides. A man goes in safety here – for at every few *koss* is a police-station. The police are thieves and extortioners (I myself would patrol it with cavalry – young recruits under a strong captain), but at least they do not suffer any rivals. All castes and kinds of men move here. Look! Brahmins and chumars, bankers and tinkers, barbers and bunnias, pilgrims and potters – all the world going and coming. It is to me as a river from which I am withdrawn like a log after a flood.'

And truly the Grand Trunk Road is a wonderful spectacle. It runs straight, bearing without crowding India's traffic for fifteen hundred miles – such a river of life as nowhere else exists in the world. They looked at the green-arched, shade-flecked length of it, the white breadth speckled with slow-pacing folk; and the two-roomed police-station opposite.

'Who bears arms against the law?' a constable called out laughingly, as he caught sight of the soldier's sword. 'Are not the police enough to destroy evil-doers?'

'It was because of the police I bought it,' was the answer. 'Does all go well in Hind?'

'Rissaldar Sahib, all goes well.'

'I am like an old tortoise, look you, who puts his head out from the bank and draws it in again. Ay, this is the Road of Hindustan. All men come by this way ...'

'Son of a swine, is the soft part of the road meant for thee to scratch thy back upon? Father of all the daughters of shame and husband of ten thousand virtueless ones, thy mother was devoted to a devil, being led thereto by her mother. Thy aunts have never had a nose for seven generations! Thy sister – What owl's folly told thee to draw thy carts across the road? A broken wheel? Then take a broken head and put the two together at leisure!'

The voice and a venomous whip-cracking came out of a pillar of dust fifty yards away, where a cart had broken down. A thin, high Kathiawar mare, with eyes and nostrils aflame, rocketed out of the jam, snorting and wincing as her rider bent her across the road in chase of a shouting man. He was tall and grey-bearded, sitting the almost mad beast as a piece of her, and scientifically lashing his victim between plunges.

The old man's face lit with pride. 'My child!' said he briefly, and strove to rein the pony's neck to a fitting arch.

'Am I to be beaten before the police?' cried the carter. 'Justice! I will have Justice –'

'Am I to be blocked by a shouting ape who upsets ten thousand sacks under a young horse's nose? That is the way to ruin a mare.'

'He speaks truth. He speaks truth. But she follows her man close,' said the old man. The carter ran under the wheels of his cart and thence threatened all sorts of vengeance.

'They are strong men, thy sons,' said the policeman serenely, picking his teeth.

The horseman delivered one last vicious cut with his whip and came on at a canter.

'My father!' He reigned back ten yards and dismounted.

The old man was off his pony in an instant, and they embraced as do father and son in the East.

Chapter 4

Good Luck, she is never a lady,
But the cursedest quean alive,
Tricksy, wincing, and jady –
Kittle to lead or drive.
Greet her – she's hailing a stranger!
Meet her – she's busking to leave!
Let her alone for a shrew to the bone
And the hussy comes plucking your sleeve!
Largesse! Largesse, O Fortune!
Give or hold at your will.
If I've no care for Fortune,
Fortune must follow me still!

The Wishing-Caps.

THEN, lowering their voices, they spoke together. Kim came to rest under a tree, but the lama tugged impatiently at his elbow.

'Let us go on. The River is not here.'

'*Hai mai!* Have we not walked enough for a little? Our River will not run away. Patience, and he will give us a dole.'

'This,' said the old soldier suddenly, 'is the Friend of the Stars. He brought me the news yesterday. Having seen the very man Himself, in a vision, giving orders for the war.'

'Hm!' said his son, all deep in his broad chest. 'He came by a bazar-rumour and made profit of it.'

His father laughed. 'At least he did not ride to me begging for a new charger, and the Gods know how many rupees. Are thy brothers' regiments also under orders?'

'I do not know. I took leave and came swiftly to thee in case –'

'In case they ran before thee to beg. O gamblers and spend-thrifts all! But thou hast never yet ridden in a charge. A good horse is needed there, truly. A good follower and a good pony also for the marching. Let us see – let us see.' He thrummed on the pommel.

64

'This is no place to cast accounts in, my father. Let us go to thy house.'

'At least pay the boy, then: I have no pice with me, and he brought auspicious news. Ho! Friend of all the World, a war is toward as thou hast said.'

'Nay, as I know, *the* war,' returned Kim composedly.

'Eh?' said the lama, fingering his beads, all eager for the road.

'My master does not trouble the Stars for hire. We brought the news – bear witness, we brought the news, and now we go.' Kim half-crooked his hand at his side.

The son tossed a silver coin through the sunlight, grumbling something about beggars and jugglers. It was a four-anna piece, and would feed them well for days. The lama, seeing the flash of the metal, droned a blessing.

'Go thy way, Friend of all the World,' piped the old soldier, wheeling his scrawny mount. 'For once in all my days I have met a true prophet – who was not in the Army.'

Father and son swung round together: the old man sitting as erect as the younger.

A Punjabi constable in yellow linen trousers slouched across the road. He had seen the money pass.

'Halt!' he cried in impressive English. 'Know ye not that there is a *takkus* of two annas a head, which is four annas, on those who enter the Road from this side-road? It is the order of the Sirkar, and the money is spent for the planting of trees and the beautification of the ways.'

'And the bellies of the police,' said Kim, slipping out of arm's reach. 'Consider for a while, man with a mud head. Think you we came from the nearest pond like the frog, thy father-in-law? Hast thou ever heard the name of thy brother?'

'And who was he? Leave the boy alone,' cried a senior constable, immensely delighted, as he squatted down to smoke his pipe in the veranda.

'He took a label from a bottle of *belaitee-pani* [soda-water], and, affixing it to a bridge, collected taxes for a month from those who passed, saying that it was the Sirkar's order. Then

came an Englishman and broke his head. Ah, brother, I am a
town-crow, not a village-crow!'

The policeman drew back abashed, and Kim hooted at him
all down the road.

'Was there ever such a disciple as I?' he cried merrily to the
lama. 'All earth would have picked thy bones within ten mile
of Lahore city if I had not guarded thee.'

'I consider in my own mind whether thou art a spirit,
sometimes, or sometimes an evil imp,' said the lama, smiling
slowly.

'I am thy *chela*.' Kim dropped into step at his side – that
indescribable gait of the long-distance tramp all the world
over.

'Now let us walk,' muttered the lama, and to the click of his
rosary they walked in silence mile upon mile. The lama, as
usual, was deep in meditation, but Kim's bright eyes were
open wide. This broad, smiling river of life, he considered,
was a vast improvement on the cramped and crowded Lahore
streets. There were new people and new sights at every stride
– castes he knew and castes that were altogether out of his
experience.

They met a troop of long-haired, strong-scented Sansis
with baskets of lizards and other unclean food on their backs,
their lean dogs sniffing at their heels. These people kept their
own side of the road, moving at a quick, furtive jog-trot, and
all other castes gave them ample room; for the Sansi is deep
pollution. Behind them, walking wide and stiffly across the
strong shadows, the memory of his leg-irons still on him,
strode one newly released from the jail; his full stomach and
shiny skin to prove that the Government fed its prisoners
better than most honest men could feed themselves. Kim
knew that walk well, and made broad jest of it as they passed.
Then an Akali, a wild-eyed, wild-haired Sikh devotee in the
blue-checked clothes of his faith, with polished-steel quoits
glistening on the cone of his tall blue turban, stalked past,
returning from a visit to one of the independent Sikh States,
where he had been singing the ancient glories of the Khalsa to

College-trained princelings in top-boots and white-cord breeches. Kim was careful not to irritate that man; for the Akali's temper is short and his arm quick. Here and there they met or were overtaken by the gaily dressed crowds of whole villages turning out to some local fair; the women, with their babes on their hips, walking behind the men, the older boys prancing on sticks of sugar-cane, dragging rude brass models of locomotives such as they sell for a half-penny, or flashing the sun into the eyes of their betters from cheap toy mirrors. One could see at a glance what each had bought; and if there were any doubt it needed only to watch the wives comparing, brown arm against brown arm, the newly purchased dull glass bracelets that come from the North-West. These merry-makers stepped slowly, calling one to the other and stopping to haggle with sweetmeat-sellers, or to make a prayer before one of the wayside shrines – sometimes Hindu, sometimes Mussalman – which the low-caste of both creeds share with beautiful impartiality. A solid line of blue, rising and falling like the back of a caterpillar in haste, would swing up through the quivering dust and trot past to a chorus of quick cackling. That was a gang of *changars* – the women who have taken all the embankments of all the Northern railways under their charge – a flat-footed, big-bosomed, strong-limbed, blue-petticoated clan of earth-carriers, hurrying north on news of a job, and wasting no time by the road. They belong to the caste whose men do not count, and they walked with squared elbows, swinging hips, and heads on high, as suits women who carry heavy weights. A little later a marriage procession would strike into the Grand Trunk with music and shoutings, and a smell of marigold and jasmine stronger even than the reek of the dust. One could see the bride's litter, a blur of red and tinsel, staggering through the haze, while the bride-groom's bewreathed pony turned aside to snatch a mouthful from a passing fodder-cart. Then Kim would join the Kentish-fire of good wishes and bad jokes, wishing the couple a hundred sons and no daughters, as the saying is. Still more interesting and more to be shouted over it was when a

strolling juggler with some half-trained monkeys, or a pant-
ing, feeble bear, or a woman who tied goats' horns to her feet,
and with these danced on a slack-rope, set the horses to
shying and the women to shrill, long-drawn quavers of
amazement.

The lama never raised his eyes. He did not note the money-
lender on his goose-rumped pony, hastening along to collect
the cruel interest; or the long-shouting, deep-voiced little
mob – still in military formation – of native soldiers on leave,
rejoicing to be rid of their breeches and puttees, and saying
the most outrageous things to the most respectable women in
sight. Even the seller of Ganges-water he did not see, and
Kim expected that he would at least buy a bottle of that
precious stuff. He looked steadily at the ground, and strode as
steadily hour after hour, his soul busied elsewhere. But Kim
was in the seventh heaven of joy. The Grand Trunk at this
point was built on an embankment to guard against winter
floods from the foothills, so that one walked, as it were, a little
above the country, along a stately corridor, seeing all India
spread out to left and right. It was beautiful to behold the
many-yoked grain and cotton wagons crawling over the
country roads: one could hear their axles, complaining a mile
away, coming nearer, till with shouts and yells and bad words
they climbed up the steep incline and plunged on to the hard
main road, carter reviling carter. It was equally beautiful to
watch the people, little clumps of red and blue and pink and
white and saffron, turning aside to go to their own villages,
dispersing and growing small by twos and threes across the
level plain. Kim felt these things, though he could not give
tongue to his feelings, and so contented himself with buying
peeled sugar-cane and spitting the pith generously about his
path. From time to time the lama took snuff, and at last Kim
could endure the silence no longer.

'This is a good land – the land of the South!' said he. 'The
air is good; the water is good. Eh?'

'And they are all bound upon the Wheel,' said the lama.

'Bound from life after life. To none of these has the Way been shown.' He shook himself back to this world.

'And now we have walked a weary way,' said Kim. 'Surely we shall soon come to a *parao* [a resting-place]. Shall we stay there? Look, the sun is sloping.'

'Who will receive us this evening?'

'That is all one. This country is full of good folk. Besides' – he sunk his voice beneath a whisper – 'we have money.'

The crowd thickened as they neared the resting-place which marked the end of their day's journey. A line of stalls selling very simple food and tobacco, a stack of firewood, a police-station, a well, a horse-trough, a few trees, and, under them, some trampled ground dotted with the black ashes of old fires, are all that mark a *parao* on the Grand Trunk; if you except the beggars and the crows – both hungry.

By this time the sun was driving broad golden spokes through the lower branches of the mango-trees; the parakeets and doves were coming home in their hundreds; the chattering, grey-backed Seven Sisters, talking over the day's adventures, walked back and forth in twos and threes almost under the feet of the travellers; and shufflings and scufflings in the branches showed that the bats were ready to go out on the night-picket. Swiftly the light gathered itself together, painted for an instant the faces and the cart-wheels and the bullocks' horns as red as blood. Then the night fell, changing the touch of the air, drawing a low, even haze, like a gossamer veil of blue, across the face of the country, and bringing out, keen and distinct, the smell of wood-smoke and cattle and the good scent of wheaten cakes cooked on ashes. The evening patrol hurried out of the police-station with important coughings and reiterated orders; and a live charcoal ball in the cup of a wayside carter's hookah glowed red while Kim's eye mechanically watched the last flicker of the sun on the brass tweezers.

The life of the *parao* was very like that of the Kashmir Serai on a small scale. Kim dived into the happy Asiatic disorder which, if you only allow time, will bring you everything that a simple man needs.

His wants were few, because, since the lama had no caste scruples, cooked food from the nearest stall would serve; but, for luxury's sake, Kim bought a handful of dung-cakes to build a fire. All about, coming and going round the little flames, men cried for oil, or grain, or sweetmeats, or tobacco, jostling one another while they waited their turn at the well; and under the men's voices you heard from halted, shuttered carts the high squeals and giggles of women whose faces should not be seen in public.

Nowadays, well-educated natives are of opinion that when their womenfolk travel – and they visit a good deal – it is better to take them quickly by rail in a properly screened compartment; and that custom is spreading. But there are always those of the old rock who hold by the use of their forefathers; and, above all, there are always the old women – more conservative than the men – who toward the end of their days go on a pilgrimage. They, being withered and undesirable, do not, under certain circumstances, object to unveiling. After their long seclusion, during which they have always been in business touch with a thousand outside interests, they love the bustle and stir of the open road, the gatherings at the shrines, and the infinite possibilities of gossip with likeminded dowagers. Very often it suits a long-suffering family that a strong-tongued, iron-willed old lady should disport herself about India in this fashion; for certainly pilgrimage is grateful to the Gods. So all about India, in the most remote places, as in the most public, you find some knot of grizzled servitors in nominal charge of an old lady who is more or less curtained and hid away in a bullock-cart. Such men are staid and discreet, and when a European or a high-caste native is near will net their charge with most elaborate precautions; but in the ordinary haphazard chances of pilgrimage the precautions are not taken. The old lady is, after all, intensely human, and lives to look upon life.

Kim marked down a gaily ornamented *ruth* or family bullock-cart, with a broidered canopy of two domes, like a double-humped camel, which had just been drawn into the *parao*. Eight men made its retinue, and two of the eight were armed with rusty sabres – sure signs that they followed a person of distinction, for the common folk do not bear arms. An increasing cackle of complaints, orders, and jests, and what to a European would have been bad language, came from behind the curtains. Here was evidently a woman used to command.

Kim looked over the retinue critically. Half of them were thin-legged, grey-bearded Ooryas from down country. The other half were duffle-clad, felt-hatted hillmen of the North; and that mixture told its own tale, even if he had not overheard the incessant sparring between the two divisions. The old lady was going south on a visit – probably to a rich relative, most probably to a son-in-law, who had sent up an escort as a mark of respect. The hillmen would be of her own people – Kulu or Kangra folk. It was quite clear that she was not taking her daughter down to be wedded, or the curtains would have been laced home and the guard would have allowed no one near the car. A merry and a high-spirited dame, thought Kim, balancing the dung-cake in one hand, the cooked food in the other, and piloting the lama with a nudging shoulder. Something might be made out of the meeting. The lama would give him no help, but, as a conscientious *chela*, Kim was delighted to beg for two.

He built his fire as close to the cart as he dared, waiting for one of the escort to order him away. The lama dropped wearily to the ground, much as a heavy fruit-eating bat cowers, and returned to his rosary.

'Stand farther off, beggar!' The order was shouted in broken Hindustani by one of the hillmen.

'Huh! It is only a *pahari* [a hillman],' said Kim over his shoulder. 'Since when have the hill-asses owned all Hindustan?'

The retort was a swift and brilliant sketch of Kim's pedigree for three generations.

'Ah!' Kim's voice was sweeter than ever, as he broke the dung-cake into fit pieces. 'In *my* country we call that the beginning of love-talk.'

A harsh, thin cackle behind the curtains put the hillman on his mettle for a second shot.

'Not so bad – not so bad,' said Kim with calm. 'But have a care, my brother, lest we – *we*, I say – be minded to give a curse or so in return. And our curses have the knack of biting home.'

The Ooryas laughed; the hillman sprang forward threateningly. The lama suddenly raised his head, bringing his huge tam-o'-shanter hat into the full light of Kim's new-started fire.

'What is it?' said he.

The man halted as though struck to stone. 'I – I – am saved from a great sin,' he stammered.

'The foreigner has found him a priest at last,' whispered one of the Ooryas.

'*Hai!* Why is that beggar-brat not well beaten?' the old woman cried.

The hillman drew back to the cart and whispered something to the curtain. There was dead silence, then a muttering.

'This goes well,' thought Kim, pretending neither to see nor hear.

'When – when – he has eaten' – the hillman fawned on Kim – 'it – it is requested that the Holy One will do the honour to talk to one who would speak to him.'

'After he has eaten he will sleep,' Kim returned loftily. He could not quite see what new turn the game had taken, but stood resolute to profit by it. 'Now I will get him his food.' The last sentence, spoken loudly, ended with a sigh as of faintness.

'I – I myself and the others of my people will look to that – if it is permitted.'

'It is permitted,' said Kim, more loftily than ever. 'Holy One, these people will bring us food.'

'The land is good. All the country of the South is good – a great and a terrible world,' mumbled the lama drowsily.

'Let him sleep,' said Kim, 'but look to it that we are well fed when he wakes. He is a very holy man.'

Again one of the Ooryas said something contemptuously.

'He is not a *fakir*. He is not a down-country beggar,' Kim went on severely, addressing the stars. 'He is the most holy of holy men. He is above all castes. I am his *chela*.'

'Come here!' said the flat thin voice behind the curtain; and Kim came, conscious that eyes he could not see were staring at him. One skinny brown finger heavy with rings lay on the edge of the cart, and the talk went this way:

'Who is that one?'

'An exceedingly holy one. He comes from far off. He comes from Tibet.'

'Where in Tibet?'

'From behind the snows – from a very far place. He knows the stars; he makes horoscopes; he reads nativities. But he does not do this for money. He does it for kindness and great charity. I am his disciple. I am called also the Friend of the Stars.'

'Thou art no hillman.'

'Ask him. He will tell thee I was sent to him from the Stars to show him an end to his pilgrimage.'

'Humph! Consider, brat, that I am an old woman and not altogether a fool. Lamas I know, and to these I give reverence, but thou art no more a lawful *chela* than this my finger is the pole of this wagon. Thou art a casteless Hindu – a bold and unblushing beggar, attached, belike, to the Holy One for the sake of gain.'

'Do we not all work for gain?' Kim changed his tone promptly to match that altered voice. 'I have heard' – this was a bow drawn at a venture – 'I have heard –'

'What hast thou heard?' she snapped, rapping with the finger.

'Nothing that I well remember, but some talk in the bazars, which is doubtless a lie, that even Rajahs – small Hill Rajahs –'

'But none the less of good Rajput blood.'

'Assuredly of good blood. That these even sell the more comely of their womenfolk for gain. Down south they sell them – to zemindars and such-all of Oudh.'

If there be one thing in the world that the small Hill Rajahs deny it is just this charge; but it happens to be one thing that the bazars believe, when they discuss the mysterious slave-traffics of India. The old lady explained to Kim, in a tense, indignant whisper, precisely what manner and fashion of malignant liar he was. Had Kim hinted this when she was a girl, he would have been pommelled to death that same evening by an elephant. This was perfectly true.

'*Ahai!* I am only a beggar's brat, as the Eye of Beauty has said,' he wailed in extravagant terror.

'Eye of Beauty, forsooth! Who am I that thou shouldst fling beggar-endearments at me?' And yet she laughed at the long-forgotten word. 'Forty years ago that might have been said, and not without truth. Ay, thirty years ago. But it is the fault of this gadding up and down Hind that a king's widow must jostle all the scum of the land, and be made a mock by beggars.'

'Great Queen,' said Kim promptly, for he heard her shaking with indignation, 'I am even what the Great Queen says I am; but none the less is my master holy. He has not yet heard the Great Queen's order that –'

'Order? I order a Holy One – a Teacher of the Law – to come and speak to a woman? Never!'

'Pity my stupidity. I thought it was given as an order –'

'It was not. It was a petition. Does this make all clear?'

A silver coin clicked on the edge of the cart. Kim took it and salaamed profoundly. The old lady recognized that, as the eyes and the ears of the lama, he was to be propitiated.

'I am but the Holy One's disciple. When he has eaten perhaps he will come.'

'Oh, villain and shameless rogue!' The jewelled forefinger shook itself at him reprovingly; but he could hear the old lady's chuckle.

'Nay, what is it?' he said, dropping into his most caressing and confidential tone – the one, he well knew, that few could resist. 'Is – is there any need of a son in thy family? Speak freely, for we priests –' That last was a direct plagiarism from a *fakir* by the Taksali Gate.

'We priests! Thou art not yet old enough to –' She checked the joke with another laugh. 'Believe me, now and again, we women, O priest, think of other matters than sons. Moreover, my daughter has borne her man-child.'

'Two arrows in the quiver are better than one; and three are better still.' Kim quoted the proverb with a meditative cough, looking discreetly earthward.

'True – oh, true. But perhaps that will come. Certainly those down-country Brahmins are utterly useless. I sent gifts and monies and gifts again to them, and they prophesied.'

'Ah,' drawled Kim, with infinite contempt, 'they prophesied!' A professional could have done no better.

'And it was not till I remembered my own Gods that my prayers were heard. I chose an auspicious hour, and – perhaps thy Holy One has heard of the Abbot of the Lung-Cho lamassery. It was to him I put the matter, and behold in the due time all came about as I desired. The Brahmin in the house of the father of my daughter's son has since said that it was through his prayers – which is a little error that I will explain to him when we reach our journey's end. And so afterwards I go to Buddh Gaya, to make *shraddha* for the father of my children.'

'Thither go we.'

'Doubly auspicious,' chirruped the old lady. 'A second son at least!'

'O Friend of all the World!' The lama had waked, and, simply as a child bewildered in a strange bed, called for Kim.

'I come! I come, Holy One!' He dashed to the fire, where

he found the lama already surrounded by dishes of food, the hillmen visibly adoring him and the Southerners looking sourly.

'Go back! Withdraw!' Kim cried. 'Do we eat publicly like dogs?' They finished the meal in silence, each turned a little from the other, and Kim topped it with a native-made cigarette.

'Have I not said an hundred times that the South is a good land? Here is a virtuous and high-born widow of a Hill Rajah on pilgrimage, she says, to Buddh Gaya. She it is sends us those dishes; and when thou art well rested she would speak to thee.'

'Is this also thy work?' The lama dipped deep into his snuff-gourd.

'Who else watched over thee since our wonderful journey began?' Kim's eyes danced in his head as he blew the rank smoke through his nostrils and stretched him on the dusty ground. 'Have I failed to oversee thy comforts, Holy One?'

'A blessing on thee.' The lama inclined his solemn head. 'I have known many men in my so long life, and disciples not a few. But to none among men, if so be thou art woman-born, has my heart gone out as it has to thee – thoughtful, wise, and courteous; but something of a small imp.'

'And I have never seen such a priest as thou.' Kim considered the benevolent yellow face wrinkle by wrinkle. 'It is less than three days since we took the road together, and it is as though it were a hundred years.'

'Perhaps in a former life it was permitted that I should have rendered thee some service. Maybe' – he smiled – 'I freed thee from a trap; or, having caught thee on a hook in the days when I was not enlightened, cast thee back into the river.'

'Maybe,' said Kim quietly. He had heard this sort of speculation again and again, from the mouths of many whom the English would not consider imaginative. 'Now, as regards that woman in the bullock-cart, *I* think she needs a second son for her daughter.'

'That is no part of the Way,' sighed the lama. 'But at least she is from the Hills. Ah, the Hills, and the snow of the Hills!'

He rose and stalked to the cart. Kim would have given his ears to come too, but the lama did not invite him; and the few words he caught were in an unknown tongue, for they spoke some common speech of the mountains. The woman seemed to ask questions which the lama turned over in his mind before answering. Now and again he heard the sing-song cadence of a Chinese quotation. It was a strange picture that Kim watched between drooped eyelids. The lama, very straight and erect, the deep folds of his yellow clothing slashed with black in the light of the *parao* fires precisely as a knotted tree-trunk is slashed with the shadows of the low sun, addressed a tinsel and lacquered *ruth* which burned like a many-coloured jewel in the same uncertain light. The patterns on the gold-worked curtains ran up and down, melting and re-forming as the folds shook and quivered to the night wind; and when the talk grew more earnest the jewelled forefinger snapped out little sparks of light between the embroideries. Behind the cart was a wall of uncertain darkness speckled with little flames and alive with half-caught forms and faces and shadows. The voices of early evening had settled down to one soothing hum whose deepest note was the steady chumping of the bullocks above their chopped straw, and whose highest was the tinkle of a Bengali dancing-girl's *sitar*. Most men had eaten and pulled deep at their gurgling, grunting hookahs, which in full blast sound like bull-frogs.

At last the lama returned. A hillman walked behind him with a wadded cotton-quilt and spread it carefully by the fire.

'She deserves ten thousand grandchildren,' thought Kim. 'None the less, but for me, those gifts would not have come.'

'A virtuous woman – and a wise one.' The lama slackened off, joint by joint, like a slow camel. 'The world is full of charity to those who follow the Way.' He flung a fair half of the quilt over Kim.

'And what said she?' Kim rolled up in his share of it.

'She asked me many questions and propounded many problems – the most of which were idle tales which she had heard from devil-serving priests who pretend to follow the Way. Some I answered, and some I said were foolish. Many wear the Robe, but few keep the Way.'

'True. That is true.' Kim used the thoughtful, conciliatory tone of those who wish to draw confidences.

'But by her lights she is most right-minded. She desires greatly that we should go with her to Buddh Gaya; her road being ours, as I understand, for many days' journey to the southward.'

'And?'

'Patience a little. To this I said that my Search came before all things. She had heard many foolish legends, but this great truth of my River she had never heard. Such are the priests of the lower hills! She knew the Abbot of Lung-Cho, but she did not know of my River – nor the tale of the Arrow.'

'And?'

'I spoke therefore of the Search, and of the Way, and of matters that were profitable; she desiring only that I should accompany her and make prayer for a second son.'

'Aha! "We women" do *not* think of anything save children,' said Kim sleepily.

'Now, since our roads run together for a while, I do not see that we in any way depart from our Search if so be we accompany her – at least as far as – I have forgotten the name of the city.'

'*Ohé!*' said Kim, turning and speaking in a sharp whisper to one of the Ooryas a few yards away. 'Where is your master's house?'

'A little behind Saharunpore, among the fruit gardens.' He named the village.

'That was the place,' said the lama. 'So far, at least, we can go with her.'

'Flies go to carrion,' said the Oorya, in an abstracted voice.

'For the sick cow a crow; for the sick man a Brahmin.' Kim

breathed the proverb impersonally to the shadow-tops of the trees overhead.

The Oorya grunted and held his peace.

'So then we go with her, Holy One?'

'Is there any reason against? I can still step aside and try all the rivers that the road overpasses. She desires that I should come. She very greatly desires it.'

Kim stifled a laugh in the quilt. When once that imperious old lady had recovered from her natural awe of a lama he thought it probable that she would be worth listening to.

He was nearly asleep when the lama suddenly quoted a proverb: 'The husbands of the talkative have a great reward hereafter.' Then Kim heard him snuff thrice, and dozed off, still laughing.

The diamond-bright dawn woke men and crows and bullocks together. Kim sat up and yawned, shook himself, and thrilled with delight. This was seeing the world in real truth; this was life as he would have it – bustling and shouting, the buckling of belts, and beating of bullocks and creaking of wheels, lighting of fires and cooking of food, and new sights at every turn of the approving eye. The morning mist swept off in a whorl of silver, the parrots shot away to some distant river in shrieking green hosts: all the well-wheels within ear-shot went to work. India was awake, and Kim was in the middle of it, more awake and more excited than anyone, chewing on a twig that he would presently use as a toothbrush; for he borrowed right- and left-handedly from all the customs of the country he knew and loved. There was no need to worry about food – no need to spend a cowrie at the crowded stalls. He was the disciple of a holy man annexed by a strong-willed old lady. All things would be prepared for them, and when they were respectfully invited so to do they would sit and eat. For the rest – Kim giggled here as he cleaned his teeth – his hostess would rather heighten the enjoyment of the road. He inspected her bullocks critically, as they came up grunting and blowing under the yokes. If they went too fast – it was not likely – there would be a pleasant seat for himself along the pole; the lama would sit beside the driver. The escort, of course, would walk. The old lady, equally of course, would talk a great deal, and by what he had heard that conversation would not lack salt. She was already ordering, haranguing, rebuking, and, it must be said, cursing her servants for delays.

'Get her her pipe. In the name of the Gods, get her her pipe and stop her ill-omened mouth,' cried an Oorya, tying up his shapeless bundles of bedding. 'She and the parrots are alike. They screech in the dawn.'

'The lead-bullocks! *Hai!* Look to the lead-bullocks!' They were backing and wheeling as a grain-cart's axle caught them by the horns. 'Son of an owl, where dost thou go?' This to the grinning carter.

'*Ai! Yai! Yai!* That within there is the Queen of Delhi going to pray for a son,' the man called back over his high load. 'Room for the Queen of Delhi and her Prime Minister the grey monkey climbing up his own sword!' Another cart loaded with bark for a down-country tannery followed close behind, and its driver added a few compliments as the *ruth*-bullocks backed and backed again.

From behind the shaking curtains came one volley of invective. It did not last long, but in kind and quality, in blistering, biting appropriateness, it was beyond anything that even Kim had heard. He could see the carter's bare chest collapse with amazement, as the man salaamed reverently to the voice, leaped from the pole, and helped the escort haul their volcano on to the main road. Here the voice told him truthfully what sort of wife he had wedded, and what she was doing in his absence.

'Oh, *shabash!*' murmured Kim, unable to contain himself, as the man slunk away.

'Well done, indeed? It is a shame and a scandal that a poor woman may not go to make prayer to her Gods except she be jostled and insulted by all the refuse of Hindustan – that she must eat *gâli* [abuse] as men eat *ghi*. But I have yet a wag left to my tongue – a word or two well spoken that serves the occasion. And *still* am I without my tobacco! Who is the one-eyed and luckless son of shame that has not yet prepared my pipe?'

It was hastily thrust in by a hillman, and a trickle of thick smoke from each corner of the curtains showed that peace was restored.

If Kim had walked proudly the day before, disciple of a holy man, today he paced with tenfold pride in the train of a semi-royal procession, with a recognized place under the patronage of an old lady of charming manners and infinite resource. The escort, their heads tied up native-fashion, fell in on either side the cart, shuffling enormous clouds of dust.

The lama and Kim walked a little to one side; Kim chewing his stick of sugar-cane, and making way for no one under the status of a priest. They could hear the old lady's tongue clack as steadily as a rice-husker. She bade the escort tell her what was going on on the road; and so soon as they were clear of the *parao* she flung back the curtains and peered out, her veil a third across her face. Her men did not eye her directly when she addressed them, and thus the proprieties were more or less observed.

A dark, sallowish District Superintendent of Police, fault-lessly uniformed, an Englishman, trotted by on a tired horse, and, seeing from her retinue what manner of person she was, chaffed her.

'O mother,' he cried, 'do they do this in the zenanas? Suppose an Englishman came by and saw that thou hadst no nose?'

'What?' she shrilled back. 'Thine own mother has no nose? Why say so, then, on the open road?'

It was a fair counter. The Englishman threw up his hand with the gesture of a man hit at sword-play. She laughed and nodded.

'Is this a face to tempt virtue aside?' She withdrew all her veil and stared at him.

It was by no means lovely, but as the man gathered up his

reins he called it a Moon of Paradise, a Disturber of Integrity, and a few other fantastic epithets which doubled her up with mirth.

'That is a *nut-cut* [rogue],' she said. 'All police-constables are *nut-cuts*; but the police-wallahs are the worst. *Hai*, my son, thou hast never learned all that since thou camest from *Belait* [Europe]. Who suckled thee?'

'A *pahareen* – a hillwoman of Dalhousie, my mother. Keep thy beauty under a shade – O Dispenser of Delights,' and he was gone.

'These be the sort' – she took a fine judicial tone, and stuffed her mouth with *pan* – 'These be the sort to oversee justice. They know the land and the customs of the land. The others, all new from Europe, suckled by white women and learning our tongues from books, are worse than the pestilence. They do harm to Kings.' Then she told a long, long tale to the world at large, of an ignorant young policeman who had disturbed some small Hill Rajah, a ninth cousin of her own, in the matter of a trivial land-case, winding up with a quotation from a work by no means devotional.

Then her mood changed, and she bade one of the escort ask whether the lama would walk alongside and discuss matters of religion. So Kim dropped back into the dust and returned to his sugar-cane. For an hour or more the lama's tam-o'-shanter showed like a moon through the haze; and, from all he heard, Kim gathered that the old woman wept. One of the Ooryas half apologized for his rudeness overnight, saying that he had never known his mistress of so bland a temper, and he ascribed it to the presence of the strange priest. Personally, he believed in Brahmins, though, like all natives, he was acutely aware of their cunning and their greed. Still, when Brahmins but irritated with begging demands the mother of his master's wife, and when she sent them away so angry that they cursed the whole retinue (which was the real reason of the second off-side bullock going lame, and of the pole breaking the night before), he was prepared to accept any priest of any other denomination in or out of India. To this Kim assented with wise nods, and bade the Oorya observe that the lama took no money, and that the cost of his and Kim's food would be repaid a hundred times in the good luck that would attend the caravan henceforward. He also told stories of Lahore city, and sang a song or two which made the escort laugh. As a town-mouse well acquainted with the latest songs by the most fashionable composers – they are women for the most part – Kim had a distinct advantage over men from a little fruit-village behind Saharunpore, but he let that advantage be inferred.

At noon they turned aside to eat, and the meal was good, plentiful, and well-served on plates of clean leaves, in decency, out of drift of the dust. They gave the scraps to certain beggars, that all requirements might be fulfilled, and sat down to a long, luxurious smoke. The old lady had retreated behind her curtains, but mixed most freely in the talk, her servants arguing with and contradicting her as servants do throughout the East. She compared the cool and the pines of the Kangra and Kulu hills with the dust and the mangoes of the South; she told a tale of some old local Gods at the edge of her husband's territory; she roundly abused the tobacco which she was then smoking, reviled all Brahmins, and speculated without reserve on the coming of many grandsons.

Chapter 5

Here come I to my own again –
Fed, forgiven, and known again –
Claimed by bone of my bone again,
   And sib to flesh of my flesh!
The fatted calf is dressed for me,
But the husks have greater zest for me ...
I think my pigs will be best for me,
   So I'm off to the styes afresh.
                  The Prodigal Son.

ONCE more the lazy, string-tied, shuffling procession got under way, and she slept till they reached the next halting-stage. It was a very short march, and time lacked an hour to sundown, so Kim cast about for means of amusement.

'But why not sit and rest?' said one of the escort. 'Only the devils and the English walk to and fro without reason.'

'Never make friends with the Devil, a Monkey, or a Boy. No man knows what they will do next,' said his fellow.

Kim turned a scornful back – he did not want to hear the old story how the Devil played with the boys and repented of it – and walked idly across country.

The lama strode after him. All that day, whenever they passed a stream, he had turned aside to look at it, but in no case had he received any warning that he had found his River. Insensibly, too, the comfort of speaking to someone in a reasonable tongue, and of being properly considered and respected as her spiritual adviser by a well-born woman, had weaned his thoughts a little from the Search. And further, he was prepared to spend serene years in his quest; having nothing of the white man's impatience, but a great faith.

'Where goest thou?' he called after Kim.

'Nowhither – it was a small march, and all this' – Kim waved his hands abroad – 'is new to me.'

'She is beyond question a wise and a discerning woman. But it is hard to meditate when –'

'All women are thus.' Kim spoke as might have Solomon.

'Before the lamassery was a broad platform,' the lama muttered, looping up the well-worn rosary, 'of stone. On that I have left the marks of my feet – pacing to and fro with these.' He clicked the beads, and began the '*Om mane pudme hum*'s of his devotion; grateful for the cool, the quiet, and the absence of dust.

One thing after another drew Kim's idle eye across the plain. There was no purpose in his wanderings, except that the build of the huts near by seemed new, and he wished to investigate.

They came out on a broad tract of grazing-ground, brown and purple in the afternoon light, with a heavy clump of mangoes in the centre. It struck Kim as curious that no shrine stood in so eligible a spot: the boy was observing as any priest for these things. Far across the plain walked side by side four men, made small by the distance. He looked intently under his curved palms and caught the sheen of brass.

'Soldiers. White soldiers!' said he. 'Let us see.'

'It is always soldiers when thou and I go out alone together. But I have never seen the white soldiers.'

'They do no harm except when they are drunk. Keep behind this tree.'

They stepped behind the thick trunks in the cool dark of the mango-tope. Two little figures halted; the other two came forward uncertainly. They were the advance-party of a regiment on the march, sent out, as usual, to mark the camp. They bore five-foot sticks with fluttering flags, and called to each other as they spread over the flat earth. At last they entered the mango-grove, walking heavily.

'It's here or hereabouts – officers' tents under the trees, I take it, an' the rest of us can stay outside. Have they marked out for the baggage-wagons behind?'

They cried again to their comrades in the distance, and the rough answer came back faint and mellowed.

'Shove the flag in here, then,' said one.

'What do they prepare?' said the lama, wonderstruck. 'This is a great and terrible world. What is the device on the flag?'

A soldier thrust a stave within a few feet of them, grunted discontentedly, pulled it up again, conferred with his companion, who looked up and down the shaded cave of greenery, and returned it.

Kim stared with all his eyes, his breath coming short and sharp between his teeth. The soldiers stamped off into the sunshine.

'O Holy One!' he gasped. 'My horoscope! The drawing in the dust by the priest at Umballa! Remember what he said. First come two – *ferashes* – to make all things ready – in a dark place, as it is always at the beginning of a vision.'

'But this is not vision,' said the lama. 'It is the world's Illusion, and no more.'

'And after them comes the Bull – the Red Bull on the green field. Look! It is he!'

He pointed to the flag that was snap-snapping in the evening breeze not ten feet away. It was no more than an ordinary camp marking-flag; but the regiment, always punctilious in matters of millinery, had charged it with the regimental device, the Red Bull, which is the crest of the Mavericks – the great Red Bull on a background of Irish green.

'I see, and now I remember,' said the lama. 'Certainly it is thy Bull. Certainly, also, the two men came to make all ready.'

'They are soldiers – white soldiers. What said the priest? "The sign over against the Bull is the sign of War and armed men." Holy One, this thing touches my Search.'

'True. It is true.' The lama stared fixedly at the device that flamed like a ruby in the dusk. 'The priest at Umballa said that thine was the sign of War.'

'What is to do now?'

'Wait. Let us wait.'

'Even now the darkness clears,' said Kim. It was only natural that the descending sun should at last strike through the tree-trunks, across the grove, filling it with mealy gold

light for a few minutes; but to Kim it was the crown of the
Umballa Brahmin's prophecy.

'Hark!' said the lama. 'One beats a drum – far off!'

At first the sound, carrying diluted through the still air,
resembled the beating of an artery in the head. Soon a
sharpness was added.

'Ah! The music,' Kim explained. He knew the sound of a
regimental band, but it amazed the lama.

At the far end of the plain a heavy, dusty column crawled in
sight. Then the wind brought the tune:

> We crave your condescension
> To tell you what we know
> Of marching in the Mulligan Guards
> To Sligo Port below!

Here broke in the shrill-tongued fifes:

> We shouldered arms,
> We marched – we marched away.
> From Phoenix Park
> We marched to Dublin Bay.
> The drums and the fifes,
> Oh, sweetly they did play,
> As we marched – marched – marched – with the
> Mulligan Guards!

It was the band of the Mavericks playing the regiment to
camp; for the men were route-marching with their baggage.
The rippling column swung into the level – carts behind it –
divided left and right, ran about like an ant-hill, and ...

'But this is sorcery!' said the lama.

The plain dotted itself with tents that seemed to rise, all
spread, from the carts. Another rush of men invaded the
grove, pitched a huge tent in silence, ran up yet eight or nine
more by the side of it, unearthed cooking-pots, pans, and
bundles, which were taken possession of by a crowd of native
servants; and behold the mango-tope turned into an orderly
town as they watched!

'Let us go,' said the lama, sinking back afraid, as the fires twinkled and white officers with jingling swords stalked into the Mess-tent.

'Stand back in the shadow. No one can see beyond the light of a fire,' said Kim, his eyes still on the flag. He had never before watched the routine of a seasoned regiment pitching camp in thirty minutes.

'Look! look! look!' clucked the lama. 'Yonder comes a priest.' It was Bennett, the Church of England Chaplain of the regiment, limping in dusty black. One of his flock had made some rude remarks about the Chaplain's mettle; and to abash him Bennett had marched step by step with the men that day. The black dress, gold cross on the watch-chain, the hairless face, and the soft, black wideawake hat would have marked him as a holy man anywhere in all India. He dropped into a camp-chair by the door of the Mess-tent and slid off his boots. Three or four officers gathered round him, laughing and joking over his exploit.

'The talk of white men is wholly lacking in dignity,' said the lama, who judged only by tone. 'But I considered the countenance of that priest and I think he is learned. Is it likely that he will understand our talk? I would talk to him of my Search.'

'Never speak to a white man till he is fed,' said Kim, quoting a well-known proverb. 'They will eat now, and – and I do not think they are good to beg from. Let us go back to the resting-place. After we have eaten we will come again. It certainly was a Red Bull – *my* Red Bull.'

They were both noticeably absent-minded when the old lady's retinue set their meal before them; so none broke their reserve, for it is not lucky to annoy guests.

'Now,' said Kim, picking his teeth, 'we will return to that place; but thou, O Holy One, must wait a little way off, because thy feet are heavier than mine and I am anxious to see more of that Red Bull.'

'But how canst thou understand the talk? Walk slowly. The road is dark,' the lama replied uneasily.

Kim put the question aside. 'I marked a place near to the

trees,' said he, 'where thou canst sit till I call. Nay,' as the lama made some sort of protest, 'remember this is my Search – the Search for my Red Bull. The sign in the Stars was not for thee. I know a little of the customs of white soldiers, and I always desire to see some new things.'

'What dost thou not know of this world?' The lama squatted obediently in a little hollow of the ground not a hundred yards from the hump of the mango-trees dark against the star-powdered sky.

'Stay till I call.' Kim flitted into the dusk. He knew that in all probability there would be sentries round the camp, and smiled to himself as he heard the thick boots of one. A boy who can dodge over the roofs of Lahore city on a moonlight night, using every little patch and corner of darkness to discomfit his pursuer, is not likely to be checked by a line of well-trained soldiers. He paid them the compliment of crawling between a couple, and, running and halting, crouching and dropping flat, worked his way toward the lighted Mess-tent where, close pressed behind the mango-tree, he waited till some chance word should give him a returnable lead.

The one thing now in his mind was further information as to the Red Bull. For aught he knew, and Kim's limitations were as curious and sudden as his expansions, the men, the nine hundred thorough devils of his father's prophecy, might pray to the beast after dark, as Hindus pray to the Holy Cow. That at least would be entirely right and logical, and the padre with the gold cross would be therefore the man to consult in the matter. On the other hand, remembering sober-faced padres whom he had avoided in Lahore city, the priest might be an inquisitive nuisance who would bid him learn. But had it not been proven at Umballa that his sign in the high heavens portended War and armed men? Was he not the Friend of the Stars as well as of all the World, crammed to the teeth with dreadful secrets? Lastly – and firstly as the undercurrent of all his quick thoughts – this adventure, though he did not know the English word, was a stupendous lark – a delightful continuation of his old flights across the housetops, as well as the fulfilment of sublime prophecy. He lay belly-flat and wriggled towards the Mess-tent door, a hand on the amulet round his neck.

It was as he suspected. The Sahibs prayed to their God; for in the centre of the Mess-table – its sole ornament when they were on the line of march – stood a golden bull fashioned from old-time loot of the Summer Palace at Pekin – a red-gold bull with lowered head, ramping upon a field of Irish green. To him the Sahibs held out their glasses and cried aloud confusedly.

Now the Reverend Arthur Bennett always left Mess after that toast, and being rather tired by his march his movements were more abrupt than usual. Kim, with slightly raised head, was still staring at his totem on the table, when the Chaplain stepped on his right shoulder-blade. Kim flinched under the leather, and, rolling sideways, brought down the Chaplain, who, ever a man of action, caught him by the throat and nearly choked the life out of him. Kim then kicked him desperately in the stomach. Mr Bennett gasped and doubled up, but without relaxing his grip, rolled over again, and silently hauled Kim to his own tent. The Mavericks were incurable practical jokers; and it occurred to the Englishman that silence was best till he had made complete inquiry.

'Why, it's a boy!' he said, as he drew his prize under the light of the tent-pole lantern, then shaking him severely cried: 'What were you doing? You're a thief. *Choor? Mallum?*' His Hindustani was very limited, and the ruffled and disgusted Kim intended to keep to the character laid down for him. As he recovered his breath he was inventing a beautifully plausible tale of his relations to some scullion, and at the same time keeping a keen eye on and a little under the Chaplain's left arm-pit. The chance came; he ducked for the doorway, but a long arm shot out and clutched at his neck, snapping the amulet-string and closing on the amulet.

'Give it me. O, give it me. Is it lost? Give me the papers.'

The words were in English – the tinny, saw-cut English of the native-bred, and the Chaplain jumped.

'A scapular,' said he, opening his hand. 'No, some sort of heathen charm. Why – why, do you speak English? Little boys who steal are beaten. You know that?'

'I do not – I did not steal.' Kim danced in agony like a terrier at a lifted stick. 'Oh, give it me. It is my charm. Do not thieve it from me.'

The Chaplain took no heed, but, going to the tent door, called aloud. A fattish, clean-shaven man appeared.

'I want your advice, Father Victor,' said Bennett. 'I found this boy in the dark outside the Mess-tent. Ordinarily, I should have chastised him and let him go, because I believe him to be a thief. But it seems he talks English, and he attaches some sort of value to a charm round his neck. I thought perhaps you might help me.'

Between himself and the Roman Catholic Chaplain of the Irish contingent lay, as Bennett believed, an unbridgeable gulf, but it was noticeable that whenever the Church of England dealt with a human problem she was very likely to call in the Church of Rome. Bennett's official abhorrence of the Scarlet Woman and all her ways was only equalled by his private respect for Father Victor.

'A thief talking English, is it? Let's look at his charm. No, it's not a scapular, Bennett.' He held out his hand.

'But have we any right to open it? A sound whipping –'

'I did *not* thieve,' protested Kim. 'You have hit me kicks all over my body. Now give me my charm and I will go away.'

'Not quite so fast. We'll look first,' said Father Victor, leisurely rolling out poor Kimball O'Hara's *'ne varietur'* parchment, his clearance-certificate, and Kim's baptismal certificate. On this last O'Hara – with some confused idea that he was doing wonders for his son – had scrawled scores of times: *'Look after the boy. Please look after the boy'* – signing his name and regimental number in full.

'Powers of Darkness below!' said Father Victor, passing all over to Mr Bennett. 'Do you know what these things are?'

'Yes,' said Kim. 'They are mine, and I want to go away.'

'I do not quite understand,' said Mr Bennett. 'He probably

brought them on purpose. It may be a begging trick of some kind.'

'I never saw a beggar less anxious to stay with his company, then. There's the makings of a gay mystery here. Ye believe in Providence, Bennett?'

'I hope so.'

'Well, I believe in miracles, so it comes to the same thing. Powers of Darkness! Kimball O'Hara! And his son! But then he's a native, and I saw Kimball married myself to Annie Shott. How long have you had these things, boy?'

'Ever since I was a little baby.'

Father Victor stepped forward quickly and opened the front of Kim's upper garment. 'You see, Bennett, he's not very black. What's your name?'

'Kim.'

'Or Kimball?'

'Perhaps. Will you let me go away?'

'What else?'

'They call me Kim Rishti ke. That is Kim of the Rishti.'

'What is that – "Rishti"?'

'*Eye*-rishti – that was the Regiment – my father's.'

'Irish – oh, I see.'

'Yess. That was how my father told me. My father, he has lived.'

'Has lived where?'

'Has lived. Of *course* he is dead – gone-out.'

'Oh! That's your abrupt way of putting it, is it?'

Bennett interrupted. 'It is possible I have done the boy an injustice. He is certainly white, though evidently neglected. I am sure I must have bruised him. I do not think spirits –'

'Get him a glass of sherry, then, and let him squat on the cot. Now, Kim,' continued Father Victor, 'no one is going to hurt you. Drink that down and tell us about yourself. The truth, if you've no objection.'

Kim coughed a little as he put down the empty glass, and considered. This seemed a time for caution and fancy. Small boys who prowl about camps are generally turned out after a whipping. But he had received no stripes; the amulet was evidently working in his favour, and it looked as though the Umballa horoscope and the few words that he could remember of his father's maunderings fitted in most miraculously. Else why did the fat padre seem so impressed, and why the glass of hot yellow drink from the lean one?

'My father, he is dead in Lahore city since I was very little. The woman, she kept *kabarri* shop near where the hire-carriages are.' Kim began with a plunge, not quite sure how far the truth would serve him.

'Your mother?'

'*No!*' – with a gesture of disgust. 'She went out when I was born. My father, he got these papers from the Jadoo-Gher – what do you call that?' (Bennett nodded) 'because he was in – good-standing. What do you call that?' (again Bennett nodded). 'My father told me that. He said, too, and also the Brahmin who made the drawing in the dust at Umballa two days ago, *he* said, that I shall find a Red Bull on a green field and that the Bull shall help me.'

'A phenomenal little liar,' muttered Bennett.

'Powers of Darkness below, what a country!' murmured Father Victor. 'Go on, Kim.'

'I did *not* thieve. Besides, I am just now disciple of a very holy man. He is sitting outside. We saw two men come with flags, making the place ready. That is *always* so in a dream, or on account of a – a – prophecy. So I knew it was come true. I saw the Red Bull on the green field, and my father he said: "Nine hundred *pukka* devils and the Colonel riding on a horse will look after you when you find the Red Bull!" I did not know what to do when I saw the Bull, but I went away and I came again when it was dark. I wanted to see the Bull again, and I saw the Bull again with the – the Sahibs praying to it. I think the Bull shall help me. The holy man said so too. He is sitting outside. Will you hurt him, if I call him a shout now? He is very holy. He can witness to all the things I say, and he knows I am not a thief.'

' "Sahibs praying to a bull!" What in the world do you

make of that?' said Bennett. ' "Disciple of a holy man!" Is the boy mad?'

'It's O'Hara's boy, sure enough. O'Hara's boy leagued with all the Powers of Darkness. It's very much what his father would have done – if he was drunk. We'd better invite the holy man. He may know something.'

'He does not know anything,' said Kim. 'I will show you him if you come. He is my master. Then afterwards we can go.'

'Powers of Darkness!' was all that Father Victor could say, as Bennett marched off, with a firm hand on Kim's shoulder.

They found the lama where he had dropped.

'The Search is at an end for me,' shouted Kim in the vernacular. 'I have found the Bull, but God knows what comes next. They will not hurt you. Come to the fat priest's tent with this thin man and see the end. It is all new, and they cannot talk Hindi. They are only uncurried donkeys.'

'Then it is not well to make a jest of their ignorance,' the lama returned. 'I am glad if thou art rejoiced, *chela*.'

Dignified and unsuspicious, he strode into the little tent, saluted the Churches as a Churchman, and sat down by the open charcoal brazier. The yellow lining of the tent reflected in the lamplight made his face red-gold.

Bennett looked at him with the triple-ringed uninterest of the creed that lumps nine-tenths of the world under the title of 'heathen'.

'And what was the end of the Search? What gift has the Red Bull brought?' The lama addressed himself to Kim.

'He says, "What are you going to do?" ' Bennett was staring uneasily at Father Victor, and Kim, for his own ends, took upon himself the office of interpreter.

'I do not see what concern this *fakir* has with the boy, who is probably his dupe or his confederate,' Bennett began. 'We cannot allow an English boy – Assuming that he is the son of a Mason, the sooner he goes to the Masonic Orphanage the better.'

'Ah! That's your opinion as Secretary to the Regimental

Lodge,' said Father Victor; 'but we might as well tell the old man what we are going to do. He doesn't look like a villain.'

'My experience is that one can never fathom the Oriental mind. Now, Kimball, I wish you to tell this man what I say – word for word.'

Kim gathered the import of the next few sentences and began thus:

'Holy One, the thin fool who looks like a camel says that I am the son of a Sahib.'

'But how?'

'Oh, it is true. I knew it since my birth, but *he* could only find it out by rending the amulet from my neck and reading all the papers. He thinks that once a Sahib is always a Sahib, and between the two of them they purpose to keep me in this Regiment or to send me to a *madrissah* [a school]. It has happened before. I have always avoided it. The fat fool is of one mind and the camel-like one of another. But that is no odds. I may spend one night here and perhaps the next. It has happened before. Then I will run away and return to thee.'

'But tell them that thou art my *chela*. Tell them how thou didst come to me when I was faint and bewildered. Tell them of our Search, and they will surely let thee go now.'

'I have already told them. They laugh, and they talk of the police.'

'What are you saying?' asked Mr Bennett.

'Oah. He only says that if you do not let me go it will stop him in his business – his ur-gent private af-fairs.' This last was a reminiscence of some talk with a Eurasian clerk in the Canal Department, but it only drew a smile, which nettled him. 'And if you *did* know what his business was you would not be in such a beastly hurry to interfere.'

'What is it then?' said Father Victor, not without feeling, as he watched the lama's face.

'There is a River in this country which he wishes to find so verree much. It was put out by an Arrow which –' Kim tapped his foot impatiently as he translated in his own mind from the vernacular to his clumsy English. 'Oah, it was made by our Lord God Buddha, you know, and if you wash there you are washed away from all your sins and made as white as cotton-wool.' (Kim had heard mission-talk in his time.) 'I am his disciple, and we *must* find that River. It is so verree valuable to us.'

'Say that again,' said Bennett. Kim obeyed, with amplifications.

'But this is gross blasphemy!' cried the Church of England.

'Tck! Tck!' said Father Victor sympathetically. 'I'd give a good deal to be able to talk the vernacular. A river that washes away sin! And how long have you two been looking for it?'

'Oh, many days. Now we wish to go away and look for it again. It is not here, you see.'

'I see,' said Father Victor gravely. 'But he can't go on in that old man's company. It would be different, Kim, if you were not a soldier's son. Tell him that the Regiment will take care of you and make you as good a man as your – as good a man as can be. Tell him that if he believes in miracles he must believe that –'

'There is no need to play on his credulity,' Bennett interrupted.

'I'm doing no such thing. He must believe that the boy's coming here – to his own Regiment – in search of his Red Bull is in the nature of a miracle. Consider the chances against it, Bennett. This one boy in all India, and our Regiment of all others on the line o' march for him to meet with! It's predestined on the face of it. Yes, tell him it's *Kismet. Kismet, mallum?* [Do you understand?]'

He turned towards the lama, to whom he might as well have talked of Mesopotamia.

'They say,' – the old man's eye lighted at Kim's speech – 'they say that the meaning of my horoscope is now accomplished, and that being led back – though as thou knowest I went out of curiosity – to these people and their Red Bull I must needs go to a *madrissah* and be turned into a Sahib. Now I make pretence of agreement, for at the worst it will be but a few meals eaten away from thee. Then I will slip away and follow down the road to Saharunpore. Therefore, Holy One, keep with that Kulu woman – on no account stray far from her cart till I come again. Past question, my sign is of War and of armed men. See how they have given me wine to drink and set me upon a bed of honour! My father must have been some great person. So if they raise me to honour among them, good. If not, good again. However it goes, I will run back to thee when I am tired. But stay with the Rajputni, or I shall miss thy feet ... Oah yess,' said the boy, 'I have told him everything you tell me to say.'

'And I cannot see any need why he should wait,' said Bennett, feeling in his trouser-pocket. 'We can investigate the details later – and I will give him a ru –'

'Give him time. Maybe he's fond of the lad,' said Father Victor, half arresting the clergyman's motion.

The lama dragged forth his rosary and pulled his huge hat-brim over his eyes.

'What can he want now?'

'He says' – Kim put up one hand. 'He says: Be quiett. He wants to speak to me by himself. You see, you do not know one little word of what he says, and I think if you talk he will perhaps give you very bad curses. When he takes those beads like that, you see, he always wants to be quiett.'

The two Englishmen sat overwhelmed, but there was a look in Bennett's eye that promised ill for Kim when he should be relaxed to the religious arm.

'A Sahib and the son of a Sahib –' The lama's voice was harsh with pain. 'But no white man knows the land and the customs of the land as thou knowest. How comes it this is true?'

'What matter, Holy One? – but remember it is only for a night or two. Remember, I can change swiftly. It will all be as it was when I first spoke to thee under Zam-Zammah the great gun –'

'As a boy in the dress of white men – when I first went to the Wonder House. And a second time thou wast a Hindu. What shall the third incarnation be?' He chuckled drearily.

'Ah, *chela*, thou hast done a wrong to an old man because my heart went out to thee.'

'And mine to thee. But how could I know that the Red Bull would bring me to this business?'

The lama covered his face afresh, and nervously rattled the rosary. Kim squatted beside him and laid hold upon a fold of his clothing.

'Now it is understood that the boy is a Sahib?' he went on in a muffled tone. 'Such a Sahib as was he who kept the images in the Wonder House.' The lama's experience of white men was limited. He seemed to be repeating a lesson. 'So then it is not seemly that he should do other than as the Sahibs do. He must go back to his own people.'

'For a day and a night and a day,' Kim pleaded.

'No, ye don't!' Father Victor saw Kim edging towards the door, and interposed a strong leg.

'I do not understand the customs of white men. The Priest of the Images in the Wonder House in Lahore was more courteous than the thin one here. This boy will be taken from me. They will make a Sahib of my disciple? Woe to me! How shall I find my River? Have *they* no disciples? Ask.'

'He says he is very sorree that he cannot find the River now any more. He says, Why have you no disciples, and stop bothering him? He wants to be washed of his sins.'

Neither Bennett nor Father Victor found any answer ready.

Said Kim in English, distressed for the lama's agony: 'I think if you will let me go now we will walk away quietly and not steal. We will look for that River like before I was caught. I wish I did not come here to find the Red Bull and all that sort of thing. I do not want it.'

'It's the very best day's work you ever did for yourself, young man,' said Bennett.

'Good heavens, I don't know how to console him,' said Father Victor, watching the lama intently. 'He can't take the boy away with him, and yet he's a good man – I'm sure he's a good man. Bennett, if you give him that rupee he'll curse you root and branch!'

They listened to each other's breathing – three – five full minutes. Then the lama raised his head, and looked forth across them into space and emptiness.

'And I am a Follower of the Way,' he said bitterly. 'The sin is mine and the punishment is mine. I made believe to myself – for now I see it was but make-belief – that thou wast sent to me to aid in the Search. So my heart went out to thee for thy charity and thy courtesy and the wisdom of thy little years. But those who follow the Way must permit not the fire of any desire or attachment, for that is all Illusion. As says ...' He quoted an old, old Chinese text, backed it with another, and reinforced these with a third. 'I stepped aside from the Way, my *chela*. It was no fault of thine. I delighted in the sight of life, the new people upon the roads, and in thy joy at seeing these things. I was pleased with thee who should have considered my Search and my Search alone. Now I am sorrowful because thou art taken away and my River is far from me. It is the Law which I have broken!'

'Powers of Darkness below!' said Father Victor, who, wise in the confessional, heard the pain in every sentence.

'I see now that the sign of the Red Bull was a sign for me as well as for thee. All Desire is red – and evil. I will do penance and find my River alone.'

'At least go back to the Kulu woman,' said Kim, 'otherwise thou wilt be lost upon the roads. She will feed thee till I run back to thee.'

The lama waved a hand to show that the matter was finally settled in his mind.

'Now,' – his tone altered as he turned to Kim, – 'what will they do with thee? At least I may, acquiring merit, wipe out past ill.'

'Make me a Sahib – so they think. The day after tomorrow I return. Do not grieve.'

'Of what sort? Such an one as this or that man?' He pointed

to Father Victor. 'Such an one as those I saw this evening – men wearing swords and stamping heavily?'

'Maybe.'

'That is not well. These men follow desire and come to emptiness. Thou must not be of their sort.'

'The Umballa priest said that my Star was War,' Kim interjected. 'I will ask these fools – but there is truly no need. I will run away this night, for all I wanted to see the new things.'

Kim put two or three questions in English to Father Victor, translating the replies to the lama.

Then: 'He says, "You take him from me and you cannot say what you will make him." He says, "Tell me before I go, for it is not a small thing to make a child."'

'You will be sent to a school. Later on, we shall see. Kimball, I suppose you'd like to be a soldier?'

'*Gorah-log* [white-folk]. No-ah! No-ah!' Kim shook his head violently. There was nothing in his composition to which drill and routine appealed. 'I will *not* be a soldier.'

'You will be what you're told to be,' said Bennett; 'and you should be grateful that we're going to help you.'

Kim smiled compassionately. If these men lay under the delusion that he would do anything that he did not fancy, so much the better.

Another long silence followed. Bennett fidgeted with impatience, and suggested calling a sentry to evict the *fakir*.

'Do they give or sell learning among the Sahibs? Ask them,' said the lama, and Kim interpreted.

'They say that money is paid to the teacher – but that money the Regiment will give ... What need? It is only for a night.'

'And – the more money is paid the better learning is given?' The lama disregarded Kim's plans for an early flight. 'It is no wrong to pay for learning. To help the ignorant to wisdom is always a merit.' The rosary clicked furiously as an abacus. Then he faced his oppressors.

'Ask them for how much money do they give a wise and suitable teaching? And in what city is that teaching given?'

'Well,' said Father Victor in English, when Kim had translated, 'that depends. The Regiment would pay for you all the time you are at the Military Orphanage; or you might go on the Punjab Masonic Orphanage's list (not that he or you 'ud understand what that means); but the best schooling a boy can get in India is, of course, at St Xavier's in Partibus at Lucknow.' This took some time to interpret, for Bennett wished to cut it short.

'He wants to know how much?' said Kim placidly.

'Two or three hundred rupees a year.' Father Victor was long past any sense of amazement. Bennett, impatient, did not understand.

'He says: "Write that name and the money upon a paper and give it him." And he says you must write your name below, because he is going to write a letter in some days to you. He says you are a good man. He says the other man is a fool. He is going away.'

The lama rose suddenly. 'I follow my Search,' he cried, and was gone.

'He'll run slap into the sentries,' cried Father Victor, jumping up as the lama stalked out; 'but I can't leave the boy.' Kim made swift motion to follow, but checked himself. There was no sound of challenge outside. The lama had disappeared.

Kim settled himself composedly on the Chaplain's cot. At least the lama had promised that he would stay with the Rajput woman from Kulu, and the rest was of the smallest importance. It pleased him that the two padres were so evidently excited. They talked long in undertones, Father Victor urging some scheme on Mr Bennett, who seemed incredulous. All this was very new and fascinating, but Kim felt sleepy. They called men into the tent – one of them certainly was the Colonel, as his father had prophesied – and they asked him an infinity of questions, chiefly about the woman who looked after him, all of which Kim answered truthfully. They did not seem to think the woman a good guardian.

After all, this was the newest of his experiences. Sooner or later, if he chose, he could escape into great, grey, formless India, beyond tents and padres and colonels. Meantime, if the Sahibs were to be impressed, he would do his best to impress them. He too was a white man.

After much talk that he could not comprehend, they handed him over to a sergeant, who had strict instructions not to let him escape. The Regiment would go on to Umballa, and Kim would be sent up, partly at the expense of the Lodge and in part by subscription, to a place called Sanawar.

'It's miraculous past all whooping, Colonel,' said Father Victor, when he had talked without a break for ten minutes. 'His Buddhist friend has levanted after taking my name and address. I can't quite make out whether he'll pay for the boy's education or whether he is preparing some sort of witchcraft on his own account.' Then to Kim: 'You'll live to be grateful to your friend the Red Bull yet. We'll make a man of you at Sanawar – even at the price o' making you a Protestant.'

'Certainly – most certainly,' said Bennett.

'But you will not go to Sanawar,' said Kim.

'But we *will* go to Sanawar, little man. That's the order of the Commander-in-Chief, who's a trifle more important than O'Hara's son.'

'You will not go to Sanawar. You will go to thee War.'

There was a shout of laughter from the full tent.

'When you know your own Regiment a trifle better you won't confuse the line of march with line of battle, Kim. We hope to go to "thee War" sometime.'

'Oah, I know all thatt.' Kim drew his bow again at a venture. If they were not going to the war, at least they did not know what he knew of the talk in the veranda at Umballa.

'I know you are not at thee war now; but I tell *you* that as soon as you get to Umballa you will be sent to the war – the new war. It is a war of eight thousand men, besides the guns.'

'That's explicit. D'you add prophecy to your other gifts? Take him along, sergeant. Take up a suit for him from the Drums, an' take care he doesn't slip through your fingers. Who says the age of miracles is gone by? I think I'll go to bed. My poor mind's weakening.'

At the far end of the camp, silent as a wild animal, an hour later sat Kim, newly washed all over, in a horrible stuff suit that rasped his arms and legs.

'A most amazin' young bird,' said the sergeant. 'He turns up in charge of a yellow-headed buck-Brahmin priest, with his father's Lodge certificates round his neck, talkin' God knows what all of a red bull. The buck-Brahmin evaporates without explanations, an' the bhoy sets cross-legged on the Chaplain's bed prophesyin' bloody war to the men at large. Injia's a wild land for a God-fearin' man. I'll just tie his leg to the tent-pole in case he'll go through the roof. What did ye say about the war?'

'Eight thousand men, besides guns,' said Kim. 'Very soon you will see.'

'You're a consolin' little imp. Lie down between the Drums an' go to bye-bye. Those two boys will watch your slumbers.'

Chapter 6

Now I remember comrades –
  Old playmates on new seas –
Whenas we traded orpiment
  Among the savages.
Ten thousand leagues to southward,
  And thirty years removed –
They knew not noble Valdez,
  But me they knew and loved.
            Song of Diego Valdez.

V<small>ERY</small> early in the morning the white tents came down and disappeared as the Mavericks took a side-road to Umballa. It did not skirt the resting-place, and Kim, trudging beside a baggage-cart under fire of comments from soldiers' wives, was not so confident as overnight. He discovered that he was closely watched – Father Victor on the one side, and Mr Bennett on the other.

In the forenoon the column checked. A camel-orderly handed the Colonel a letter. He read it, and spoke to a Major. Half a mile in the rear, Kim heard a hoarse and joyful clamour rolling down on him through the thick dust. Then someone beat him on the back, crying: 'Tell us how ye knew, ye little limb of Satan? Father dear, see if ye can make him tell.'

A pony ranged alongside, and he was hauled on to the priest's saddle-bow.

'Now, my son, your prophecy of last night has come true. Our orders are to entrain at Umballa for the Front tomorrow.'

'What is thatt?' said Kim, for '*front*' and '*entrain*' were newish words to him.

'We are going to "thee War," as you called it.'

'Of course you are going to thee War. I said last night.'

'Ye did; but, Powers o' Darkness, how did ye know?'

Kim's eyes sparkled. He shut his lips, nodded his head, and

looked unspeakable things. The Chaplain moved on through
the dust, and privates, sergeants, and subalterns called one
another's attention to the boy. The Colonel, at the head of the
column, stared at him curiously. 'It was probably some bazar
rumour,' he said; 'but even then –' He referred to the paper in
his hand. 'Hang it all, the thing was only decided within the
last forty-eight hours.'

'Are there many more like you in India?' said Father
Victor, 'or are you by way o' being a *lusus naturae*?'

'Now I have told you,' said the boy, 'will you let me go
back to my old man? If he has not stayed with that woman
from Kulu, I am afraid he will die.'

'By what I saw of him he's as well able to take care of
himself as you. No. Ye've brought us luck, an' we're goin' to
make a man of you. I'll take ye back to your baggage–cart and
ye'll come to me this evening.'

For the rest of the day Kim found himself an object of
distinguished consideration among a few hundred white men.
The story of his appearance in camp, the discovery of his
parentage, and his prophecy, had lost nothing in the telling. A
big, shapeless white woman on a pile of bedding asked him
mysteriously whether he thought her husband would come
back from the war. Kim reflected gravely, and said that he
would, and the woman gave him food. In many respects, this
big procession that played music at intervals – this crowd that
talked and laughed so easily – resembled a festival in Lahore
city. So far, there was no sign of hard work, and he resolved to
lend the spectacle his patronage. At evening there came out to
meet them bands of music, and played the Mavericks into
camp near Umballa railway station. That was an interesting
night. Men of other regiments came to visit the Mavericks.
The Mavericks went visiting on their own account. Their
pickets hurried forth to bring them back, met pickets of
strange regiments on the same duty; and, after a while, the
bugles blew madly for more pickets with officers to control
the tumult. The Mavericks had a reputation for liveliness to
live up to. But they fell in on the platform next morning in

perfect shape and condition; and Kim, left behind with the sick, women, and boys, found himself shouting farewells excitedly as the trains drew away. Life as a Sahib was amusing so far; but he touched it with a cautious hand. Then they marched him back in charge of a drummer-boy to empty, lime-washed barracks, whose floors were covered with rubbish and string and paper, and whose ceilings gave back his lonely footfall. Native-fashion, he curled himself up on a stripped cot and went to sleep. An angry man stumped down the veranda, woke him up, and said he was a schoolmaster. This was enough for Kim, and he retired into his shell. He could just puzzle out the various English Police notices in Lahore city, because they affected his comfort; and among the many guests of the woman who looked after him had been a queer German who painted scenery for the Parsee travelling theatre. He told Kim that he had been 'on the barricades in 'Forty-eight,' and therefore – at least that was how it struck Kim – he would teach the boy to write in return for food. Kim had been kicked as far as single letters, but did not think well of them.

'I do not know anything. Go away!' said Kim, scenting evil. Hereupon the man caught him by the ear, dragged him to a room in a far-off wing where a dozen drummer-boys were sitting on forms, and told him to be still if he could do nothing else. This he managed very successfully. The man explained something or other with white lines on a black board for at least half an hour, and Kim continued his interrupted nap. He much disapproved of the present aspect of affairs, for this was the very school and discipline he had spent two-thirds of his young life in avoiding. Suddenly a beautiful idea occurred to him, and he wondered that he had not thought of it before.

The man dismissed them, and first to spring through the veranda into the open sunshine was Kim.

' 'Ere, you! 'Alt! Stop!' said a high voice at his heels. 'I've got to look after you. My orders are not to let you out of my sight. Where are you goin'?'

It was the drummer-boy who had been hanging round him

all the forenoon – a fat and freckled person of about fourteen, and Kim loathed him from the soles of his boots to his cap-ribbons.

'To the bazar – to get sweets – for you,' said Kim, after thought.

'Well, the bazar's out o' bounds. If we go there we'll get a dressing-down. You come back.'

'How near can we go?' Kim did not know what bounds meant, but he wished to be polite – for the present.

' 'Ow near? 'Ow far, you mean! We can go as far as that tree down the road.'

'Then I will go there.'

'All right. I ain't goin'. It's too 'ot. I can watch you from 'ere. It's no good your runnin' away. If you did, they'd spot you by your clothes. That's regimental stuff you're wearin'. There ain't a picket in Umballa wouldn't 'ead you back quicker than you started out.'

This did not impress Kim as much as the knowledge that his raiment would tire him out if he tried to run. He slouched to the tree at the corner of a bare road leading towards the bazar, and eyed the natives passing. Most of them were barrack-servants of the lowest caste. Kim hailed a sweeper, who promptly retorted with a piece of unnecessary insolence, in the natural belief that the European boy could not follow it. The low, quick answer undeceived him. Kim put his fettered soul into it, thankful for the late chance to abuse somebody in the tongue he knew best. 'And now, go to the nearest letter-writer in the bazar and tell him to come here. I would write a letter.'

'But – but what manner of white man's son art thou to need a bazar letter-writer? Is there not a schoolmaster in the barracks?'

'Ay; and Hell is full of the same sort. Do my order, you – you Od! Thy mother was married under a basket! Servant of Lal Beg' (Kim knew the God of the sweepers), 'run on my business or we will talk again.'

The sweeper shuffled off in haste. 'There is a white boy by

the barracks waiting under a tree who is not a white boy,' he stammered to the first bazar letter-writer he came across. 'He needs thee.'

'Will he pay?' said the spruce scribe, gathering up his desk and pens and sealing-wax all in order.

'I do not know. He is not like other boys. Go and see. It is well worth.'

Kim danced with impatience when the slim young Kayeth hove in sight. As soon as his voice could carry he cursed him volubly.

'First I will take my pay,' the letter-writer said. 'Bad words have made the price higher. But who art thou, dressed in that fashion, to speak in this fashion?'

'Aha! That is in the letter which thou shalt write. Never was such a tale. But I am in no haste. Another writer will serve me. Umballa city is as full of them as is Lahore.'

'Four annas,' said the writer, sitting down and spreading his cloth in the shade of a deserted barrack-wing.

Mechanically Kim squatted beside him – squatted as only the natives can – in spite of the abominable clinging trousers.

The writer regarded him sideways.

'That is the price to ask of Sahibs,' said Kim. 'Now fix me a true one.'

'An anna and a half. How do I know, having written the letter, that thou wilt not run away?'

'I must not go beyond this tree, and there is also the stamp to be considered.'

'I get no commission on the price of the stamp. Once more, what manner of white boy art thou?'

'That shall be said in the letter, which is to Mahbub Ali, the horse-dealer in the Kashmir Serai, at Lahore. He is my friend.'

'Wonder on wonder!' murmured the letter-writer, dipping a reed in the inkstand. 'To be written in Hindi?'

'Assuredly. To Mahbub Ali then. Begin! *I have come down with the old man as far as Umballa in the train. At Umballa I carried the news of the bay mare's pedigree.*' After what he had seen in the garden, he was not going to write of white stallions.

'Slower a little. What has a bay mare to do . . . Is it Mahbub Ali, the great dealer?'

'Who else? I have been in his service. Take more ink. Again. *As the order was, so I did it. We then went on foot towards Benares, but on the third day we found a certain regiment.* Is that down?'

'Ay, *pulton*,' murmured the writer, all ears.

'*I went into their camp and was caught, and by means of the charm about my neck, which thou knowest, it was established that I was the son of some man in the regiment: according to the prophecy of the Red Bull, which thou knowest was common talk of our bazar.*' Kim waited for this shaft to sink into the letter-writer's heart, cleared his throat, and continued: '*A priest clothed me and gave me a new name . . . One priest, however, was a fool. The clothes are very heavy, but I am a Sahib and my heart is heavy too. They send me to a school and beat me. I do not like the air and water here. Come then and help me, Mahbub Ali, or send me some money, for I have not sufficient to pay the writer who writes this.*'

' "Who writes this." It is my own fault that I was tricked. Thou art as clever as Husain Bux that forged the Treasury stamps at Nucklao. But what a tale! What a tale! Is it true by any chance?'

'It does not profit to tell lies to Mahbub Ali. It is better to help his friends by lending them a stamp. When the money comes I will repay.'

The writer grunted doubtfully, but took a stamp out of his desk, sealed the letter, handed it over to Kim, and departed. Mahbub Ali's was a name of power in Umballa.

'That is the way to win a good account with the Gods,' Kim shouted after him.

'Pay me twice over when the money comes,' the man cried over his shoulder.

'What was you bukkin' to that nigger about?' said the drummer-boy when Kim returned to the veranda. 'I was watchin' you.'

'I was only talkin' to him.'

'You talk the same as a nigger, don't you?'

'No-ah! No-ah! I onlee speak a little. What shall we do now?'

'The bugles'll go for dinner in arf a minute. My Gawd! I wish I'd gone up to the Front with the Regiment. It's awful doin' nothin' but school down 'ere. Don't you 'ate it?'

'Oah yess!'

'I'd run away if I knew where to go to, but, as the men say, in this bloomin' Injia you're only a prisoner at large. You can't desert without bein' took back at once. I'm fair sick of it.'

'You have been in Be – England?'

'W'y, I only come out last troopin' season with my mother. I should think I *'ave* been in England. What a ignorant little beggar you are! You was brought up in the gutter, wasn't you?'

'Oah yess. Tell me something about England. My father he came from there.'

Though he would not say so, Kim of course disbelieved every word the drummer-boy spoke about the Liverpool suburb which was his England. It passed the heavy time till dinner – a most unappetizing meal served to the boys and a few invalids in a corner of a barrack-room. But that he had written to Mahbub Ali, Kim would have been almost depressed. The indifference of native crowds he was used to; but this strong loneliness among white men preyed on him. He was grateful when, in the course of the afternoon, a big soldier took him over to Father Victor, who lived in another wing across another dusty parade-ground. The priest was reading an English letter written in purple ink. He looked at Kim more curiously than ever.

'An' how do you like it, my son, as far as you've gone? Not much, eh? It must be hard – very hard on a wild animal. Listen now. I've an amazin' epistle from your friend.'

'Where is he? Is he well? Oah! If he knows to write me letters, it is all right.'

'You're fond of him then?'

'*Of* course I am fond of him. He was fond of me.'

'It seems so by the look of this. He can't write English, can he?'

'Oah no. Not that I know, but *of* course he found a letter-writer who can write English verree well, and so he wrote. I *do* hope you understand.'

'That accounts for it. D'you know anything about his money affairs?' Kim's face showed that he did not.

'How can I tell?'

'That's what I'm askin'. Now listen if you can make head or tail o' this. We'll skip the first part ... It's written from Jagadhir Road ... "*Sitting on wayside in grave meditation, trusting to be favoured with your Honour's applause of present step, which recommend your Honour to execute for Almighty God's sake. Education is greatest blessing if of best sorts. Otherwise no earthly use.*" Faith, the old man's hit the bull's-eye that time! "*If your Honour condescending giving my boy best educations Xavier*" (I suppose that's St Xavier's in Partibus) "*in terms of our conversation dated in your tent 15th instant*" (a business-like touch there!) "*then Almighty God blessing your Honour's succeedings to third an' fourth generation and*" – now listen! – "*confide in your Honour's humble servant for adequate remuneration per hoondi per annum three hundred rupees a year to one expensive education St Xavier, Lucknow, and allow small time to forward same per hoondi sent to any part of India as your Honour shall address yourself. This servant of your Honour has presently no place to lay crown of his head, but going to Benares by train on account of persecution of old woman talking so much and unanxious residing Saharunpore in any domestic capacity.*" Now what in the world does that mean?'

'She has asked him to be her *puro* -- her clergyman – at Saharunpore, *I* think. He would not do that on account of his River. She *did* talk.'

'It's clear to you, is it? It beats me altogether. "*So going to Benares, where will find address and forward rupees for boy who is apple of eye, and for Almighty God's sake execute this education,*

*and your petitioner as in duty bound shall ever awfully pray.
Written by Sobrao Satai, Failed Entrance Allahabad University,
for Venerable Teshoo Lama the priest of Such-zen looking for a
River, address care of Tirthankars' Temple, Benares. P.M. –
Please note boy is apple of eye, and rupees shall be sent per hoondi
three hundred per annum. For God Almighty's sake.*" Now, is that
ravin' lunacy or a business proposition? I ask you, because
I'm fairly at my wits' end.'

'He says he will give me three hundred rupees a year? So he
will give me them.'

'Oh, that's the way you look at it, is it?'

'*Of* course. If he says so!'

The priest whistled; then he addressed Kim as an equal.

'I don't believe it; but we'll see. You were goin' off today to
the Military Orphanage at Sanawar, where the Regiment
would keep you till you were old enough to enlist. Ye'd be
brought up to the Church of England. Bennett arranged for
that. On the other hand, if ye go to St Xavier's ye'll get a
better education an' – an' can have the religion. D'ye see my
dilemma?'

Kim saw nothing save a vision of the lama going south in a
train with none to beg for him.

'Like most people, I'm going to temporize. If your friend
sends the money from Benares – Powers of Darkness below,
where's a street-beggar to raise three hundred rupees? – ye'll
go down to Lucknow and I'll pay your fare, because I can't
touch the subscription-money if I intend, as I do, to make ye
a Catholic. If he doesn't, ye'll go to the Military Orphanage at
the Regiment's expense. I'll allow him three days' grace,
though I don't believe it at all. Even then, if he fails in his
payments later on ... but it's beyond me. We can only walk
one step at a time in this world, praise God! An' they sent
Bennett to the Front an' left me behind. Bennett can't expect
everything.'

'Oah yess,' said Kim vaguely.

The priest leaned forward. 'I'd give a month's pay to find
what's goin' on inside that little round head of yours.'

'There is nothing,' said Kim, and scratched it. He was wondering whether Mahbub Ali would send him as much as a whole rupee. Then he could pay the letter-writer and write letters to the lama at Benares. Perhaps Mahbub Ali would visit him next time he came south with horses. Surely he must know that Kim's delivery of the letter to the officer at Umballa had caused the great war which the men and boys had discussed so loudly over the barrack dinner-tables. But if Mahbub Ali did not know this, it would be very unsafe to tell him so. Mahbub Ali was hard upon boys who knew, or thought they knew, too much.

'Well, till I get further news' – Father Victor's voice interrupted the reverie. 'Ye can run along now and play with the other boys. They'll teach ye something – but I don't think ye'll like it.'

The day dragged to its weary end. When he wished to sleep he was instructed how to fold up his clothes and set out his boots; the other boys deriding. Bugles waked him in the dawn; the schoolmaster caught him after breakfast, thrust a page of meaningless characters under his nose, gave them senseless names, and whacked him without reason. Kim meditated poisoning him with opium borrowed from a barrack-sweeper, but reflected that, as they all ate at one table in public (this was peculiarly revolting to Kim, who preferred to turn his back on the world at meals), the stroke might be dangerous. Then he attempted running off to the village where the priest had tried to drug the lama – the village where the old soldier lived. But far-seeing sentries at every exit headed back the little scarlet figure. Trousers and jacket crippled body and mind alike, so he abandoned the project and fell back, Oriental-fashion, on time and chance. Three days of torment passed in the big, echoing white rooms. He walked out of afternoons under escort of the drummer-boy, and all he heard from his companions were the few useless words which seemed to make two-thirds of the white man's abuse. Kim knew and despised them all long ago. The boy resented his silence and lack of interest by beating him, as was

only natural. He did not care for any of the bazars which were
in bounds. He styled all natives 'niggers'; yet servants and
sweepers called him abominable names to his face, and,
misled by their deferential attitude, he never understood.
This somewhat consoled Kim for the beatings.

On the morning of the fourth day a judgement overtook
that drummer. They had gone out together towards Umballa
racecourse. He returned alone, weeping, with news that
young O'Hara, to whom he had been doing nothing in
particular, had hailed a scarlet-bearded nigger on horseback;
that the nigger had then and there laid into him with a
peculiarly adhesive quirt, picked up young O'Hara, and borne
him off at full gallop. These tidings came to Father Victor,
and he drew down his long upper lip. He was already
sufficiently startled by a letter from the Temple of the
Tirthankars at Benares, enclosing a native banker's note of
hand for three hundred rupees, and an amazing prayer to
'Almighty God'. The lama would have been more annoyed
than the priest had he known how the bazar letter-writer had
translated his phrase 'to acquire merit'.

'Powers of Darkness below!' Father Victor fumbled with
the note. 'An' now he's off with another of his peep-o'-day
friends. I don't know whether it will be a greater relief to me
to get him back or to have him lost. He's beyond my
comprehension. How the Divil – yes, *he's* the man I mean –
can a street-beggar raise money to educate white boys?'

Three miles off, on Umballa racecourse, Mahbub Ali,
reining a grey Kabuli stallion with Kim in front of him, was
saying:

'But, Little Friend of all the World, there is my honour and
reputation to be considered. All the officer-Sahibs in all the
regiments, and all Umballa, know Mahbub Ali. Men saw me
pick thee up and chastise that boy. We are seen now from far
across this plain. How can I take thee away, or account for thy
disappearing if I set thee down and let thee run off into the
crops? They would put me in jail. Be patient. Once a Sahib,

always a Sahib. When thou art a man – who knows? – thou
wilt be grateful to Mahbub Ali.'

'Take me beyond their sentries where I can change this
red. Give me money and I will go to Benares and be with my
lama again. I do not want to be a Sahib, and remember I *did*
deliver that message.'

The stallion bounded wildly. Mahbub Ali had incautiously
driven home the sharp-edged stirrup. (He was not the new
sort of fluent horse-dealer who wears English boots and
spurs.) Kim drew his own conclusions from that betrayal.

'That was a small matter. It lay on the straight road to
Benares. I and the Sahib have by this time forgotten it. I send
so many letters and messages to men who ask questions about
horses, I cannot well remember one from the other. Was it
some matter of a bay mare that Peters Sahib wished the
pedigree of?'

Kim saw the trap at once. If he had said 'bay mare'
Mahbub would have known by his very readiness to fall in
with the amendment that the boy suspected something. Kim
replied therefore:

'Bay mare. No. *I* do not forget my messages thus. It was a
white stallion.'

'Ay, so it was. A white Arab stallion. But thou didst write
"bay mare" to me.'

'Who cares to tell truth to a letter-writer?' Kim answered,
feeling Mahbub's palm on his heart.

'Hi! Mahbub, you old villain, pull up!' cried a voice, and an
Englishman raced alongside on a little polo-pony. 'I've been
chasing you half over the country. That Kabuli of yours can
go. For sale, I suppose?'

'I have some young stuff coming on made by Heaven for
the delicate and difficult polo-game. He has no equal. He –'

'Plays polo and waits at table. Yes. We know all that. What
the deuce have you got there?'

'A boy,' said Mahbub gravely. 'He was being beaten by
another boy. His father was once a white soldier in the big

war. The boy was a child in Lahore city. He played with my horses when he was a babe. Now I think they will make him a soldier. He has been newly caught by his father's Regiment that went up to the war last week. But I do not think he wants to be a soldier. I take him for a ride. Tell me where thy barracks are and I will set thee there.'

'Let me go. I can find the barracks alone.'

'And if thou runnest away who will say it is not my fault?'

'He'll run back to his dinner. Where has he to run to?' the Englishman asked.

'He was born in the land. He has friends. He goes where he chooses. He is a *chabuk sawai* [a sharp chap]. It needs only to change his clothing, and in a twinkling he would be a low-caste Hindu boy.'

'The deuce he would!' The Englishman looked critically at the boy as Mahbub headed towards the barracks. Kim ground his teeth. Mahbub was mocking him, as faithless Afghans will; for he went on:

'They will send him to a school and put heavy boots on his feet and swaddle him in these clothes. Then he will forget all he knows. Now, which of the barracks is thine?'

Kim pointed – he could not speak – to Father Victor's wing, all staring white near by.

'Perhaps he will make a good soldier,' said Mahbub reflectively. 'He will make a good orderly at least. I sent him to deliver a message once from Lahore. A message concerning the pedigree of a white stallion.'

Here was deadly insult on deadlier injury – and the Sahib to whom he had so craftily given that war-waking letter heard it all. Kim beheld Mahbub Ali frying in flame for his treachery, but for himself he saw one long grey vista of barracks, schools, and barracks again. He gazed imploringly at the clear-cut face in which there was no glimmer of recognition; but even at this extremity it never occurred to him to throw himself on the white man's mercy or to denounce the Afghan. And Mahbub stared deliberately at the

Englishman, who stared as deliberately at Kim, quivering and tongue-tied.

'My horse is well trained,' said the dealer. 'Others would have kicked, Sahib.'

'Ah,' said the Englishman at last, rubbing his pony's damp withers with his whip-butt. 'Who makes the boy a soldier?'

'He says the Regiment that found him, and especially the Padre-sahib of that regiment.'

'There is the Padre!' Kim choked as bare-headed Father Victor sailed down upon them from the veranda.

'Powers o' Darkness below, O'Hara! How many more mixed friends do you keep in Asia?' he cried, as Kim slid down and stood helplessly before him.

'Good morning, Padre,' the Englishman said cheerily. 'I know you by reputation well enough. Meant to have come over and called before this. I'm Creighton.'

'Of the Ethnological Survey?' said Father Victor. The Englishman nodded. 'Faith, I'm glad to meet ye then; an' I owe you some thanks for bringing back the boy.'

'No thanks to me, Padre. Besides, the boy wasn't going away. You don't know old Mahbub Ali.' The horse-dealer sat impassive in the sunlight. 'You will when you have been in the station a month. He sells us all our crocks. That boy is rather a curiosity. Can you tell me anything about him?'

'Can I tell you?' puffed Father Victor. 'You'll be the one man that could help me in my quandaries. Tell you! Powers o' Darkness, I'm bursting to tell someone who knows something o' the native!'

A groom came round the corner. Colonel Creighton raised his voice, speaking in Urdu. 'Very good, Mahbub Ali, but what is the use of telling me all those stories about the pony? Not one pice more than three hundred and fifty rupees will I give.'

'The Sahib is a little hot and angry after riding,' the horse-dealer returned, with the leer of a privileged jester. 'Presently, he will see my horse's points more clearly. I will wait till he has finished his talk with the Padre. I will wait under that tree.'

'Confound you!' The Colonel laughed. 'That comes of looking at one of Mahbub's horses. He's a regular old leech, Padre. Wait, then, if thou hast so much time to spare, Mahbub. Now I'm at your service, Padre. Where is the boy? Oh, he's gone off to collogue with Mahbub. Queer sort of boy. Might I ask you to send my mare round under cover?'

He dropped into a chair which commanded a clear view of Kim and Mahbub Ali in conference beneath the tree. The Padre went indoors for cheroots.

Creighton heard Kim say bitterly: 'Trust a Brahmin before a snake, and a snake before an harlot, and an harlot before a Pathan, Mahbub Ali.'

'That is all one.' The great red beard wagged solemnly. 'Children should not see a carpet on the loom till the pattern is made plain. Believe me, Friend of all the World, I do thee great service. They will not make a soldier of thee.'

'You crafty old sinner!' thought Creighton. 'But you're not far wrong. That boy mustn't be wasted if he is as advertised.'

'Excuse me half a minute,' cried the Padre from within, 'but I'm gettin' the documents in the case.'

'If through me the favour of this bold and wise Colonel Sahib comes to thee, and thou art raised to honour, what thanks wilt thou give Mahbub Ali when thou art a man?'

'Nay, nay! I begged thee to let me take the Road again, where I should have been safe; and thou hast sold me back to the English. What will they give thee for blood-money?'

'A cheerful young demon!' The Colonel bit his cigar, and turned politely to Father Victor.

'What are the letters that the fat priest is waving before the Colonel? Stand behind the stallion as though looking at my bridle!' said Mahbub Ali.

'A letter from my lama which he wrote from Jagadhir Road, saying that he will pay three hundred rupees by the year for my schooling.'

'Oho! Is old Red Hat of that sort? At which school?'

'God knows. I think in Nucklao.'

'Yes. There is a big school there for the sons of Sahibs – and half-Sahibs. I have seen it when I sell horses there. So the lama also loved the Friend of all the World?'

'Ay; and *he* did not tell lies, or return me to captivity.'

'Small wonder the Padre does not know how to unravel the thread. How fast he talks to the Colonel Sahib!' Mahbub Ali chuckled. 'By Allah!' – the keen eyes swept the veranda for an instant – 'thy lama has sent what to me looks like a note of hand. I have had some few dealings in *hoondis*. The Colonel Sahib is looking at it.'

'What good is all this to me?' said Kim wearily. 'Thou wilt go away, and they will return me to those empty rooms where there is no good place to sleep and where the boys beat me.'

'I do not think that. Have patience, child. All Pathans are not faithless – except in horseflesh.'

Five – ten – fifteen minutes passed, Father Victor talking energetically or asking questions which the Colonel answered.

'Now I've told you everything that I know about the boy from beginnin' to end; and it's a blessed relief to me. Did ye ever hear the like?'

'At any rate, the old man has sent the money. Gobind Sahai's notes of hand are good from here to China,' said the Colonel. 'The more one knows about natives the less can one say what they will or won't do.'

'That's consolin' – from the head of the Ethnological Survey. It's this mixture of Red Bulls and Rivers of Healing (poor heathen, God help him!) an' notes of hand and Masonic certificates. Are you a Mason, by any chance?'

'By Jove, I am, now I come to think of it. That's an additional reason,' said the Colonel absently.

'I'm glad ye see a reason in it. But as I said, it's the mixture o' things that's beyond me. An' his prophesyin' to our Colonel sitting on my bed with his little shimmy torn open showing his white skin; an' the prophecy comin' true! They'll cure all that nonsense at St Xavier's, eh?'

'Sprinkle him with holy water,' the Colonel laughed.

'On my word, I fancy I ought to sometimes. But I'm hoping he'll be brought up as a good Catholic. All that troubles me is what'll happen if the old beggar-man –'

'Lama, lama, my dear sir; and some of them are gentlemen in their own country.'

'The lama, then, fails to pay next year. He's a fine business head to plan on the spur of the moment, but he's bound to die some day. An' takin' a heathen's money to give a child a Christian education –'

'But he said explicitly what he wanted. As soon as he knew the boy was white he seems to have made his arrangements accordingly. I'd give a month's pay to hear how he explained it all at the Tirthankars' Temple at Benares. Look here, Padre, I don't pretend to know much about natives, but if he says he'll pay, he'll pay – dead or alive. I mean, his heirs will assume the debt. My advice to you is, send the boy down to Lucknow. If your Anglican Chaplain thinks you've stolen a march on him –'

'Bad luck to Bennett! He was sent to the Front instead o' me. Doughty certified me medically unfit. I'll excommunicate Doughty if he comes back alive! Surely Bennett ought to be content with –'

'Glory, leaving you the religion. Quite so! As a matter of fact I don't think Bennett will mind. Put the blame on me. I – er – strongly recommend sending the boy to St Xavier's. He can go down on pass as a soldier's orphan, so the railway fare will be saved. You can buy him an outfit from the Regimental subscription. The Lodge will be saved the expense of his education, and that will put the Lodge in a good temper. It's perfectly easy. I've got to go down to Lucknow next week. I'll look after the boy on the way – give him in charge of my servants, and so on.'

'You're a good man.'

'Not in the least. Don't make that mistake. The lama has sent us money for a definite end. We can't very well return it. We shall have to do as he says. Well, that's settled, isn't it? Shall we say that, Tuesday next, you'll hand him over to me at the night train south? That's only three days. He can't do much harm in three days.'

'It's a weight off my mind, but – this thing here?' – he waved the note of hand – 'I don't know Gobind Sahai: or his bank, which may be a hole in a wall.'

'*You've* never been a subaltern in debt. I'll cash it if you like, and send you the vouchers in proper order.'

'But with all your own work too! It's askin' –'

'It's not the least trouble indeed. You see, as an ethnologist, the thing's very interesting to me. I'd like to make a note of it for some Government work that I'm doing. The transformation of a regimental badge like your Red Bull into a sort of fetish that the boy follows is very interesting.'

'But I can't thank you enough.'

'There's one thing you can do. All we Ethnological men are as jealous as jackdaws of one another's discoveries. They're of no interest to anyone but ourselves, of course, but you know what book-collectors are like. Well, don't say a word, directly or indirectly, about the Asiatic side of the boy's character – his adventures and his prophecy, and so on. I'll worm them out of the boy later on and – you see?'

'I do. Ye'll make a wonderful account of it. Never a word will I say to anyone till I see it in print.'

'Thank you. That goes straight to an ethnologist's heart. Well, I must be getting back to my breakfast. Good Heavens! Old Mahbub here still?' He raised his voice, and the horse-dealer came out from under the shadow of the tree, 'Well, what is it?'

'As regards that young horse,' said Mahbub, 'I say that when a colt is born to be a polo-pony, closely following the ball without teaching – when such a colt knows the game by divination – then I say it is a great wrong to break that colt to a heavy cart, Sahib!'

'So say I also, Mahbub. The colt will be entered for polo only. (These fellows think of nothing in the world but horses, Padre.) I'll see you tomorrow, Mahbub, if you've anything likely for sale.'

The dealer saluted, horseman-fashion, with a sweep of the off hand. 'Be patient a little, Friend of all the World,' he whispered to the agonized Kim. 'Thy fortune is made. In a little while thou goest to Nucklao, and – here is something to pay the letter-writer. I shall see thee again, I think, many times,' and he cantered off down the road.

'Listen to me,' said the Colonel from the veranda, speaking in the vernacular. 'In three days thou wilt go with me to Lucknow, seeing and hearing new things all the while. Therefore sit still for three days and do not run away. Thou wilt go to school at Lucknow.'

'Shall I meet my Holy One there?' Kim whimpered.

'At least Lucknow is nearer to Benares than Umballa. It may be thou wilt go under my protection. Mahbub Ali knows this, and he will be angry if thou returnest to the Road now. Remember – much has been told me which I do not forget.'

'I will wait,' said Kim, 'but the boys will beat me.'

Then the bugles blew for dinner.

Chapter 7

Unto whose use the pregnant suns are poised
　　With idiot moons and stars retracing stars?
Creep thou betweene – thy coming's all unnoised.
　　Heaven hath her high, as Earth her baser, wars.
Heir to these tumults, this affright, that fraye
(By Adam's, fathers', own, sin bound alway);
Peer up, draw out thy horoscope and say
　　Which planet mends thy threadbare fate or mars!
　　　　　　　　　　　　　　　　Sir John Christie.

IN the afternoon the red-faced schoolmaster told Kim that he had been 'struck off the strength', which conveyed no meaning to him till he was ordered to go away and play. Then he ran to the bazar, and found the young letter-writer to whom he owed a stamp.

'Now I pay,' said Kim royally, 'and now I need another letter to be written.'

'Mahbub Ali is in Umballa,' said the writer jauntily. He was, by virtue of his office, a bureau of general misinformation.

'This is not to Mahbub, but to a priest. Take thy pen and write quickly. *To Teshoo Lama, the Holy One from Bhotiyal seeking for a River, who is now in the Temple of the Tirthankars at Benares.* Take more ink! *In three days I am to go down to Nucklao to the school at Nucklao. The name of the school is Xavier. I do not know where that school is, but it is at Nucklao.*'

'But I know Nucklao,' the writer interrupted. 'I know the school.'

'Tell him where it is, and I give half an anna.'

The reed pen scratched busily. 'He cannot mistake.' The man lifted his head. 'Who watches us across the street?'

Kim looked up hurriedly and saw Colonel Creighton in tennis-flannels.

'Oh, that is some Sahib who knows the fat priest in the barracks. He is beckoning me.'

'What dost thou?' said the Colonel, when Kim trotted up.

'I – I am not running away. I send a letter to my Holy One at Benares.'

'I had not thought of that. Hast thou said that I take thee to Lucknow?'

'Nay, I have not. Read the letter, if there be a doubt.'

'Then why hast thou left out my name in writing to that Holy One?' The Colonel smiled a queer smile. Kim took his courage in both hands.

'It was said once to me that it is inexpedient to write the names of strangers concerned in any matter, because by the naming of names many good plans are brought to confusion.'

'Thou hast been well taught,' the Colonel replied, and Kim flushed. 'I have left my cheroot-case in the Padre's veranda. Bring it to my house this even.'

'Where is the house?' said Kim. His quick wit told him that he was being tested in some fashion or another, and he stood on guard.

'Ask anyone in the big bazar.' The Colonel walked on.

'He has forgotten his cheroot-case,' said Kim, returning. 'I must bring it to him this evening. That is all my letter except, thrice over, *Come to me! Come to me! Come to me!* Now I will pay for a stamp and put it in the post.' He rose to go, and as an afterthought asked: 'Who is that angry-faced Sahib who lost the cheroot-case?'

'Oh, he is only Creighton Sahib – a very foolish Sahib, who is a Colonel Sahib without a regiment.'

'What is his business?'

'God knows. He is always buying horses which he cannot ride, and asking riddles about the works of God – such as plants and stones and the customs of people. The dealers call him the father of fools, because he is so easily cheated about a horse. Mahbub Ali says he is madder than most other Sahibs.'

'Oh!' said Kim, and departed. His training had given him some small knowledge of character, and he argued that fools are not given information which leads to calling out eight thousand men besides guns. The Commander-in-Chief of all India does not talk, as Kim had heard him talk, to fools. Nor would Mahbub Ali's tone have changed, as it did every time he mentioned the Colonel's name, if the Colonel had been a fool. Consequently – and this set Kim to skipping – there was a mystery somewhere, and Mahbub Ali probably spied for the Colonel much as Kim had spied for Mahbub. And, like the horse-dealer, the Colonel evidently respected people who did not show themselves to be too clever.

He rejoiced that he had not betrayed his knowledge of the Colonel's house; and when, on his return to barracks, he discovered that no cheroot-case had been left behind, he beamed with delight. Here was a man after his own heart – a tortuous and indirect person playing a hidden game. Well, if he could be a fool, so could Kim.

He showed nothing of his mind when Father Victor, for three long mornings, discoursed to him of an entirely new set of Gods and Godlings – notably of a Goddess called Mary, who, he gathered, was one with Bibi Miriam of Mahbub Ali's theology. He betrayed no emotion when, after the lecture, Father Victor dragged him from shop to shop buying articles of outfit, nor when envious drummer-boys kicked him because he was going to a superior school did he complain, but awaited the play of circumstances with an interested soul. Father Victor, good man, took him to the station, put him into an empty second-class next to Colonel Creighton's first, and bade him farewell with genuine feeling.

'They'll make a man o' you, O'Hara, at St Xavier's – a white man, an', I hope, a good man. They know all about your comin', an' the Colonel will see that ye're not lost or mislaid anywhere on the road. I've given you a notion of religious matters, – at least I hope so, – and you'll remember, when they ask you your religion, that you're a Cath'lic. Better say Roman Cath'lic, tho' I'm not fond of the word.'

Kim lit a rank cigarette – he had been careful to buy a stock in the bazar – and lay down to think. This solitary passage was very different from that joyful down-journey in the third-class with the lama. 'Sahibs get little pleasure of travel,' he reflected. '*Hai mai!* I go from one place to another as it might be a kick-ball. It is my *Kismet*. No man can escape his *Kismet*. But I am to pray to Bibi Miriam, and I am a Sahib.' He looked at his boots ruefully. 'No; I am Kim. This is the great world, and I am only Kim. Who is Kim?' He considered his own identity, a thing he had never done before, till his head swam. He was one insignificant person in all this roaring whirl of India, going southward to he knew not what fate.

Presently the Colonel sent for him, and talked for a long time. So far as Kim could gather, he was to be diligent and enter the Survey of India as a chain-man. If he were very good, and passed the proper examinations, he would be earning thirty rupees a month at seventeen years old, and Colonel Creighton would see that he found suitable employment.

Kim pretended at first to understand perhaps one word in three of this talk. Then the Colonel, seeing his mistake, turned to fluent and picturesque Urdu and Kim was contented. No man could be a fool who knew the language so intimately, who moved so gently and silently, and whose eyes were so different from the dull fat eyes of other Sahibs.

'Yes, and thou must learn how to make pictures of roads and mountains and rivers – to carry these pictures in thine eye till a suitable time comes to set them upon paper. Perhaps some day, when thou art a chain-man, I may say to thee when we are working together: "Go across those hills and see what lies beyond." Then one will say: "There are bad people living in those hills who will slay the chain-man if he be seen to look like a Sahib." What then?'

Kim thought. Would it be safe to return the Colonel's lead?

'I would tell what that other man had said.'

'But if I answered: "I will give thee a hundred rupees for knowledge of what is behind those hills – for a picture of a river and a little news of what the people say in the villages there"?'

'How can I tell? I am only a boy. Wait till I am a man.'
Then, seeing the Colonel's brow clouded, he went on: 'But I
think I should in a few days earn the hundred rupees.'

'By what road?'

Kim shook his head resolutely. 'If I said how I would earn
them, another man might hear and forestall me. It is not good
to sell knowledge for nothing.'

'Tell now.' The Colonel held up a rupee. Kim's hand half
reached towards it, and dropped.

'Nay, Sahib; nay. I know the price that will be paid for the
answer, but I do not know why the question is asked.'

'Take it for a gift, then,' said Creighton, tossing it over.
'There is a good spirit in thee. Do not let it be blunted at St
Xavier's. There are many boys there who despise the black
men.'

'Their mothers were bazar-women,' said Kim. He knew
well there is no hatred like that of the half-caste for his
brother-in-law.

'True; but thou art a Sahib and the son of a Sahib.
Therefore, do not at any time be led to contemn the black
men. I have known boys newly entered into the service of the
Government who feigned not to understand the talk or the
customs of black men. Their pay was cut for ignorance. There
is no sin so great as ignorance. Remember this.'

Several times in the course of the long twenty-four hours'
run south did the Colonel send for Kim, always developing
this latter text.

'We be all on one lead-rope, then,' said Kim at last, 'the
Colonel, Mahbub Ali, and I – when I become a chain-man.
He will use me as Mahbub Ali employed me, I think. That is
good, if it allows me to return to the Road again. This
clothing grows no easier by wear.'

When they came to the crowded Lucknow station there
was no sign of the lama. He swallowed his disappointment,
while the Colonel bundled him into a *ticca-gharri* with his neat
belongings and despatched him alone to St Xavier's.

'I do not say farewell, because we shall meet again,' he

cried. 'Again, and many times, if thou art one of good spirit. But thou art not yet tried.'

'Not when I brought thee' – Kim actually dared to use the *tum* of equals – 'a white stallion's pedigree that night?'

'Much is gained by forgetting, little brother,' said the Colonel, with a look that pierced through Kim's shoulder-blades as he scuttled into the carriage.

It took him nearly five minutes to recover. Then he sniffed the new air appreciatively. 'A rich City,' he said. 'Richer than Lahore. How good the bazars must be! Coachman, drive me a little through the bazars here.'

'My order is to take thee to the school.' The driver used the 'thou', which is rudeness when applied to a white man. In the clearest and most fluent vernacular Kim pointed out his error, climbed on to the box-seat. and, perfect understanding established, drove for a couple of hours up and down, estimating, comparing, and enjoying. There is no city – except Bombay, the queen of all – more beautiful in her garish style than Lucknow, whether you see her from the bridge over the river, or from the top of the Imambara looking down on the gilt umbrellas of the Chutter Munzil, and the trees in which the town is bedded. Kings have adorned her with fantastic buildings, endowed her with charities, crammed her with pensioners, and drenched her with blood. She is the centre of all idleness, intrigue, and luxury, and shares with Delhi the claim to talk the only pure Urdu.

'A fair city – a beautiful city.' The driver, as a Lucknow man, was pleased with the compliment, and told Kim many astounding things where an English guide would have talked of the Mutiny.

'Now we will go to the school,' said Kim at last. The great old school of St Xavier's in Partibus, block on block of low white buildings, stands in vast grounds over against the Gumti River, at some distance from the city.

'What like of folk are they within?' said Kim.

'Young Sahibs – all devils. But to speak truth, and I drive

many of them to and fro from the railway station, I have never seen one that had in him the making of a more perfect devil than thou – this young Sahib whom I am now driving.'

Naturally, for he was never trained to consider them in any way improper, Kim had passed the time of day with one or two frivolous ladies at upper windows in a certain street, and naturally, in the exchange of compliments, had acquitted himself well. He was about to acknowledge the driver's last insolence, when his eye – it was growing dusk – caught a figure sitting by one of the white plaster gate-pillars in the long sweep of wall.

'Stop!' he cried. 'Stay here. I do not go to the school at once.'

'But what is to pay me for this coming and re-coming?' said the driver petulantly. 'Is the boy mad? Last time it was a dancing-girl. This time it is a priest.'

Kim was in the road headlong, patting the dusty feet beneath the dirty yellow robe.

'I have waited here a day and a half,' the lama's level voice began. 'Nay, I had a disciple with me. He that was my friend at the Temple of the Tirthankars gave me a guide for this journey. I came from Benares in the *te-rain*, when thy letter was given me. Yes, I am well fed. I need nothing.'

'But why didst thou not stay with the Kulu woman, O Holy One? In what way didst thou get to Benares? My heart has been heavy since we parted.'

'The woman wearied me by constant flux of talk and requiring charms for children. I separated myself from that company, permitting her to acquire merit by gifts. She is at least a woman of open hands, and I made a promise to return to her house if need arose. Then, perceiving myself alone in this great and terrible world, I bethought me of the *te-rain* to Benares, where I knew one abode in the Tirthankars' Temple who was a Seeker, even as I.'

'Ah! Thy River,' said Kim. 'I had forgotten the River.'

'So soon, my *chela*? I have never forgotten it. But when I had left thee it seemed better that I should go to the Temple

and take counsel, for, look you, India is very large, and it may
be that wise men before us, some two or three, have left a
record of the place of our River. There is debate in the
Temple of the Tirthankars on this matter; some saying one
thing, and some another. They are courteous folk.'

'So be it; but what dost thou do now?'

'I acquire merit in that I help thee, my *chela*, to wisdom.
The priest of that body of men who serve the Red Bull wrote
me that all should be as I desired for thee. I sent the money to
suffice for one year, and then I came, as thou seest me, to
watch for thee going up into the Gates of Learning. A day and
a half have I waited – not because I was led by any affection
towards thee – that is no part of the Way – but, as they said at
the Tirthankars' Temple, because, money having been paid
for learning, it was right that I should oversee the end of the
matter. They resolved my doubts most clearly. I had a fear
that, perhaps, I came because I wished to see thee –
misguided by the Red Mist of affection. It is not so ...
Moreover, I am troubled by a dream.'

'But surely, Holy One, thou hast not forgotten the Road
and all that befell on it. Surely it was a little to see me that
thou didst come?'

'The horses are cold, and it is past their feeding-time,'
whined the driver.

'Go to Jehannum and abide there with thy reputationless
aunt!' Kim snarled over his shoulder. 'I am all alone in this
land; I know not where I go nor what shall befall me. My
heart was in that letter I sent thee. Except for Mahbub Ali,
and he is a Pathan, I have no friend save thee, Holy One. Do
not altogether go away.'

'I have considered that also,' the lama replied, in a shaking
voice. 'It is manifest that from time to time I shall acquire
merit – if before that I have not found my River – by assuring
myself that thy feet are set on wisdom. What they will teach
thee I do not know, but the priest wrote me that no son of a
Sahib in all India will be better taught than thou. So from
time to time, therefore, I will come again. Maybe thou wilt be

such a Sahib as he who gave me these spectacles' – the lama wiped them elaborately – 'in the Wonder House at Lahore. That is my hope, for he was a Fountain of Wisdom – wiser than many abbots ... Again, maybe thou wilt forget me and our meetings.'

'If I eat thy bread,' cried Kim passionately, 'how shall I ever forget thee?'

'No – no.' He put the boy aside. 'I must go back to Benares. From time to time, now that I know the customs of letter-writers in this land, I will send thee a letter, and from time to time I will come and see thee.'

'But whither shall I send my letters?' wailed Kim, clutching at the robe, all forgetful that he was a Sahib.

'To the Temple of the Tirthankars at Benares. That is the place I have chosen till I find my River. Do not weep; for, look you, all Desire is Illusion and a new binding upon the Wheel. Go up to the Gates of Learning. Let me see thee go ... Dost thou love me? Then go, or my heart cracks ... I will come again. Surely I will come again.'

The lama watched the *ticca-gharri* rumble into the compound, and strode off, snuffing between each long stride.

'The Gates of Learning' shut with a clang.

The country born and bred boy has his own manners and customs, which do not resemble those of any other land; and his teachers approach him by roads which an English master would not understand. Therefore, you would scarcely be interested in Kim's experiences as a St Xavier's boy among two or three hundred precocious youths, most of whom had never seen the sea. He suffered the usual penalties for breaking out of bounds when there was cholera in the city. This was before he had learned to write fair English, and so was obliged to find a bazar letter-writer. He was, of course, indicted for smoking and for the use of abuse more full-flavoured than even St Xavier's had ever heard. He learned to wash himself with the Levitical scrupulosity of the native-born, who in his heart considers the Englishman rather dirty.

He played the usual tricks on the patient coolies pulling the punkahs in the sleeping-rooms where the boys threshed through the hot nights telling tales till the dawn; and quietly he measured himself against his self-reliant mates.

They were sons of subordinate officials in the Railway, Telegraph, and Canal Services; of warrant-officers, sometimes retired and sometimes acting as commanders-in-chief to a feudatory Rajah's army; of captains of the Indian Marine Government pensioners, planters, Presidency shopkeepers, and missionaries. A few were cadets of the old Eurasian houses that have taken strong root in Dhurrumtollah – Pereiras, De Souzas, and D'Silvas. Their parents could well have educated them in England, but they loved the school that had served their own youth, and generation followed sallow-hued generation at St Xavier's. Their homes ranged from Howrah of the railway people to abandoned cantonments like Monghyr and Chunar; lost tea-gardens Shillongway; villages where their fathers were large landholders in Oudh or the Deccan; Mission-stations a week from the nearest railway line; seaports a thousand miles south, facing the brazen Indian surf; and cinchona-plantations south of all. The mere story of their adventures, which to them were no adventures, on their road to and from school would have crisped a Western boy's hair. They were used to jogging off alone through a hundred miles of jungle, where there was always the delightful chance of being delayed by tigers; but they would no more have bathed in the English Channel in an English August than their brothers across the world would have lain still while a leopard snuffed at their palanquin. There were boys of fifteen who had spent a day and a half on an islet in the middle of a flooded river, taking charge, as by right, of a camp of frantic pilgrims returning from a shrine. There were seniors who had requisitioned a chance-met Rajah's elephant, in the name of St Francis Xavier, when the Rains once blotted out the cart-track that led to their father's estate, and had all but lost the huge beast in a quicksand. There was a boy who, he said, and none doubted, had helped

his father to beat off with rifles from the veranda a rush of
Akas in the days when those head-hunters were bold against
lonely plantations.

And every tale was told in the even, passionless voice of the
native-born, mixed with quaint reflections, borrowed uncon-
sciously from native foster-mothers, and turns of speech that
showed they had been that instant translated from the
vernacular. Kim watched, listened, and approved. This was
not insipid, single-word talk of drummer-boys. It dealt with a
life he knew and in part understood. The atmosphere suited
him, and he throve by inches. They gave him a white drill suit
as the weather warmed, and he rejoiced in the new-found
bodily comforts as he rejoiced to use his sharpened mind over
the tasks they set him. His quickness would have delighted an
English master; but at St Xavier's they know the first rush of
minds developed by sun and surroundings, as they know the
half-collapse that sets in at twenty-two or twenty-three.

None the less he remembered to hold himself lowly. When
tales were told of hot nights, Kim did not sweep the board
with his reminiscences; for St Xavier's looks down on boys
who 'go native all-together.' One must never forget that one is
a Sahib, and that some day, when examinations are passed,
one will command natives. Kim made a note of this, for he
began to understand where examinations led.

Then came the holidays from August to October – the long
holidays imposed by the heat and the Rains. Kim was
informed that he would go north to some station in the hills
behind Umballa, where Father Victor would arrange for him.

'A barrack-school?' said Kim, who had asked many questions and thought more.

'Yes, I suppose so,' said the master. 'It will not do you any
harm to keep you out of mischief. You can go up with young
De Castro as far as Delhi.'

Kim considered it in every possible light. He had been
diligent, even as the Colonel advised. A boy's holiday was his
own property – of so much the talk of his companions had
advised him, – and a barrack-school would be torment after

St Xavier's. Moreover – this was magic worth anything else –
he could write. In three months he had discovered how men
can speak to each other without a third party, at the cost of
half an anna and a little knowledge. No word had come from
the lama, but there remained the Road. Kim yearned for the
caress of soft mud squashing up between the toes, as his
mouth watered for mutton stewed with butter and cabbages,
for rice speckled with strong-scented cardamoms, for the
saffron-tinted rice, garlic and onions, and the forbidden
greasy sweetmeats of the bazars. They would feed him raw
beef on a platter at the barrack-school, and he must smoke by
stealth. But again, he was a Sahib and was at St Xavier's, and
that pig Mahbub Ali ... No, he would not test Mahbub's
hospitality – and yet ... He thought it out alone in the
dormitory, and came to the conclusion he had been unjust to
Mahbub.

The school was empty; nearly all the masters had gone
away; Colonel Creighton's railway pass lay in his hand, and
Kim puffed himself that he had not spent Colonel Creighton's or Mahbub's money in riotous living. He was still lord
of two rupees seven annas. His new bullock-trunk, marked
'K. O'H.', and bedding-roll lay in the empty sleeping-room.
'Sahibs are always tied to their baggage,' said Kim, nodding
at them. 'You will stay here.' He went out into the warm rain,
smiling sinfully, and sought a certain house whose outside he
had noted down some time before ...

'*Arré!* Dost thou know what manner of women we be in
this quarter? Oh, shame!'

'Was I born yesterday?' Kim squatted native-fashion on
the cushions of that upper room. 'A little dyestuff and three
yards of cloth to help out a jest. Is it much to ask?'

'Who is *she*? Thou art full young, as Sahibs go, for this
devilry.'

'Oh, she? She is the daughter of a certain schoolmaster of a
regiment in the cantonments. He has beaten me twice because
I went over their wall in these clothes. Now I would go as a
gardener's boy. Old men are very jealous.'

'That is true. Hold thy face still while I dab on the juice.'

'Not too black, *Naikan*. I would not appear to her as a *hubshi* [nigger].'

'Oh, love makes nought of these things. And how old is she?'

'Twelve years, I think,' said the shameless Kim. 'Spread it also on the breast. It may be her father will tear my clothes off me, and if I am piebald –' he laughed.

The girl worked busily, dabbing a twist of cloth into a little saucer of brown dye that holds longer than any walnut-juice.

'Now send out and get me a cloth for the turban. Woe is me, my head is all unshaved! And he will surely knock off my turban.'

'I am not a barber, but I will make shift. Thou wast born to be a breaker of hearts! All this disguise for one evening? Remember, the stuff does not wash away.' She shook with laughter till her bracelets and anklets jingled. 'But who is to pay me for this? Huneefa herself could not have given thee better stuff.'

'Trust in the Gods, my sister,' said Kim gravely, screwing his face round as the stain dried. 'Besides, hast thou ever helped to paint a Sahib thus before?'

'Never indeed. But a jest is not money.'

'It is worth much more.'

'Child, thou art beyond all dispute the most shameless son of Shaitan that I have ever known to take up a poor girl's time with this play, and then to say: "Is not the jest enough?" Thou wilt go very far in this world.' She gave the dancing-girls' salutation in mockery.

'All one. Make haste and rough-cut my head.' Kim shifted from foot to foot, his eyes ablaze with mirth as he thought of the fat days before him. He gave the girl four annas, and ran down the stairs in the likeness of a low-caste Hindu boy – perfect in every detail. A cookshop was his next point of call, where he feasted in extravagance and greasy luxury.

On Lucknow station platform he watched young De Castro, all covered with prickly-heat, get into a second-class compartment. Kim patronized a third, and was the life and soul of it. He explained to the company that he was assistant to a juggler who had left him behind sick with fever, and that he would pick up his master at Umballa. As the occupants of the carriage changed, he varied this tale, or adorned it with all the shoots of a budding fancy, the more rampant for being held off native speech so long. In all India that night was no human being so joyful as Kim. At Umballa he got out and headed eastward, plashing over the sodden fields to the village where the old soldier lived.

About this time Colonel Creighton at Simla was advised from Lucknow by wire that young O'Hara had disappeared. Mahbub Ali was in town selling horses, and to him the Colonel confided the affair one morning cantering round Annandale racecourse.

'Oh, that is nothing,' said the horse-dealer. 'Men are like horses. At certain times they need salt, and if that salt is not in the mangers they will lick it up from the earth. He has gone back to the Road again for a while. The *madrissah* wearied him. I knew it would. Another time, I will take him upon the Road myself. Do not be troubled, Creighton Sahib. It is as though a polo-pony, breaking loose, ran out to learn the game alone.'

'Then he is not dead, think you?'

'Fever might kill him. I do not fear for the boy otherwise. A monkey does not fall among trees.'

Next morning, on the same course, Mahbub's stallion ranged alongside the Colonel.

'It is as I had thought,' said the horse-dealer. 'He has come through Umballa at least, and there he has written a letter to me, having learned in the bazar that I was here.'

'Read,' said the Colonel, with a sigh of relief. It was absurd that a man of his position should take an interest in a little country-bred vagabond; but the Colonel remembered the conversation in the train, and often in the past few months had caught himself thinking of the queer, silent, self-possessed boy. His evasion, of course, was the height of insolence, but it argued some resource and nerve.

Mahbub's eyes twinkled as he reined out into the centre of the cramped little plain, where none could come near unseen.

'"*The Friend of the Stars, who is the Friend of all the World –*"'

'What is this?'

'A name we give him in Lahore city. "*The Friend of all the World takes leave to go to his own places. He will come back upon the appointed day. Let the box and the bedding-roll be sent for; and if there has been a fault, let the Hand of Friendship turn aside the Whip of Calamity.*" There is yet a little more, but –'

'No matter, read.'

'"*Certain things are not known to those who eat with forks. It is better to eat with both hands for a while. Speak soft words to those who do not understand this that the return may be propitious.*" Now the manner in which that was cast is, of course, the work of the letter-writer, but see how wisely the boy has devised the matter of it so that no hint is given except to those who know!'

'Is this the Hand of Friendship to avert the Whip of Calamity?' laughed the Colonel.

'See how wise is the boy. He would go back to the Road again, as I said. Not knowing yet thy trade –'

'I am not at all sure of that,' the Colonel muttered.

'He turns to me to make a peace between you. Is he not wise? He says he will return. He is but perfecting his knowledge. Think, Sahib! He has been three months at the school. And he is not mouthed to that bit. For my part, I rejoice. The pony learns the game.'

'Ay, but another time he must not go alone.'

'Why? He went alone before he came under the Colonel Sahib's protection. When he comes to the Great Game he must go alone – alone, and at peril of his head. *Then*, if he spits, or sneezes, or sits down other than as the people do whom he watches, he may be slain. Why hinder him now? Remember how the Persians say: The jackal that lives in the wilds of Mazanderan can only be caught by the hounds of Mazanderan.'

'True. It is true, Mahbub Ali. And if he comes to no harm, I do not desire anything better. But it is great insolence on his part.'

'He does not tell me, even, whither he goes,' said Mahbub. 'He is no fool. When his time is accomplished he will come to me. It is time the healer of pearls took him in hand. He ripens too quickly – as Sahibs reckon.'

This prophecy was fulfilled to the letter a month later. Mahbub had gone down to Umballa to bring up a fresh consignment of horses, and Kim met him on the Kalka road at dusk riding alone, begged an alms of him, was sworn at, and replied in English. There was nobody within earshot to hear Mahbub's gasp of amazement.

'Oho! And where hast thou been?'

'Up and down – down and up.'

'Come under a tree, out of the wet, and tell.'

'I stayed for a while with an old man near Umballa; anon with a household of my acquaintance in Umballa. With one of these I went as far as Delhi to the southward. That is a wondrous city. Then I drove a bullock for a *teli* [an oilman] coming north; but I heard of a great feast forward in Patiala, and thither went I in the company of a firework-maker. It was a great feast' (Kim rubbed his stomach). 'I saw Rajahs, and elephants with gold and silver trappings; and they lit all the fireworks at once, whereby eleven men were killed, my fire-work-maker among them, and I was blown across a tent but took no harm. Then I came back to the *rêl* with a Sikh horseman, to whom I was groom for my bread; and so here.'

'*Shabash!*' said Mahbub Ali.

'But what does the Colonel Sahib say? I do not wish to be beaten.'

'The Hand of Friendship has averted the Whip of Calamity; but another time, when thou takest the Road it will be with me. This is too early.'

'Late enough for me. I have learned to read and to write

English a little at the *madrissah*. I shall soon be altogether a Sahib.'

'Hear him!' laughed Mahbub, looking at the little drenched figure dancing in the wet. 'Salaam – Sahib,' and he saluted ironically. 'Well, art tired of the Road, or wilt thou come on to Umballa with me and work back with the horses?'

'I come with thee, Mahbub Ali.'

Chapter 8

Something I owe to the soil that grew –
  More to the life that fed –
But most to Allah Who gave me two
  Separate sides to my head.

I would go without shirts or shoes,
  Friends, tobacco or bread
Sooner than for an instant lose
  Either side of my head.
                    The Two-Sided Man.

'THEN in God's name take blue for red,' said Mahbub, alluding to the Hindu colour of Kim's disreputable turban.

Kim countered with the old proverb, 'I will change my faith and my bedding, but *thou* must pay for it.'

The dealer laughed till he nearly fell from his horse. At a shop on the outskirts of the city the change was made, and Kim stood up, externally at least, a Mohammedan.

Mahbub hired a room over against the railway station, sent for a cooked meal of the finest with the almond-curd sweet-meats [*balushai* we call it] and fine-chopped Lucknow tobacco.

'This is better than some other meat that I ate with the Sikh,' said Kim, grinning as he squatted, 'and assuredly they give no such victuals at my *madrissah*.'

'I have a desire to hear of that same *madrissah*.' Mahbub stuffed himself with great boluses of spiced mutton fried in fat with cabbage and golden-brown onions. 'But tell me first, altogether and truthfully, the manner of thy escape. For, O Friend of all the World,' – he loosed his cracking belt – 'I do not think it is often that a Sahib and the son of a Sahib runs away from there.'

'How should they? They do not know the land. It was nothing,' said Kim, and began his tale. When he came to the disguisement and the interview with the girl in the bazar, Mahbub Ali's gravity went from him. He laughed aloud and beat his hand on his thigh.

'*Shabash! Shabash!* Oh, well done, little one! What will the healer of turquoises say to this? Now, slowly, let us hear what befell afterwards – step by step, omitting nothing.'

Step by step then, Kim told his adventures between coughs as the full-flavoured tobacco caught his lungs.

'I said,' growled Mahbub Ali to himself, 'I *said* it was the pony breaking out to play polo. The fruit is ripe already – except that he must learn his distances and his pacings, and his rods and his compasses. Listen now. I have turned aside the Colonel's whip from thy skin, and that is no small service.'

'True.' Kim pulled serenely. 'That is true.'

'But it is not to be thought that this running out and in is any way good.'

'It was my holiday, Hajji. I was a slave for many weeks. Why should I not run away when the school was shut? Look, too, how I, living upon my friends or working for my bread, as I did with the Sikh, have saved the Colonel Sahib a great expense.'

Mahbub's lips twitched under his well-pruned Mohamme-dan moustache.

'What are a few rupees' – the Pathan threw out his open hand carelessly – 'to the Colonel Sahib? He spends them for a purpose, not in any way for love of thee.'

'That,' said Kim slowly, 'I knew a very long time ago.'

'Who told?'

'The Colonel Sahib himself. Not in those many words, but plainly enough for one who is not altogether a mud-head. Yea, he told me in the *te-rain* when we went down to Lucknow.'

'Be it so. Then I will tell thee more, Friend of all the World, though in the telling I lend thee my head.'

'It was forfeit to me,' said Kim, with deep relish, 'in Umballa, when thou didst pick me up on the horse after the drummer-boy beat me.'

'Speak a little plainer. All the world may tell lies save thou and I. For equally is thy life forfeit to me if I chose to raise my finger here.'

'And this is known to me also,' said Kim, readjusting the live charcoal-ball on the weed. 'It is a very sure tie between us. Indeed, thy hold is surer even than mine; for who would miss a boy beaten to death, or, it may be, thrown into a well by the roadside? Most people here and in Simla and across the passes behind the Hills would, on the other hand, say: "What has come to Mahbub Ali?" if he were found dead among his horses. Surely, too, the Colonel Sahib would make inquiries. But again,' – Kim's face puckered with cunning, – 'he would not make overlong inquiry, lest people should ask: "What has this Colonel Sahib to do with that horse-dealer?" But I – if I lived –'

'As thou wouldst surely die –'

'Maybe; but I say, *if* I lived, I, and I alone, would know that one had come by night, as a common thief perhaps, to Mahbub Ali's bulkhead in the serai, and there had slain him, either before or after that thief had made a full search into his saddle-bags and between the soles of his slippers. Is that news to tell to the Colonel, or would he say to me – (I have not forgotten when he sent me back for a cigar-case that he had not left behind him) – "What is Mahbub Ali to me?"?'

Up went a gout of heavy smoke. There was a long pause: then Mahbub Ali spoke in admiration: 'And with these things on thy mind, dost thou lie down and rise again among all the Sahibs' little sons at the *madrissah* and meekly take instruction from thy teachers?'

'It is an order,' said Kim blandly. 'Who am I to dispute an order?'

'A most finished Son of Eblis,' said Mahbub Ali. 'But what is this tale of the thief and the search?'

'That which I saw,' said Kim, 'the night that my lama and I lay next thy place in the Kashmir Serai. The door was left unlocked, which I think is not thy custom, Mahbub. He came in as one assured that thou wouldst not soon return. My eye was against a knot-hole in the plank. He searched as it were for something – not a rug, not stirrups, nor a bridle, nor brass pots – something little and most carefully hid. Else why did he prick with an iron between the soles of thy slippers?'

'Ha!' Mahbub Ali smiled gently. 'And seeing these things, what tale didst thou fashion to thyself, Well of the Truth?'

'None. I put my hand upon my amulet, which lies always next to my skin, and, remembering the pedigree of a white stallion that I had bitten out of a piece of Mussalmani bread, I went away to Umballa perceiving that a heavy trust was laid upon me. At that hour, had I chosen, thy head was forfeit. It needed only to say to that man, "I have here a paper concerning a horse which I cannot read." And then?' Kim peered at Mahbub under his eyebrows.

'Then thou wouldst have drunk water twice – perhaps thrice, afterwards. I do not think more than thrice,' said Mahbub simply.

'It is true. I thought of that a little, but most I thought that I loved thee, Mahbub. Therefore I went to Umballa, as thou knowest, but (and this thou dost not know) I lay hid in the garden-grass to see what Colonel Creighton Sahib might do upon reading the white stallion's pedigree.'

'And what did he?' for Kim had bitten off the conversation.

'Dost *thou* give news for love, or dost thou sell it?' Kim asked.

'I sell and – I buy.' Mahbub took a four-anna piece out of his belt and held it up.

'Eight!' said Kim, mechanically following the huckster instinct of the East.

Mahbub laughed, and put away the coin. 'It is too easy to deal in that market, Friend of all the World. Tell me for love. Our lives lie in each other's hand.'

'Very good. I saw the Jang-i-Lat Sahib [the Commander-in-Chief] come to a big dinner. I saw him in Creighton Sahib's office. I saw the two read the white stallion's pedigree. I heard the very orders given for the opening of a great war.'

'Hah!' Mahbub nodded with deepest eyes afire. 'The game is well played. That war is done now, and the evil, we hope, nipped before the flower – thanks to me – and thee. What didst thou later?'

'I made the news as it were a hook to catch me victual and honour among the villagers in a village whose priest drugged my lama. But I bore away the old man's purse, and the Brahmin found nothing. So next morning he was angry. Ho! Ho! And I also used the news when I fell into the hands of that white Regiment with their Bull!'

'That was foolishness.' Mahbub scowled. 'News is not meant to be thrown about like dung-cakes, but used sparingly – like *bhang*.'

'So I think now, and moreover, it did me no sort of good. But that was very long ago,' – he made as to brush it all away with a thin brown hand – 'and since then, and especially in the nights under the punkah at the *madrissah*, I have thought very greatly.'

'Is it permitted to ask whither the Heaven-born's thought might have led?' said Mahbub, with an elaborate sarcasm, smoothing his scarlet beard.

'It is permitted,' said Kim, and threw back the very tone. 'They say at Nucklao that no Sahib must tell a black man that he has made a fault.'

Mahbub's hand shot into his bosom, for to call a Pathan a 'black man' [*kala admi*] is a blood-insult. Then he remembered and laughed. 'Speak, Sahib. Thy black man hears.'

'But,' said Kim, 'I am *not* a Sahib, and I say I made a fault to curse thee, Mahbub Ali, on that day at Umballa when I thought I was betrayed by a Pathan. I was senseless; for I was but newly caught, and I wished to kill that low-caste drummer-boy. I say now, Hajji, that it was well done; and I see my road all clear before me to a good service. I will stay in the *madrissah* till I am ripe.'

'Well said. Especially are distances and numbers and the manner of using compasses to be learned in that game. One waits in the Hills above to show thee.'

'I will learn their teaching upon a condition – that my time is given to me without question when the *madrissah* is shut. Ask that for me of the Colonel.'

'But why not ask the Colonel in the Sahibs' tongue?'

'The Colonel is the servant of the Government. He is sent hither and yon at a word, and must consider his own advancement. (See how much I have already learned at Nucklao!) Moreover, the Colonel I know since three months only. I have known one Mahbub Ali for six years. So! To the *madrissah* I will go. At the *madrissah* I will learn. In the *madrissah* I will be a Sahib. But when the *madrissah* is shut, then must I be free and go among my people. Otherwise I die!'

'And who are thy people, Friend of all the World?'

'This great and beautiful land,' said Kim, waving his paw round the little clay-walled room where the oil-lamp in its niche burned heavily through the tobacco-smoke. 'And, further, I would see my lama again. And, further, I need money.'

'That is the need of everyone,' said Mahbub ruefully. 'I will give thee eight annas, for much money is not picked out of horses' hooves, and it must suffice for many days. As to all the rest, I am well pleased, and no further talk is needed. Make haste to learn, and in three years, or it may be less, thou wilt be an aid – even to me.'

'Have I been such a hindrance till now?' said Kim, with a boy's giggle.

'Do not give answers,' Mahbub grunted. 'Thou art my new horse-boy. Go and bed among my men. They are near the north end of the station, with the horses.'

'They will beat me to the south end of the station if I come without authority.'

Mahbub felt in his belt, wetted his thumb on a cake of Chinese ink, and dabbed the impression on a piece of soft native paper. From Balkh to Bombay men know that tough-ridged print with the old scar running diagonally across it.

'That is enough to show my headman. I come in the morning.'

'By which road?' said Kim.

'By the road from the city. There is but one, and then we return to Creighton Sahib. I have saved thee a beating.'

'Allah! What is a beating when the very head is loose on the shoulders?

Kim slid out quietly into the night, walked half round the house, keeping close to the walls, and headed away from the station for a mile or so. Then, fetching a wide compass, he worked back at leisure, for he needed time to invent a story if any of Mahbub's retainers asked questions.

They were camped on a piece of waste ground beside the railway, and, being natives, had not, of course, unloaded the two trucks in which Mahbub's animals stood among a consignment of country-breds bought by the Bombay tram-company. The headman, a broken-down, consumptive-looking Mohammedan, promptly challenged Kim, but was pacified at sight of Mahbub's sign-manual.

'The Hajji has of his favour given me service,' said Kim testily. 'If this be doubted, wait till he comes in the morning. Meantime, a place by the fire.'

Followed the usual aimless babble that every low-caste native must raise on every occasion. It died down, and Kim lay out behind the little knot of Mahbub's followers, almost under the wheels of a horse-truck, a borrowed blanket for covering. Now a bed among brickbats and ballast-refuse on a damp night, between overcrowded horses and unwashed Baltis, would not appeal to many white boys; but Kim was utterly happy. Change of scene, service, and surroundings were the breath of his little nostrils, and thinking of the neat white cots of St Xavier's all arow under the punkah gave him joy as keen as the repetition of the multiplication-table in English.

'I am very old,' he thought sleepily. 'Every month I become a year more old. I was very young, and a fool to boot, when I took Mahbub's message to Umballa. Even when I was with that white Regiment I was very young and small and had no wisdom. But now I learn every day, and in three years the Colonel will take me out of the *madrissah* and let me go upon the Road with Mahbub hunting for horses' pedigrees, or maybe I shall go by myself; or maybe I shall find the lama and go with him. Yes; that is best. To walk again as a *chela* with my lama when he comes back to Benares.' The thoughts came more slowly and disconnectedly. He was plunging into a beautiful dreamland when his ears caught a whisper, thin and sharp, above the monotonous babble round the fire. It came from behind the iron-skinned horse-truck.

'He is not here, then?'

'Where should he be but roystering in the city. Who looks for a rat in a frog-pond? Come away. He is not our man.'

'He must not go back beyond the Passes a second time. It is the order.'

'Hire some woman to drug him. It is a few rupees only, and there is no evidence.'

'Except the woman. It must be more certain; and remember the price upon his head.'

'Ay, but the police have a long arm, and we are far from the Border. If it were in Peshawur, now!'

'Yes – in Peshawur,' the second voice sneered. 'Peshawur, full of his blood-kin – full of bolt-holes and women behind whose clothes he will hide. Yes, Peshawur or Jehannum would suit us equally well.'

'Then what is the plan?'

'O fool, have I not told it a hundred times? Wait till he comes to lie down, and then one sure shot. The trucks are between us and pursuit. We have but to run back over the lines and go our way. They will not see whence the shot came. Wait here at least till the dawn. What manner of *fakir* art thou, to shiver at a little watching?'

'Oho!' thought Kim, behind close-shut eyes. 'Once again it is Mahbub. Indeed a white stallion's pedigree is not a good thing to peddle to Sahibs! Or maybe Mahbub has been selling other news. Now what is to do, Kim? I know not where

Mahbub houses, and if he comes here before the dawn they will shoot him. That would be no profit for thee, Kim. And this is not a matter for the police. That would be no profit for Mahbub; and' – he giggled almost aloud –'I do not remember any lesson at Nucklao which will help me. Allah! Here is Kim and yonder are they. First, then, Kim must wake and go away, so that they shall not suspect. A bad dream wakes a man – thus –'

He threw the blanket off his face, and raised himself suddenly with the terrible, bubbling, meaningless yell of the Asiatic roused by nightmare.

'Urr-urr-urr-urr! Ya-la-la-la-la! *Narain!* The *churel*! The *churel*!'

A *churel* is the peculiarly malignant ghost of a woman who has died in child-bed. She haunts lonely roads, her feet are turned backwards on the ankles, and she leads men to torment.

Louder rose Kim's quavering howl, till at last he leaped to his feet and staggered off sleepily, while the camp cursed him for waking them. Some twenty yards farther up the line he lay down again, taking care that the whisperers should hear his grunts and groans as he recomposed himself. After a few minutes he rolled towards the road and stole away into the thick darkness.

He paddled along swiftly till he came to a culvert, and dropped behind it, his chin on a level with the coping-stone. Here he could command all the night-traffic, himself unseen.

Two or three carts passed, jingling out to the suburbs; a coughing policeman and a hurrying foot-passenger or two who sang to keep off evil spirits. Then rapped the shod feet of a horse.

'Ah! This is more like Mahbub,' thought Kim, as the beast shied at the little head above the culvert.

'Ohé, Mahbub Ali,' he whispered, 'have a care!'

The horse was reined back almost on its haunches, and forced towards the culvert.

'Never again,' said Mahbub, 'will I take a shod horse for

night-work. They pick up all the bones and nails in the city.' He stooped to lift its forefoot, and that brought his head within a foot of Kim's. 'Down – keep down,' he muttered. 'The night is full of eyes.'

'Two men wait thy coming behind the horse-trucks. They will shoot thee at thy lying down, because there is a price on thy head. I heard, sleeping near the horses.'

'Didst thou see them? ... Hold still, Sire of Devils!' This furiously to the horse.

'No.'

'Was one dressed belike as a *fakir*?'

'One said to the other, "What manner of *fakir* art thou, to shiver at a little watching?"'

'Good. Go back to the camp and lie down. I do not die tonight.'

Mahbub wheeled his horse and vanished. Kim tore back down the ditch till he reached a point opposite his second resting-place, slipped across the road like a weasel, and re-coiled himself in the blanket.

'At least Mahbub knows,' he thought contentedly. 'And certainly he spoke as one expecting it. I do not think those two men will profit by tonight's watch.'

An hour passed, and, with the best will in the world to keep awake all night, he slept deeply. Now and again a night train roared along the metals within twenty feet of him; but he had all the Oriental's indifference to mere noise, and it did not even weave a dream through his slumber.

Mahbub was anything but asleep. It annoyed him vehemently that people outside his tribe and unaffected by his casual amours should pursue him for the life. His first and natural impulse was to cross the line lower down, work up again, and, catching his well-wishers from behind, summarily slay them. Here, he reflected with sorrow, another branch of the Government, totally unconnected with Colonel Creighton, might demand explanations which would be hard to supply; and he knew that south of the Border a perfectly ridiculous fuss is made about a corpse or so. He had not been troubled in this way since he sent Kim to Umballa with the message, and hoped that suspicion had been finally diverted.

Then a most brilliant notion struck him.

'The English do eternally tell the truth,' he said, 'therefore we of this country are eternally made foolish. By Allah, I will tell the truth to an Englishman! Of what use is the Government police if a poor Kabuli be robbed of his horses in their very trucks. This is as bad as Peshawur! I should lay a complaint at the station. Better still, some young Sahib on the Railway! They are zealous, and if they catch thieves it is remembered to their honour.'

He tied up his horse outside the station, and strode on to the platform.

'Hullo, Mahbub Ali!' said a young Assistant District Traffic Superintendent who was waiting to go down the line – a tall, tow-haired, horsey youth in dingy white linen. 'What are you doing here? Selling weeds – eh?'

'No; I am not troubled for my horses. I come to look for Lutuf Ullah. I have a truck-load up the line. Could anyone take them out without the Railway's knowledge?'

'Shouldn't think so, Mahbub. You can claim against us if they do.'

'I have seen two men crouching under the wheels of one of the trucks nearly all night. *Fakirs* do not steal horses, so I gave them no more thought. I would find Lutuf Ullah, my partner.'

'The deuce you did? And you didn't bother your head about it? 'Pon my word, it's just almost as well that I met you. What were they like, eh?'

'They were only *fakirs*. They will no more than take a little grain, perhaps, from one of the trucks. There are many up the line. The State will never miss the dole. I came here seeking for my partner, Lutuf Ullah –'

'Never mind your partner. Where are your horse-trucks?'

'A little to this side of the farthest place where they make lamps for the trains.'

'The signal-box! Yes.'

'And upon the rail nearest to the road upon the right-hand side – looking up the line thus. But as regards Lutuf Ullah – a tall man with a broken nose, and a Persian greyhound – Aie!'

The boy had hurried off to wake up a young and enthusiastic policeman; for, as he said, the Railway had suffered much from depredations in the goods-yard. Mahbub Ali chuckled in his dyed beard.

'They will walk in their boots, making a noise, and then they will wonder why there are no *fakir*s. They are very clever boys – Barton Sahib and Young Sahib.'

He waited idly for a few minutes, expecting to see them hurry up the line girt for action. A light engine slid through the station, and he caught a glimpse of young Barton in the cab.

'I did that child an injustice. He is not altogether a fool,' said Mahbub Ali. 'To take a fire-carriage for a thief is a new game!'

When Mahbub Ali came to his camp in the dawn, no one thought it worth while to tell him any news of the night. No one, at least, but one small horseboy, newly advanced to the great man's service, whom Mahbub called to his tiny tent to assist in some packing.

'It is all known to me,' whispered Kim, bending above saddle-bags. 'Two Sahibs came up on a *te-rain*. I was running to and fro in the dark on this side of the trucks as the *te-rain* moved up and down slowly. They fell upon two men sitting under this truck – Hajji, what shall I do with this lump of tobacco? Wrap it in paper and put it under the salt-bag? Yes – and struck them down. But one man struck at a Sahib with a *fakir*'s buck's horn' (Kim meant the conjoined black-buck horns, which are a *fakir*'s sole temporal weapon) – 'the blood came. So the other Sahib, first smiting his own man senseless, smote the stabber with a short gun which had rolled from the first man's hand. They all raged as though mad together.'

Mahbub smiled with heavenly resignation. 'No! That is

not so much *dewanee* [madness, or a case for the civil court –
the word can be punned upon both ways] as *nizamut* [a
criminal case]. A gun, sayest thou? Ten good years in jail.'

'Then they both lay still, but I think they were nearly dead
when they were put on the *te-rain*. Their heads moved thus.
And there is much blood on the line. Come and see?'

'I have seen blood before. Jail is the sure place – and
assuredly they will give false names, and assuredly no man
will find them for a long time. They were unfriends of mine.
Thy fate and mine seem on one string. What a tale for the
healer of pearls! Now swiftly with the saddle-bags and the
cooking-platter. We will take out the horses and away to
Simla.'

Swiftly – as Orientals understand speed – with long,
explanations, with abuse and windy talk, carelessly, amid a
hundred checks for little things forgotten, the untidy camp
broke up and led the half-dozen stiff and fretful horses along
the Kalka road in the fresh of the rain-swept dawn. Kim,
regarded as Mahbub Ali's favourite by all who wished to
stand well with the Pathan, was not called upon to work.
They strolled on by the easiest of stages, halting every few
hours at a wayside shelter. Very many Sahibs travel along the
Kalka road; and, as Mahbub Ali says, every young Sahib
must needs esteem himself a judge of a horse, and, though he
be over head in debt to the money-lender, must make as if to
buy. That was the reason that Sahib after Sahib, rolling along
in a stage-carriage, would stop and open talk. Some would
even descend from their vehicles and feel the horses' legs;
asking inane questions, or, through sheer ignorance of the
vernacular, grossly insulting the imperturbable trader.

'When first I dealt with Sahibs, and that was when Colonel
Soady Sahib was Governor of Fort Abazai and flooded the
Commissioner's camping-ground for spite,' Mahbub confided to Kim as the boy filled his pipe under a tree, 'I did not
know how greatly they were fools, and this made me wroth.
As thus –' and he told Kim a tale of an expression, misused in
all innocence, that doubled Kim up with mirth. 'Now I see,

however,' – he exhaled smoke slowly – 'that it is with them as with all men – in certain matters they are wise, and in others most foolish. Very foolish it is to use the wrong word to a stranger; for though the heart may be clean of offence, how is the stranger to know that? He is more like to search truth with a dagger.'

'True. True talk,' said Kim solemnly. 'Fools speak of a cat when a woman is brought to bed, for instance. I have heard them.'

'Therefore, in one situate as thou art, it particularly behoves thee to remember this with both kinds of faces. Among Sahibs, never forgetting thou art a Sahib; among the folk of Hind, always remembering thou art –' He paused, with a puzzled smile.

'What am I? Mussalman, Hindu, Jain, or Buddhist? That is a hard knot.'

'Thou art beyond question an unbeliever, and therefore thou wilt be damned. So says my Law – or I think it does. But thou art also my Little Friend of all the World, and I love thee. So says my heart. This matter of creeds is like horse-flesh. The wise man knows horses are good – that there is a profit to be made from all; and for myself – but that I am a good *Sunni* and hate the men of Tirah – I could believe the same of all the Faiths. Now manifestly a Kathiawar mare taken from the sands of her birthplace and removed to the west of Bengal founders – nor is even a Balkh stallion (and there are no better horses than those of Balkh, were they not so heavy in the shoulder) of any account in the great Northern deserts beside the snow-camels I have seen. Therefore I say in my heart the Faiths are like the horses. Each has merit in its own country.'

'But my lama said altogether a different thing.'

'Oh, he is an old dreamer of dreams from Bhotiyal. My heart is a little angry, Friend of all the World, that thou shouldst see such worth in a man so little known.'

'It is true, Hajji; but that worth do I see, and to him my heart is drawn.'

'And his to thine, I hear. Hearts are like horses. They come and they go against bit or spur. Shout Gul Sher Khan yonder to drive in that bay stallion's pickets more firmly. We do not want a horse-fight at every resting-stage, and the dun and the black will be locked in a little . . . Now hear me. Is it necessary to the comfort of thy heart to see that lama?'

'It is one part of my bond,' said Kim. 'If I do not see him, and if he is taken from me, I will go out of that *madrissah* in Nucklao and, and – once gone, who is to find me again?'

'It is true. Never was colt held on a lighter heel-rope than thou.' Mahbub nodded his head.

'Do not be afraid.' Kim spoke as though he could have evanished on the moment. 'My lama has said that he will come to see me at the *madrissah* –'

'A beggar and his bowl in the presence of those young Sa –'

'Not all!' Kim cut in with a snort. 'Their eyes are blued and their nails are blackened with low-caste blood, many of them. Sons of *mehteranees* – brothers-in-law to the *bhungi* [sweeper].'

We need not follow the rest of the pedigree; but Kim made his little point clearly and without heat, chewing a piece of sugar-cane the while.

'Friend of all the World,' said Mahbub, pushing over the pipe for the boy to clean, 'I have met many men, women, and boys, and not a few Sahibs. I have never in all my days met such an imp as thou art.'

'And why? When I always tell thee the truth.'

'Perhaps the very reason, for this is a world of danger to honest men.' Mahbub Ali hauled himself off the ground, girt in his belt, and went over to the horses.

'Or sell it?'

There was that in the tone that made Mahbub halt and turn. 'What new devilry?'

'Eight annas, and I will tell,' said Kim, grinning. 'It touches thy peace.'

'O Shaitan!' Mahbub gave the money.

'Rememberest thou the little business of the thieves in the dark, down yonder at Umballa?'

'Seeing they sought my life, I have not altogether forgotten. Why?'

'Rememberest thou the Kashmir Serai?'

'I will twist thy ears in a moment – Sahib.'

'No need – Pathan. Only, the second *fakir*, whom the Sahibs beat senseless, was the man who came to search thy bulkhead at Lahore. I saw his face as they helped him on the engine. The very same man.'

'Why didst thou not tell before?'

'Oh, he will go to jail, and be safe for some years. There is no need to tell more than is necessary at any one time. Besides, I did not then need money for sweetmeats.'

'*Allah kerim!*' said Mahbub Ali. 'Wilt thou some day sell my head for a few sweetmeats if the fit takes thee?'

Kim will remember till he dies that long, lazy journey from Umballa, through Kalka and the Pinjore Gardens near by, up to Simla. A sudden spate in the Gugger River swept down one horse (the most valuable, be sure), and nearly drowned Kim among the dancing boulders. Farther up the road the horses were stampeded by a Government elephant, and being in high condition of grass food, it cost a day and a half to get them together again. Then they met Sikandar Khan coming down with a few unsaleable screws – remnants of his string – and Mahbub, who has more of horse-coping in his little fingernail than Sikandar Khan in all his tents, must needs buy two of the worst, and that meant eight hours' laborious diplomacy and untold tobacco. But it was all pure delight – the wandering road, climbing, dipping, and sweeping about the growing spurs; the flush of the morning laid along the distant snows; the branched cacti, tier upon tier on the stony hillsides; the voices of a thousand water-channels; the chatter of the monkeys; the solemn deodars, climbing one after another with down-drooped branches; the vista of the Plains rolled out far beneath them; the incessant twanging of the tonga-horns and the wild rush of the led horses when a tonga swung round a curve; the halts for prayers (Mahbub was very religious in dry-washings and bellowings when time did not press); the evening conferences by the halting-places, when camels and bullocks chewed solemnly together and the stolid drivers told the news of the Road – all these things lifted Kim's heart to song within him.

'But, when the singing and dancing is done,' said Mahbub Ali, 'comes the Colonel Sahib's, and that is not so sweet.'

'A fair land – a most beautiful land is this of Hind – and the land of the Five Rivers is fairer than all,' Kim half chanted. 'Into it I will go again if Mahbub Ali or the Colonel lift hand or foot against me. Once gone, who shall find me? Look, Hajji, is yonder the city of Simla? Allah, what a city!'

'My father's brother, and he was an old man when Mackerson Sahib's well was new at Peshawur, could recall when there were but two houses in it.'

He led the horses below the main road into the lower Simla bazar – the crowded rabbit-warren that climbs up from the valley to the Town Hall at an angle of forty-five. A man who knows his way there can defy all the police of India's summer capital, so cunningly does veranda communicate with veranda, alley-way with alley-way, and bolt-hole with bolt-hole. Here live those who minister to the wants of the glad city – *jhampanis* pull the pretty ladies' rickshaws by night and gamble till the dawn; grocers, oil-sellers, curio-vendors, firewood-dealers, priests, pickpockets, and native employees of the Government. Here are discussed by courtesans the things which are supposed to be profoundest secrets of the India Council; and here gather all the sub-sub-agents of half the Native States. Here, too, Mahbub Ali rented a room, much more securely locked than his bulkhead at Lahore, in the house of a Mohammedan cattle-dealer. It was a place of miracles, too, for there went in at twilight a Mohammedan horseboy, and there came out an hour later a Eurasian lad – the Lucknow girl's dye was of the best – in badly-fitting shop-clothes.

'I have spoken with Creighton Sahib,' quoth Mahbub Ali, 'and a second time has the Hand of Friendship averted the

Whip of Calamity. He says that thou hast altogether wasted sixty days upon the Road, and it is too late, therefore, to send thee to any Hill-school.'

'I have said that my holidays are my own. I do not go to school twice over. That is one part of my bond.'

'The Colonel Sahib is not yet aware of that contract. Thou art to lodge in Lurgan Sahib's house till it is time to go again to Nucklao.'

'I had sooner lodge with thee, Mahbub.'

'Thou dost not know the honour. Lurgan Sahib himself asked for thee. Thou wilt go up the hill and along the road atop, and there thou must forget for a while that thou hast ever seen or spoken to me, Mahbub Ali, who sells horses to Creighton Sahib, whom thou dost not know. Remember this order.'

Kim nodded. 'Good,' said he, 'and who is Lurgan Sahib? Nay' – he caught Mahbub's sword-keen glance – 'indeed I have never heard his name. Is he by chance' – he lowered his voice – 'one of us?'

'What talk is this of *us*, Sahib?' Mahbub Ali returned, in the tone he used towards Europeans. 'I am a Pathan; thou art a Sahib and the son of a Sahib. Lurgan Sahib has a shop among the European shops. All Simla knows it. Ask there . . . and, Friend of all the World, he is one to be obeyed to the last wink of his eyelashes. Men say he does magic, but that should not touch thee. Go up the hill and ask. Here begins the Great Game.'

Chapter 9

S'doaks was son of Yelth the wise –
  Chief of the Raven clan.
Itswoot the Bear had him in care
  To make him a medicine-man.

He was quick and quicker to learn –
  Bold and bolder to dare:
He danced the dread Kloo-Kwallie Dance
  To tickle Itswoot the Bear!
                              Oregon Legend

K IM flung himself wholeheartedly upon the next turn of
  the wheel. He would be a Sahib again for a while. In that
idea, so soon as he had reached the broad road under Simla
Town Hall, he cast about for one to impress. A Hindu child,
some ten years old, squatted under a lamp-post.

'Where is Mr Lurgan's house?' demanded Kim.

'I do not understand English,' was the answer, and Kim
shifted his speech accordingly.

'I will show.'

Together they set off through the mysterious dusk, full of
the noises of a city below the hillside, and the breath of a cool
wind in deodar-crowned Jakko, shouldering the stars. The
house-lights, scattered on every level, made, as it were, a
double firmament. Some were fixed, others belonged to the
rickshaws of the careless, open-spoken English folk, going out
to dinner.

'It is here,' said Kim's guide, and halted in a veranda flush
with the main road. No door stayed them, but a curtain of
beaded reeds that split up the lamplight beyond.

'He is come,' said the boy, in a voice little louder than a
sigh, and vanished. Kim felt sure that the boy had been
posted to guide him from the first, but, putting a bold face on
it, parted the curtain. A black-bearded man, with a green

shade over his eyes, sat at a table, and, one by one, with short, white hands, picked up globules of light from a tray before him, threaded them on a glancing silken string, and hummed to himself the while. Kim was conscious that beyond the circle of light the room was full of things that smelt like all the temples of all the East. A whiff of musk, a puff of sandal-wood, and a breath of sickly jessamine-oil caught his opened nostrils.

'I am here,' said Kim at last, speaking in the vernacular: the smells made him forget that he was to be a Sahib.

'Seventy-nine, eighty, eighty-one,' the man counted to himself, stringing pearl after pearl so quickly that Kim could scarcely follow his fingers. He slid off the green shade and looked fixedly at Kim for a full half-minute. The pupils of the eye dilated and closed to pin-pricks, as if at will. There was a *fakir* by the Taksali Gate who had just this gift and made money by it, especially when cursing silly women. Kim stared with interest. His disreputable friend could further twitch his ears, almost like a goat, and Kim was disappointed that this new man could not imitate him.

'Do not be afraid,' said Lurgan Sahib suddenly.

'Why should I fear?'

'Thou wilt sleep here tonight, and stay with me till it is time to go again to Nucklao. It is an order.'

'It is an order,' Kim repeated. 'But where shall I sleep?'

'Here, in this room.' Lurgan Sahib waved his hand towards the darkness behind him.

'So be it,' said Kim composedly. 'Now?'

He nodded and held the lamp above his head. As the light swept them, there leaped out from the walls a collection of Tibetan devil-dance masks, hanging above the fiend-embroidered draperies of those ghastly functions – horned masks, scowling masks, and masks of idiotic terror. In a corner, a Japanese warrior, mailed and plumed, menaced him with a halberd, and a score of lances and *khandas* and *kuttars* gave back the unsteady gleam. But what interested Kim more than all these things – he had seen devil-dance masks at the Lahore Museum – was a glimpse of the soft-eyed Hindu child who had left him in the doorway, sitting cross-legged under the table of pearls with a little smile on his scarlet lips.

'I think that Lurgan Sahib wishes to make me afraid. And I am sure that that devil's brat below the table wishes to see me afraid. This place,' he said aloud, 'is like a Wonder House. Where is my bed?'

Lurgan Sahib pointed to a native quilt in a corner by the loathsome masks, picked up the lamp, and left the room black.

'Was that Lurgan Sahib?' Kim asked as he cuddled down. No answer. He could hear the Hindu boy breathing, however, and, guided by the sound, crawled across the floor, and cuffed into the darkness, crying: 'Give answer, devil! Is this the way to lie to a Sahib?'

From the darkness he fancied he could hear the echo of a chuckle. It could not be his soft-fleshed companion, because he was weeping. So Kim lifted up his voice and called aloud: 'Lurgan Sahib! O Lurgan Sahib! Is it an order that thy servant does not speak to me?'

'It is an order.' The voice came from behind him and he started.

'Very good. But remember,' he muttered, as he resought the quilt, 'I will beat thee in the morning. I do not love Hindus.'

That was no cheerful night; the room being overfull of voices and music. Kim was waked twice by someone calling his name. The second time he set out in search, and ended by bruising his nose against a box that certainly spoke with a human tongue, but in no sort of human accent. It seemed to end in a tin trumpet and to be joined by wires to a smaller box on the floor – so far, at least, as he could judge by touch. And the voice, very hard and whirring, came out of the trumpet. Kim rubbed his nose and grew furious, thinking, as usual, in Hindi.

'This with a beggar from the bazar might be good, but – I

am a Sahib and the son of a Sahib and, which is twice as much
more beside, a student of Nucklao. Yess' (here he turned to
English), 'a boy of St Xavier's. Damn Mr Lurgan's eyes! – It
is some sort of machinery like a sewing-machine. Oh, it is a
great cheek of him – we are not frightened that way at
Lucknow – No!' Then in Hindi: 'But what does *he* gain? He is
only a trader – I am in his shop. But Creighton Sahib is a
Colonel – and I think Creighton Sahib gave orders that it
should be done. *How* I will beat that Hindu in the morning!
What is this?'

The trumpet-box was pouring out a string of the most
elaborate abuse that even Kim had ever heard, in a high
uninterested voice, that for a moment lifted the short hairs of
his neck. When the vile thing drew breath, Kim was reassured
by the soft, sewing-machine-like whirr.

'*Chûp!* [Be still]' he cried, and again he heard a chuckle that
decided him. '*Chûp* – or I break your head.'

The box took no heed. Kim wrenched at the tin trumpet
and something lifted with a click. He had evidently raised a
lid. If there were a devil inside, now was its time, for – he
sniffed – thus did the sewing-machines of the bazar smell. He
would clean that *shaitan*. He slipped off his jacket, and
plunged it into the box's mouth. Something long and round
bent under the pressure, there was a whirr and the voice
stopped – as voices must if you ram a thrice-doubled coat on
to the wax cylinder and into the works of an expensive
phonograph. Kim finished his slumbers with a serene mind.

In the morning he was aware of Lurgan Sahib looking
down on him.

'Oah!' said Kim, firmly resolved to cling to his Sahib-dom.
'There was a box in the night that gave me bad talk. So I
stopped it. Was it your box?'

The man held out his hand.

'Shake hands, O'Hara,' he said. 'Yes, it was my box. I keep
such things because my friends the Rajahs like them. That
one is broken, but it was cheap at the price. Yes, my friends,
the Kings, are very fond of toys – and so am I sometimes.'

Kim looked him over out of the corners of his eyes. He was
a Sahib in that he wore Sahib's clothes; the accent of his
Urdu, the intonation of his English, showed that he was
anything but a Sahib. He seemed to understand what moved
in Kim's mind ere the boy opened his mouth, and he took no
pains to explain himself as did Father Victor or the Lucknow
masters. Sweetest of all – he treated Kim as an equal on the
Asiatic side.

'I am sorry you cannot beat my boy this morning. He says
he will kill you with a knife or poison. He is jealous, so I have
put him in the corner and I shall not speak to him today. He
has just tried to kill me. You must help me with the breakfast.
He is almost too jealous to trust, just now.'

Now a genuine imported Sahib from England would have
made a great to-do over this tale. Lurgan Sahib stated it as
simply as Mahbub Ali was used to record his little affairs in
the North.

The back veranda of the shop was built out over the sheer
hillside, and they looked down into their neighbours'
chimney-pots, as is the custom of Simla. But even more than
the purely Persian meal cooked by Lurgan Sahib with his own
hands, the shop fascinated Kim. The Lahore Museum was
larger, but here were more wonders – ghost-daggers and
prayer-wheels from Tibet; turquoise and raw amber necklaces; green jade bangles; curiously packed incense-sticks in
jars crusted over with raw garnets; the devil-masks of overnight and a wall full of peacock-blue draperies; gilt figures of
Buddha, and little portable lacquer altars; Russian samovars
with turquoises on the lid; egg-shell china sets in quaint
octagonal cane boxes; yellow ivory crucifixes – from Japan of
all places in the world, so Lurgan Sahib said; carpets in dusty
bales, smelling atrociously, pushed back behind torn and
rotten screens of geometrical work; Persian water-jugs for the
hands after meals; dull copper incense-burners neither Chinese nor Persian, with friezes of fantastic devils running
round them; tarnished silver belts that knotted like raw hide;
hairpins of jade, ivory, and plasma; arms of all sorts and

kinds, and a thousand other oddments were cased, or piled, or merely thrown into the room, leaving a clear space only round the rickety deal table, where Lurgan Sahib worked.

'Those things are nothing,' said his host, following Kim's glance. 'I buy them because they are pretty, and sometimes I sell – if I like the buyer's look. My work is on the table – some of it.'

It blazed in the morning light – all red and blue and green flashes, picked out with the vicious blue-white spurt of a diamond here and there. Kim opened his eyes.

'Oh, they are quite well, those stones. It will not hurt them to take the sun. Besides, they are cheap. But with sick stones it is very different.' He piled Kim's plate anew. 'There is no one but *me* can doctor a sick pearl and re-blue turquoises. I grant you opals – any fool can cure an opal – but for a sick pearl there is only me. Suppose I were to die! Then there would be no one . . . Oh no! *You* cannot do anything with jewels. It will be quite enough if you understand a little about the Turquoise – some day.'

He moved to the end of the veranda to refill the heavy, porous clay water-jug from the filter.

'Do you want drink?'

Kim nodded. Lurgan Sahib, fifteen feet off, laid one hand on the jar. Next instant, it stood at Kim's elbow, full to within half an inch of the brim – the white cloth only showing, by a small wrinkle, where it had slid into place.

'Wah!' said Kim in most utter amazement. 'That is magic.' Lurgan Sahib's smile showed that the compliment had gone home.

'Throw it back.'

'It will break.'

'I say, throw it back.'

Kim pitched it at random. It fell short and crashed into fifty pieces, while the water dripped through the rough veranda boarding.

'I said it would break.'

'All one. Look at it. Look at the largest piece.'

That lay with a sparkle of water in its curve, as it were a star on the floor. Kim looked intently. Lurgan Sahib laid one hand gently on the nape of his neck, stroked it twice or thrice, and whispered: 'Look! It shall come to life again, piece by piece. First the big piece shall join itself to two others on the right and the left – on the right and the left. Look!'

To save his life, Kim could not have turned his head. The light touch held him as in a vice, and his blood tingled pleasantly through him. There was one large piece of the jar where there had been three, and above them the shadowy outline of the entire vessel. He could see the veranda through it, but it was thickening and darkening with each beat of his pulse. Yet the jar – how slowly the thoughts came! – the jar had been smashed before his eyes. Another wave of prickling fire raced down his neck, as Lurgan Sahib moved his hand.

'Look! It is coming into shape,' said Lurgan Sahib.

So far Kim had been thinking in Hindi, but a tremor came on him, and with an effort like that of a swimmer before sharks, who hurls himself half out of the water, his mind leaped up from a darkness that was swallowing it and took refuge in – the multiplication-table in English!

'Look! It is coming into shape,' whispered Lurgan Sahib.

The jar had been smashed – yess, smashed – not the native word, he would not think of that – but smashed – into fifty pieces, and twice three was six, and thrice three was nine, and four times three was twelve. He clung desperately to the repetition. The shadow-outline of the jar cleared like a mist after rubbing eyes. There were the broken shards; there was the spilt water drying in the sun, and through the cracks of the veranda showed, all ribbed, the white house-wall below – and thrice twelve was thirty-six!

'Look! Is it coming into shape?' asked Lurgan Sahib.

'But it *is* smashed – smashed,' he gasped – Lurgan Sahib had been muttering softly for the last half-minute. Kim wrenched his head aside. 'Look! *Dekho!* It is there as it was there.'

'It is there as it was there,' said Lurgan, watching Kim

closely while the boy rubbed his neck. 'But you are the first of many who has ever seen it so.' He wiped his broad forehead.

'Was that more magic?' Kim asked suspiciously. The tingle had gone from his veins; he felt unusually wide awake.

'No, that was not magic. It was only to see if there was – a flaw in a jewel. Sometimes very fine jewels will fly all to pieces if a man holds them in his hand, and knows the proper way. That is why one must be careful before one sets them. Tell me, did you see the shape of the pot?'

'For a little time. It began to grow like a flower from the ground.'

'And then what did you do? I mean, how did you think?'

'Oah! I knew it was broken, and so, I think, that was what I thought – and it *was* broken.'

'Hm! Has anyone ever done that same sort of magic to you before?'

'If it was,' said Kim, 'do you think I should let it again? I should run away.'

'And now you are not afraid – eh?'

'Not now.'

Lurgan Sahib looked at him more closely than ever. 'I shall ask Mahbub Ali – not now, but some day later,' he muttered. 'I am pleased with you – yes; and I am pleased with you – no. You are the first that ever saved himself. I wish I knew what it was that ... But you are right. You should not tell that – not even to me.'

He turned into the dusky gloom of the shop, and sat down at the table, rubbing his hands softly. A small, husky sob came from behind a pile of carpets. It was the Hindu child obediently facing towards the wall. His thin shoulders worked with grief.

'Ah! He is jealous, so jealous. I wonder if he will try to poison me again in my breakfast, and make me cook it twice.'

'*Kubbee – kubbee nahin* [Never – never. No!]', came the broken answer.

'And whether he will kill this other boy?'

'*Kubbee – kubbee nahin.*'

'What do *you* think he will do?' He turned suddenly on Kim.

'Oah! I do not know. Let him go, perhaps. Why did he want to poison you?'

'Because he is so fond of me. Suppose you were fond of someone, and you saw someone come, and the man you were fond of was more pleased with him than he was with you, what would you do?'

Kim thought. Lurgan repeated the sentence slowly in the vernacular.

'I should not poison that man,' said Kim reflectively, 'but I should beat that boy – *if* that boy was fond of my man. But first, I would ask that boy if it were true.'

'Ah! He thinks everyone must be fond of me.'

'Then I think he is a fool.'

'Hearest thou?' said Lurgan Sahib to the shaking shoulders. 'The Sahib's son thinks thou art a little fool. Come out, and next time thy heart is troubled, do not try white arsenic quite so openly. Surely the Devil Dasim was lord of our table-cloth that day! It might have made me ill, child, and then a stranger would have guarded the jewels. Come!'

The child, heavy-eyed with much weeping, crept out from behind the bale and flung himself passionately at Lurgan Sahib's feet, with an extravagance of remorse that impressed even Kim.

'I will look into the ink-pools – I will faithfully guard the jewels! Oh, my Father and my Mother, send *him* away!' He indicated Kim with a backward jerk of his bare heel.

'Not yet – not yet. In a little while he will go away again. But now he is at school – at a new *madrissah* – and thou shalt be his teacher. Play the Play of the Jewels against him. I will keep tally.'

The child dried his tears at once, and dashed to the back of the shop, whence he returned with a copper tray.

'Give me!' he said to Lurgan Sahib. 'Let them come from thy hand, for he may say that I knew them before.'

'Gently – gently,' the man replied, and from a drawer

under the table dealt a half-handful of clattering trifles into the tray.

'Now,' said the child, waving an old newspaper. 'Look on them as long as thou wilt, stranger. Count and, if need be, handle. One look is enough for *me*.' He turned his back proudly.

'But what is the game?'

'When thou hast counted and handled and art sure that thou canst remember them all, I cover them with this paper, and thou must tell over the tally to Lurgan Sahib. *I* will write mine.'

'Oah!' The instinct of competition waked in his breast. He bent over the tray. There were but fifteen stones on it. 'That is easy,' he said after a minute. The child slipped the paper over the winking jewels and scribbled in a native account-book.

'There are under that paper five blue stones – one big, one smaller, and three small,' said Kim, all in haste. 'There are four green stones, and one with a hole in it; there is one yellow stone that I can see through, and one like a pipe-stem. There are two red stones, and – and – I made the count fifteen, but two I have forgotten. No! Give me time. One was of ivory, little and brownish; and – and – give me time ...'

'One – two' – Lurgan Sahib counted him out up to ten. Kim shook his head.

'Hear my count!' the child burst in, trilling with laughter. 'First, are two flawed sapphires – one of two ruttees and one of four as I should judge. The four-ruttee sapphire is chipped at the edge. There is one Turkestan turquoise, plain with black veins, and there are two inscribed – one with a Name of God in gilt, and the other being cracked across, for it came out of an old ring, I cannot read. We have now all five blue stones. Four flawed emeralds there are, but one is drilled in two places, and one is a little carven –'

'Their weights?' said Lurgan Sahib impassively.

'Three – five – five – and four ruttees as I judge it. There is one piece of old greenish pipe amber, and a cut topaz from

Europe. There is one ruby of Burma, of two ruttees, without a flaw, and there is a balas-ruby, flawed, of two ruttees. There is a carved ivory from China representing a rat sucking an egg; and there is last – ah ha! – a ball of crystal as big as a bean set on a gold leaf.'

He clapped his hands at the close.

'He is thy master,' said Lurgan Sahib, smiling.

'Huh! He knew the names of the stones,' said Kim, flushing. 'Try again! With common things such as he and I both know.'

They heaped the tray again with odds and ends gathered from the shop, and even the kitchen, and every time the child won, till Kim marvelled.

'Bind my eyes – let me feel once with my fingers, and even *then* I will leave thee open-eyed behind,' he challenged.

Kim stamped with vexation when the lad made his boast good.

'If it were men – or horses,' he said, 'I could do better. This playing with tweezers and knives and scissors is too little.'

'Learn first – teach later,' said Lurgan Sahib. 'Is he thy master?'

'Truly. But how is it done?'

'By doing it many times over till it is done perfectly – for it is worth doing.'

The Hindu boy, in highest feather, actually patted Kim on the back.

'Do not despair,' he said. 'I myself will teach thee.'

'And I will see that thou art well taught,' said Lurgan Sahib, still speaking in the vernacular, 'for except my boy here – it was foolish of him to buy so much white arsenic when, if he had asked, I could have given it – except my boy here I have not in a long time met with one better worth teaching. And there are ten days more ere thou canst return to Lucknao where they teach nothing – at the long price. We shall, I think, be friends.'

They were a most mad ten days, but Kim enjoyed himself too much to reflect on their craziness. In the morning they played the Jewel Game – sometimes with veritable stones, sometimes with piles of swords and daggers, sometimes with photographs of natives. Through the afternoons he and the Hindu boy would mount guard in the shop, sitting dumb behind a carpet-bale or a screen and watching Mr Lurgan's many and very curious visitors. There were small Rajahs, escorts coughing in the veranda, who came to buy curiosities – such as phonographs and mechanical toys. There were ladies in search of necklaces, and men, it seemed to Kim – but his mind may have been vitiated by early training – in search of the ladies; natives from independent and feudatory Courts whose ostensible business was the repair of broken necklaces – rivers of light poured out upon the table – but whose true end seemed to be to raise money for angry Maharanees or young Rajahs. There were Babus to whom Lurgan Sahib talked with austerity and authority, but at the end of each interview he gave them money in coined silver and currency notes. There were occasional gatherings of long-coated theatrical natives who discussed metaphysics in English and Bengali, to Mr Lurgan's great edification. He was always interested in religions. At the end of the day, Kim and the Hindu boy – whose name varied at Lurgan's pleasure – were expected to give a detailed account of all that they had seen and heard – their view of each man's character, as shown in his face, talk, and manner, and their notions of his real errand. After dinner, Lurgan Sahib's fancy turned more to what might be called dressing-up, in which game he took a most informing interest. He could paint faces to a marvel; with a brush-dab here and a line there changing them past recognition. The shop was full of all manner of dresses and turbans, and Kim was apparelled variously as a young Mohammedan of good family, an oilman, and once – which was a joyous evening – as the son of an Oudh landholder in the fullest of full dress. Lurgan Sahib had a hawk's eye to detect the least flaw in the make-up; and lying on a worn teak-wood couch, would explain by the half-hour together how such and such a caste talked, or walked, or coughed, or spat, or sneezed, and, since 'hows' matter little in this world, the 'why' of everything. The Hindu child played this game clumsily. That little mind, keen as an icicle where tally of jewels was concerned, could not temper itself to enter another's soul; but a demon in Kim woke up and sang with joy as he put on the changing dresses, and changed speech and gesture therewith.

Carried away by enthusiasm, he volunteered to show Lurgan Sahib one evening how the disciples of a certain caste of *fakir*, old Lahore acquaintances, begged doles by the roadside; and what sort of language he would use to an Englishman, to a Punjabi farmer going to a fair, and to a woman without a veil. Lurgan Sahib laughed immensely, and begged Kim to stay as he was, immobile for half an hour – cross-legged, ash-smeared, and wild-eyed, in the back room. At the end of that time entered a hulking, obese Babu whose stockinged legs shook with fat, and Kim opened on him with a shower of wayside chaff. Lurgan Sahib – this annoyed Kim – watched the Babu and not the play.

'I think,' said the Babu heavily, lighting a cigarette, 'I am of opeenion that it is most extraordinary and effeecient performance. Except that you had told me I should have opined that – that – that you were pulling my legs. How soon can he become approximately effeecient chain-man? Because *then* I shall indent for him.'

'That is what he must learn at Lucknow.'

'Then order him to be jolly-dam'-quick. Good-night, Lurgan.' The Babu swung out with the gait of a bogged cow.

When they were telling over the day's list of visitors, Lurgan Sahib asked Kim who he thought the man might be.

'God knows!' said Kim cheerily. The tone might almost have deceived Mahbub Ali, but it failed entirely with the healer of sick pearls.

'That is true. God, He knows; but I wish to know what you think.'

Kim glanced sideways at his companion, whose eye had a way of compelling truth.

'I – I think he will want me when I come from the school, but' – confidentially, as Lurgan Sahib nodded approval – 'I do not understand how *he* can wear many dresses and talk many tongues.'

'Thou wilt understand many things later. He is a writer of tales for a certain Colonel. His honour is great only in Simla, and it is noticeable that he has no name, but only a number and a letter – that is a custom among us.'

'And is there a price upon his head too – as upon Mah – all the others?'

'Not yet; but if a boy rose up who is now sitting here and went – look, the door is open! – as far as a certain house with a red-painted veranda, behind that which was the old theatre in the Lower Bazar, and whispered through the shutters: "Hurree Chunder Mookerjee bore the bad news of last month", that boy might take away a belt full of rupees.'

'How many?' said Kim promptly.

'Five hundred – a thousand – as many as he might ask for.'

'Good. And for how long might such a boy live after the news was told?' He smiled merrily at Lurgan Sahib's very beard.

'Ah! That is to be well thought of. Perhaps if he were very clever, he might live out the day – but not the night. By no means the night.'

'Then what is the Babu's pay if so much is put upon his head?'

'Eighty – perhaps a hundred – perhaps a hundred and fifty rupees; but the pay is the least part of the work. From time to time, God causes men to be born – and thou art one of them – who have a lust to go abroad at the risk of their lives and discover news – today it may be of far-off things, tomorrow of some hidden mountain, and the next day of some near-by men who have done a foolishness against the State. These souls are very few; and of these few, not more than ten are of the best. Among these ten I count the Babu, and that is curious. How great, therefore, and desirable must be a business that brazens the heart of a Bengali!'

'True. But the days go slowly for me. I am yet a boy, and it is only within two months I learned to write Angrezi. Even now I cannot read it well. And there are yet years and years and long years before I can be even a chain-man.'

'Have patience, Friend of all the World' – Kim started at the title. 'Would I had a few of the years that so irk thee. I have proved thee in several small ways. This will not be forgotten when I make my report to the Colonel Sahib.' Then, changing suddenly into English with a deep laugh:

'By Jove! O'Hara, I think there is a great deal in you; but you must not become proud and you must not talk. You must go back to Lucknow and be a good little boy and mind your book, as the English say, and perhaps, next holidays if you care, you can come back to me!' Kim's face fell. 'Oh, I mean *if* you like. I know where you want to go.'

Four days later a seat was booked for Kim and his small trunk at the rear of a Kalka tonga. His companion was the whale-like Babu, who, with a fringed shawl wrapped round his head, and his fat openwork-stockinged left leg tucked under him, shivered and grunted in the morning chill.

'How comes it that this man is one of *us*?' thought Kim considering the jelly back as they jolted down the road; and the reflection threw him into most pleasant day-dreams. Lurgan Sahib had given him five rupees – a splendid sum – as well as the assurance of his protection if he worked. Unlike Mahbub, Lurgan Sahib had spoken most explicitly of the reward that would follow obedience, and Kim was content. If only, like the Babu, he could enjoy the dignity of a letter and a number – and a price upon his head! Some day he would be all that and more. Some day he might be almost as great as Mahbub Ali! The housetops of his search should be half India; he would follow Kings and Ministers, as in the old days he had followed *vakils* and lawyers' touts across Lahore city for Mahbub Ali's sake. Meantime, there was the present, and not at all unpleasant, fact of St Xavier's immediately before him. There would be new boys to condescend to, and there would be tales of holiday adventures to hear. Young Martin, son of the tea-planter at Manipur, had boasted that he would go to war, with a rifle, against the head-hunters. That might be, but it was certain young Martin had not been blown half across the forecourt of a Patiala palace by an explosion of fireworks; nor had he ... Kim fell to telling himself the story of his own adventures through the last three months. He could paralyse St Xavier's – even the biggest boys who shaved – with the recital, were that permitted. But it was, of course, out of the question. There would be a price upon his head in good time, as Lurgan Sahib had assured him; and if he talked foolishly now, not only would that price never be set, but Colonel Creighton would cast him off – and he would be left to the wrath of Lurgan Sahib and Mahbub Ali – for the short space of life that would remain to him.

'So I should lose Delhi for the sake of a fish,' was his proverbial philosophy. It behoved him to forget his holidays (there would always remain the fun of inventing imaginary adventures) and, as Lurgan Sahib had said, to work.

Of all the boys hurrying back to St Xavier's, from Sukkur in the sands to Galle beneath the palms, none was so filled with virtue as Kimball O'Hara, jiggering down to Umballa behind Hurree Chunder Mookerjee, whose name on the books of one section of the Ethnological Survey was R17.

And if additional spur were needed, the Babu supplied it. After a huge meal at Kalka, he spoke uninterruptedly. Was Kim going to school? Then he, an MA of Calcutta University, would explain the advantages of education. There were marks to be gained by due attention to Latin and Wordsworth's *Excursion* (all this was Greek to Kim). French, too, was vital, and the best was to be picked up in Chandernagore a few miles from Calcutta. Also a man might go far, as he himself had done, by strict attention to plays called *Lear* and *Julius Caesar*, both much in demand by examiners. *Lear* was not so full of historical allusions as *Julius Caesar*; the book cost four annas, but could be bought second-hand in Bow Bazar for two. Still more important than Wordsworth, or the eminent authors, Burke and Hare, was the art and science of mensuration. A boy who had passed his examination in these branches – for which, by the way, there were no cram-books – could, by merely marching over a country with a compass and a level and a straight eye, carry away a picture of that country which might be sold for large sums in coined silver. But as it was occasionally inexpedient to carry about measuring-chains a boy would do well to know the precise length of his own foot-pace, so that when he was deprived of what Hurree Chunder called 'adventitious aids' he might still tread his distances. To keep count of thousands of paces, Hurree Chunder's experience had shown him nothing more valuable than a rosary of eighty-one or a hundred and eight beads, for 'it was divisible and sub-divisible into many multiples and sub-multiples'. Through the volleying drifts of English, Kim caught the general trend of the talk, and it interested him very much. Here was a new craft that a man could tuck away in his head and by the look of the large wide world unfolding itself before him, it seemed that the more a man knew the better for him.

Said the Babu when he had talked for an hour and a half, 'I hope some day to enjoy your offeecial acquaintance. *Ad interim*, if I may be pardoned that expression, I shall give you this betel-box, which is highly valuable article and cost me two rupees only four years ago.' It was a cheap, heart-shaped brass thing with three compartments for carrying the eternal betel-nut, lime and *pan*-leaf; but it was filled with little tabloid-bottles. 'That is reward of merit for your performance in character of that holy man. You see, you are so young you think you will last for ever and not take care of your body. It is great nuisance to go sick in the middle of business. I am fond of drugs myself, and they are handy to cure poor people too. These are good Departmental drugs – quinine and so on. I give it you for souvenir. Now good-bye. I have urgent private business here by the roadside.'

He slipped out noiselessly as a cat, on the Umballa road, hailed a passing cart and jingled away, while Kim, tongue-tied, twiddled the brass betel-box in his hands.

The record of a boy's education interests few save his parents, and, as you know, Kim was an orphan. It is written in the books of St Xavier's in Partibus that a report of Kim's progress was forwarded at the end of each term to Colonel Creighton and to Father Victor, from whose hands duly came the money for his schooling. It is further recorded in the same books that he showed a great aptitude for mathematical studies as well as map-making, and carried away a prize (*The Life of Lord Lawrence*, tree-calf, two vols., nine rupees, eight annas) for proficiency therein; and the same term played in St Xavier's eleven against the Alighur Mohammedan College, his age being fourteen years and ten months. He was also re-vaccinated (from which we may assume that there had been another epidemic of smallpox at Lucknow) about the same time. Pencil notes on the edge of an old muster-roll record that he was punished several times for 'conversing with improper persons', and it seems that he was once sentenced to heavy pains for 'absenting himself for a day in the company of a street beggar'. That was when he got over the gate and pleaded with the lama through a whole day down the banks of the Gumti to accompany him on the Road next holidays – for one month – for a little week; and the lama set his face as a flint against it, averring that the time had not yet come. Kim's business, said the old man as they ate cakes together, was to get all the wisdom of the Sahibs and then he would see. The Hand of Friendship must in some way have averted the Whip of Calamity, for six weeks later Kim seems to have passed an examination in elementary surveying 'with great credit', his age being fifteen years and eight months. From this date the record is silent. His name does not appear in the year's batch of those who entered for the subordinate Survey of India, but against it stand the words 'removed on appointment'.

Several times in those three years, cast up at the Temple of the Tirthankars in Benares the lama, a little thinner and a shade yellower, if that were possible, but gentle and untainted as ever. Sometimes it was from the South that he came – from south of Tuticorin, whence the wonderful fire-boats go to

Ceylon where are priests who know Pali; sometimes it was
from the wet green West and the thousand cotton-factory
chimneys that ring Bombay; and once from the North, where
he had doubled back eight hundred miles to talk for a day
with the Keeper of the Images in the Wonder House. He
would stride to his cell in the cool, cut marble – the priests of
the Temple were good to the old man, – wash off the dust of
travel, make prayer, and depart for Lucknow, well accus-
tomed now to the way of the rail, in a third-class carriage.
Returning, it was noticeable, as his friend the Seeker pointed
out to the head-priest, that he ceased for a while to mourn the
loss of his River, or to draw wondrous pictures of the Wheel
of Life, but preferred to talk of the beauty and wisdom of a
certain mysterious *chela* whom no man of the Temple had
ever seen. Yes, he had followed the traces of the Blessed Feet
throughout all India. (The Curator has still in his possession a
most marvellous account of his wanderings and meditations.)
There remained nothing more in life but to find the River of
the Arrow. Yet it was shown to him in dreams that it was a
matter not to be undertaken with any hope of success unless
that seeker had with him the one *chela* appointed to bring the
event to a happy issue, and versed in great wisdom – such
wisdom as white-haired Keepers of Images possess. For
example (here came out the snuff-gourd, and the kindly Jain
priests made haste to be silent):

'Long and long ago, when Devadatta was King of Benares
– let all listen to the *Jâtaka*! – an elephant was captured for a
time by the king's hunters and, ere he broke free, beringed
with a grievous leg-iron. This he strove to remove with hate
and frenzy in his heart, and hurrying up and down the forests,
besought his brother-elephants to wrench it asunder. One by
one, with their strong trunks, they tried and failed. At the last
they gave it as their opinion that the ring was not to be broken
by any bestial power. And in a thicket, new-born, wet with
moisture of birth, lay a day-old calf of the herd whose mother
had died. The fettered elephant, forgetting his own agony,
said: "If I do not help this suckling it will perish under our

feet." So he stood above the young thing, making his legs buttresses against the uneasily moving herd; and he begged milk of a virtuous cow, and the calf throve, and the ringed elephant was the calf's guide and defence. Now the days of an elephant – let all listen to the *Jâtaka*! – are thirty-five years to his full strength, and through thirty-five Rains the ringed elephant befriended the younger, and all the while the fetter ate into the flesh.

'Then one day the young elephant saw the half-buried iron, and turning to the elder said: "What is this?" "It is even my sorrow," said he who had befriended him. Then that other put out his trunk and in the twinkling of an eyelash abolished the ring, saying: "The appointed time has come." So the virtuous elephant who had waited temperately and done kind acts was relieved, at the appointed time, by the very calf whom he had turned aside to cherish – let all listen to the *Jâtaka*! – for the Elephant was Ananda, and the Calf that broke the ring was none other than The Lord Himself ...'

Then he would shake his head benignly, and over the ever-clicking rosary point out how free that elephant-calf was from the sin of pride. He was as humble as a *chela* who, seeing his master sitting in the dust outside the Gates of Learning, over-leapt the gates (though they were locked) and took his master to his heart in the presence of the proud-stomached city. Rich would be the reward of such a master and such a *chela* when the time came for them to seek freedom together!

So did the lama speak, coming and going across India as softly as a bat. A sharp-tongued old woman in a house among the fruit-trees behind Saharunpore honoured him as the woman honoured the prophet, but his chamber was by no means upon the wall. In an apartment of the forecourt overlooked by cooing doves he would sit, while she laid aside her useless veil and chattered of spirits and fiends of Kulu, of grandchildren unborn, and of the free-tongued brat who had talked to her in the resting-place. Once, too, he strayed alone from the Grand Trunk Road below Umballa to the very village whose priest had tried to drug him; but the kind

Heaven that guards lamas sent him at twilight through the crops, absorbed and unsuspicious, to the Rissaldar's door. Here was like to have been a grave misunderstanding, for the old soldier asked him why the Friend of the Stars had gone that way only six days before.

'That may not be,' said the lama. 'He has gone back to his own people.'

'He sat in that corner telling a hundred merry tales five nights ago,' his host insisted. 'True, he vanished somewhat suddenly in the dawn after foolish talk with my grand-daughter. He grows apace, but he is the same Friend of the Stars as brought me true word of the war. Have ye parted?'

'Yes – and no,' the lama replied. 'We – we have not altogether parted, but the time is not ripe that we should take the Road together. He acquires wisdom in another place. We must wait.'

'All one – but if it were not the boy how did he come to speak so continually of thee?'

'And what said he?' asked the lama eagerly.

'Sweet words – an hundred thousand – that thou art his father and mother and such all. Pity that he does not take the Queen's service. He is fearless.'

This news amazed the lama, who did not then know how religiously Kim kept to the contract made with Mahbub Ali, and perforce ratified by Colonel Creighton ...

'There is no holding the young pony from the game,' said the horse-dealer when the Colonel pointed out that vaga-bonding over India in holiday time was absurd. 'If permission be refused to go and come as he chooses, he will make light of the refusal. Then who is to catch him? Colonel Sahib, only once in a thousand years is a horse born so well fitted for the game as this our colt. And we need men.'

Chapter 10

Your tiercel's too long at hack, Sire. He's no eyass
But a passage-hawk that footed ere we caught him,
Dangerously free o' the air. Faith! were he mine
(As mine's the glove he binds to for his tirings)
I'd fly him with a make-hawk. He's in yarak
Plumed to the very point – so manned, so weathered ...
Give him the firmament God made him for,
And what shall take the air of him?

Gow's Watch.

L URGAN Sahib did not use as direct speech, but his advice
tallied with Mahbub's; and the upshot was good for
Kim. He knew better now than to leave Lucknow city in
native garb, and if Mahbub were anywhere within reach of a
letter, it was to Mahbub's camp he headed, and made his
change under the Pathan's wary eye. Could the little Survey
paint-box that he used for map-tinting in term-time have
found a tongue to tell of holiday doings, he might have been
expelled. Once Mahbub and he went together as far as the
beautiful city of Bombay, with three truckloads of tram-
horses, and Mahbub nearly melted when Kim proposed a sail
in a dhow across the Indian Ocean to buy Gulf Arabs, which,
he understood from a hanger-on of the dealer Abdul Rahman,
fetched better prices than mere Kabulis.

He dipped his hand into the dish with that great trader
when Mahbub and a few co-religionists were invited to a big
Haj dinner. They came back by way of Karachi by sea, when
Kim took his first experience of sea-sickness sitting on the
fore-hatch of a coasting-steamer, well persuaded he had been
poisoned. The Babu's famous drug-box proved useless,
though Kim had restocked it at Bombay. Mahbub had
business at Quetta, and there Kim, as Mahbub admitted,
earned his keep, and perhaps a little over, by spending four

curious days as scullion in the house of a fat Commissariat
sergeant, from whose office-box, in an auspicious moment, he
removed a little vellum ledger which he copied out – it
seemed to deal entirely with cattle and camel sales – by
moonlight, lying behind an outhouse, all through one hot
night. Then he returned the ledger to its place, and, at
Mahbub's word, left that service unpaid, rejoining him six
miles down the road, the clean copy in his bosom.

'That soldier is a small fish,' Mahbub Ali explained, 'but in
time we shall catch the larger one. He only sells oxen at two
prices – one for himself and one for the Government – which
I do not think is a sin.'

'Why could not I take away the little book and be done
with it?'

'Then he would have been frightened, and he would have
told his master. Then we should miss, perhaps, a great
number of new rifles which seek their way up from Quetta to
the North. The Game is so large that one sees but a little at a
time.'

'Oho!' said Kim, and held his tongue. That was in the
monsoon holidays, after he had taken the prize for mathematics. The Christmas holidays he spent – deducting ten days
for private amusements – with Lurgan Sahib, where he sat for
the most part in front of a roaring wood-fire – Jakko road was
four feet deep in snow that year – and – the small Hindu had
gone away to be married – helped Lurgan to thread pearls. He
made Kim learn whole Chapters of the Koran by heart, till he
could deliver them with the very roll and cadence of a mullah.
Moreover, he told Kim the names and properties of many
native drugs, as well as the runes proper to recite when you
administer them. And in the evenings he wrote charms on
parchment – elaborate pentagrams crowned with the names
of devils – Murra, and Awan the Companion of Kings – all
fantastically written in the corners. More to the point, he
advised Kim as to the care of his own body, the cure of fever-
fits, and simple remedies of the Road. A week before it was
time to go down, Colonel Creighton Sahib – this was unfair –

sent Kim a written examination-paper that concerned itself solely with rods and chains and links and angles.

Next holidays he was out with Mahbub, and here, by the way, he nearly died of thirst, plodding through the sand on a camel to the mysterious city of Bikanir, where the wells are four hundred feet deep, and lined throughout with camel-bone. It was not an amusing trip from Kim's point of view, because – in defiance of the contract – the Colonel ordered him to make a map of that wild, walled city; and since Mohammedan horse-boys and pipe-tenders are not expected to drag Survey-chains round the capital of an independent Native State, Kim was forced to pace all his distances by means of a bead rosary. He used the compass for bearings as occasion served – after dark chiefly, when the camels had been fed – and by the help of his little Survey paint-box of six colour-cakes and three brushes, he achieved something not remotely unlike the city of Jeysulmir. Mahbub laughed a great deal, and advised him to make up a written report as well; and in the back of the big account-book that lay under the flap of Mahbub's pet saddle Kim fell to work.

'It must hold everything that thou hast seen or touched or considered. Write as though the Jung-i-Lat Sahib himself had come by stealth with a vast army outsetting to war.'

'How great an army?'

'Oh, half a lakh of men.'

'Folly! Remember how few and bad were the wells in the sand. Not a thousand thirsty men could come near by here.'

'Then write that down – also all the old breaches in the walls – and whence the firewood is cut – and what is the temper and disposition of the King. I stay here till all my horses are sold. I will hire a room by the gateway, and thou shalt be my accountant. There is a good lock to the door.'

The report in its unmistakable St Xavier's running script, and the brown, yellow, and lake-daubed map, was on hand a few years ago (a careless clerk filed it with the rough notes of E23's second Seistan survey), but by now the pencil characters must be almost illegible. Kim translated it, sweating

under the light of an oil-lamp, to Mahbub, the second day of
their return-journey. The Pathan rose and stooped over his
dappled saddle-bags.

'I knew it would be worthy a dress of honour, and so I
made one ready,' he said, smiling. 'Were I Amir of Afghanistan (and some day we may see him), I would fill thy mouth
with gold.' He laid the garments formally at Kim's feet.
There was a gold-embroidered Peshawur turban-cap, rising
to a cone, and a big turban-cloth ending in a broad fringe of
gold. There was a Delhi embroidered waistcoat to slip over a
milky white shirt, fastening to the right, ample and flowing;
green pyjamas with twisted silk waist-string; and that nothing
might be lacking, russia-leather slippers, smelling divinely,
with arrogantly curled tips.

'Upon a Wednesday, and in the morning, to put on new
clothes is auspicious,' said Mahbub solemnly. 'But we must
not forget the wicked folk in the world. So!'

He capped all the splendour, that was taking Kim's
delighted breath away, with a mother-of-pearl, nickel-plated,
self-extracting .450 revolver.

'I had thought of a smaller bore, but reflected that this
takes Government bullets. A man can always come by those –
especially across the Border. Stand up and let me look.' He
clapped Kim on the shoulder. 'May you never be tired,
Pathan! Oh, the hearts to be broken! Oh, the eyes under the
eyelashes, looking sideways!'

Kim turned about, pointed his toes, stretched, and felt
mechanically for the moustache that was just beginning.
Then he stooped towards Mahbub's feet to make proper
acknowledgment with fluttering, quick-patting hands; his
heart too full for words. Mahbub forestalled and embraced
him.

'My son,' said he, 'what need of words between us? But is
not the little gun a delight? All six cartridges come out at one
twist. It is borne in the bosom next the skin, which, as it were,
keeps it oiled. Never put it elsewhere, and please God, thou
shalt some day kill a man with it.'

'*Hai mai!*' said Kim ruefully. 'If a Sahib kills a man he is hanged in the jail.'

'True: but one pace beyond the Border, men are wiser. Put it away; but fill it first. Of what use is a gun unfed?'

'When I go back to the *madrissah* I must return it. They do not allow little guns. Thou wilt keep it for me?'

'Son, I am wearied of that *madrissah*, where they take the best years of a man to teach him what he can only learn upon the Road. The folly of the Sahibs has neither top nor bottom. No matter. Maybe thy written report shall save thee further bondage; and God He knows we need men more and more in the Game.'

They marched, jaw-bound against blowing sand, across the salt desert to Jodhpur, where Mahbub and his handsome nephew Habib Ullah did much trading; and then sorrowfully, in European clothes, which he was fast outgrowing, Kim went second-class to St Xavier's. Three weeks later, Colonel Creighton, pricing Tibetan ghost-daggers at Lurgan's shop, faced Mahbub Ali openly mutinous. Lurgan Sahib operated as support in reserve.

'The pony is made – finished – mouthed and paced, Sahib! From now on, day by day, he will lose his manners if he is kept at tricks. Drop the rein on his back and let go,' said the horse-dealer. 'We need him.'

'But he is so young, Mahbub – not more than sixteen – is he?'

'When I was fifteen, I had shot my man and begot my man, Sahib.'

'You impenitent old heathen!' Creighton turned to Lurgan. The black beard nodded assent to the wisdom of the Afghan's dyed scarlet.

'*I* should have used him long ago,' said Lurgan. 'The younger the better. That is why I always have my really valuable jewels watched by a child. You sent him to me to try. I tried him in every way: he is the only boy I could not make to see things.'

'In the crystal – in the ink-pool?' demanded Mahbub.

'No. Under my hand, as I told you. That has never happened before. It means that he is strong enough – but you think it skittles, Colonel Creighton – to make anyone do anything he wants. And that is three years ago. I have taught him a good deal since, Colonel Creighton. I think you waste him now.'

'Hmm! Maybe you're right. But, as you know, there is no Survey work for him at present.'

'Let him out – let him go,' Mahbub interrupted. 'Who expects any colt to carry heavy weight at first? Let him run with the caravans – like our white camel-colts – for luck. I would take him myself, but –'

'There is a little business where he would be most useful – in the South,' said Lurgan, with peculiar suavity, dropping his heavy blued eyelids.

'E23 has that in hand,' said Creighton quickly. 'He must not go down there. Besides, he knows no Turki.'

'Only tell him the shape and the smell of the letters we want and he will bring them back,' Lurgan insisted.

'No. That is a man's job,' said Creighton.

It was a wry-necked matter of unauthorized and incendiary correspondence between a person who claimed to be the ultimate authority in all matters of the Mohammedan religion throughout the world, and a younger member of a royal house who had been brought to book for kidnapping women within British territory. The Moslem Archbishop had been emphatic and over-arrogant; the young prince was merely sulky at the curtailment of his privileges, but there was no need he should continue a correspondence which might some day compromise him. One letter indeed had been procured, but the finder was later found dead by the roadside in the habit of an Arab trader, as E23, taking up the work, duly reported.

These facts, and a few others not to be published, made both Mahbub and Creighton shake their heads.

'Let him go out with his Red Lama,' said the horse-dealer with visible effort. 'He is fond of the old man. He can learn his paces by the rosary at least.'

'I have had some dealings with the old man – by letter,' said Colonel Creighton, smiling to himself. 'Whither goes he?'

'Up and down the land, as he has these three years. He seeks a River of Healing. God's curse upon all –' Mahbub checked himself. 'He beds down at the Temple of the Tirthankars or at Buddh Gaya when he is in from the Road. Then he goes to see the boy at the *madrissah*, as we know, for the boy was punished for it twice or thrice. He is quite mad, but a peaceful man. I have met him. The Babu also has had dealings with him. We have watched him for three years. Red Lamas are not so common in Hind that one loses track.'

'Babus are very curious,' said Lurgan meditatively. 'Do you know what Hurree Babu really wants? He wants to be made a member of the Royal Society by taking ethnological notes. I tell you, I tell him about the lama everything which Mahbub and the boy have told me. Hurree Babu goes down to Benares – at his own expense, I think.'

'I don't,' said Creighton briefly. He had paid Hurree's travelling expenses, out of a most lively curiosity to learn what the lama might be.

'And he applies to the lama for information on lamaism, and devil-dances, and spells and charms, several times in these few years. Holy Virgin! I could have told him all that yee-ars ago. I think Hurree Babu is getting too old for the Road. He likes better to collect manners and customs information. Yes, he wants to be an FRS.'

'Hurree thinks well of the boy, doesn't he?'

'Oh, very indeed – we have had some pleasant evenings at my little place – but I think it would be waste to throw him away with Hurree on the Ethnological side.'

'Not for a first experience. How does that strike you, Mahbub? Let the boy run with the lama for six months. After that we can see. He will get experience.'

'He has it already, Sahib – as a fish controls the water he swims in. But for every reason it will be well to loose him from the school.'

'Very good, then,' said Creighton, half to himself. 'He can go with the lama, and if Hurree Babu cares to keep an eye on them so much the better. He won't lead the boy into any danger as Mahbub would. Curious – his wish to be an FRS. Very human, too. He *is* best on the Ethnological side – Hurree.'

No money and no preferment would have drawn Creighton from his work on the Indian Survey, but deep in his heart also lay the ambition to write 'FRS' after his name. Honours of a sort he knew could be obtained by ingenuity and the help of friends, but, to the best of his belief, nothing save work – papers representing a life of it – took a man into the Society which he had bombarded for years with monographs on strange Asiatic cults and unknown customs. Nine men out of ten would flee from a Royal Society soirée in extremity of boredom; but Creighton was the tenth, and at times his soul yearned for the crowded rooms in easy London where silver-haired, bald-headed gentlemen who know nothing of the Army move among spectroscopic experiments, the lesser plants of the frozen tundras, electric flight-measuring machines, and apparatus for slicing into fractional millimetres the left eye of the female mosquito. By all right and reason, it was the Royal Geographical that should have appealed to him, but men are as chancy as children in their choice of playthings. So Creighton smiled, and thought the better of Hurree Babu, moved by like desire.

He dropped the ghost-dagger and looked up at Mahbub.

'How soon can we get the colt from the stable?' said the horse-dealer, reading his eyes.

'Hmm! If I withdraw him by order now – what will he do, think you? I have never before assisted at the teaching of such an one.'

'He will come to me,' said Mahbub promptly. 'Lurgan Sahib and I will prepare him for the Road.'

'So be it, then. For six months he shall run at his choice. But who will be his sponsor?'

Lurgan slightly inclined his head. 'He will not tell any-thing, if that is what you are afraid of, Colonel Creighton.'

'It's only a boy, after all.'

'Ye-es; but first, he has nothing to tell; and secondly, he knows what would happen. Also, he is very fond of Mahbub, and of me a little.'

'Will he draw pay?' demanded the practical horse-dealer.

'Food and water allowance only. Twenty rupees a month.'

One advantage of the Secret Service is that it has no worrying audit. That Service is ludicrously starved, of course, but the funds are administered by a few men who do not call for vouchers or present itemized accounts. Mahbub's eyes lighted with almost a Sikh's love of money. Even Lurgan's impassive face changed. He considered the years to come when Kim would have been entered and made to the Great Game that never ceases day and night, throughout India. He foresaw honour and credit in the mouths of a chosen few, coming to him from his pupil. Lurgan Sahib had made E23 what E23 was, out of a bewildered, impertinent, lying, little North-West Province man.

But the joy of these masters was pale and smoky beside the joy of Kim when St Xavier's Head called him aside, with word that Colonel Creighton had sent for him.

'I understand, O'Hara, that he has found you a place as an assistant chain-man in the Canal Department: that comes of taking up mathematics. It is great luck for you, for you are only sixteen; but of course you understand that you do not become *pukka* [permanent] till you have passed the autumn examination. So you must not think you are going out into the world to enjoy yourself, or that your fortune is made. There is a great deal of hard work before you. Only, if you succeed in becoming *pukka*, you can rise, you know, to four hundred and fifty a month.' Whereat the Principal gave him much good advice as to his conduct, and his manners, and his morals; and others, his elders, who had not been wafted into billets, talked as only Anglo-Indian lads can, of favouritism and corruption.

Indeed, young Cazalet, whose father was a pensioner at Chunar, hinted very broadly that Colonel Creighton's interest in Kim was directly paternal; and Kim, instead of retaliating, did not even use language. He was thinking of the immense fun to come, of Mahbub's letter of the day before, all neatly written in English, making appointment for that afternoon in a house the very name of which would have crisped the Principal's hair with horror ...

Said Kim to Mahbub in Lucknow railway station that evening, above the luggage-scales: 'I feared lest, at the last, the roof would fall upon me and cheat me. It is indeed all finished, O my father?'

Mahbub snapped his fingers to show the utterness of that end, and his eyes blazed like red coals.

'Then where is the pistol that I may wear it?'

'Softly! A half-year, to run without heel-ropes. I begged that much from Colonel Creighton Sahib. At twenty rupees a month. Old Red Hat knows that thou art coming.'

'I will pay thee *dustoorie* [commission] on my pay for three months,' said Kim gravely. 'Yea, two rupees a month. But first we must get rid of these.' He plucked his thin linen trousers and dragged at his collar. 'I have brought with me all that I need on the Road. My trunk has gone up to Lurgan Sahib's.'

'Who sends his salaams to thee – Sahib.'

'Lurgan Sahib is a very clever man. But what dost thou do?'

'I go North again, upon the Great Game. What else? Is thy mind still set on following old Red Hat?'

'Do not forget he made me that I am – though he did not know it. Year by year, he sent the money that taught me.'

'I would have done as much – had it struck my thick head,' Mahbub growled. 'Come away. The lamps are lit now, and none will mark thee in the bazar. We go to Huneefa's house.'

On the way thither, Mahbub gave him much the same sort of advice as his mother gave to Lemuel, and curiously enough, Mahbub was exact to point out how Huneefa and her likes destroyed kings.

'And I remember,' he quoted maliciously, 'one who said, "Trust a snake before an harlot, and an harlot before a Pathan, Mahbub Ali." Now, excepting as to Pathans, of whom I am one, all that is true. Most true is it in the Great Game, for it is by means of women that all plans come to ruin and we lie out in the dawning with our throats cut. So it happened to such a one.' He gave the reddest particulars.

'Then why –?' Kim paused before a filthy staircase that climbed to the warm darkness of an upper chamber, in the ward that is behind Azim Ullah's tobacco-shop. Those who know it call it The Birdcage – it is so full of whisperings and whistlings and chirrupings.

The room, with its dirty cushions and half-smoked hookahs, smelt abominably of stale tobacco. In one corner lay a huge and shapeless woman clad in greenish gauzes, and decked, brow, nose, ear, neck, wrist, arm, waist, and ankle with heavy native jewellery. When she turned it was like the clashing of copper pots. A lean cat in the balcony outside the window mewed hungrily. Kim checked, bewildered, at the door-curtain.

'Is that the new stuff, Mahbub?' said Huneefa lazily, scarce troubling to remove the mouthpiece from her lips. 'O Buktanoos!' – like most of her kind, she swore by the Djinns – 'O Buktanoos! He is very good to look upon.'

'That is part of the selling of the horse,' Mahbub explained to Kim, who laughed.

'I have heard that talk since my Sixth Day,' he replied, squatting by the light. 'Whither does it lead?'

'To protection. Tonight we change thy colour. This sleeping under roofs has blanched thee like an almond. But Huneefa has the secret of a colour that catches. No painting of a day or two. Also, we fortify thee against the chances of the Road. That is *my* gift to thee, my son. Take out all metals on thee and lay them here. Make ready, Huneefa.'

Kim dragged forth his compass, Survey paint-box, and the new-filled medicine-box. They had all accompanied his travels, and boylike he valued them immensely.

The woman rose slowly and moved with her hands a little spread before her. Then Kim saw that she was blind. 'No, no,' she muttered, 'the Pathan speaks truth – my colour does not go in a week or a month, and those whom I protect are under strong guard.'

'When one is far off and alone, it would not be well to grow blotched and leprous of a sudden,' said Mahbub. 'When thou wast with me I could oversee the matter. Besides, a Pathan is a fair-skin. Strip to the waist now and look how thou art whitened.' Huneefa felt her way back from an inner room. 'It is no matter, she cannot see.' He took a pewter bowl from her ringed hand.

The dye-stuff showed blue and gummy. Kim experimented on the back of his wrist, with a dab of cotton-wool; but Huneefa heard him.

'No, no,' she cried, 'the thing is not done thus, but with the proper ceremonies. The colouring is the least part. I give thee the full protection of the Road.'

'*Jadoo?* [magic],' said Kim, with a half start. He did not like the white, sightless eyes. Mahbub's hand on his neck bowed him to the floor, nose within an inch of the boards.

'Be still. No harm comes to thee, my son. I am thy sacrifice!'

He could not see what the woman was about, but heard the clish-clash of her jewellery for many minutes. A match lit up the darkness; he caught the well-known purr and fizzle of grains of incense. Then the room filled with smoke – heavy, aromatic, and stupefying. Through growing drowse he heard the names of devils – of Zulbazan, Son of Eblis, who lives in bazars and *paraos*, making all the sudden lewd wickedness of wayside halts; of Dulhan, invisible about mosques, the dweller among the slippers of the faithful, who hinders folk from their prayers; and Musboot, Lord of lies and panic.

Huneefa, now whispering in his ear, now talking as from an immense distance, touched him with horrible soft fingers, but Mahbub's grip never shifted from his neck till, relaxing with a sigh, the boy lost his senses.

'Allah! How he fought! We should never have done it but for the drugs. That was his white blood, I take it,' said Mahbub testily. 'Go on with the *dawut* [invocation]. Give him full Protection.'

'*O Hearer! Thou that hearest with ears, be present. Listen, O Hearer!*' Huneefa moaned, her dead eyes turned to the west. The dark room filled with moanings and snortings.

From the outer balcony, a ponderous figure raised a round bullet head and coughed nervously.

'Do not interrupt this ventriloquial necromanciss, my friend,' it said in English. 'I opine that it is very disturbing to you, but no enlightened observer is jolly-well upset.'

'*. . . I will lay a plot for their ruin! O Prophet, bear with the unbelievers. Let them alone awhile!*' Huneefa's face, turned to the northward, worked horribly, and it was as though voices from the ceiling answered her.

Hurree Babu returned to his notebook, balanced on the window-sill, but his hand shook. Huneefa, in some sort of drugged ecstasy, wrenched herself to and fro as she sat cross-legged by Kim's still head, and called upon devil after devil, in the ancient order of the ritual, binding them to avoid the boy's every action.

'*With Him are the keys of the Secret Things! None knoweth them besides Himself. He knoweth that which is in the dry land and in the sea!*' Again broke out the unearthly whistling responses.

'I – I apprehend it is not at all malignant in its operation?' said the Babu, watching the throat-muscles quiver and jerk as Huneefa spoke with tongues. 'It – it is not likely that she has killed the boy? If so, I decline to be witness at the trial . . . What was the last hypothetical devil mentioned?'

'Babuji,' said Mahbub in the vernacular. 'I have no regard for the devils of Hind, but the Sons of Eblis are far otherwise, and whether they be *jumalee* [well-affected] or *jullalee* [terrible] they love not Kafirs.'

'Then you think I had better go?' said Hurree Babu, half rising. 'They are, of course, dematerialized phenomena. Spencer says –'

Huneefa's crisis passed, as these things must, in a paroxysm of howling, with a touch of froth at the lips. She lay spent and motionless beside Kim, and the crazy voices ceased.

'Wah! That work is done. May the boy be better for it; and Huneefa is surely a mistress of *dawut*. Help haul her aside, Babu. Do not be afraid.'

'How am I to fear the absolutely non-existent?' said Hurree Babu, talking English to reassure himself. It is an awful thing still to dread the magic that you contemptuously investigate – to collect folk-lore for the Royal Society with a lively belief in all Powers of Darkness.

Mahbub chuckled. He had been out with Hurree on the Road ere now. 'Let us finish the colouring,' said he. 'The boy is well protected if – if the Lords of the Air have ears to hear. I am a *Sufi* [free-thinker], but when one can get blind-sides of a woman, a stallion, or a devil, why go round to invite a kick? Set him upon the way, Babu, and see that old Red Hat does not lead him beyond our reach. I must get back to my horses.'

'All raight,' said Hurree Babu. 'He is at present curious spectacle.'

About third cockcrow, Kim woke after a sleep of thousands of years. Huneefa, in her corner, snored heavily, but Mahbub was gone.

'I hope you were not frightened,' said an oily voice at his elbow. 'I superintended entire operation, which was most interesting from ethnological point of view. It was high-class *dawut*.'

'Huh!' said Kim, recognizing Hurree Babu, who smiled ingratiatingly.

'And also I had honour to bring down from Lurgan your

present costume. I am not in the habit offeecially of carrying such gauds to subordinates, but' – he giggled – 'your case is noted as exceptional on the books. I hope Mr Lurgan will note my action.'

Kim yawned and stretched himself. It was good to turn and twist within loose clothes once again.

'What is this?' He looked curiously at the heavy duffle-stuff loaded with the scents of the far North.

'Oho! That is inconspicuous dress of *chela* attached to service of lamaistic lama. *Com*plete in every particular,' said Hurree Babu, rolling into the balcony to clean his teeth at a goglet. 'I am of opeenion it is not your old gentleman's precise releegion, but rather sub-variant of same. I have contributed rejected notes to *Asiatic Quarterly Review* on these subjects. Now it is curious that the old gentleman himself is totally devoid of releegiosity. He is not a dam' particular.'

'Do you know him?'

Hurree Babu held up his hand to show he was engaged in the prescribed rites that accompany tooth-cleaning and such things among decently bred Bengalis. Then he recited in English an Arya-Somaj prayer of a theistical nature, and stuffed his mouth with *pan* and betel.

'Oah yes. I have met him several times at Benares, and also at Buddh Gaya, to interrogate him on releegious points and devil-worship. He is pure agnostic – same as me.'

Huneefa stirred in her sleep, and Hurree Babu jumped nervously to the copper incense-burner, all black and discoloured in morning-light, rubbed a finger in the accumulated lamp-black and drew it diagonally across his face.

'Who has died in thy house?' asked Kim in the vernacular.

'None. But she may have the Evil Eye – that sorceress,' the Babu replied.

'What dost thou do now, then?'

'I will set thee on thy way to Benares, if thou goest thither, and tell thee what must be known by Us.'

'I go. At what hour runs the *te-rain*?' He rose to his feet,

looked round the desolate chamber and at the yellow-wax face
of Huneefa as the low sun stole across the floor. 'Is there
money to be paid that witch?'

'No. She has charmed thee against all devils and all dangers
– in the name of her devils. It was Mahbub's desire.' In
English: 'He is highly obsolete, *I* think, to indulge in such
supersteetion. Why, it is all ventri*lo*quy. Belly-speak – eh?'

Kim snapped his fingers mechanically to avert whatever
evil – Mahbub, he knew, meditated none – might have crept
in through Huneefa's ministrations; and Hurree giggled once
more. But as he crossed the room he was careful not to step in
Huneefa's blotched, squat shadow on the boards. Witches –
when their time is on them – can lay hold of the heels of a
man's soul if he does that.

'Now you must well listen,' said the Babu when they were
in the fresh air. 'Part of these ceremonies which we witnessed
they include supply of effeecient amulet to those of our
Department. If you feel in your neck you will find one small
silver amulet, verree cheap. That is *ours*. Do you understand?'

'Oah yes, *hawa-dilli* [a heart-lifter],' said Kim, feeling at his
neck.

'Huneefa she makes them for two rupees twelve annas with
– oh, all sorts of exorcisms. They are quite common, except
they are partially black enamel, and there is a paper inside
each one full of names of local saints and such things. *Thatt* is
Huneefa's look-out, you see? Huneefa makes them onlee for
us, but in case she does not, when we get them we put in,
before issue, one small piece of turquoise. Mr Lurgan he gives
them. There is no other source of supply; but it was me
invented all this. It is strictly unoffeecial of course, but
convenient for subordinates. Colonel Creighton he does not
know. He is European. The turquoise is wrapped in the paper
... Yes, that is road to railway station ... Now suppose you go
with the lama, or with me, I hope, some day, or with
Mahbub. Suppose we get into a dam'-tight place. I am a
fearful man – most fearful – but I tell you I have been in

dam'-tight places more than hairs on my head. You say: "I am Son of the Charm." Verree good.'

'I do not understand quite. We must not be heard talking English here.'

'That is all raight. I am only Babu showing off my English to you. All we Babus talk English to show off,' said Hurree, flinging his shoulder-cloth jauntily. 'As I was about to say, "Son of the Charm" means that you may be member of the *Sat Bhai* – the Seven Brothers, which is Hindi *and* Tantric. It is popularly supposed to be extinct Society, but I have written notes to show it is still extant. You see, it is all my invention. Verree good. *Sat Bhai* has many members, and perhaps before they jolly-well-cut-your-throat they may give you just a chance of life. That is useful, anyhow. And moreover, these foolish natives – if they are not too excited – they always stop to think before they kill a man who says he belongs to any speecific organization. You see? You say then when you are in tight place, "I am Son of the Charm", and you get – perhaps – ah – your second wind. That is only in extreme instances, or to open negotiations with a stranger. Can you quite see? Verree good. But suppose now, I, or any one of the Department, come to you dressed quite different. You would not know me at all unless I choose, I bet you. Some day I will prove it. I come as Ladakhi trader – oh, anything – and I say to you: "You want to buy precious stones?" You say: "Do I look like a man who buys precious stones?" Then I say: "Even verree poor man can buy a turquoise or *tarkeean*."'

'That is *kichree* – vegetable curry,' said Kim.

'Of course it is. You say: "Let me see the *tarkeean*." Then I say: "It was cooked by a woman, and perhaps it is bad for your caste." Then you say: "There is no caste when men go to – look for *tarkeean*." You stop a little between those words, "to – look". That is thee whole secret. The little stop before the words.'

Kim repeated the test-sentence.

'That is all right. Then I will show you my turquoise if

there is time, and then you know who I am, and then we exchange views and documents and those-all things. And so it is with any other man of us. We talk sometimes about turquoises and sometimes about *tarkeean*, but always with that little stop in the words. It is verree easy. First, "Son of the Charm", if you are in a tight place. Perhaps that may help you – perhaps not. Then what I have told you about the *tarkeean*, if you want to transact offeecial business with a strange man. Of course, at present, you have no offeecial business. You are – ah ha! – supernumerary on probation. Quite unique specimen. If you were Asiatic of birth you might be employed right off; but this half-year of leave is to make you de-Englishized, you see? The lama he expects you, because I have demi-offeecially informed him you have passed all your examinations, and will soon obtain Government appointment. Oh ho! You are on acting-allowance, you see: so if you are called upon to help Sons of the Charm mind you jolly-well try. Now I shall say good-bye, my dear fellow, and I hope you – ah – will come out top-side all raight.'

Hurree Babu stepped back a pace or two into the crowd at the entrance of Lucknow station and – was gone. Kim drew a deep breath and hugged himself all over. The nickel-plated revolver he could feel in the bosom of his sad-coloured robe, the amulet was on his neck; begging-gourd, rosary, and ghost-dagger (Mr Lurgan had forgotten nothing) were all to hand, with medicine, paint-box, and compass, and in a worn old purse-belt embroidered with porcupine-quill patterns lay a month's pay. Kings could be no richer. He bought sweet-meats in a leaf-cup from a Hindu trader, and ate them with glad rapture till a policeman ordered him off the steps.

Chapter 11

Give the man who is not made
      To his trade
Swords to fling and catch again,
Coins to ring and snatch again,
Men to harm and cure again,
Snakes to charm and lure again –
He'll be hurt by his own blade,
By his serpents disobeyed,
By his clumsiness bewrayed,
By the people mocked to scorn –
    So 'tis not with juggler born!
Pinch of dust or withered flower,
      Chance-flung fruit or borrowed staff,
Serve his need and shore his power,
      Bind the spell, or loose the laugh!
             But a man who, etc.
      The Juggler's Song, op. 15

FOLLOWED a sudden natural reaction.

'Now am I alone – all alone,' he thought. 'In all India is no one so alone as I! If I die today, who shall bring the news – and to whom? If I live and God is good, there will be a price upon my head, for I am a Son of the Charm – I, Kim.'

A very few white people, but many Asiatics, can throw themselves into a mazement as it were by repeating their own names over and over again to themselves, letting the mind go free upon speculation as to what is called personal identity. When one grows older, the power, usually, departs, but while it lasts it may descend upon a man at any moment.

'Who is Kim – Kim – Kim?'

He squatted in a corner of the clanging waiting-room, rapt from all other thoughts; hands folded in lap, and pupils contracted to pin-points. In a minute – in another half-second – he felt he would arrive at the solution of the tremendous puzzle; but here, as always happens, his mind dropped away from those heights with a rush of a wounded bird, and passing his hand before his eyes, he shook his head.

A long-haired Hindu *bairagi* [holy man], who had just bought a ticket, halted before him at that moment and stared intently.

'I also have lost it,' he said sadly. 'It is one of the Gates to the Way, but for me it has been shut many years.'

'What is the talk?' said Kim, abashed.

'Thou wast wondering there in thy spirit what manner of thing thy soul might be. The seizure came of a sudden. I know. Who should know but I? Whither goest thou?'

'Toward Kashi [Benares].'

'There are no Gods there. I have proved them. I go to Prayag [Allahabad] for the fifth time – seeking the Road to Enlightenment. Of what faith art thou?'

'I too am a Seeker,' said Kim, using one of the lama's pet words. 'Though' – he forgot his Northern dress for the moment – 'though Allah alone knoweth what I seek.'

The old fellow slipped the *bairagi*'s crutch under his armpit and sat down on a patch of ruddy leopard's skin as Kim rose at the call for the Benares train.

'Go in hope, little brother,' he said. 'It is a long road to the feet of the One; but thither do we all travel.'

Kim did not feel so lonely after this, and ere he had sat out twenty miles in the crowded compartment, was cheering his neighbours with a string of most wonderful yarns about his own and his master's magical gifts.

Benares struck him as a peculiarly filthy city, though it was pleasant to find how his cloth was respected. At least one-third of the population prays eternally to some group or other of the many million deities, and so reveres every sort of holy man. Kim was guided to the Temple of the Tirthankars, about a mile outside the city, near Sarnath, by a chance-met Punjabi farmer – a Kamboh from Jullundur-way who had appealed in vain to every God of his homestead to cure his small son, and was trying Benares as a last resort.

'Thou art from the North?' he asked, shouldering through

the press of the narrow, stinking streets much like his own pet bull at home.

'Ay, I know the Punjab. My mother was a *pahareen*, but my father came from Amritzar – by Jandiala,' said Kim, oiling his ready tongue for the needs of the Road.

'Jandiala – Jullundur? Oho! Then we be neighbours in some sort, as it were.' He nodded tenderly to the wailing child in his arms. 'Whom dost thou serve?'

'A most holy man at the Temple of the Tirthankars.'

'They are all most holy and – most greedy,' said the Jat with bitterness. 'I have walked the pillars and trodden the temples till my feet are flayed, and the child is no whit better. And the mother being sick too ... Hush, then, little one ... We changed his name when the fever came. We put him into girl's clothes. There was nothing we did not do, except – I said to his mother when she bundled me off to Benares she should have come with me – I *said* Sakhi Sarwar Sultan would serve us best. We know His generosity, but these down-country Gods are strangers.'

The child turned on the cushion of the huge corded arms and looked at Kim through heavy eyelids.

'And was it all worthless?' Kim asked, with easy interest.

'All worthless – all worthless,' said the child, lips cracking with fever.

'The Gods have given him a good mind, at least,' said the father proudly. 'To think he should have listened so cleverly. Yonder is thy Temple. Now I am a poor man – many priests have dealt with me – but my son is my son, and if a gift to thy master can cure him – I am at my very wits' end.'

Kim considered for a while, tingling with pride. Three years ago he would have made prompt profit on the situation and gone his way without a thought; but now, the very respect the Jat paid him proved that he was a man. Moreover, he had tasted fever once or twice already, and knew enough to recognize starvation when he saw it.

'Call him forth and I will give him a bond on my best yoke, so that the child is cured.'

Kim halted at the carved outer door of the temple. A white-clad Oswal banker from Ajmir, his sins of usury new wiped out, asked him what he did.

'I am *chela* to Teshoo Lama, an Holy One from Bhotiyal – within there. He bade me come. I wait. Tell him.'

'Do not forget the child,' cried the importunate Jat over his shoulder, and then bellowed in Punjabi: 'O Holy One – O disciple of the Holy One – O Gods above all the Worlds – behold affliction sitting at the gate!' That cry is so common in Benares that the passers never turned their heads.

The Oswal, at peace with mankind, carried the message into the darkness behind him, and the easy, uncounted Eastern minutes slid by; for the lama was asleep in his cell, and no priest would wake him. When the click of his rosary again broke the hush of the inner court where the calm images of the Arhats stand, a novice whispered, 'Thy *chela* is here,' and the old man strode forth, forgetting the end of that prayer.

Hardly had the tall figure shown in the doorway than the Jat ran before him, and, lifting up the child, cried: 'Look upon this, Holy One; and if the Gods will, he lives – he lives!'

He fumbled in his waist-belt and drew out a small silver coin.

'What is now?' The lama's eyes turned to Kim. It was noticeable he spoke far clearer Urdu than long ago, under Zam-Zammah; but the father would allow no private talk.

'It is no more than a fever,' said Kim. 'The child is not well fed.'

'He sickens at everything, and his mother is not here.'

'If it be permitted, I may cure, Holy One.'

'What! Have they made thee a healer? Wait here,' said the lama, and he sat down by the Jat upon the lowest step of the temple, while Kim, looking out of the corner of his eyes, slowly opened the little betel-box. He had dreamed dreams at school of returning to the lama as a Sahib – of chaffing the old man before he revealed himself – boy's dreams all. There was more drama in this abstracted, brow-puckered search through the tabloid-bottles, with a pause here and there for thought and a muttered invocation between whiles. Quinine he had in tablets, and dark brown meat-lozenges – beef most probably, but that was not *his* business. The little thing would not eat, but it sucked at a lozenge greedily, and said it liked the salt taste.

'Take then these six.' Kim handed them to the man. 'Praise the Gods, and boil three in milk; other three in water. After he has drunk the milk give him this' (it was the half of a quinine pill), 'and wrap him warm. Give him the water of the other three, and the other half of this white pill when he wakes. Meantime, here is another brown medicine that he may suck at on the way home.'

'Gods, what wisdom!' said the Kamboh, snatching.

It was as much as Kim could remember of his own treatment in a bout of autumn malaria – if you except the patter that he added to impress the lama.

'Now go! Come again in the morning.'

'But the price – the price,' said the Jat, and threw back his sturdy shoulders. 'My son is my son. Now that he will be whole again, how shall I go back to his mother and say I took help by the wayside and did not even give a bowl of curds in return?'

'They are alike, these Jats,' said Kim softly. 'The Jat stood on his dunghill and the King's elephants went by. "O driver," said he, "what will you sell those little donkeys for?" '

The Jat burst into a roar of laughter, stifled with apologies to the lama. 'It is the saying of my own country – the very talk of it. So are we Jats all. I will come tomorrow with the child; and the blessing of the Gods of the Homesteads – who are good little Gods – be on you both … Now, son, we grow strong again. Do not spit it out, little Princeling! King of my Heart, do not spit it out, and we shall be strong men, wrestlers and club-wielders, by morning.'

He moved away, crooning and mumbling. The lama turned to Kim, and all the loving old soul of him looked out through his narrow eyes.

'To heal the sick is to acquire merit; but first one gets knowledge. That was wisely done, O Friend of all the World.'

'I was made wise by thee, Holy One,' said Kim, forgetting the little play just ended; forgetting St Xavier's; forgetting his white blood; forgetting even the Great Game as he stooped, Mohammedan-fashion, to touch his master's feet in the dust of the Jain temple. 'My teaching I owe to thee. I have eaten thy bread three years. My time is finished. I am loosed from the schools. I come to thee.'

'Herein is my reward. Enter! Enter! And is all well?' They passed to the inner court, where the afternoon sun sloped golden across. 'Stand that I may see. So!' He peered critically. 'It is no longer a child, but a man, ripened in wisdom, walking as a physician. I did well – I did well when I gave thee up to the armed men on that black night. Dost thou remember our first day under Zam-Zammah?'

'Ay,' said Kim. 'Dost thou remember when I leapt off the carriage the first day I went to –'

'The Gates of Learning? Truly. And the day that we ate the cakes together at the back of the river by Nucklao. Aha! Many times hast thou begged for me, but that day I begged for thee.'

'Good reason,' quoth Kim. 'I was then a scholar in the Gates of Learning, and attired as a Sahib. Do not forget, Holy One,' he went on playfully. 'I am still a Sahib – by thy favour.'

'True. And a Sahib in most high esteem. Come to my cell, *chela*.'

'How is that known to thee?'

The lama smiled. 'First by means of letters from the kindly priest whom we met in the camp of armed men; but he is now gone to his own country, and I sent the money to his brother.' Colonel Creighton, who had succeeded to the trusteeship when Father Victor went to England with the Mavericks, was hardly the Chaplain's brother. 'But I do not well understand Sahibs' letters. They must be interpreted to me. I chose a surer way. Many times when I returned from my Search to this Temple, which has always been a nest to me, there came one seeking Enlightenment – a man from Leh – that had been, he said, a Hindu, but wearied of all those Gods.' The lama pointed to the Arhats.

'A fat man?' said Kim, a twinkle in his eye.

'Very fat; but I perceived in a little his mind was wholly given up to useless things – such as devils and charms and the form and fashion of our tea-drinkings in the monasteries, and by what road we initiated the novices. A man abounding in questions; but he was a friend of thine, *chela*. He told me that thou wast on the road to much honour as a scribe. And I see thou art a physician.'

'Yes, that am I – a scribe, when I am a Sahib, but it is set aside when I come as thy disciple. I have accomplished the years appointed for a Sahib.'

'As it were a novice?' said the lama, nodding his head. 'Art thou freed from the schools? I would not have thee unripe.'

'I am all free. In due time I take service under the Government as a scribe –'

'Not as a warrior. That is well.'

'But first I come to wander – with thee. Therefore I am here. Who begs for thee, these days?' he went on quickly. The ice was thin.

'Very often I beg myself; but, as thou knowest, I am seldom here, except when I come to look again at my disciple. From one end to another of Hind have I travelled afoot and in the *te-rain*. A great and a wonderful land! But here, when I put in, is as though I were in my own Bhotiyal.'

He looked round the little clean cell complacently. A low cushion gave him a seat, on which he had disposed himself in the cross-legged attitude of the Bodhisat emerging from meditation; a black teak-wood table, not twenty inches high, set with copper tea-cups, was before him. In one corner stood a tiny altar, also of heavily carved teak, bearing a copper-gilt image of the seated Buddha and fronted by a lamp, an incense-holder, and a pair of copper flower-pots.

'The Keeper of the Images in the Wonder House acquired

merit by giving me these a year since,' he said, following Kim's eye. 'When one is far from one's own land such things carry remembrance; and we must reverence the Lord for that He showed the Way. See!' He pointed to a curiously-built mound of coloured rice crowned with a fantastic metal ornament. 'When I was Abbot in my own place – before I came to better knowledge – I made that offering daily. It is the Sacrifice of the Universe to the Lord. Thus do we of Bhotiyal offer all the world daily to the Excellent Law. And I do it even now, though I know that the Excellent One is beyond all pinchings and pattings.' He snuffed from his gourd.

'It is well done, Holy One,' Kim murmured, sinking at ease on the cushions, very happy and rather tired.

'And also,' the old man chuckled, 'I write pictures of the Wheel of Life. Three days to a picture. I was busied on it – or it may be I shut my eyes a little – when they brought word of thee. It is good to have thee here: I will show thee my art – not for pride's sake, but because thou must learn. The Sahibs have not all this world's wisdom.'

He drew from under the table a sheet of strangely scented yellow Chinese paper, the brushes, and slab of Indian ink. In cleanest, severest outline he had traced the Great Wheel with its six spokes, whose centre is the conjoined Hog, Snake, and Dove (Ignorance, Anger, and Lust), and whose compartments are all the Heavens and Hells, and all the chances of human life. Men say that the Bodhisat Himself first drew it with grains of rice upon dust, to teach His disciples the cause of things. Many ages have crystallized it into a most wonderful convention crowded with hundreds of little figures whose every line carries a meaning. Few can translate the picture-parable; there are not twenty in all the world who can draw it surely without a copy: of those who can both draw and expound are but three.

'I have a little learned to draw,' said Kim. 'But this is a marvel beyond marvels.'

'I have written it for many years,' said the lama. 'Time was when I could write it all between one lamp-lighting and the next. I will teach thee the art – after due preparation; and I will show thee the meaning of the Wheel.'

'We take the Road, then?'

'The Road and our Search. I was but waiting for thee. It was made plain to me in a hundred dreams – notably one that came upon the night of the day that the Gates of Learning first shut – that without thee I should never find my River. Again and again, as thou knowest, I put this from me, fearing an illusion. Therefore I would not take thee with me that day at Lucknow, when we ate the cakes. I would not take thee till the time was ripe and auspicious. From the Hills to the Sea, from the Sea to the Hills have I gone, but it was vain. Then I remembered the *Jâtaka*.'

He told Kim the story of the elephant with the leg-iron, as he had told it so often to the Jain priests.

'Further testimony is not needed,' he ended serenely. 'Thou wast sent for an aid. That aid removed, my Search came to naught. Therefore we will go out again together, and our Search is sure.'

'Whither go we?'

'What matters, Friend of all the World? The Search, I say, is sure. If need be, the River will break from the ground before us. I acquired merit when I sent thee to the Gates of Learning, and gave thee the jewel that is Wisdom. Thou didst return, I saw even now, a follower of Sakyamuni, the Physician, whose altars are many in Bhotiyal. It is sufficient. We are together, and all things are as they were – Friend of all the World – Friend of the Stars – my *chela*!'

Then they talked of matters secular; but it was noticeable that the lama never demanded any details of life at St Xavier's, nor showed the faintest curiosity as to the manners and customs of Sahibs. His mind moved all in the past, and he revived every step of their wonderful first journey together, rubbing his hands and chuckling, till it pleased him to curl himself up into the sudden sleep of old age.

Kim watched the last dusty sunshine fade out of the court,

and played with his ghost-dagger and rosary. The clamour of
Benares, oldest of all earth's cities awake before the Gods, day
and night, beat round the walls as the sea's roar round a
breakwater. Now and again, a Jain priest crossed the court,
with some small offering to the images, and swept the path
about him lest by chance he should take the life of a living
thing. A lamp twinkled, and there followed the sound of a
prayer. Kim watched the stars as they rose one after another
in the still, sticky dark, till he fell asleep at the foot of the altar.
That night he dreamed in Hindustani, with never an English
word . . .

'Holy One, there is the child to whom we gave the
medicine,' he said, about three o'clock in the morning, when
the lama, also waking from dreams, would have fared forth on
pilgrimage. 'The Jat will be here at the light.'

'I am well answered. In my haste I would have done a
wrong.' He sat down on the cushions and returned to his
rosary. 'Surely old folk are as children,' he said pathetically.
'They desire a matter – behold, it must be done at once, or
they fret and weep! Many times when I was upon the Road I
have been ready to stamp with my feet at the hindrance of an
ox-cart in the way, or a mere cloud of dust. It was not so when
I was a man – a long time ago. None the less it is wrongful – '

'But thou art indeed old, Holy One.'

'The thing was done. A Cause was put out into the world,
and, old or young, sick or sound, knowing or unknowing, who
can rein in the effect of that Cause? Does the Wheel hang still
if a child spin it – or a drunkard? *Chela*, this is a great and a
terrible world.'

'I think it good,' Kim yawned. 'What is there to eat? I have
not eaten since yesterday even.'

'I had forgotten thy need. Yonder is good Bhotiyal tea and
cold rice.'

'We cannot walk far on such stuff.' Kim felt all the
European's lust for flesh-meat, which is not accessible in a
Jain temple. Yet, instead of going out at once with the
begging-bowl, he stayed his stomach on slabs of cold rice till

the full dawn. It brought the farmer, voluble, stuttering with gratitude.

'In the night the fever broke and the sweat came,' he cried. 'Feel here his skin is fresh and new! He esteemed the salt lozenges, and took milk with greed.' He drew the cloth from the child's face, and it smiled sleepily at Kim. A little knot of Jain priests, silent but all-observant, gathered by the temple door. They knew, and Kim knew that they knew, how the old lama had met his disciple. Being courteous folk, they had not obtruded themselves overnight by presence, word, or gesture. Wherefore Kim repaid them as the sun rose.

'Thank the Gods of the Jains, brother,' he said, not knowing how those Gods were named. 'The fever is indeed broken.'

'Look! See!' The lama beamed in the background upon his hosts of three years. 'Was there ever such a *chela*? He follows our Lord the Healer.'

Now the Jains officially recognize all the Gods of the Hindu creed, as well as the Lingam and the Snake. They wear the Brahminical thread; they adhere to every claim of Hindu caste-law. But, because they knew and loved the lama, because he was an old man, because he sought the Way, because he was their guest, and because he collogued long of nights with the head-priest – as free-thinking a metaphysician as ever split one hair into seventy – they murmured assent.

'Remember,' – Kim bent over the child – 'this trouble may come again.'

'Not if thou hast the proper spell,' said the father.

'But in a little while we go away.'

'True,' said the lama to all the Jains. 'We go now together upon the Search whereof I have often spoken. I waited till my *chela* was ripe. Behold him! We go North. Never again shall I look upon this place of my rest, O people of good will.'

'But I am not a beggar.' The cultivator rose to his feet, clutching the child.

'Be still. Do not trouble the Holy One,' a priest cried.

'Go,' Kim whispered. 'Meet us again under the big railway

bridge, and for the sake of all the Gods of our Punjab, bring food – curry, pulse, cakes fried in fat, and sweetmeats. Specially sweetmeats. Be swift!'

The pallor of hunger suited Kim very well as he stood, tall and slim, in his sand-coloured, sweeping robes, one hand on his rosary and the other in the attitude of benediction, faithfully copied from the lama. An English observer might have said that he looked rather like the young saint of a stained-glass window, whereas he was but a growing lad faint with emptiness.

Long and formal were the farewells, thrice ended and thrice renewed. The Seeker – he who had invited the lama to that haven from far-away Tibet, a silver-faced, hairless ascetic – took no part in it, but meditated, as always, alone among the images. The others were very human; pressing small comforts upon the old man – a betel-box, a fine new iron pencase, a food-bag, and such-like – warning him against the dangers of the world without, and prophesying a happy end to the Search. Meantime Kim, lonelier than ever, squatted on the steps, and swore to himself in the language of St Xavier's.

'But it is my own fault,' he concluded. 'With Mahbub, I ate Mahbub's bread, or Lurgan Sahib's. At St Xavier's, three meals a day. Here I must jolly-well look out for myself. Besides, I am not in good training. *How* I could eat a plate of beef now! ... Is it finished, Holy One?'

The lama, both hands raised, intoned a final blessing in ornate Chinese. 'I must lean on thy shoulder,' said he, as the temple gates closed. 'We grow stiff, I think.'

The weight of a six-foot man is not light to steady through miles of crowded streets, and Kim, loaded down with bundles and packages for the way, was glad to reach the shadow of the railway bridge.

'Here we eat,' he said resolutely, as the Kamboh, blue-robed and smiling, hove in sight, a basket in one hand and the child in the other.

'Fall to, Holy Ones!' he cried from fifty yards. (They were by the shoal under the first bridge-span, out of sight of hungry priests.) 'Rice and good curry, cakes all warm and well scented with *hing* [asafoetida], curds and sugar. King of my fields,' – this to the small son – 'let us show these holy men that we Jats of Jullundur can pay a service ... I had heard the Jains would eat nothing that they had not cooked, but truly' – he looked away politely over the broad river – 'where there is no eye there is no caste.'

'And we,' said Kim, turning his back and heaping a leafplatter for the lama, 'are beyond all castes.'

They gorged themselves on the good food in silence. Nor till he had licked the last of the sticky sweetstuff from his little finger did Kim note that the Kamboh too was girt for travel.

'If our roads lie together,' he said roughly, 'I go with thee. One does not often find a worker of miracles, and the child is still weak. But *I* am not altogether a reed.' He picked up his *lathi* – a five-foot male-bamboo ringed with bands of polished iron – and flourished it in the air. 'The Jats are called quarrelsome, but that is not true. Except when we are crossed, we are like our own buffaloes.'

'So be it,' said Kim. 'A good stick is a good reason.'

The lama gazed placidly up-stream, where in long, smudged perspective the ceaseless columns of smoke go up from the burning-ghats by the river. Now and again, despite all municipal regulations, the fragment of a half-burned body bobbed by on the full current.

'But for thee,' said the Kamboh to Kim, drawing the child into his hairy breast, 'I might today have gone thither – with this one. The priests tell us that Benares is holy – which none doubt – and desirable to die in. But I do not know their Gods, and they ask for money; and when one has done one worship a shaved-head vows it is of none effect except one do another. Wash here! Wash there! Pour, drink, lave, and scatter flowers – but always pay the priests. No, the Punjab for me, and the soil of the Jullundur-*doab* for the best soil in it.'

'I have said many times – in the Temple, I think – that if need be, the River will open at our feet. We will therefore go North,' said the lama, rising. 'I remember a pleasant place, set

about with fruit-trees, where one can walk in meditation –
and the air is cooler there. It comes from the Hills and the
snow of the Hills.'

'What is the name?' said Kim.

'How should I know? Didst thou not – no, that was after
the Army rose out of the earth and took thee away. I abode
there in meditation in a room against the dovecot – except
when she talked eternally.'

'Oho! the woman from Kulu. That is by Saharunpore.'
Kim laughed.

'How does the spirit move thy master? Does he go afoot,
for the sake of past sins?' the Jat demanded cautiously. 'It is a
far cry to Delhi.'

'No,' said Kim. 'I will beg a *tikkut* for the *te-rain*.' One does
not own to the possession of money in India.

'Then, in the name of the Gods, let us take the fire-
carriage. My son is best in his mother's arms. The Government has brought on us many taxes, but it gives us one good
thing – the *te-rain* that joins friends and unites the anxious. A
wonderful matter is the *te-rain*.'

They all piled into it a couple of hours later, and slept
through the heat of the day. The Kamboh plied Kim with ten
thousand questions as to the lama's walk and work in life, and
received some curious answers. Kim was content to be where
he was, to look out upon the flat North-Western landscape,
and to talk to the changing mob of fellow-passengers. Even
today, tickets and ticket-clipping are dark oppression to
Indian rustics. They do not understand why, when they have
paid for a magic piece of paper, strangers should punch great
pieces out of the charm. So, long and furious are the debates
between travellers and Eurasian ticket-collectors. Kim
assisted at two or three with grave advice, meant to darken
counsel and to show off his wisdom before the lama and the
admiring Kamboh. But at Somna Road the Fates sent him a
matter to think upon. There tumbled into the compartment,
as the train was moving off, a mean, lean little person – a
Mahratta, so far as Kim could judge by the cock of the tight

turban. His face was cut, his muslin upper-garment was badly torn, and one leg was bandaged. He told them that a country-cart had upset and nearly slain him: he was going to Delhi, where his son lived. Kim watched him closely. If, as he asserted, he had been rolled over and over on the earth, there should have been signs of gravel-rash on the skin. But all his injuries seemed clean cuts, and a mere fall from a cart could not cast a man into such extremity of terror. As, with shaking fingers, he knotted up the torn cloth about his neck he laid bare an amulet of the kind called a keeper-up of the heart. Now, amulets are common enough, but they are not generally strung on square-plaited copper wire, and still fewer amulets bear black enamel on silver. There were none except the Kamboh and the lama in the compartment, which, luckily, was of an old type with solid ends. Kim made as to scratch in his bosom, and thereby lifted his own amulet. The Mahratta's face changed altogether at the sight, and he disposed the amulet fairly on his breast.

'Yes,' he went on to the Kamboh, 'I was in haste, and the cart, driven by a bastard, bound its wheel in a water-cut, and besides the harm done to me there was lost a full dish of *tarkeean*. I was not a Son of the Charm [a lucky man] that day.'

'That was a great loss,' said the Kamboh, withdrawing interest. His experience of Benares had made him suspicious.

'Who cooked it?' said Kim.

'A woman.' The Mahratta raised his eyes.

'But all women can cook *tarkeean*,' said the Kamboh. 'It is a good curry, as I know.'

'Oh yes, it is a good curry,' said the Mahratta.

'And cheap,' said Kim. 'But what about caste?'

'Oh, there is no caste where men go to – look for *tarkeean*,' the Mahratta replied, in the prescribed cadence. 'Of whose service art thou?'

'Of the service of this Holy One.' Kim pointed to the happy, drowsy lama, who woke with a jerk at the well-loved word.

'Ah, he was sent from Heaven to aid me. He is called the Friend of all the World. He is also called the Friend of the Stars. He walks as a physician – his time being ripe. Great is his wisdom.'

'And a Son of the Charm,' said Kim under his breath, as the Kamboh made haste to prepare a pipe lest the Mahratta should beg.

'And who is *that*?' the Mahratta asked, glancing sideways nervously.

'One whose child I – we have cured, who lies under great debt to us. – Sit by the window, man from Jullundur. Here is a sick one.'

'Humph! *I* have no desire to mix with chance-met wastrels. *My* ears are not long. *I* am not a woman wishing to overhear secrets.' The Jat slid himself heavily into a far corner.

'Art thou anything of a healer? I am ten leagues deep in calamity,' cried the Mahratta, picking up the cue.

'This man is cut and bruised all over. I go about to cure him,' Kim retorted. 'None interfered between thy babe and me.'

'I am rebuked,' said the Kamboh meekly. 'I am thy debtor for the life of my son. Thou art a miracle-worker – I know it.'

'Show me the cuts.' Kim bent over the Mahratta's neck, his heart nearly choking him; for this was the Great Game with a vengeance. 'Now, tell thy tale swiftly, brother, while I say a charm.'

'I come from the South, where my work lay. One of us they slew by the roadside. Hast thou heard?' Kim shook his head. He, of course, knew nothing of E23's predecessor, slain down South in the habit of an Arab trader. 'Having found a certain letter which I was sent to seek, I came away. I escaped from the city and ran to Mhow. So sure was I that none knew, I did not change my face. At Mhow a woman brought charge against me of theft of jewellery in that city which I had left. Then I saw the cry was out against me. I ran from Mhow by night, bribing the police, who had been bribed to hand me over without question to my enemies in the South. Then I lay in old Chitor city a week, a penitent in a temple, but I could not get rid of the letter which was my charge. I buried it under the Queen's Stone, at Chitor, in the place known to us all.'

Kim did not know, but not for worlds would he have broken the thread.

'At Chitor, look you, I was all in Kings' country; for Kotah to the east is beyond the Queen's law, and east again lie Jaipur and Gwalior. Neither love spies, and there is no justice. I was hunted like a wet jackal; but I broke through at Bandakui, where I heard there was a charge against me of murder in the city I had left – of the murder of a boy. They have both the corpse and the witnesses waiting.'

'But cannot the Government protect?'

'We of the Game are beyond protection. If we die, we die. Our names are blotted from the book. That is all. At Bandakui, where lives one of Us, I thought to slip the scent by changing my face, and so made me a Mahratta. Then I came to Agra, and would have turned back to Chitor to recover the letter. So sure I was I had slipped them. Therefore I did not send a *tar* [telegram] to any one saying where the letter lay. I wished the credit of it all.'

Kim nodded. He understood that feeling well.

'But at Agra, walking in the streets, a man cried a debt against me, and approaching with many witnesses, would hale me to the courts then and there. Oh, they are clever in the South! He recognized me as his agent for cotton. May he burn in Hell for it!'

'And wast thou?'

'O fool! I was the man they sought for the matter of the letter! I ran into the Fleshers' Ward and came out by the House of the Jew, who feared a riot and pushed me forth. I came afoot to Somna Road – I had only money for my *tikkut* to Delhi – and there, while I lay in a ditch with a fever, one sprang out of the bushes and beat me and cut me and searched me from head to foot. Within earshot of the *te-rain* it was!'

'Why did he not slay thee out of hand?'

'They are not so foolish. If I am taken in Delhi at the instance of lawyers, upon a proven charge of murder, my body is handed over to the State that desires it. I go back guarded, and then – I die slowly for an example to the rest of Us. The South is not my country. I run in circles – like a goat with one eye. I have not eaten for two days. I am marked' – he touched the filthy bandage on his leg – 'so that they will know me at Delhi.'

'Thou art safe in the *te-rain*, at least.'

'Live a year at the Great Game and tell me that again! The wires will be out against me at Delhi, describing every tear and rag upon me. Twenty – a hundred, if need be – will have seen me slay that boy. And thou art useless!'

Kim knew enough of native methods of attack not to doubt that the case would be deadly complete – even to the corpse. The Mahratta twitched his fingers with pain from time to time. The Kamboh in his corner glared sullenly; the lama was busy over his beads; and Kim, fumbling doctor-fashion at the man's neck, thought out his plan between invocations.

'Hast thou a charm to change my shape? Else I am dead. Five – ten minutes alone, if I had not been so pressed, and I might –'

'Is he cured yet, miracle-worker?' said the Kamboh jealously. 'Thou hast chanted long enough.'

'Nay. There is no cure for his hurts, as I see, except he sit for three days in the habit of a *bairagi*.' This is a common penance, often imposed on a fat trader by his spiritual teacher.

'One priest always goes about to make another priest,' was the retort. Like most grossly superstitious folk, the Kamboh could not keep his tongue from deriding his Church.

'Will thy son be a priest, then? It is time he took more of my quinine.'

'We Jats are all buffaloes,' said the Kamboh, softening anew.

Kim rubbed a finger-tip of bitterness on the child's

trusting little lips. 'I have asked for nothing,' he said sternly to the father, 'except food. Dost thou grudge me that? I go to heal another man. Have I thy leave – Prince?'

Up flew the man's huge paws in supplication. 'Nay – nay. Do not mock me thus.'

'It pleases me to cure this sick one. Thou shalt acquire merit by aiding. What colour ash is there in thy pipe-bowl? White. That is auspicious. Was there raw turmeric among thy food-stuffs?'

'I – I –'

'Open thy bundle!'

It was the usual collection of small oddments: bits of cloth, quack medicines, cheap fairings, a clothful of *atta* – greyish, rough-ground native flour – twists of down-country tobacco, tawdry pipe-stems, and a packet of curry-stuff, all wrapped in a quilt. Kim turned it over with the air of a wise warlock, muttering a Mohammedan invocation.

'This is wisdom I learned from the Sahibs,' he whispered to the lama; and here, when one thinks of his training at Lurgan's, he spoke no more than the truth. 'There is a great evil in this man's fortune, as shown by the Stars, which – which troubles him. Shall I take it away?'

'Friend of the Stars, thou hast done well in all things. Let it be at thy pleasure. Is it another healing?'

'Quick! Be quick!' gasped the Mahratta. 'The train may stop.'

'A healing against the shadow of death,' said Kim, mixing the Kamboh's flour with the mingled charcoal and tobacco ash in the red-earth bowl of the pipe. E23, without a word, slipped off his turban and shook down his long black hair.

'That is my food – priest,' the Jat growled.

'A buffalo in the temple! Hast thou dared to look even thus far?' said Kim. 'I must do mysteries before fools; but have a care for thine eyes. Is there a film before them already? I save the babe, and for return thou – oh, shameless!' The man flinched at the direct gaze, for Kim was wholly in earnest. 'Shall I curse thee, or shall I –' He picked up the outer cloth of the bundle and threw it over the bowed head. 'Dare so much as to think a wish to see, and – and – even I cannot save thee. Sit! Be dumb!'

'I am blind – dumb. Forbear to curse! Co – come, child; we will play a game of hiding. Do not, for my sake, look from under the cloth.'

'I see hope,' said E23. 'What is thy scheme?'

'This comes next,' said Kim, plucking the thin body-shirt. E23 hesitated, with all a North-West man's dislike of baring his body.

'What is caste to a cut throat?' said Kim, rending it to the waist. 'We must make thee a yellow Saddhu all over. Strip – strip swiftly, and shake thy hair over thine eyes while I scatter the ash. Now, a caste-mark on thy forehead.' He drew from his bosom the little Survey paint-box and a cake of crimson lake.

'Art thou only a beginner?' said E23, labouring literally for the dear life, as he slid out of his body-wrappings and stood clear in the loin-cloth while Kim splashed in a noble caste-mark on the ash-smeared brow.

'But two days entered to the Game, brother,' Kim replied. 'Smear more ash on the bosom.'

'Hast thou met – a physician of sick pearls?' He switched out his long, tight-rolled turban-cloth and, with swiftest hands, rolled it over and under about his loins into the intricate devices of a Saddhu's cincture.

'Hah! Dost thou know his touch, then? He was my teacher for a while. We must bare thy legs. Ash cures wounds. Smear it again.'

'I was his pride once, but thou art almost better. The Gods are kind to us! Give me *that*.'

It was a tin box of opium pills among the rubbish of the Jat's bundle. E23 gulped down a half handful. 'They are good against hunger, fear, and chill. And they make the eyes red too,' he explained. 'Now I shall have heart to play the Game. We lack only a Saddhu's tongs. What of the old clothes?'

Kim rolled them small, and stuffed them into the slack

folds of his tunic. With a yellow-ochre paint cake he smeared the legs and the breast, great streaks against the background of flour, ash, and turmeric.

'The blood on them is enough to hang thee, brother.'

'Maybe; but no need to throw them out of the window ... It is finished.' His voice thrilled with a boy's pure delight in the Game. 'Turn and look, O Jat!'

'The Gods protect us,' said the hooded Kamboh, emerging like a buffalo from the reeds. 'But – whither went the Mahratta? What hast thou done?'

Kim had been trained by Lurgan Sahib; E23, by virtue of his business, was no bad actor. In place of the tremulous, shrinking trader there lolled against the corner an all but naked, ash-smeared, ochre-barred, dusty-haired Saddhu, his swollen eyes – opium takes quick effect on an empty stomach – luminous with insolence and bestial lust, his legs crossed under him, Kim's brown rosary round his neck, and a scant yard of worn, flowered chintz on his shoulders. The child buried his face in his amazed father's arms.

'Look up, Princeling! We travel with warlocks, but they will not hurt thee. Oh, do not cry ... What is the sense of curing a child one day and killing him with fright the next?'

'The child will be fortunate all his life. He has seen a great healing. When I was a child I made clay men and horses.'

'I have made them too. Sír Banás, he comes in the night and makes them all alive at the back of our kitchen-midden,' piped the child.

'And so thou art not frightened at anything. Eh, Prince?'

'I was frightened because my father was frightened. I felt his arms shake.'

'Oh, chicken-man!' said Kim, and even the abashed Jat laughed. 'I have done a healing on this poor trader. He must forsake his gains and his account-books, and sit by the wayside three nights to overcome the malignity of his enemies. The Stars are against him.'

'The fewer money-lenders the better, say I; but, Saddhu or no Saddhu, he should pay for my stuff on his shoulders.'

'So? But that is thy child on thy shoulder – given over to the burning-ghat not two days ago. There remains one thing more. I did this charm in thy presence because need was great. I changed his shape and his soul. None the less, if, by any chance, O man from Jullundur, thou rememberest what thou hast seen, either among the elders sitting under the village tree, or in thine own house, or in company of thy priest when he blesses thy cattle, a murrain will come among the buffaloes, and a fire in thy thatch, and rats in the corn-bins, and the curse of our Gods upon thy fields that they may be barren before thy feet and after thy ploughshare.' This was part of an old curse picked up from a *fakir* by the Taksali Gate in the days of Kim's innocence. It lost nothing by repetition.

'Cease, Holy One! In mercy, cease!' cried the Jat. 'Do not curse the household. I saw nothing! I heard nothing! I am thy cow!' and he made to grab at Kim's bare foot beating rhythmically on the carriage floor.

'But since thou hast been permitted to aid me in the matter of a pinch of flour and a little opium and such trifles as I have honoured by using in my art, so will the Gods return a blessing,' and he gave it at length, to the man's immense relief. It was one that he had learned from Lurgan Sahib.

The lama stared through his spectacles as he had not stared at the business of disguisement.

'Friend of the Stars,' he said at last, 'thou hast acquired great wisdom. Beware that it do not give birth to pride. No man having the Law before his eyes speaks hastily of any matter which he has seen or encountered.'

'No – no – no, indeed,' cried the farmer, fearful lest the master should be minded to improve on the pupil. E23, with relaxed mouth, gave himself up to the opium that is meat, tobacco, and medicine to the spent Asiatic.

So, in a silence of awe and great miscomprehension, they slid into Delhi about lamp-lighting time.

Chapter 12

Who hath desired the Sea – the sight of salt-water unbounded?
The heave and the halt and the hurl and the crash of the comber
      wind-hounded?
The sleek-barrelled swell before storm – grey, foamless, enormous, and
      growing?
Stark calm on the lap of the Line – or the crazy-eyed hurricane
      blowing?
His Sea in no showing the same – his Sea and the same 'neath all
      showing –
    His Sea that his being fulfils?
So and no otherwise – so and no otherwise hill-men desire their Hills!
                      The Sea and the Hills.

'I HAVE found my heart again,' said E23, under cover of the platform's tumult. 'Hunger and fear make men dazed, or I might have thought of this escape before. I was right. They come to hunt for me. Thou hast saved my head.'

A group of yellow-trousered Punjab policemen, headed by a hot and perspiring young Englishman, parted the crowd about the carriages. Behind them, inconspicuous as a cat, ambled a small fat person who looked like a lawyer's tout.

'See the young Sahib reading from a paper. My description is in his hand,' said E23. 'They go carriage by carriage, like fisher-folk netting a pool.'

When the procession reached their compartment, E23 was counting his beads with a steady jerk of the wrist; while Kim jeered at him for being so drugged as to have lost the ringed fire-tongs which are the Saddhu's distinguishing mark. The lama, deep in meditation, stared straight before him; and the farmer, glancing furtively, gathered up his belongings.

'Nothing here but a parcel of holy-bolies,' said the Englishman aloud, and passed on amid a ripple of uneasiness; for native police mean extortion to the native all India over.

'The trouble now,' whispered E23, 'lies in sending a wire

as to the place where I hid that letter I was sent to find. I
cannot go to the *tar*-office in this guise.'

'Is it not enough I have saved thy neck?'

'Not if the work be left unfinished. Did never the healer of
sick pearls tell thee so? Comes another Sahib! Ah!'

This was a tallish, sallowish District Superintendent of
Police – belt, helmet, polished spurs and all – strutting and
twirling his dark moustache.

'What fools are these Police Sahibs!' said Kim genially.

E23 glanced up under his eyelids. 'It is well said,' he
muttered in a changed voice. 'I go to drink water. Keep my
place.'

He blundered out almost into the Englishman's arms, and
was bad-worded in clumsy Urdu.

Tum mut? You drunk? You mustn't bang about as though
Delhi station belonged to you, my friend.'

E23, not moving a muscle of his countenance, answered
with a stream of the filthiest abuse, at which Kim naturally
rejoiced. It reminded him of the drummer-boys and the
barrack-sweepers at Umballa in the terrible time of his first
schooling.

'My good fool,' the Englishman drawled. '*Nickle-jao!* Go
back to your carriage.'

Step by step, withdrawing deferentially, and dropping his
voice, the yellow Saddhu clomb back to the carriage, cursing
the D.S.P. to remotest posterity by – here Kim almost
jumped – by the curse of the Queen's Stone, by the writing
under the Queen's Stone, and by an assortment of Gods with
wholly new names.

'I don't know what you're saying,' – the Englishman
flushed angrily – 'but it's some piece of blasted impertinence.
Come out of that!'

E23, affecting to misunderstand, gravely produced his
ticket, which the Englishman wrenched angrily from his
hand.

'Oh, *zoolum*! What oppression!' growled the Jat from his

corner. 'All for the sake of a jest too.' He had been grinning at the freedom of the Saddhu's tongue. 'Thy charms do not work well today, Holy One!'

The Saddhu followed the policeman, fawning and supplicating. The ruck of passengers, busy with their babies and their bundles, had not noticed the affair. Kim slipped out behind him; for it flashed through his head that he had heard this angry, stupid Sahib discoursing loud personalities to an old lady near Umballa three years ago.

'It is well,' the Saddhu whispered, jammed in the calling, shouting, bewildered press – a Persian greyhound between his feet and a cageful of yelling hawks under charge of a Rajput falconer in the small of his back. 'He has gone now to send word of the letter which I hid. They told me he was in Peshawur. I might have known that he is like the crocodile – always at the other ford. He has saved me from present calamity, but I owe my life to thee.'

'Is he also one of Us?' Kim ducked under a Mewar cameldriver's greasy armpit and cannoned off a covey of jabbering Sikh matrons.

'Not less than the greatest. We are both fortunate! I will make report to him of what thou hast done. I am safe under his protection.'

He bored through the edge of the crowd besieging the carriages, and squatted by the bench near the telegraph-office.

'Return, or they take thy place! Have no fear for the work, brother – or my life. Thou hast given me breathing-space, and Strickland Sahib has pulled me to land. We may work together at the Game yet. Farewell!'

Kim hurried to his carriage: elated, bewildered, but a little nettled in that he had no key to the secrets about him.

'I am only a beginner at the Game, that is sure. *I* could not have leaped into safety as did the Saddhu. He knew it was darkest under the lamp. *I* could not have thought to tell news under pretence of cursing ... and how clever was the Sahib!

No matter, I saved the life of one ... Where is the Kamboh gone, Holy One?' he whispered, as he took his seat in the now crowded compartment.

'A fear gripped him,' the lama replied, with a touch of tender malice. 'He saw thee change the Mahratta to a Saddhu in the twinkling of an eye, as a protection against evil. That shook him. Then he saw the Saddhu fall sheer into the hands of the *polis* – all the effect of thy art. Then he gathered up his son and fled; for he said that thou didst change a quiet trader into an impudent bandier of words with the Sahibs, and he feared a like fate. Where is the Saddhu?'

'With the *polis*,' said Kim ... 'Yet I saved the Kamboh's child.'

The lama snuffed blandly.

'Ah, *chela*, see how thou art overtaken! Thou didst cure the Kamboh's child solely to acquire merit. But thou didst put a spell on the Mahratta with prideful workings – I watched thee – and with sidelong glances to bewilder an old old man and a foolish farmer: whence calamity and suspicion.'

Kim controlled himself with an effort beyond his years. Not more than any other youngster did he like to eat dirt or to be misjudged, but he saw himself in a cleft stick. The train rolled out of Delhi into the night.

'It is true,' he murmured. 'Where I have offended thee I have done wrong.'

'It is more, *chela*. Thou hast loosed an Act upon the world, and as a stone thrown into a pool so spread the consequences thou canst not tell how far.'

This ignorance was well both for Kim's vanity and for the lama's peace of mind, when we think that there was then being handed in at Simla a code-wire reporting the arrival of E23 at Delhi, and, more important, the whereabouts of a letter he had been commissioned to – abstract. Incidentally, an over-zealous policeman had arrested, on charge of murder done in a far southern State, a horribly indignant Ajmir cotton-broker, who was explaining himself to a Mr Strickland on Delhi platform, while E23 was paddling through byways into the locked heart of Delhi city. In two hours several telegrams had reached the angry minister of a southern State reporting that all trace of a somewhat bruised Mahratta had been lost; and by the time the leisurely train halted at Saharunpore the last ripple of the stone Kim had helped to heave was lapping against the steps of a mosque in far-away Roum – where it disturbed a pious man at prayers.

The lama made his in ample form near the dewy bougainvillea-trellis near the platform, cheered by the clear sunshine and the presence of his disciple. 'We will put these things behind us,' he said, indicating the brazen engine and the gleaming track. 'The jolting of the *te-rain* – though a wonderful thing – has turned my bones to water. We will use clean air henceforward.'

'Let us go to the Kulu woman's house,' said Kim, and stepped forth cheerily under the bundles. Early morning Saharunporeway is clean and well scented. He thought of the other mornings at St Xavier's, and it topped his already thrice-heaped contentment.

'Where is this new haste born from? Wise men do not run about like chickens in the sun. We have come hundreds upon hundreds of *koss* already, and, till now, I have scarcely been alone with thee an instant. How canst thou receive instruction all jostled of crowds? How can I, whelmed by a flux of talk, meditate upon the Way?'

'Her tongue grows no shorter with the years, then?' the disciple smiled.

'Nor her desire for charms. I remember once when I spoke of the Wheel of Life' – the lama fumbled in his bosom for his latest copy – 'she was only curious about the devils that besiege children. She shall acquire merit by entertaining us – in a little while – at an after-occasion – softly, softly. Now we will wander loose-foot, waiting upon the Chain of Things. The Search is sure.'

So they travelled very easily across and among the broad bloomful fruit-gardens – by way of Aminabad, Sahaigunge, Akrola of the Ford, and little Phulesa – the line of the

Siwaliks always to the north, and behind them again the snows. After long, sweet sleep under the dry stars came the lordly, leisurely passage through a waking village – begging-bowl held forth in silence, but eyes roving in defiance of the Law from sky's edge to sky's edge. Then would Kim return soft-footed through the soft dust to his master under the shadow of a mango-tree or the thinner shade of a white Doon *siris*, to eat and drink at ease. At mid-day, after talk and a little wayfaring, they slept; meeting the world refreshed when the air was cooler. Night found them adventuring into new territory – some chosen village spied three hours before across the fat land, and much discussed upon the road.

There they told their tale – a new one each evening so far as Kim was concerned – and there were they made welcome, either by priest or headman, after the custom of the kindly East.

When the shadows shortened and the lama leaned more heavily upon Kim, there was always the Wheel of Life to draw forth, to hold flat under wiped stones, and with a long straw to expound cycle by cycle. Here sat the Gods on high – and they were dreams of dreams. Here was our Heaven and the world of the demi-Gods – horsemen fighting among the hills. Here were the agonies done upon the beasts, souls ascending or descending the ladder and therefore not to be interfered with. Here were the Hells, hot and cold, and the abodes of tormented ghosts. Let the *chela* study the troubles that come from over-eating – bloated stomach and burning bowels. Obediently, then, with bowed head and brown finger alert to follow the pointer, did the *chela* study; but when they came to the Human World, busy and profitless, that is just above the Hells, his mind was distracted; for by the roadside trundled the very Wheel itself, eating, drinking, trading, marrying, and quarrelling – all warmly alive. Often the lama made the living pictures the matter of his text, bidding Kim – too ready – note how the flesh takes a thousand shapes, desirable or detestable as men reckon, but in truth of no account either way; and how the stupid spirit, bond-slave to the Hog, the Dove, and the Serpent – lusting after betel-nut, a new yoke of oxen, women, or the favour of kings – is bound to follow the body through all the Heavens and all the Hells, and strictly round again. Sometimes a woman or a poor man, watching the ritual – it was nothing less – when the great yellow chart was unfolded, would throw a few flowers or a handful of cowries upon its edge. It sufficed these humble ones that they had met a Holy One who might be moved to remember them in his prayers.

'Cure them if they are sick,' said the lama, when Kim's sporting instincts woke. 'Cure them if they have fever, but by no means work charms. Remember what befell the Mahratta.'

'Then all Doing is evil?' Kim replied, lying out under a big tree at the fork of the Doon road, watching the little ants run over his hand.

'To abstain from action is well – except to acquire merit.'

'At the Gates of Learning we were taught that to abstain from action was unbefitting a Sahib. And I am a Sahib.'

'Friend of all the World,' – the lama looked directly at Kim – 'I am an old man – pleased with shows as are children. To those who follow the Way there is neither black nor white, Hind nor Bhotiyal. We be all souls seeking escape. No matter what thy wisdom learned among Sahibs, when we come to my River thou wilt be freed from all illusion – at my side. *Hai!* my bones ache for that River, as they ached in the *te-rain*; but my spirit sits above my bones, waiting. The Search is sure!'

'I am answered. Is it permitted to ask a question?'

The lama inclined his stately head.

'I ate thy bread for three years – as thou knowest. Holy One, whence came –?'

'There is much wealth, as men count it, in Bhotiyal,' the lama returned with composure. 'In my own place I have the illusion of honour. I ask for that I need. I am not concerned with the account. That is for my monastery. *Ai!* The black high seats in the monastery, and novices all in order!'

And he told stories, tracing with a finger in the dust, of the immense and sumptuous ritual of avalanche-guarded cathedrals; of processions and devil-dances; of the changing of monks and nuns into swine; of holy cities fifteen thousand feet in the air; of intrigue between monastery and monastery; of voices among the hills, and of that mysterious mirage that dances on dry snow. He spoke even of Lhassa and of the Dalai Lama, whom he had seen and adored.

Each long, perfect day rose behind Kim for a barrier to cut him off from his race and his mother-tongue. He slipped back to thinking and dreaming in the vernacular, and mechanically followed the lama's ceremonial observances at eating, drinking, and the like. The old man's mind turned more and more to his monastery as his eyes turned to the steadfast snows. His River troubled him nothing. Now and again, indeed, he would gaze long and long at a tuft or a twig, expecting, he said, the earth to cleave and deliver its blessing; but he was content to be with his disciple, at ease in the temperate wind that comes down from the Doon. This was not Ceylon, nor Buddh Gaya, nor Bombay, nor some grass-tangled ruins that he seemed to have stumbled upon two years ago. He spoke of those places as a scholar removed from vanity, as a Seeker walking in humility, as an old man, wise and temperate, illumining knowledge with brilliant insight. Bit by bit, disconnectedly, each tale called up by some wayside thing, he spoke of all his wanderings up and down Hind; till Kim, who had loved him without reason, now loved him for fifty good reasons. So they enjoyed themselves in high felicity, abstaining, as the Rule demands, from evil words, covetous desires; not over-eating, not lying on high beds, nor wearing rich clothes. Their stomachs told them the time, and the people brought them their food, as the saying is. They were lords of the villages of Aminabad, Sahaigunge, Akrola of the Ford, and little Phulesa, where Kim gave the soulless woman a blessing.

But news travels fast in India, and too soon shuffled across the crop-land, bearing a basket of fruits with a box of Kabul grapes and gilt oranges, a white-whiskered servitor – a lean, dry Oorya – begging them to bring the honour of their presence to his mistress, distressed in her mind that the lama had neglected her so long.

'Now do I remember' – the lama spoke as though it were a wholly new proposition. 'She is virtuous, but an inordinate talker.'

Kim was sitting on the edge of a cow's manger, telling stories to a village smith's children.

'She will only ask for another son for her daughter. I have not forgotten her,' he said. 'Let her acquire merit. Send word that we will come.'

They covered eleven miles through the fields in two days, and were overwhelmed with attentions at the end; for the old lady held a fine tradition of hospitality, to which she forced her son-in-law, who was under the thumb of his women-folk and bought peace by borrowing of the money-lender. Age had not weakened her tongue or her memory, and from a discreetly barred upper window, in the hearing of not less than a dozen servants, she paid Kim compliments that would have flung European audiences into unclean dismay.

'But thou art still the shameless beggar-brat of the *parao*,' she shrilled. 'I have not forgotten thee. Wash ye and eat. The father of my daughter's son is gone away awhile. So we poor women are dumb and useless.'

For proof, she harangued the entire household unsparingly till food and drink were brought; and in the evening – the smoke-scented evening, copper-dun and turquoise across the fields – it pleased her to order her palanquin to be set down in the untidy forecourt by smoky torchlight; and there, behind not too closely drawn curtains, she gossiped.

'Had the Holy One come alone, I should have received him otherwise; but with this rogue, who can be too careful?'

'Maharanee,' said Kim, choosing as always the amplest title, 'is it my fault that none other than a Sahib – a *polis*-Sahib – called the Maharanee whose face he –'

'Chutt! That was on the pilgrimage. When we travel – thou knowest the proverb.'

'Called the Maharanee a Breaker of Hearts and a Dispenser of Delights?'

'To remember that! It was true. So he did. That was in the time of the bloom of my beauty.' She chuckled like a contented parrot above the sugar lump. 'Now tell me of thy goings and comings – as much as may be without shame. How many maids, and whose wives, hang upon thine eyelashes? Ye hail from Benares? I would have gone there again this year, but my daughter – we have only two sons. Phaii! Such is the effect of these low plains. Now in Kulu men are elephants. But I would ask thy Holy One – stand aside, rogue – a charm against most lamentable windy colics that in mango-time overtake my daughter's eldest. Two years back he gave me a powerful spell.'

'Oh, Holy One!' said Kim, bubbling with mirth at the lama's rueful face.

'It is true. I gave her one against wind.'

'Teeth – teeth – teeth,' snapped the old woman.

'"Cure them if they are sick,"' Kim quoted relishingly, '"but by no means work charms. Remember what befell the Mahratta."'

'That was two Rains ago; she wearied me with her continual importunity.' The lama groaned as the Unjust Judge had groaned before him. 'Thus it comes – take note, my *chela* – that even those who would follow the Way are thrust aside by idle women. Three days through, when the child was sick, she talked to me.'

'*Arré!* and to whom else should I talk? The boy's mother knew nothing, and the father – in the nights of the cold weather it was – "Pray to the Gods," said he, forsooth, and turning over, snored!'

'I gave her the charm. What is an old man to do?'

'"To abstain from action is well – except to acquire merit."'

'Ah *chela*, if thou desertest me, I am all alone.'

'He found his milk-teeth easily at any rate,' said the old lady. 'But all priests are alike.'

Kim coughed severely. Being young, he did not approve of her flippancy. 'To importune the wise out of season is to invite calamity.'

'There is a talking *mynah*' – the thrust came back with the well-remembered snap of the jewelled fore-finger – 'over the stables which has picked up the very tone of the family priest. Maybe I forget honour to my guests, but if ye had seen *him* double his fists into his belly, which was like a half-grown gourd, and cry: "Here is the pain!" ye would forgive. I am half minded to take the *hakim*'s medicine. He sells it cheap, and certainly it makes him fat as Shiv's own bull. *He* does not deny remedies, but I doubted for the child because of the inauspicious colour of the bottles.'

The lama, under cover of the monologue, had faded out into the darkness towards the room prepared.

'Thou hast angered him, belike,' said Kim.

'Not he. He is wearied, and I forgot, being a grandmother. (None but a grandmother should ever oversee a child. Mothers are only fit for bearing.) Tomorrow, when he sees how my daughter's son is grown, he will write the charm. Then, too, he can judge of the new *hakim*'s drugs.'

'Who is the *hakim*, Maharanee?'

'A wanderer, as thou art, but a most sober Bengali from Dacca – a master of medicine. He relieved me of an oppression after meat by means of a small pill that wrought like a devil unchained. He travels about now, vending preparations of great value. He has even papers, printed in Angrezi, telling what things he has done for weak-backed men and slack women. He has been here four days; but hearing ye were coming (*hakims* and priests are snake and tiger the world over) he has, as I take it, gone to cover.'

While she drew breath after this volley, the ancient servant, sitting unrebuked on the edge of the torchlight, muttered: 'This house is a cattle-pound, as it were, for all charlatans and – priests. Let the boy stop eating mangoes . . . but who can argue with a grandmother?' He raised his voice respectfully: 'Sahiba, the *hakim* sleeps after his meat. He is in the quarters behind the dovecot.'

Kim bristled like an expectant terrier. To outface and down-talk a Calcutta-taught Bengali, a voluble Dacca drug-vendor, would be a good game. It was not seemly that the lama, and incidentally himself, should be thrown aside for such an one. He knew those curious bastard English advertisements at the backs of native newspapers. St Xavier's boys sometimes brought them in by stealth to snigger over among their mates; for the language of the grateful patient recounting his symptoms is most simple and revealing. The Oorya, not unanxious to play off one parasite against the other, slunk away towards the dovecot.

'Yes,' said Kim, with measured scorn. 'Their stock-in-trade is a little coloured water and a very great shamelessness. Their prey are broken-down kings and overfed Bengalis. Their profit is in children – who are not born.'

The old lady chuckled. 'Do not be envious. Charms are better, eh? *I* never gainsaid it. See that thy Holy One writes me a good amulet by the morning.'

'None but the ignorant deny' – a thick, heavy voice boomed through the darkness, as a figure came to rest squatting – 'None but the ignorant deny the value of charms. None but the ignorant deny the value of medicines.'

'A rat found a piece of turmeric. Said he: "I will open a grocer's shop,"' Kim retorted.

Battle was fairly joined now, and they heard the old lady stiffen to attention.

'The priest's son knows the names of his nurse and three Gods. Says he: "Hear me, or I will curse you by the three million Great Ones."' Decidedly this invisible had an arrow or two in his quiver. He went on: 'I am but a teacher of the alphabet. I have learned all the wisdom of the Sahibs.'

'The Sahibs never grow old. They dance and they play like children when they are grandfathers. A strong-backed breed,' piped the voice inside the palanquin.

'I have, too, our drugs which loosen humours of the head in hot and angry men. *Siná* well compounded when the moon stands in the proper House; yellow earths I have – *arplan* from China that makes a man renew his youth and astonish his household; saffron from Kashmir, and the best salep of Kabul. Many people have died before –'

'That I surely believe,' said Kim.

'They knew the value of my drugs. I do not give *my* sick the mere ink in which a charm is written, but hot and rending drugs which descend and wrestle with the evil.'

'Very mightily they do so,' sighed the old lady.

The voice launched into an immense tale of misfortune and bankruptcy, studded with plentiful petitions to the Government. 'But for my fate, which overrules all, I had been now in Government employ. I bear a degree from the great school at Calcutta – whither, maybe, the son of this House shall go.'

'He shall indeed. If our neighbour's brat can in a few years be made an F A' (First Arts – she used the English word, of which she had heard so often), 'how much more shall children clever as some that I know bear away prizes at rich Calcutta.'

'Never,' said the voice, 'have I seen such a child! Born in an auspicious hour, and – but for that colic which, alas! turning into black cholers, may carry him off like a pigeon – destined to many years, he is enviable.'

'*Hai mai!*' said the old lady. 'To praise children is inauspicious, or I could listen to this talk. But the back of the house is unguarded, and even in this soft air men think themselves to be men, and women we know ... The child's father is away too, and I must be *chowkedar* [watchman] in my old age. Up! Up! Take up the palanquin. Let the *hakim* and the young priest settle between them whether charms or medicine most avail. Ho! worthless people, fetch tobacco for the guests, and – round the homestead go I!'

The palanquin reeled off, followed by straggling torches and a horde of dogs. Twenty villages knew the Sahiba – her failings, her tongue, and her large charity. Twenty villages cheated her after immemorial custom, but no man would have stolen or robbed within her jurisdiction for any gift under heaven. None the less, she made great parade of her formal inspections, the riot of which could be heard half-way to Mussoorie.

Kim relaxed, as one augur must when he meets another. The *hakim*, still squatting, slid over his hookah with a friendly foot, and Kim pulled at the good weed. The hangers-on expected grave professional debate, and perhaps a little free doctoring.

'To discuss medicine before the ignorant is of one piece with teaching the peacock to sing,' said the *hakim*.

'True courtesy,' Kim echoed, 'is very often inattention.'

These, be it understood, were company-manners, designed to impress.

'Hi! I have an ulcer on my leg,' cried a scullion. 'Look at it!'

'Get hence! Remove!' said the *hakim*. 'Is it the habit of the place to pester honoured guests? Ye crowd in like buffaloes.'

'If the Sahiba knew –' Kim began.

'Ai! Ai! Come away. They are meat for our mistress. When her young Shaitan's colics are cured perhaps we poor people may be suffered to –'

'The mistress fed thy wife when thou wast in jail for breaking the money-lender's head. Who speaks against her?' The old servitor curled his white moustaches savagely in the young moonlight. '*I* am responsible for the honour of this house. Go!' and he drove the underlings before him.

Said the *hakim*, hardly more than shaping the words with his lips: 'How do you do, Mister O'Hara? I am jolly glad to see you again.'

Kim's hand clenched about the pipe-stem. Anywhere on the open road, perhaps, he would not have been astonished; but here, in this quiet backwater of life, he was not prepared for Hurree Babu. It annoyed him, too, that he had been hoodwinked.

'Ah ha! I told you at Lucknow – *resurgam* – I shall rise again and you shall not know me. How much did you bet – eh?'

He chewed leisurely upon a few cardamom seeds, but he breathed uneasily.

'But why come here, Babuji?'

'Ah! *Thatt* is the question, as Shakespeare hath it. I come to congratulate you on your extraordinary effeecient performance at Delhi. Oah! I tell you we are all proud of you. It was verree neat and handy. Our mutual friend, he is old friend of mine. He has been in some dam'-tight places. Now he will be in some more. He told me; I tell Mr Lurgan; and he is pleased you graduate so nicely. All the Department is pleased.'

For the first time in his life, Kim thrilled to the clean pride (it can be a deadly pitfall, none the less) of Departmental praise – ensnaring praise from an equal of work appreciated by fellow-workers. Earth has nothing on the same plane to compare with it. But, cried the Oriental in him, Babus do not travel far to retail compliments.

'Tell thy tale, Babu,' he said authoritatively.

'Oah, it is nothing. Onlee I was at Simla when the wire came in about what our mutual friend said he had hidden, and old Creighton –' He looked to see how Kim would take this piece of audacity.

'The Colonel Sahib,' the boy from St Xavier's corrected.

'*Of* course. He found me at a loose string, and I had to go down to Chitor to find that beastly letter. I do not like the South – too much railway travel; but I drew good travelling allowance. Ha! Ha! I meet our mutual at Delhi on the way back. He lies quiett just now, and says Saddhu-disguise suits him to the ground. Well, there I hear what you have done so well, so quickly, upon the instantaneous spur of the moment. I tell our mutual you take the bally bun, by Jove! It was splendid. I come to tell you so.'

'Umm!'

The frogs were busy in the ditches, and the moon slid to her setting. Some happy servant had gone out to commune with the night and to beat upon a drum. Kim's next sentence was in the vernacular.

'How didst thou follow us?'

'Oah. Thatt was nothing. I know from our mutual friend you go to Saharunpore. So I come on. Red Lamas are not inconspicuous persons. I buy myself my drug-box, and I am very good doctor really. I go to Akrola of the Ford, and hear all about you, and I talk here and talk there. All the common people know what you do. I knew when the hospitable old lady sent the *dooli*. They have great recollections of the old lama's visits here. I know old ladies cannot keep their hands from medicines. So I am a doctor, and – you hear my talk? *I* think it is verree good. My word, Mister O'Hara, they know about you and the lama for fifty miles – the common people. So I come. Do you mind?'

'Babuji,' said Kim, looking up at the broad, grinning face, 'I am a Sahib.'

'My dear Mister O'Hara –'

'And I hope to play the Great Game.'

'You are subordinate to me departmentally at present.'

'Then why talk like an ape in a tree? Men do not come after one from Simla and change their dress, for the sake of a few sweet words. I am not a child. Talk Hindi and let us get to the yolk of the egg. Thou art here – speaking not one word of truth in ten. Why art thou here? Give a straight answer.'

'That is so verree disconcerting of the Europeans, Mister O'Hara. You should know a heap better at your time of life.'

'But I want to know,' said Kim, laughing. 'If it is the Game, I may help. How can I do anything if you *bukh* [babble] all round the shop?'

Hurree Babu reached for the pipe, and sucked it till it guggled again.

'Now I will speak vernacular. You sit tight, Mister O'Hara ... It concerns the pedigree of a white stallion.'

'Still? That was finished long ago.'

'When everyone is dead the Great Game is finished. Not before. Listen to me till the end. There were Five Kings who prepared a sudden war three years ago, when thou wast given the stallion's pedigree by Mahbub Ali. Upon them, because of that news, and ere they were ready, fell our Army.'

'Ay – eight thousand men with guns. I remember that night.'

'But the war was not pushed. That is the Government custom. The troops were recalled because the Government believed the Five Kings were cowed; and it is not cheap to feed men among the high Passes. Hilás and Bunár – Rajahs with guns – undertook for a price to guard the Passes against all coming from the North. They protested both fear and friendship.' He broke off with a giggle into English: 'Of course, I tell you this unoffeecially to elucidate political situation, Mister O'Hara. Offeecially, I am debarred from criticizing any action of superiors. Now I go on. – This pleased the Government, anxious to avoid expense, and a bond was made for so many rupees a month that Hilás and Bunár should guard the Passes as soon as the State's troops were withdrawn. At that time – it was after we two met – I, who had been selling tea in Leh, became a clerk of accounts in the Army. When the troops were withdrawn, I was left behind to pay the coolies who made new roads in the Hills. This road-making was part of the bond between Bunár, Hilás, and the Government.'

'So? And then?'

'I tell you, it was jolly-beastly cold up there too, after summer,' said Hurree Babu confidentially. 'I was afraid these Bunár men would cut my throat every night for thee pay-chest. My native sepoy-guard, they laughed at me! By Jove! I was such a fearful man. Nevar mind thatt. I go on colloquially ... I send word many times that these two Kings were sold to the North; and Mahbub Ali, who was yet farther North, amply confirmed it. Nothing was done. Only my feet were frozen, and a toe dropped off. I sent word that the roads for which I was paying money to the diggers were being made for the feet of strangers and enemies.'

'For?'

'For the Russians. The thing was an open jest among the coolies. Then I was called down to tell what I knew by speech of tongue. Mahbub came South too. See the end! Over the Passes, this year after snow-melting' – he shivered afresh – 'come two strangers under cover of shooting wild goats. They bear guns, but they bear also chains and levels and compasses.'

'Oho! The thing gets clearer.'

'They are well received by Hilás and Bunár. They make great promises; they speak as the mouthpiece of a Kaisar with gifts. Up the valleys, down the valleys go they, saying, "Here is a place to build a breastwork; here can ye pitch a fort. Here can ye hold the road against an army" – the very roads for which I paid out the rupees monthly. The Government knows, but does nothing. The three other Kings, who were *not* paid for guarding the Passes, tell them by runner of the bad faith of Bunár and Hilás. When all the evil is done, look you – when these two strangers with the levels and the compasses make the Five Kings to believe that a great army will sweep the Passes tomorrow or the next day – Hill-people are all fools – comes the order to me, Hurree Babu, "Go North and see what those strangers do." I say to Creighton Sahib, "This is not a lawsuit, that we go about to collect evidence." ' Hurree returned to his English with a jerk: ' "By Jove," I said, "why the dooce do you not issue demi-offeecial orders to some brave man to poison them, for an example? It is, if you permit the observation, most reprehensible laxity on your part." And Colonel Creighton, he laughed at me! It is all your beastly English pride. You think no one dare conspire! That is all tommy-rott.'

Kim smoked slowly, revolving the business, so far as he understood it, in his quick mind.

'Then thou goest forth to follow the strangers?'

'No. To meet them. They are coming in to Simla to send down their horns and heads to be dressed at Calcutta. They are exclusively sporting gentlemen, and they are allowed

special faceelities by the Government. Of course, we always
do that. It is our British pride.'

'Then what is to fear from them?'

'By Jove, they are not black people. I can do all sorts of
things with black people, of course. They are Russians, and
highly unscrupulous people. I – I do not want to consort with
them without a witness.'

'Will they kill thee?'

'Oah, thatt is nothing. I am good enough Herbert Spencer-
ian, I trust, to meet little thing like death, which is all in my
fate, you know. But – but they may beat me.'

'Why?'

Hurree Babu snapped his fingers with irritation. 'Of *course*
I shall affeeliate myself to their camp in supernumerary
capacity as perhaps interpreter, or person mentally impotent
and hungree, or some such thing. And then I must pick
up what I can, I suppose. That is as easy for me as playing
Mister Doctor to the old lady. Onlee – onlee – you see, Mister
O'Hara, I am unfortunately Asiatic, which is serious detri-
ment in some respects. And *all*-so I am Bengali – a fearful
man.'

'God made the Hare and the Bengali. What shame?' said
Kim, quoting the proverb.

'It was process of Evolution, *I* think, from Primal Necessity, but the fact remains in all the *cui bono*. I am, oh, awfully
fearful! – I remember once they wanted to cut off my head on
the road to Lhassa. (No, I have never reached to Lhassa.) I sat
down and cried, Mister O'Hara, anticipating Chinese tor-
tures. I do not suppose these two gentlemen will torture me,
but I like to provide for possible contingency with European
assistance in emergency.' He coughed and spat out the
cardamoms. 'It is purely unoffeecial indent, to which you can
say "No, Babu". If you have no pressing engagement with
your old man – perhaps you might divert him; perhaps I can
seduce his fancies – I should like you to keep in Departmental
touch with me till I find those sporting coves. I have great

opeenion of you since I met my friend at Delhi. And also I will embody your name in my offeecial report when matter is finally adjudicated. It will be a great feather in your cap. That is why I come really.'

'Humph! The end of the tale, I think, is true; but what of the fore-part?'

'About the Five Kings? Oah! there is ever so much truth in it. A lots more than you would suppose,' said Hurree earnestly. 'You come – eh? I go from here straight into the Doon. It is verree verdant and painted meads. I shall go to Mussoorie – to good old Munsoorie Pahar, as the gentlemen and ladies say. Then by Rampur into Chini. That is the only way they can come. I do not like waiting in the cold, but we must wait for them. I want to walk with them to Simla. You see, one Russian is a Frenchman, and I know my French pretty well. I have friends in Chandernagore.'

'*He* would certainly rejoice to see the Hills again,' said Kim meditatively. 'All his speech these ten days past has been of little else. If we go together –'

'Oah! We can be quite strangers on the road, if your lama prefers. I shall just be four or five miles ahead. There is no hurry for Hurree – that is an Europe pun, ha! ha! – and you come after. There is plenty of time; they will plot and survey and map, of course. I shall go tomorrow, and you the next day, if you choose. Eh? You go think on it till morning. By Jove, it is near morning now.' He yawned ponderously, and with never a civil word lumbered off to his sleeping-place. But Kim slept little, and his thoughts ran in Hindustani:

'Well is the Game called great! I was four days a scullion at Quetta, waiting on the wife of the man whose book I stole. And that was part of the Great Game! From the South – God knows how far came up the Mahratta, playing the Great Game in fear of his life. Now I shall go far and far into the North playing the Great Game. Truly, it runs like a shuttle throughout all Hind. And my share and my joy' – he smiled to the darkness –'I owe to the lama here. Also to Mahbub Ali – also to Creighton Sahib, but chiefly to the Holy One. He is right – a great and a wonderful world – and I am Kim – Kim – Kim – alone – one person – in the middle of it all. But I will see these strangers with their levels and chains ...'

'What was the upshot of last night's babble?' said the lama, after his orisons.

'There came a strolling seller of drugs – a hanger-on of the Sahiba's. Him I abolished by arguments and prayers, proving that our charms are worthier than his coloured waters.'

'Alas, my charms! Is the virtuous woman still bent upon a new one?'

'Very strictly.'

'Then it must be written, or she will deafen me with her clamour.' He fumbled at his pencase.

'In the Plains,' said Kim, 'are always too many people. In the Hills, as I understand, there are fewer.'

'Oh! the Hills, and the snows upon the Hills.' The lama tore off a tiny square of paper fit to go in an amulet. 'But what dost thou know of the Hills?'

'They are very close.' Kim thrust open the door and looked at the long, peaceful line of the Himalayas flushed in morning-gold. 'Except in the dress of a Sahib, I have never set foot among them.'

The lama snuffed the wind wistfully.

'If we go North,' – Kim put the question to the waking sunrise – 'would not much mid-day heat be avoided by walking among the lower hills at least? ... Is the charm made, Holy One?'

'I have written the names of seven silly devils – not one of whom is worth a grain of dust in the eye. Thus do foolish women drag us from the Way!'

Hurree Babu came out from behind the dovecot, washing his teeth with ostentatious ritual. Full-fleshed, heavy-haunched, bull-necked, and deep-voiced, he did not look like 'a fearful man'. Kim signed almost imperceptibly that matters were in good train, and when the morning toilet was over, Hurree Babu, in flowery speech, came to do honour to the lama. They ate, of course, apart, and afterwards the old lady, more or less veiled behind a window, returned to the vital business of green-mango colics in the young. The lama's knowledge of medicine was, of course, sympathetic only. He believed that the dung of a black horse, mixed with sulphur, and carried in a snakeskin, was a sound remedy for cholera; but the symbolism interested him far more than the science. Hurree Babu deferred to these views with enchanting politeness, so that the lama called him a courteous physician. Huffee Babu replied that he was no more than an inexpert dabbler in the mysteries; but at least – he thanked the Gods therefore – he knew when he sat in the presence of a master. He himself had been taught by the Sahibs, who do not consider expense, in the lordly halls of Calcutta; but, as he was ever first to acknowledge, there lay a wisdom behind earthly wisdom – the high and lonely lore of meditation. Kim looked on with envy. The Hurree Babu of his knowledge – oily, effusive, and nervous – was gone; gone, too, was the brazen drug-vendor of overnight. There remained – polished, polite, attentive – a sober, learned son of experience and adversity, gathering wisdom from the lama's lips. The old lady confided to Kim that these rare levels were beyond her. She liked charms with plenty of ink that one could wash off in water, swallow, and be done with. Else what was the use of the Gods? She liked men and women, and she spoke of them – of kinglets she had known in the past; of her own youth and beauty; of the depredations of leopards and the eccentricities of love Asiatic; of the incidence of taxation, rack-renting, funeral ceremonies, her son-in-law (this by allusion, easy to be followed), the care of the young, and the age's lack of decency. And Kim, as interested in the life of this world as she soon to leave it, squatted with his feet under the hem of his robe, drinking all in, while the lama demolished one after another every theory of body-curing put forward by Hurree Babu.

At noon the Babu strapped up his brass-bound drug-box, took his patent-leather shoes of ceremony in one hand, a gay blue-and-white umbrella in the other, and set off northwards to the Doon, where, he said, he was in demand among the lesser kings of those parts.

'We will go in the cool of the evening, *chela*,' said the lama. 'That doctor, learned in physic and courtesy, affirms that the people among these lower hills are devout, generous, and much in need of a teacher. In a very short time – so says the *hakim* – we come to cool air and the smell of pines.'

'Ye go to the Hills? And by Kulu road? Oh, thrice happy!' shrilled the old lady. 'But that I am a little pressed with the care of the homestead I would take palanquin ... but that would be shameless, and my reputation would be cracked. Ho! Ho! I know the road – every march of the road I know. Ye will find charity throughout – it is not denied to the well-looking. I will give orders for provision. A servant to set you forth upon your journey? No ... Then I will at least cook ye good food.'

'What a woman is the Sahiba!' said the white-bearded Oorya, when a tumult rose by the kitchen quarters. 'She has never forgotten a friend: she has never forgotten an enemy in all her years. And her cookery – wah!' He rubbed his slim stomach.

There were cakes, there were sweetmeats, there was cold fowl stewed to rags with rice and prunes – enough to burden Kim like a mule.

'I am old and useless,' she said. 'None now love me – and none respect – but there are few to compare with me when I call on the Gods and squat to my cooking-pots. Come again, O people of good will. Holy One and disciple, come again. The room is always prepared; the welcome is always ready ... See the women do not follow thy *chela* too openly. *I* know the women of Kulu. Take heed, *chela*, lest he run away when he smells his Hills again ... *Hai!* Do not tilt the rice-bag upside down ... Bless the household, Holy One, and forgive thy servant her stupidities.'

She wiped her red old eyes on a corner of her veil, and clucked throatily.

'Women talk,' said the lama at last, 'but that is a woman's

infirmity. I gave her a charm. She is upon the Wheel and
wholly given over to the shows of this life, but none the less,
chela, she is virtuous, kindly, hospitable – of a whole and
zealous heart. Who shall say she does not acquire merit?'

'Not I, Holy One,' said Kim, reslinging the bountiful
provision on his shoulders. 'In my mind – behind my eyes – I
have tried to picture such an one altogether freed from the
Wheel – desiring nothing, causing nothing – a nun, as it
were.'

'And, O imp?' The lama almost laughed aloud.

'I cannot make the picture.'

'Nor I. But there are many, many millions of lives before
her. She will get wisdom a little, it may be, in each one.'

'And will she forget how to make stews with saffron upon
that road?'

'Thy mind is set on things unworthy. But she has skill. I
am refreshed all over. When we reach the lower hills I shall be
yet stronger. The *hakim* spoke truly to me this morn when he
said a breath from the snows blows away twenty years from
the life of a man. We will go up into the Hills – the high hills –
up to the sound of snow-waters and the sound of the trees –
for a little while. The *hakim* said that at any time we may
return to the Plains, for we do no more than skirt the pleasant
places. The *hakim* is full of learning; but he is in no way
proud. I spoke to him – when thou wast talking to the Sahiba
– of a certain dizziness that lays hold upon the back of my
neck in the night, and he said it rose from excessive heat – to
be cured by cool air. Upon consideration, I marvelled that I
had not thought of such a simple remedy.'

'Didst thou tell him of thy Search?' said Kim, a little
jealously. He preferred to sway the lama by his own speech –
not through the wiles of Hurree Babu.

'Assuredly. I told him of my dream, and of the manner by
which I had acquired merit by causing thee to be taught
wisdom.'

'Thou didst not say I was a Sahib?'

'What need? I have told thee many times we be but two

souls seeking escape. He said – and he is just herein – that the River of Healing will break forth even as I dreamed – at my feet, if need be. Having found the Way, seest thou, that shall free me from the Wheel, need I trouble to find a way about the mere fields of earth – which are illusion? That were senseless. I have my dreams, night upon night repeated; I have the *Jâtaka*; and I have thee, Friend of all the World. It was written in thy horoscope that a Red Bull on a green field – I have not forgotten – should bring thee to honour. Who but I saw that prophecy accomplished? Indeed, I was the instrument. Thou shalt find me my River, being in return the instrument. The Search is sure!'

He set his ivory-yellow face, serene and untroubled, towards the beckoning Hills; his shadow shouldering far before him in the dust.

Chapter 13

Who hath desired the Sea – the immense and contemptuous surges?
The shudder, the stumble, the swerve ere the star-stabbing bowsprit
      emerges –
The orderly clouds of the Trades and the ridged roaring sapphire
      thereunder –
Unheralded cliff-lurking flaws and the head-sails' low-volleying
      thunder?
His Sea in no wonder the same – his Sea and the same in each wonder –
      His Sea that his being fulfils?
So and no otherwise – so and no otherwise hill-men desire their hills!
                       The Sea and the Hills.

'WHO goes to the hills goes to his mother.'
They had crossed the Siwaliks and the half-tropical
Doon, left Mussoorie behind them, and headed north along
the narrow hill-roads. Day after day they struck deeper into
the huddled mountains, and day after day Kim watched the
lama return to a man's strength. Among the terraces of the
Doon he had leaned on the boy's shoulder, ready to profit by
wayside halts. Under the great ramp to Mussoorie he drew
himself together as an old hunter faces a well-remembered
bank, and where he should have sunk exhausted swung his
long draperies about him, drew a deep double-lungful of the
diamond air, and walked as only a hillman can. Kim, plains-
bred and plains-fed, sweated and panted astonished. 'This is
my country,' said the lama. 'Beside Such-zen, this is flatter
than a rice-field'; and with steady, driving strokes from the
loins he strode upwards. But it was on the steep downhill
marches, three thousand feet in three hours, that he went
utterly away from Kim, whose back ached with holding back,
and whose big toe was nigh cut off by his grass sandal-string.
Through the speckled shadow of the great deodar-forests;
through oak feathered and plumed with ferns; birch, ilex,
rhododendron, and pine, out on to the bare hillsides' slippery

sunburnt grass, and back into the woodlands' coolth again, till oak gave way to bamboo and palm of the valley, the lama swung untiring.

Glancing back in the twilight at the huge ridges behind him and the faint, thin line of the road whereby they had come, he would lay out, with a hillman's generous breadth of vision, fresh marches for the morrow; or, halting in the neck of some uplifted pass that gave on Spiti and Kulu, would stretch out his hands yearningly towards the high snows of the horizon. In the dawns they flared windy-red above stark blue, as Kedarnath and Badrinath – kings of that wilderness – took the first sunlight. All day long they lay like molten silver under the sun, and at evening put on their jewels again. At first they breathed temperately upon the travellers, winds good to meet when one crawled over some gigantic hog's-back, but in a few days, at a height of nine or ten thousand feet, those breezes bit; and Kim kindly allowed a village of hillmen to acquire merit by giving him a rough blanket-coat. The lama was mildly surprised that anyone should object to the knife-edged breezes which had cut the years off his shoulders.

'These are but the lower hills, *chela*. There is no cold till we come to the true Hills.'

'Air and water are good, and the people are devout enough, but the food is very bad,' Kim growled; 'and we walk as though we were mad – or English. It freezes at night, too.'

'A little, maybe; but only enough to make old bones rejoice in the sun. We must not always delight in soft beds and rich food.'

'We might at least keep to the road.'

Kim had all a plainsman's affection for the well-trodden track, not six feet wide, that snaked among the mountains; but the lama, being Tibetan, could not refrain from short cuts over spurs and the rims of gravel-strewn slopes. As he explained to his limping disciple, a man bred among mountains can prophesy the course of a mountain-road, and though low-lying clouds might be a hindrance to a short-cutting stranger, they made no earthly difference to a thoughtful man. Thus, after long hours of what would be reckoned very fair mountaineering in civilized countries, they would pant over a saddle-back, sidle past a few landslips, and drop through forest at an angle of forty-five on to the road again. Along their track lay the villages of the hill-folk – mud and earth huts, timbers now and then rudely carved with an axe – clinging like swallows' nests against the steeps, huddled on tiny flats half-way down a three-thousand-foot glissade; jammed into a corner between cliffs that tunnelled and focused every wandering blast; or, for the sake of summer pasture, cowering down on a neck that in winter would be ten feet deep in snow. And the people – the sallow, greasy, duffle-clad people, with short bare legs and faces almost Esquimaux – would flock out and adore. The Plains – kindly and gentle – had treated the lama as a holy man among holy men. But the Hills worshipped him as one in the confidence of all their devils. Theirs was an almost obliterated Buddhism, overlaid with a nature-worship fantastic as their own landscapes, elaborate as the terracing of their tiny fields; but they recognized the big hat, the clicking rosary, and the rare Chinese texts for great authority; and they respected the man beneath the hat.

'We saw thee come down over the black Breasts of Eua,' said a Betah who gave them cheese, sour milk, and stone-hard bread one evening. 'We do not use that often – except when calving cows stray in summer. There is a sudden wind among those stones that casts men down on the stillest day. But what should such folk care for the Devil of Eua!'

Then did Kim, aching in every fibre, dizzy with looking down, footsore with cramping desperate toes into inadequate crannies, take joy in the day's march – such joy as a boy of St Xavier's who had won the quarter-mile on the flat might take in the praises of his friends. The hills sweated the *ghi* and sugar suet off his bones; the dry air, taken sobbingly at the head of cruel passes, firmed and built out his upper ribs; and the tilted levels put new hard muscles into calf and thigh.

They meditated often on the Wheel of Life – the more so since, as the lama said, they were freed from its visible temptations. Except the grey eagle and an occasional far-seen bear grubbing and rooting on the hillside; a vision of a furious painted leopard met at dawn in a still valley devouring a goat; and now and again a bright-coloured bird, they were alone with the winds and the grass singing under the wind. The women of the smoky huts over whose roofs the two walked as they descended the mountains, were unlovely and unclean, wives of many husbands, and afflicted with goitre. The men were wood-cutters when they were not farmers – meek, and of an incredible simplicity. But that suitable discourse might not fail, Fate sent them, overtaking and overtaken upon the road, the courteous Dacca physician, who paid for his food in ointments good for goitre and counsels that restore peace between men and women. He seemed to know these hills as well as he knew the hill dialects, and gave the lama the lie of the land towards Ladakh and Tibet. He said they could return to the Plains at any moment. Meantime, for such as loved mountains, yonder road might amuse. This was not all revealed in a breath, but at evening encounters on the stone threshing-floors, when, patients disposed of, the doctor would smoke and the lama snuff, while Kim watched the wee cows grazing on the house-tops, or threw his soul after his eyes across the deep blue gulfs between range and range. And there were talks apart in the dark woods, when the doctor would seek herbs, and Kim, as budding physician, must accompany him.

'You see, Mister O'Hara, I do not know what the deuce-an'-all I shall do when I find our sporting friends; but if you will kindly keep within sight of my umbrella, which is fine fixed point for cadastral survey, I shall feel much better.'

Kim looked out across the jungle of peaks. 'This is not my country, *hakim*. Easier, I think, to find one louse in a bear-skin.'

'Oah, thatt is my strong points. There is no hurry for Hurree. They were at Leh not so long ago. They said they had come down from the Karakorum with their heads and horns and all. I am onlee afraid they will have sent back all their letters and compromising things from Leh into Russian territoree. Of course they will walk away as far to the East as possible – just to show that they were never among the Western States. You do not know the Hills?' He scratched with a twig on the earth. 'Look! They should have come in by Srinagar or Abbottabad. *Thatt* is their short road – down the river by Bunji and Astor. But they have made mischief in the West. So' – he drew a furrow from left to right – 'they march and they march away East to Leh (ah! it is cold there), and down the Indus to Hanlé (I know that road), and then down, you see, to Bushahr and Chini valley. That is ascertained by process of elimination, and also by asking questions from people that I cure so well. Our friends have been a long time playing about and producing impressions. So they are well known from far off. You will see me catch them somewhere in Chini valley. Please keep your eye on the umbrella.'

It nodded like a wind-blown harebell down the valleys and round the mountain sides, and in due time the lama and Kim, who steered by compass, would overhaul it, vending ointments and powders at eventide. 'We came by such and such a way!' The lama would throw a careless finger backward at the ridges, and the umbrella would expend itself in compliments.

They crossed a snowy pass in cold moonlight, when the lama, mildly chaffing Kim, went through up to his knees, like a Bactrian camel – the snow-bred, shag-haired sort that came into the Kashmir Serai. They dipped across beds of light snow and snow-powdered shale, where they took refuge from a gale in a camp of Tibetans hurrying down tiny sheep, each laden with a bag of borax. They came out upon grassy shoulders still snow-speckled, and through forest, to grass anew. For all their marchings, Kedarnath and Badrinath were not impressed; and it was only after days of travel that Kim, uplifted upon some insignificant ten-thousand-foot hummock, could see that a shoulder-knot or horn of the two great lords had – ever so slightly – changed outline.

At last they entered a world within a world – a valley of leagues where the high hills were fashioned of a mere rubble and refuse from off the knees of the mountains. Here one day's march carried them no farther, it seemed, than a dreamer's clogged pace bears him in a nightmare. They skirted a shoulder painfully for hours, and, behold, it was but an outlying boss in an outlying buttress of the main pile! A rounded meadow revealed itself, when they had reached it, for a vast tableland running far into the valley. Three days later, it was a dim fold in the earth to southward.

'Surely the Gods live here!' said Kim, beaten down by the silence and the appalling sweep and dispersal of the cloud-shadows after rain. 'This is no place for men!'

'Long and long ago,' said the lama, as to himself, 'it was asked of the Lord whether the world were everlasting. To this the Excellent One returned no answer ... When I was in Ceylon, a wise Seeker confirmed that from the gospel which is written in Pali. Certainly, since we know the way to Freedom, the question were unprofitable, but – look, and know illusion, *chela*! These are the true Hills! They are like my hills by Such-zen. Never were such hills!'

Above them, still enormously above them, earth towered away towards the snow-line, where from east to west across hundreds of miles, ruled as with a ruler, the last of the bold birches stopped. Above that, in scarps and blocks upheaved, the rocks strove to fight their heads above the white smother. Above these again, changeless since the world's beginning, but changing to every mood of sun and cloud, lay out the eternal snow. They could see blots and blurs on its face where storm and wandering wullie-wa got up to dance. Below them, as they stood, the forest slid away in a sheet of blue-green for mile upon mile; below the forest was a village in its sprinkle of terraced fields and steep grazing-grounds. Below the village they knew, though a thunderstorm worried and growled there for the moment, a pitch of twelve or fifteen hundred feet gave to the moist valley where the streams gather that are the mothers of young Sutluj.

As usual, the lama had led Kim by cow-track and by-road, far from the main route along which Hurree Babu, that 'fearful man', had bucketed three days before through a storm to which nine Englishmen out of ten would have given full right of way. Hurree was no game-shot – the snick of a trigger made him change colour – but, as he himself would have said, he was 'fairly effeecient stalker', and he had raked the huge valley with a pair of cheap binoculars to some purpose. Moreover, the white of worn canvas tents against green carries far. Hurree Babu had seen all he wanted to see when he sat on the threshing-floor of Ziglaur, twenty miles away as the eagle flies, and forty by road – that is to say, two small dots which one day were just below the snow-line, and the next had moved downward perhaps six inches on the hillside. Once cleaned out and set to the work, his fat bare legs could cover a surprising amount of ground, and this was the reason why, while Kim and the lama lay in a leaky hut at Ziglaur till the storm should be over-past, an oily, wet, but always smiling Bengali, talking the best of English with the vilest of phrases, was ingratiating himself with two sodden and rather rheumatic foreigners. He had arrived, revolving many wild schemes, on the heels of a thunderstorm which had split a pine over against their camp, and so convinced a dozen or two forcibly impressed baggage-coolies the day was inauspicious for farther travel that with one accord they had thrown down their loads and jibbed. They were subjects of a Hill Rajah who farmed out their services, as is the custom, for his private gain; and, to add to their personal distresses, the strange Sahibs had already threatened them with rifles. The most of them knew rifles and Sahibs of old: they were trackers and *shikarris* of the Northern valleys, keen after bear and wild goat; but they had never been thus treated in their lives. So the forest took them to her bosom, and, for all oaths and clamour, refused to restore. There was no need to feign madness or – the Babu had thought of another means of securing a welcome. He wrung out his wet clothes, slipped on his patent-leather shoes, opened the blue-and-white umbrella, and with mincing gait and a heart beating against his tonsils appeared as 'agent for His Royal Highness, the Rajah of Rampur, gentlemen. What can I do for you, please?'

The gentlemen were delighted. One was visibly French, the other Russian, but they spoke English not much inferior to the Babu's. They begged his kind offices. Their native servants had gone sick at Leh. They had hurried on because they were anxious to bring the spoils of the chase to Simla ere the skins grew moth-eaten. They bore a general letter of introduction (the Babu salaamed to it orientally) to all Government officials. No, they had not met any other shooting-parties *en route*. They did for themselves. They had plenty of supplies. They only wished to push on as soon as might be. At this he waylaid a cowering hillman among the trees, and after three minutes' talk and a little silver (one cannot be economical upon State service, though Hurree's heart bled at the waste) the eleven coolies and the three hangers-on reappeared. At least the Babu would be a witness to their oppression.

'My royal master, he will be much annoyed, but these people are onlee common people and grossly ignorant. If your honours will kindly overlook unfortunate affair, I shall be much pleased. In a little while rain will stop and we can then proceed. You have been shooting, eh? That is fine performance!'

He skipped nimbly from one *kilta* to the next, making pretence to adjust each conical basket. The Englishman is not, as a rule, familiar with the Asiatic, but he would not strike across the wrist a kindly Babu who had accidentally upset a *kilta* with a red oilskin top. On the other hand, he would not press drink upon a Babu were he never so friendly, nor would he invite him to meat. The strangers did all these things, and asked many questions – about women mostly – to which Hurree returned gay and unstudied answers. They gave him a glass of whitish fluid like to gin, and then more; and in a little time his gravity departed from him. He became thickly treasonous, and spoke in terms of sweeping indecency of a Government which had forced upon him a white man's education and neglected to supply him with a white man's salary. He babbled tales of oppression and wrong till the tears ran down his cheeks for the miseries of his land. Then he staggered off, singing love-songs of Lower Bengal, and collapsed upon a wet tree-trunk. Never was so unfortunate a product of English rule in India more unhappily thrust upon aliens.

'They are all just of that pattern,' said one sportsman to the other in French. 'When we get into India proper thou wilt see. I should like to visit his Rajah. One might speak the good word there. It is possible that he has heard of us and wishes to signify his good-will.'

'We have not time. We must get into Simla as soon as may be,' his companion replied. 'For my own part, I wish our reports had been sent back from Hilás, or even Leh.'

'The English post is better and safer. Remember we are given all facilities – and Name of God! – they give them to us too! Is it unbelievable stupidity?'

'It is pride – pride that deserves and will receive punishment.'

'Yes! To fight a fellow-Continental in our game is something. There is a risk attached, but these people – bah! It is too easy.'

'Pride – all pride, my friend.'

'Now what the deuce is good of Chandernagore being so close to Calcutta and all,' said Hurree, snoring open-mouthed on the sodden moss, 'if I cannot understand their French? They talk so par*tic*ularly fast! It would have been much better to cut their beastly throats.'

When he presented himself again he was racked with a headache – penitent, and volubly afraid that in his drunkenness he might have been indiscreet. He loved the British Government – it was the source of all prosperity and honour, and his master at Rampur held the very same opinion. Upon this the men began to deride him and to quote past words, till step by step, with deprecating smirks, oily grins, and leers of infinite cunning, the poor Babu was beaten out of his defences and forced to speak – truth. When Lurgan was told the tale later, he mourned aloud that he could not have been in the place of the stubborn, inattentive coolies, who with grass mats over their heads and the raindrops puddling in their footprints, waited on the weather. All the Sahibs of their acquaintance – rough-clad men joyously returning year after year to their chosen gullies – had servants and cooks and orderlies, very often hillmen. These Sahibs travelled without any retinue. Therefore they were poor Sahibs, and ignorant; for no Sahib in his senses would follow a Bengali's advice. But the Bengali, appearing from somewhere, had given them money, and could make shift with their dialect. Used to comprehensive ill-treatment from their own colour, they suspected a trap somewhere, and stood by to run if occasion offered.

Then through the new-washed air, steaming with delicious earth-smells, the Babu led the way down the slopes – walking ahead of the coolies in pride; walking behind the foreigners in humility. His thoughts were many and various. The least of them would have interested his companions beyond words. But he was an agreeable guide, ever keen to point out the beauties of his royal master's domain. He peopled the hills with anything they had a mind to slay – thar, ibex, or markhor, and bear by Elisha's allowance. He discoursed of botany and ethnology with unimpeachable inaccuracy, and his store of local legends – he had been a trusted agent of the State for fifteen years, remember – was inexhaustible.

'Decidedly this fellow is an original,' said the taller of the two foreigners. 'He is like the nightmare of a Viennese courier.'

'He represents in little India in transition – the monstrous hybridism of East and West,' the Russian replied. 'It is *we* who can deal with Orientals.'

'He has lost his own country and has not acquired any other. But he has a most complete hatred of his conquerors. Listen. He confided to me last night,' said the other.

Under the striped umbrella Hurree Babu was straining ear and brain to follow the quick-poured French, and keeping both eyes on a *kilta* full of maps and documents – an extra-large one with a double red oil-skin cover. He did not wish to steal anything. He only desired to know what to steal, and, incidentally, how to get away when he had stolen it. He thanked all the Gods of Hindustan, and Herbert Spencer, that there remained some valuables to steal.

On the second day the road rose steeply to a grass spur above the forest; and it was here, about sunset, that they came across an aged lama but they called him a bonze – sitting cross-legged above a mysterious chart held down by stones, which he was explaining to a young man, evidently a neophyte, of singular, though unwashen, beauty. The striped umbrella had been sighted half a march away, and Kim had suggested a halt till it came up to them.

'Ha!' said Hurree Babu, resourceful as Puss-in-Boots. 'That is eminent local holy man. Probably subject of my royal master.'

'What is he doing? It is very curious.'

'He is expounding holy picture – *all* hand-worked.'

The two men stood bareheaded in the wash of the afternoon sunlight low across the gold-coloured grass. The sullen coolies, glad of the check, halted and slid down their loads.

'Look!' said the Frenchman. 'It is like a picture for the birth of a religion – the first teacher and the first disciple. Is he a Buddhist?'

'Of some debased kind,' the other answered. 'There are no true Buddhists among the Hills. But look at the folds of the drapery. Look at his eyes – how insolent! Why does this make one feel that we are so young a people?' The speaker struck passionately at a tall weed. 'We have nowhere left our mark yet. Nowhere! *That*, do you understand, is what disquiets me.' He scowled at the placid face, and the monumental calm of the pose.

'Have patience. We shall make your mark together – we and you young people. Meantime, draw his picture.'

The Babu advanced loftily; his back out of all keeping with his deferential speech, or his wink towards Kim.

'Holy One, these be Sahibs. My medicines cured one of a flux, and I go into Simla to oversee his recovery. They wish to see thy picture –'

'To heal the sick is always good. This is the Wheel of Life,' said the lama, 'the same I showed thee in the hut at Ziglaur when the rain fell.'

'And to hear thee expound it.'

The lama's eyes lighted at the prospect of new listeners. 'To expound the Most Excellent Way is good. Have they any knowledge of Hindi, such as had the Keeper of Images?'

'A little, maybe.'

Hereat, simply as a child engrossed with a new game, the lama threw back his head and began the full-throated invocation of the Doctor of Divinity ere he opens the full doctrine. The strangers leaned on their alpenstocks and listened. Kim, squatting humbly, watched the red sunlight on their faces, and the blend and parting of their long shadows. They wore un-English leggings and curious girt-in belts that reminded him hazily of the pictures in a book in St Xavier's library: *The Adventures of a Young Naturalist in Mexico* was its name. Yes, they looked very like the wonderful M. Sumichrast of that tale, and very unlike the 'highly unscrupulous folk' of Hurree Babu's imagining. The coolies, earth-coloured and mute, crouched reverently some twenty or thirty yards away, and the Babu, the slack of his thin gear snapping like a marking-flag in the chill breeze, stood by with an air of happy proprietorship.

'These are the men,' Hurree whispered, as the ritual went on and the two whites followed the grass-blade sweeping from Hell to Heaven and back again. 'All their books are in the large *kilta*, with the reddish top – books and reports and maps – and I have seen a King's letter that either Hilás or Bunár has written. They guard it most carefully. They have sent nothing back from Hilás or Leh. That is sure.'

'Who is with them?'

'Only the *beegar*-coolies. They have no servants. They are so close they cook their own food.'

'But what am I to do?'

'Wait and see. Only if any chance comes to me thou wilt know where to seek for the papers.'

'This were better in Mahbub Ali's hands than a Bengali's,' said Kim scornfully.

'There are more ways of getting to a sweetheart than butting down a wall.'

'See here the Hell appointed for avarice and greed. Flanked upon the one side by Desire and on the other by Weariness.' The lama warmed to his work, and one of the strangers sketched him in the quick-fading light.

'That is enough,' the man said at last brusquely. 'I cannot understand him, but I want that picture. He is a better artist than I. Ask him if he will sell it.'

'He says "No, sar," ' the Babu replied. The lama, of course, would no more have parted with his chart to a casual wayfarer than an archbishop would pawn the holy vessels of his cathedral. All Tibet is full of cheap reproductions of the Wheel; but the lama was an artist, as well as a wealthy Abbot in his own place.

'Perhaps in three days, or four, or ten, if I perceive that the Sahib is a Seeker and of good understanding, I may myself draw him another. But this was used for the initiation of a novice. Tell him so, *hakim*.'

'He wishes it now – for money.'

The lama shook his head slowly and began to fold up the Wheel. The Russian, on his side, saw no more than an unclean old man haggling over a dirty piece of paper. He drew out a handful of rupees, and snatched half-jestingly at the chart, which tore in the lama's grip. A low murmur of horror went up from the coolies – some of whom were Spiti men and, by their lights, good Buddhists. The lama rose at the insult; his hand went to the heavy iron pencase that is the priest's weapon, and the Babu danced in agony.

'Now you see – you see why I wanted witnesses. They are highly unscrupulous people. Oh, sar! sar! You must *not* hit holy man!'

'*Chela!* He has defiled the Written Word!'

It was too late. Before Kim could ward him off, the Russian struck the old man full on the face. Next instant he was rolling over and over downhill with Kim at his throat. The blow had waked every unknown Irish devil in the boy's blood, and the sudden fall of his enemy did the rest. The lama dropped to his knees, half-stunned; the coolies under their loads fled up the hill as fast as plainsmen run aross the level. They had seen sacrilege unspeakable, and it behoved them to get away before the Gods and devils of the hills took vengeance. The Frenchman ran towards the lama, fumbling at his revolver with some notion of making him a hostage for his companion. A shower of cutting stones – hillmen are very straight shots – drove him away, and a coolie from Ao-chung snatched the lama into the stampede. All came about as swiftly as the sudden mountain-darkness.

'They have taken the baggage and all the guns,' yelled the Frenchman, firing blindly into the twilight.

'All right, sar! All right! Don't shoot. I go to rescue,' and Hurree, pounding down the slope, cast himself bodily upon the delighted and astonished Kim, who was banging his breathless foe's head against a boulder.

'Go back to the coolies,' whispered the Babu in his ear. 'They have the baggage. The papers are in the *kilta* with the red top, but look through all. Take their papers, and specially the *murasla* [King's letter]. Go! The other man comes!'

Kim tore uphill. A revolver-bullet rang on a rock by his side, and he cowered partridge-wise.

'If you shoot,' shouted Hurree, 'they will descend and annihilate us. I have rescued the gentleman, sar. This is par*tic*ularly dangerous.'

'By Jove!' Kim was thinking hard in English. 'This is dam'- tight place, but *I* think it is self-defence.' He felt in his bosom for Mahbub's gift, and uncertainly – save for a few practice shots in the Bikanir desert, he had never used the little gun – pulled the trigger.

'What did I say, sar!' The Babu seemed to be in tears. 'Come down here and assist to resuscitate. We are all up a tree, I tell you.'

The shots ceased. There was a sound of stumbling feet, and Kim hurried upward through the gloom, swearing like a cat – or a country-bred.

'Did they wound thee, *chela*?' called the lama above him.

'No. And thou?' He dived into a clump of stunted firs.

'Unhurt. Come away. We go with these folk to Shamlegh-under-the-Snow.'

'But not before we have done justice,' a voice cried. 'I have got the Sahibs' guns – all four. Let us go down.'

'He struck the Holy One – we saw it! Our cattle will be barren – our wives will cease to bear! The snows will slide upon us as we go home . . . Atop of all other oppression too!'

The little fir-clump filled with clamouring coolies – panic-stricken, and in their terror capable of anything. The man from Ao-chung clicked the breech-bolt of his gun impatiently, and made as to go downhill.

'Wait a little, Holy One; they cannot go far. Wait till I return,' said he.

'It is this person who has suffered wrong,' said the lama, his hand over his brow.

'For that very reason,' was the reply.

'If this person overlooks it, your hands are clean. Moreover, ye acquire merit by obedience.'

'Wait, and we will all go to Shamlegh together,' the man insisted.

For a moment, for just so long as it needs to stuff a cartridge into a breech-loader, the lama hesitated. Then he rose to his feet, and laid a finger on the man's shoulder.

'Hast thou heard? *I* say there shall be no killing – I who was Abbot of Such-zen. Is it any lust of thine to be re-born as a rat, or a snake under the eaves – a worm in the belly of the most mean beast? Is it thy wish to –'

The man from Ao-chung fell to his knees, for the voice boomed like a Tibetan devil-gong.

'Ai! ai!' cried the Spiti men. 'Do not curse us – do not curse him. It was but his zeal, Holy One! . . . Put down the rifle, fool!'

'Anger on anger! Evil on evil! There will be no killing. Let the priest-beaters go in bondage to their own acts. Just and sure is the Wheel, swerving not a hair! They will be born many times – in torment.' His head drooped, and he leaned heavily on Kim's shoulder.

'I have come near to great evil, *chela*,' he whispered in that dead hush under the pines. 'I was tempted to loose the bullet; and truly, in Tibet there would have been a heavy and a slow death for them . . . He struck me across the face . . . upon the flesh . . .' He slid to the ground, breathing heavily, and Kim could hear the over-driven heart bump and check.

'Have they hurt him to the death?' said the Ao-chung man, while the others stood mute.

Kim knelt over the body in deadly fear. 'Nay,' he cried passionately, 'this is only a weakness.' Then he remembered that he was a white man, with a white man's camp-fittings at his service. 'Open the *kiltas*! The Sahibs may have a medicine.'

'Oho! Then I know it,' said the Ao-chung man with a laugh. 'Not for five years was I Yankling Sahib's *shikarri* without knowing that medicine. I too have tasted it. Behold!'

He drew from his breast a bottle of cheap whisky – such as is sold to explorers at Leh – and cleverly forced a little between the lama's teeth.

'So I did when Yankling Sahib twisted his foot beyond Astor. Aha! I have already looked into their baskets – but we will make fair division at Shamlegh. Give him a little more. It is good medicine. Feel! His heart goes better now. Lay his head down and rub a little on the chest. If he had waited quietly while I accounted for the Sahibs this would never have come. But perhaps the Sahibs may chase us here. Then it would not be wrong to shoot them with their own guns, heh?'

'One is paid, I think, already,' said Kim between his teeth. 'I kicked him in the groin as we went downhill. Would I had killed him!'

'It is well to be brave when one does not live in Rampur,' said one whose hut lay within a few miles of the Rajah's rickety palace. 'If we get a bad name among the Sahibs, none will employ us as *shikarris* any more.'

'Oh, but these are not Angrezi Sahibs – not merry-minded men like Fostum Sahib or Yankling Sahib. They are foreigners – they cannot speak Angrezi as do Sahibs.'

Here the lama coughed and sat up, groping for the rosary.

'There shall be no killing,' he murmured. 'Just is the Wheel! Evil on evil –'

'Nay, Holy One. We are all here.' The Ao-chung man timidly patted his feet. 'Except by thy order, no one shall be slain. Rest awhile. We will make a little camp here, and later, as the moon rises, we go to Shamlegh-under-the-Snow.'

'After a blow,' said a Spiti man sententiously, 'it is best to sleep.'

'There is, as it were, a dizziness at the back of my neck, and a pinching in it. Let me lay my head on thy lap, *chela*. I am an old man, but not free from passion ... We must think of the Cause of Things.'

'Give him a blanket. We dare not light a fire lest the Sahibs see.'

'Better get away to Shamlegh. None will follow us to Shamlegh.'

This was the nervous Rampur man.

'I have been Fostum Sahib's *shikarri*, and I am Yankling Sahib's *shikarri*. I should have been with Yankling Sahib now but for this cursed *beegar* [the *corvée*]. Let two men watch below with the guns lest the Sahibs do more foolishness. *I* shall not leave this Holy One.'

They sat down a little apart from the lama, and, after listening awhile, passed round a water-pipe whose receiver was an old Day and Martin blacking-bottle. The glow of the red charcoal as it went from hand to hand lit up the narrow, blinking eyes, the high Chinese cheek-bones, and the bull-throats that melted away into the dark duffle folds round the shoulders. They looked like kobolds from some magic mine – gnomes of the hills in conclave. And while they talked, the voices of the snow-waters round them diminished one by one as the night-frost choked and clogged the runnels.

'How he stood up against us!' said a Spiti man admiring. 'I remember an old ibex, out Ladakh-way, that Dupont Sahib missed on a shoulder-shot, seven seasons back, standing up just like him. Dupont Sahib was a good *shikarri*.'

'Not as good as Yankling Sahib.' The Ao-chung man took a pull at the whisky-bottle and passed it over. 'Now hear me – unless any other man thinks he knows more.'

The challenge was not taken up.

'We go to Shamlegh when the moon rises. There we will fairly divide the baggage between us. I am content with this new little rifle and all its cartridges.'

'Are the bears only bad on thy holding?' said a mate, sucking at the pipe.

'No; but musk-pods are worth six rupees apiece now, and thy women can have the canvas of the tents and some of the cooking-gear. We will do all that at Shamlegh before dawn. Then we all go our ways, remembering that we have never seen or taken service with these Sahibs, who may, indeed, say that we have stolen their baggage.'

'That is well for thee, but what will our Rajah say?'

'Who is to tell him? Those Sahibs, who cannot speak our talk, or the Babu, who for his own ends gave us money? Will *he* lead an army against us? What evidence will remain? That we do not need we shall throw on Shamlegh-midden, where no man has yet set foot.'

'Who is at Shamlegh this summer?' The place was only a grazing centre of three or four huts.

'The Woman of Shamlegh. *She* has no love for Sahibs, as we know. The others can be pleased with little presents; and here is enough for us all.' He patted the fat sides of the nearest basket.

'But – but–'

'I have said they are not true Sahibs. *All* their skins and heads were bought in the bazar at Leh. I know the marks. I showed them to ye last march.'

'True. They were all bought skins and heads. Some had even the moth in them.'

That was a shrewd argument, and the Ao-chung man knew his fellows.

'If the worst comes to the worst, I shall tell Yankling Sahib, who is a man of a merry mind, and he will laugh. We are not doing any wrong to any Sahibs whom we know. *They* are priest-beaters. They frightened us. We fled! Who knows where we dropped the baggage? Do ye think Yankling Sahib will permit down-country police to wander all over the hills, disturbing his game? It is a far cry from Simla to Chini, and farther from Shamlegh to Shamlegh-midden.'

'So be it, but I carry the big *kilta*. The basket with the red top that the Sahibs pack themselves every morning.'

'Thus it is proved,' said the Shamlegh man adroitly, 'that they are Sahibs of no account. Who ever heard of Fostum Sahib, or Yankling Sahib, or even the little Peel Sahib that sits up of nights to shoot serow – I say, who ever heard of these Sahibs coming into the hills without a down-country cook, and a bearer, and – and all manner of well-paid, high-handed and oppressive folk in their tail? How can *they* make trouble? What of the *kilta*?'

'Nothing, but that it is full of the Written Word – books and papers in which they wrote, and strange instruments, as of worship.'

'Shamlegh-midden will take them all.'

'True! But how if we insult the Sahibs' Gods thereby! I do not like to handle the Written Word in that fashion. And their brass idols are beyond my comprehension. It is no plunder for simple hill-folk.'

'The old man still sleeps. Hst! We will ask his *chela*.' The Ao-chung man refreshed himself, and swelled with pride of leadership.

'We have here,' he whispered, 'a *kilta* whose nature we do not know.'

'But I do,' said Kim cautiously. The lama drew breath in natural, easy sleep, and Kim had been thinking of Hurree's last words. As a player of the Great Game, he was disposed just then to reverence the Babu. 'It is a *kilta* with a red top full of very wonderful things, not to be handled by fools.'

'I said it; I said it,' cried the bearer of that burden. 'Thinkest thou it will betray us?'

'Not if it be given to me. I can draw out its magic. Otherwise it will do great harm.'

'A priest always takes his share.' Whisky was demoralizing the Ao-chung man.

'It is no matter to me,' Kim answered, with the craft of his mother-country. 'Share it among you, and see what comes!'

'Not I. I was only jesting. Give the order. There is more than enough for us all. We go our way from Shamlegh in the dawn.'

They arranged and re-arranged their artless little plans for another hour, while Kim shivered with cold and pride. The humour of the situation tickled the Irish and the Oriental in his soul. Here were the emissaries of the dread Power of the North, very possibly as great in their own land as Mahbub or Colonel Creighton, suddenly smitten helpless. One of them, he privately knew, would be lame for a time. They had made promises to Kings. Tonight they lay out somewhere below him, chartless, foodless, tentless, gunless – except for Hurree Babu, guideless. And this collapse of their Great Game (Kim wondered to whom they would report it), this panicky bolt into the night, had come about through no craft of Hurree's or contrivance of Kim's, but simply, beautifully, and inevitably as the capture of Mahbub's *fakir*-friends by the zealous young policeman at Umballa.

'They are there – with nothing; and, by Jove, it is cold! I am here with all their things. Oh, they will be angry! I am sorry for Hurree Babu.'

Kim might have saved his pity, for though at that moment the Bengali suffered acutely in the flesh, his soul was puffed and lofty. A mile down the hill, on the edge of the pine-forest, two half-frozen men – one powerfully sick at intervals – were varying mutual recriminations with the most poignant abuse of the Babu, who seemed distraught with terror. They demanded a plan of action. He explained that they were very lucky to be alive; that their coolies, if not then stalking them, had passed beyond recall; that the Rajah, his master, was ninety miles away, and, so far from lending them money and a retinue for the Simla journey, would surely cast them into prison if he heard that they had hit a priest. He enlarged on this sin and its consequences till they bade him change the subject. Their one hope, said he, was unostentatious flight from village to village till they reached civilization; and, for the hundredth time dissolved in tears, he demanded of the high stars why the Sahibs 'had beaten holy man'.

Ten steps would have taken Hurree into the creaking gloom utterly beyond their reach – to the shelter and food of the nearest village, where glib-tongued doctors were scarce. But he preferred to endure cold, belly-pinch, bad words, and occasional blows in the company of his honoured employers. Crouched against a tree-trunk, he sniffed dolefully.

'And have you thought,' said the uninjured man hotly, 'what sort of spectacle we shall present wandering through these hills among these aborigines?'

Hurree Babu had thought of little else for some hours, but the remark was not to his address.

'We cannot wander! I can hardly walk,' groaned Kim's victim.

'Perhaps the holy man will be merciful in loving-kindness, sar, otherwise –'

'I promise myself a peculiar pleasure in emptying my revolver into that young bonze when next we meet,' was the unchristian answer.

'Revolvers! Vengeance! Bonzes!' Hurree crouched lower. The war was breaking out afresh. 'Have you no consideration for our loss? The baggage! The baggage!' He could hear the speaker literally dancing on the grass. 'Everything we bore! Everything we have secured! Our gains! Eight months' work! Do you know what that means? "Decidedly it is we who can deal with Orientals!" Oh, you have done well.'

They fell to it in several tongues, and Hurree smiled. Kim was with the *kiltas*, and in the *kiltas* lay eight months of good diplomacy. There was no means of communicating with the boy, but he could be trusted. For the rest, Hurree could so stage-manage the journey through the hills that Hilás, Bunár, and four hundred miles of hill-roads should tell the tale for a generation. Men who cannot control their own coolies are little respected in the Hills, and the hillman has a very keen sense of humour.

'If I had done it myself,' thought Hurree, 'it would not have been better; and, by Jove, now I think of it, of course I arranged it myself. How quick I have been! Just when I ran downhill I thought it! Thee outrage was accidental, but onlee me could have worked it – ah – for all it was dam'-well worth. Consider the moral effect upon these ignorant peoples! No treaties – no papers – no written documents at all – and *me* to interpret for them. How I shall laugh with the Colonel! I wish I had their papers also: but you cannot occupy two places in space simultaneously. Thatt is axiomatic.'

Chapter 14

My brother kneels (so saith Kabir)
   To stone and brass in heathen wise,
But in my brother's voice I hear
   My own unanswered agonies.
His God is as his Fates assign –
His prayer is all the world's – and mine.
               The Prayer.

AT moonrise the cautious coolies got under way. The
lama, refreshed by his sleep and the spirit, needed no
more than Kim's shoulder to bear him along – a silent, swift-
striding man. They held the shale-sprinkled grass for an hour,
swept round the shoulder of an immortal cliff, and climbed
into a new country entirely blocked off from all sight of Chini
valley. A huge pasture-ground ran up fan-shaped to the living
snow. At its base was perhaps half an acre of flat land, on
which stood a few soil and timber huts. Behind them – for,
hill-fashion, they were perched on the edge of all things – the
ground fell sheer two thousand feet to Shamlegh-midden,
where never yet man has set foot.

The men made no motion to divide the plunder till they
had seen the lama bedded down in the best room of the place,
with Kim shampooing his feet, Mohammedan-fashion.

'We will send food,' said the Ao-chung man, 'and the red-
topped *kilta*. By dawn there will be none to give evidence, one
way or the other. If anything is not needed in the *kilta* – see
here!'

He pointed through the window – opening into space that
was filled with moonlight reflected from the snow – and threw
out an empty whisky-bottle.

'No need to listen for the fall. This is the world's end,'
he said, and went out. The lama looked forth, a hand on
either sill, with eyes that shone like yellow opals. From the

266

enormous pit before him white peaks lifted themselves yearning to the moonlight. The rest was as the darkness of interstellar space.

'These,' he said slowly, 'are indeed my Hills. Thus should a man abide, perched above the world, separated from delights, considering vast matters.'

'Yes; if he has a *chela* to prepare tea for him, and to fold a blanket for his head, and to chase out calving cows.'

A smoky lamp burned in a niche, but the full moonlight beat it down; and by the mixed light, stooping above the food-bag and cups, Kim moved like a tall ghost.

'*Ai!* But now I have let the blood cool, my head still beats and drums, and there is a cord round the back of my neck.'

'No wonder. It was a strong blow. May he who dealt it –'

'But for my own passions there would have been no evil.'

'What evil? Thou hast saved the Sahibs from the death they deserved a hundred times.'

'The lesson is not well learnt, *chela*.' The lama came to rest on a folded blanket, as Kim went forward with his evening routine. 'The blow was but a shadow upon a shadow. Evil in itself – my legs weary apace these latter days! – it met evil in me anger, rage, and a lust to return evil. These wrought in my blood, woke tumult in my stomach, and dazzled my ears.' Here he drank scalding block-tea ceremonially, taking the hot cup from Kim's hand. 'Had I been passionless, the evil blow would have done only bodily evil – a scar, or a bruise – which is illusion. But my mind was *not* abstracted, for rushed in straightway a lust to let the Spiti men kill. In fighting that lust, my soul was torn and wrenched beyond a thousand blows. Not till I had repeated the Blessings' (he meant the Buddhist Beatitudes) 'did I achieve calm. But the evil planted in me by that moment's carelessness works out to its end. Just is the Wheel, swerving not a hair! Learn the lesson, *chela*.'

'It is too high for me,' Kim muttered. 'I am still all shaken. I am glad I hurt the man.'

'I felt that, sleeping upon thy knees, in the wood below. It disquieted me in my dreams – the evil in thy soul working through to mine. Yet on the other hand' – he loosed his rosary – 'I have acquired merit by saving two lives – the lives of those that wronged me. Now I must see into the Cause of Things. The boat of my soul staggers.'

'Sleep, and be strong. That is wisest.'

'I meditate. There is a need greater than thou knowest.'

Till the dawn, hour after hour, as the moonlight paled on the high peaks, and that which had been belted blackness on the sides of the far hills showed as tender green forest, the lama stared fixedly at the wall. From time to time he groaned. Outside the barred door, where discomfited kine came to ask for their old stable, Shamlegh and the coolies gave itself up to plunder and riotous living. The Ao-chung man was their leader, and once they had opened the Sahibs' tinned foods and found that they were very good they dared not turn back. Shamlegh kitchen-midden took the dunnage.

When Kim, after a night of bad dreams, stole forth to brush his teeth in the morning chill, a fair-coloured woman with turquoise-studded headgear drew him aside.

'The others have gone. They left thee this *kilta* as the promise was. I do not love Sahibs, but thou wilt make us a charm in return for it. We do not wish little Shamlegh to get a bad name on account of the – accident. I am the Woman of Shamlegh.' She looked him over with bold, bright eyes, unlike the usual furtive glance of hillwomen.

'Assuredly. But it must be done in secret.'

She raised the heavy *kilta* like a toy and slung it into her own hut.

'Out and bar the door! Let none come near till it is finished,' said Kim.

'But afterwards – we may talk?'

Kim tilted the *kilta* on the floor – a cascade of Survey-instruments, books, diaries, letters, maps, and queerly scented native correspondence. At the very bottom was an embroidered bag covering a sealed, gilded, and illuminated document such as one King sends to another. Kim caught his breath with delight, and reviewed the situation from a Sahib's point of view.

'The books I do not want. Besides, they are logarithms – Survey, I suppose.' He laid them aside. 'The letters I do not understand, but Colonel Creighton will. They must all be kept. The maps – they draw better maps than me – *of* course. All the native letters – oho! – and particularly the *murasla*.' He sniffed the embroidered bag. 'That must be from Hilás or Bunár, and Hurree Babu spoke truth. By Jove! It is a fine haul. I wish Hurree could know ... The rest must go out of the window.' He fingered a superb prismatic compass and the shiny top of a theodolite. But after all, a Sahib cannot very well steal, and the things might be inconvenient evidence later. He sorted out every scrap of manuscript, every map, and the native letters. They made one softish slab. The three locked ferril-backed books, with five worn pocket-books, he put aside.

'The letters and the *murasla* I must carry inside my coat and under my belt, and the hand-written books I must put into the food-bag. It will be very heavy. No. I do not think there is anything more. If there is, the coolies have thrown it down the *khud*, so *thatt* is all right. Now you go too.' He repacked the *kilta* with all he meant to lose, and hove it up on to the window-sill. A thousand feet below lay a long, lazy, round-shouldered bank of mist, as yet untouched by the morning sun. A thousand feet below that was a hundred–year-old pine-forest. He could see the green tops looking like a bed of moss when a wind-eddy thinned the cloud.

'No! I don't think any one will go after *you*!'

The wheeling basket vomited its contents as it dropped. The theodolite hit a jutting cliff-ledge and exploded like a shell; the books, inkstands, paint-boxes, compasses, and rulers showed for a few seconds like a swarm of bees. Then they vanished; and, though Kim, hanging half out of the window, strained his young ears, never a sound came up from the gulf.

'Five hundred – a thousand rupees could not buy them,' he thought sorrowfully. 'It was verree wasteful, but I have all their other stuff – everything they did – I hope. Now how the deuce am I to tell Hurree Babu, and *whatt* the deuce am I to do? And my old man is sick. I must tie up the letters in oilskin. That is something to do first – else they will get all sweated ... And I am all alone!' He bound them into a neat packet, swedging down the stiff, sticky oilskin at the corners, for his roving life had made him as methodical as an old hunter in matters of the road. Then with double care he packed away the books at the bottom of the food-bag.

The woman rapped at the door.

'But thou hast made no charm,' she said, looking about.

'There is no need.' Kim had completely overlooked the necessity for a little patter-talk. The woman laughed at his confusion irreverently.

'None – for thee. Thou canst cast a spell by the mere winking of an eye. But think of us poor people when thou art gone. They were all too drunk last night to hear a woman. Thou art not drunk?'

'I am a priest.' Kim had recovered himself, and, the woman being aught but unlovely, thought best to stand on his office.

'I warned them that the Sahibs will be angry and will make an inquisition and a report to the Rajah. There is also the Babu with them. Clerks have long tongues.'

'Is that all thy trouble?' The plan rose fully formed in Kim's mind, and he smiled ravishingly.

'Not all,' quoth the woman, putting out a hard brown hand all covered with turquoises set in silver.

'I can finish that in a breath,' he went on quickly. 'The Babu is the very *hakim* (thou hast heard of him?) who was wandering among the hills by Ziglaur. I know him.'

'He will tell for the sake of a reward. Sahibs cannot distinguish one hillman from another, but Babus have eyes for men – and women.'

'Carry a word to him from me.'

'There is nothing I would not do for thee.'

He accepted the compliment calmly, as men must in lands where women make the love, tore a leaf from a note-book, and with a patent indelible pencil wrote in gross Shikast – the script that bad little boys use when they write dirt on walls: '*I have everything that they have written: their pictures of the country, and many letters. Especially the* murasla. *Tell me what to do. I am at Shamlegh-under-the-Snow. The old man is sick.*'

'Take this to him. It will altogether shut his mouth. He cannot have gone far.'

'Indeed no. They are still in the forest across the spur. Our children went to watch them when the light came, and have cried the news as they moved.'

Kim looked his astonishment; but from the edge of the sheep-pasture floated a shrill, kite-like trill. A child tending cattle had picked it up from a brother or sister on the far side of the slope that commanded Chini valley.

'My husbands are also out there gathering wood.' She drew a handful of walnuts from her bosom, split one neatly, and began to eat. Kim affected blank ignorance.

'Dost thou not know the meaning of the walnut – priest?' she said coyly, and handed him the half-shells.

'Well thought of.' He slipped the piece of paper between them quickly. 'Hast thou a little wax to close them on this letter?'

The woman sighed aloud, and Kim relented.

'There is no payment till service has been rendered. Carry this to the Babu, and say it was sent by the Son of the Charm.'

'*Ai!* Truly! Truly! By a magician – who is like a Sahib.'

'Nay, a Son of the Charm: and ask if there be any answer.'

'But if he offer a rudeness? I – I am afraid.'

Kim laughed. 'He is, I have no doubt, very tired and very hungry. The Hills make cold bed-fellows. *Hai*, my' – it was on the tip of his tongue to say Mother, but he turned it to Sister – 'thou art a wise and witty woman. By this time all the villages know what has befallen the Sahibs – eh?'

'True. News was at Ziglaur by midnight, and by tomorrow should be at Kotgarh. The villages are both afraid and angry.'

'No need. Tell the villages to feed the Sahibs and pass them on, in peace. We must get them quietly away from our valleys. To steal is one thing – to kill another. The Babu will understand, and there will be no after-complaints. Be swift. I must tend my master when he wakes.'

'So be it. After service – thou hast said? – comes the reward. I am the Woman of Shamlegh, and I hold from the Rajah. I am no common bearer of babes. Shamlegh is thine: hoof and horn and hide, milk and butter. Take or leave.'

She turned resolutely uphill, her silver necklaces clicking on her broad breast, to meet the morning sun fifteen hundred feet above them. This time Kim thought in the vernacular as he waxed down the oilskin edges of the packets.

'How can a man follow the Way or the Great Game when he is so-always pestered by women? There was that girl at Akrola of the Ford; and there was the scullion's wife behind the dovecot – not counting the others – and now comes this one! When I was a child it was well enough, but now I am a man and they will not regard me as a man. Walnuts, indeed! Ho! ho! It is almonds in the Plains!'

He went out to levy on the village – not with a begging-bowl, which might do for down-country, but in the manner of a prince. Shamlegh's summer population is only three families – four women and eight or nine men. They were all full of tinned meats and mixed drinks, from ammoniated quinine to white vodka, for they had taken their full share in the overnight loot. The neat Continental tents had been cut up and shared long ago, and there were patent aluminium saucepans abroad.

But they considered the lama's presence a perfect safeguard against all consequences, and impenitently brought Kim of their best – even to a drink of *chang* – the barley-beer that comes from Ladakh-way. Then they thawed out in the sun, and sat with their legs hanging over infinite abysses, chattering, laughing, and smoking. They judged India and its Government solely from their experience of wandering Sahibs who had employed them or their friends as *shikarris*. Kim heard tales of shots missed upon ibex, serow, or markhor, by Sahibs twenty years in their graves – every detail lighted from behind like twigs on tree-tops seen against lightning. They told him of their little diseases, and, more important, the diseases of their tiny, sure-footed cattle; of trips as far as Kotgarh, where the strange missionaries live, and beyond even to marvellous Simla, where the streets are paved with silver, and anyone, look you, can get service with the Sahibs, who ride about in two-wheeled carts and spend money with a spade. Presently, grave and aloof, walking very heavily, the lama joined himself to the chatter under the eaves, and they gave him great room. The thin air refreshed him, and he sat on the edge of precipices with the best of them, and, when talk languished, flung pebbles into the void. Thirty miles away, as the eagle flies, lay the next range, seamed and channelled and pitted with little patches of brush – forests, each a day's dark march. Behind the village, Shamlegh hill itself cut off all view to southward. It was like sitting in a swallow's nest under the eaves of the roof of the world.

From time to time the lama stretched out his hand, and with a little low-voiced prompting would point out the road to Spiti and north across the Parungla.

'Beyond, where the hills lie thickest, lies De-ch'en' (he meant Han-lé), 'the great Monastery. s'Tag-stan-ras-ch'en built it, and of him there runs this tale.' Whereupon he told it: a fantastic piled narrative of bewitchment and miracles that set Shamlegh a-gasping. Turning west a little, he speered for the green hills of Kulu, and sought Kailung under the glaciers. 'For thither came I in the old, old days. From Leh I came, over the Baralachi.'

'Yes, yes; we know it,' said the far-faring people of Shamlegh.

'And I slept two nights with the priests of Kailung. These are the Hills of my delight! Shadows blessed above all other shadows! There my eyes opened on this world; there my eyes were opened to this world; there I found Enlightenment; and there I girt my loins for my Search. Out of the Hills I came – the high Hills and the strong winds. Oh, Just is the Wheel!' He blessed them in detail – the great glaciers, the naked rocks, the piled moraines and tumbled shale; dry upland, hidden salt-lake, age-old timber and fruitful water-shot valley one after the other, as a dying man blesses his folk; and Kim marvelled at his passion.

'Yes – yes. There is no place like our Hills,' said the people of Shamlegh. And they fell to wondering how a man could live in the hot terrible Plains where the cattle run as big as elephants, unfit to plough on a hillside; where village touches village, they had heard, for a hundred miles; where folk went about stealing in gangs, and what the robbers spared the Police carried utterly away.

So the still forenoon wore through, and at the end of it Kim's messenger dropped from the steep pasture as unbreathed as when she had set out.

'I sent a word to the *hakim*,' Kim explained, while she made reverence.

'He joined himself to the idolaters? Nay, I remember he did a healing upon one of them. He has acquired merit, though the healed employed his strength for evil. Just is the Wheel! What of the *hakim*?'

'I feared that thou hadst been bruised and – and I knew he was wise.' Kim took the waxed walnut-shell and read in English on the back of his note: *Your favour received. Cannot get away from present company at present, but shall take them into Simla. After which, hope to rejoin you. Inexpedient to follow angry gentlemen. Return by same road you came, and will overtake. Highly gratified about correspondence due to my forethought.* 'He says, Holy One, that he will escape from the idolaters, and will return to us. Shall we wait awhile at Shamlegh, then?'

The lama looked long and lovingly upon the hills and shook his head.

'That may not be, *chela*. From my bones outward I do desire it, but it is forbidden. I have seen the Cause of Things.'

'Why? When the Hills give thee back thy strength day by day? Remember we were weak and fainting down below there in the Doon.'

'I became strong to do evil and to forget. A brawler and a swashbuckler upon the hillsides was I.' Kim bit back a smile. 'Just and perfect is the Wheel, swerving not a hair. When I was a man – a long time ago – I did pilgrimage to Guru Ch'wan among the poplars' (he pointed Bhotanwards), 'where they keep the Sacred Horse.'

'Quiet, be quiet!' said Shamlegh, all arow. 'He speaks of Jam-lin-nin-k'or, the Horse That Can Go Round The World In a Day.'

'I speak to my *chela* only,' said the lama, in gentle reproof, and they scattered like frost on south eaves of a morning. 'I did not seek truth in those days, but the talk of doctrine. All illusion! I drank the beer and ate the bread of Guru Ch'wan. Next day one said: "We go out to fight Sangor Gutok down the valley to discover" (mark again how Lust is tied to Anger!) "which Abbot shall bear rule in the valley and take the profit of the prayers they print at Sangor Gutok." I went, and we fought a day.'

'But how, Holy One?'

'With our long pencases as I could have shown ... I say, we fought under the poplars, both Abbots and all the monks, and one laid open my forehead to the bone. See!' He tilted back his cap and showed a puckered silvery scar. 'Just and perfect is the Wheel! Yesterday the scar itched, and after fifty years I recalled how it was dealt and the face of him who dealt it; dwelling a little in illusion. Followed that which thou didst see – strife and stupidity. Just is the Wheel! The idolater's blow fell upon the scar. Then I was shaken in my soul: my soul was darkened, and the boat of my soul rocked upon the waters of illusion. Not till I came to Shamlegh could I meditate upon the Cause of Things, or trace the running grass-roots of Evil. I strove all the long night.'

'But, Holy One, thou art innocent of all evil. May I be thy sacrifice!'

Kim was genuinely distressed at the old man's sorrow, and Mahbub Ali's phrase slipped out unawares.

'In the dawn,' the lama went on more gravely, ready rosary clicking between the slow sentences, 'came enlightenment. It is here ... I am an old man ... hill-bred, hill-fed, never to sit down among my Hills. Three years I travelled through Hind, but – can earth be stronger than Mother Earth? My stupid body yearned to the Hills and the snows of the Hills, from below there. I said, and it is true, my Search is sure. So, at the Kulu woman's house I turned hillward, over-persuaded by myself. There is no blame to the *hakim*. He – following Desire – foretold that the Hills would make me strong. They strengthened me to do evil, to forget my Search. I delighted in life and the lust of life. I desired strong slopes to climb. I cast about to find them. I measured the strength of my body, which is evil, against the high Hills, I made a mock of thee when thy breath came short under Jamnotri. I jested when thou wouldst not face the snow of the pass.'

'But what harm? I *was* afraid. It was just. I am not a hillman; and I loved thee for thy new strength.'

'More than once I remember' – he rested his cheek dolefully on his hand – 'I sought thy praise and the *hakim*'s for the mere strength of my legs. Thus evil followed evil till the cup was full. Just is the Wheel! All Hind for three years did me all honour. From the Fountain of Wisdom in the Wonder House to' – he smiled – 'a little child playing by a big gun – the world prepared my road. And why?'

'Because we loved thee. It is only the fever of the blow. I myself am still sick and shaken.'

'No! It was because I was upon the Way – tuned as are *sinen* [cymbals] to the purpose of the Law. I departed from that ordinance. The tune was broken: followed the punishment.

In my own Hills, on the edge of my own country, in the very place of my evil desire, comes the buffet – here!' (He touched his brow.) 'As a novice is beaten when he misplaces the cups, so am I beaten, who was Abbot of Such-zen. No word, look you, but a blow, *chela*.'

'But the Sahibs did not know thee, Holy One?'

'We were well matched. Ignorance and Lust met Ignorance and Lust upon the road, and they begat Anger. The blow was a sign to me, who am no better than a strayed yak, that my place is not here. Who can read the Cause of an act is halfway to Freedom! "Back to the path," says the Blow. "The Hills are not for thee. Thou canst not choose Freedom and go in bondage to the delight of life."'

'Would we had never met that cursed Russian!'

'Our Lord Himself cannot make the Wheel swing backward. And for my merit that I had acquired I gain yet another sign.' He put his hand in his bosom, and drew forth the Wheel of Life. 'Look! I considered this after I had meditated. There remains untorn by the idolater no more than the breadth of my fingernail.'

'I see.'

'So much, then, is the span of my life in this body. I have served the Wheel all my days. Now the Wheel serves me. But for the merit I have acquired in guiding thee upon the Way, there would have been added to me yet another life ere I had found my River. Is it plain, *chela*?'

Kim stared at the brutally disfigured chart. From left to right diagonally the rent ran – from the Eleventh House where Desire gives birth to the Child (as it is drawn by Tibetans) across the human and animal worlds, to the Fifth House – the empty House of the Senses. The logic was unanswerable.

'Before our Lord won Enlightenment' – the lama folded all away with reverence – 'He was tempted. I too have been tempted, but it is finished. The Arrow fell in the Plains – not in the Hills. Therefore, what make we here?'

'Shall we at least wait for the *hakim*?'

'I know how long I shall live in this body. What can a *hakim* do?'

'But thou art all sick and shaken. Thou canst not walk.'

'How can I be sick if I see Freedom?' He rose unsteadily to his feet.

'Then I must get food from the village. Oh, the weary Road!' Kim felt that he too needed rest.

'That is lawful. Let us eat and go. The Arrow fell in the Plains ... but I yielded to Desire. Make ready, *chela*.'

Kim turned to the woman with the turquoise headgear who had been idly pitching pebbles over the cliff. She smiled very kindly.

'I found him like a strayed buffalo in a cornfield – the Babu; snorting and sneezing with cold. He was so hungry that he forgot his dignity and gave me sweet words. The Sahibs have nothing.' She flung out an empty palm. 'One is very sick about the stomach. Thy work?'

Kim nodded, with a bright eye.

'I spoke to the Bengali first – and to the people of a near-by village after. The Sahibs will be given food as they need it – nor will the people ask money. The plunder is already distributed. The Babu makes lying speeches to the Sahibs. Why does he not leave them?'

'Out of the greatness of his heart.'

''Was never a Bengali yet had one bigger than a dried walnut. But it is no matter ... Now as to walnuts. After service comes reward. I have said the village is thine.'

'It is my loss,' Kim began. 'Even now I had planned desirable things in my heart which' – there is no need to go through the compliments proper to these occasions. He sighed deeply ... 'But my master, led by a vision –'

'Huh! What can old eyes see except a full begging-bowl?'

'– turns from this village to the Plains again.'

'Bid him stay.'

Kim shook his head. 'I know my Holy One, and his rage if he be crossed,' he replied impressively. 'His curses shake the Hills.'

'Pity they did not save him from a broken head! I heard that thou wast the tiger-hearted one who smote the Sahib. Let him dream a little longer. Stay!'

'Hillwoman,' said Kim, with austerity that could not harden the outlines of his young oval face, 'these matters are too high for thee.'

'The Gods be good to us! Since when have men and women been other than men and women?'

'A priest is a priest. He says he will go upon this hour. I am his *chela*, and I go with him. We need food for the Road. He is an honoured guest in all the villages, but' – he broke into a pure boy's grin – 'the food here is good. Give me some.'

'What if I do not give it thee? I am the woman of this village.'

'Then I curse thee – a little – not greatly, but enough to remember.' He could not help smiling.

'Thou hast cursed me already by the down-dropped eyelash and the uplifted chin. Curses? What should I care for mere words?' She clenched her hands upon her bosom ... 'But I would not have thee to go in anger, thinking hardly of me – a gatherer of cow-dung and grass at Shamlegh, but still a woman of substance.'

'I think nothing,' said Kim, 'but that I am grieved to go, for I am very weary; and that we need food. Here is the bag.'

The woman snatched it angrily. 'I was foolish,' said she. 'Who is thy woman in the Plains? Fair or black? I was fair once. Laughest thou? Once, long ago, if thou canst believe, a Sahib looked on me with favour. Once, long ago, I wore European clothes at the Mission-house yonder.' She pointed towards Kotgarh. 'Once, long ago. I was Ker-lis-ti-an and spoke English – as the Sahibs speak it. Yes. My Sahib said he would return and wed me – yes, wed me. He went away – I had nursed him when he was sick – but he never returned. Then I saw that the Gods of the Kerlistians lied, and I went back to my own people ... I have never set eyes on a Sahib since. (Do not laugh at me. The fit is past, little priestling.) Thy face and thy walk and thy fashion of speech put me in mind of my Sahib, though thou art only a wandering mendicant to whom I give a dole. Curse me? Thou canst neither curse nor bless!' She set her hands on her hips and laughed bitterly. 'Thy Gods are lies; thy works are lies; thy words are lies. There are no Gods under all the Heavens. I know it ... But for awhile I thought it was my Sahib come back, and he was my God. Yes, once I made music on a *pianno* in the Mission-house at Kotgarh. Now I give alms to priests who are *heatthen*.' She wound up with the English word, and tied the mouth of the brimming bag.

'I wait for thee, *chela*,' said the lama, leaning against the door-post.

The woman swept the tall figure with her eyes. 'He walk! He cannot cover half a mile. Whither would old bones go?'

At this Kim, already perplexed by the lama's collapse and foreseeing the weight of the bag, fairly lost his temper. 'What is it to thee, woman of ill-omen, where he goes?'

'Nothing – but something to thee, priest with a Sahib's face. Wilt thou carry him on thy shoulders?'

'I go to the Plains. None must hinder my return. I have wrestled with my soul till I am strengthless. The stupid body is spent, and we are far from the Plains.'

'Behold!' she said simply, and drew aside to let Kim see his own utter helplessness. 'Curse me. Maybe it will give him strength. Make a charm! Call on thy great God. Thou art a priest.' She turned away.

The lama had squatted limply, still holding by the door-post. One cannot strike down an old man that he recovers again like a boy in the night. Weakness bowed him to the earth, but his eyes that hung on Kim were alive and imploring.

'It is all well,' said Kim. 'It is the thin air that weakens thee. In a little while we go! It is the mountain-sickness. I too am a little sick at stomach,' ... and he knelt and comforted with such poor words as came first to his lips. Then the woman returned, more erect than ever.

'Thy Gods useless, heh? Try mine. *I* am the Woman of

Shamlegh.' She hailed hoarsely, and there came out of a cow-pen her two husbands and three others with a *dooli*, the rude native litter of the Hills, that they use for carrying the sick and for visits of state. 'These cattle' – she did not condescend to look at them – 'are thine for so long as thou shalt need.'

'But we will not go Simla-way. We will not go near the Sahibs,' cried the first husband.

'They will not run away as the others did, nor will they steal baggage. Two I know for weaklings. Stand to the rear-pole, Sonoo and Taree.' They obeyed swiftly. 'Lower now, and lift in that holy man. I will see to the village and your virtuous wives till ye return.'

'When will that be?'

'Ask the priests. Do not pester me. Lay the food-bag at the foot, it balances better so.'

'Oh, Holy One, thy Hills are kinder than our Plains!' cried Kim, relieved, as the lama tottered to the litter. 'It is a very king's bed – a place of honour and ease. And we owe it to –'

'A woman of ill-omen. I need thy blessings as much as I do thy curses. It is *my* order and none of thine. Lift and away! Here! Hast thou money for the road?'

She beckoned Kim to her hut, and stooped above a battered English cash-box under her cot.

'I do not need anything,' said Kim, angered where he should have been grateful. 'I am already rudely loaded with favours.'

She looked up with a curious smile and laid a hand on his shoulder. 'At least, thank me. I am foul-faced and a hill-woman, but, as thy talk goes, I have acquired merit. Shall I show thee how the Sahibs render thanks?' and her hard eyes softened.

'I am but a wandering priest,' said Kim, his eyes lighting in answer. 'Thou needest neither my blessings nor my curses.'

'Nay. But for one little moment – thou canst overtake the *dooli* in ten strides – *if* thou wast a Sahib, shall I show thee what thou wouldst do?'

'How if I guess, though?' said Kim, and putting his arm

round her waist, he kissed her on the cheek, adding in English:

'Thank you verree much, my dear.'

Kissing is practically unknown among Asiatics, which may have been the reason that she leaned back with wide-open eyes and a face of panic.

'Next time,' Kim went on, 'you must not be so sure of your heathen priests. Now I say good-bye.' He held out his hand English-fashion. She took it mechanically. 'Good-bye, my dear.'

'Good-bye, and – and' – she was remembering her English words one by one – 'you will come back again? Good-bye, and – thee God bless you.'

Half an hour later, as the creaking litter jolted up the hill path that leads south-easterly from Shamlegh, Kim saw a tiny figure at the hut door waving a white rag.

'She has acquired merit beyond all others,' said the lama. 'For to set a man upon the way to Freedom is half as great as though she had herself found it.'

'Umm,' said Kim thoughtfully, considering the past. 'It may be that I have acquired merit also ... At least she did not treat me like a child.' He hitched the front of his robe, where lay the slab of documents and maps, re-stowed the precious food-bag at the lama's feet, laid his hand on the litter's edge, and buckled down to the slow pace of the grunting husbands.

'These also acquire merit,' said the lama after three miles.

'More than that, they shall be paid in silver,' quoth Kim. The Woman of Shamlegh had given it to him; and it was only fair, he argued, that her men should earn it back again.

Chapter 15

I'd not give room for an Emperor –
  I'd hold my road for a King.
To the Triple Crown I'd not bow down –
  But this is a different thing!
I'll not fight with the Powers of Air –
  Sentry, pass him through!
Drawbridge let fall – He's the Lord of us all –
  The Dreamer whose dream came true!
                    The Siege of the Fairies.

Two hundred miles north of Chini, on the blue shale of Ladakh, lies Yankling Sahib, the merry-minded man, spy-glassing wrathfully across the ridges for some sign of his pet tracker – a man from Ao-chung. But that renegade, with a new Männlicher rifle and two hundred cartridges, is elsewhere, shooting musk-deer for the market, and Yankling Sahib will learn next season how very ill he has been.

Up the valleys of Bushahr – the far-beholding eagles of the Himalayas swerve at his new blue-and-white gored umbrella – hurries a Bengali, once fat and well-looking, now lean and weather-worn. He has received the thanks of two foreigners of distinction, piloted not unskilfully to Mashobra tunnel, which leads to the great and gay capital of India. It was not his fault that, blanketed by wet mists, he conveyed them past the telegraph-station and European colony of Kotgarh. It was not his fault, but that of the Gods, of whom he discoursed so engagingly, that he led them into the borders of Nahan, where the Rahah of that State mistook them for deserting British soldiery. Hurree Babu explained the greatness and glory, in their own country, of his companions, till the drowsy kinglet smiled. He explained it to everyone who asked – many times – aloud – variously. He begged food, arranged accommodation, proved a skilful leech for an injury of the groin – such a blow as one may receive rolling down a rock-covered hillside in the dark – and in all things indispensable. The reason of his friendliness did him credit. With millions of fellow-serfs, he had learned to look upon Russia as the great deliverer from the North. He was a fearful man. He had been afraid that he could not save his illustrious employers from the anger of an excited peasantry. He himself would just as lief hit a holy man as not, but ... He was deeply grateful and sincerely rejoiced that he had done his 'little possible' towards bringing their venture to – barring the lost baggage – a successful issue, he had forgotten the blows; denied that any blows had been dealt that unseemly first night under the pines. He asked neither pension nor retaining fee, but, if they deemed him worthy, would they write him a testimonial? It might be useful to him later, if others, their friends, came over the Passes. He begged them to remember him in their future greatnesses, for he 'opined subtly' that he, even he, Mohendro Lal Dutt, MA of Calcutta, had 'done the State some service'.

They gave him a certificate praising his courtesy, helpfulness, and unerring skill as a guide. He put it in his waist-belt and sobbed with emotion; they had endured so many dangers together. He led them at high noon along crowded Simla Mall to the Alliance Bank of Simla, where they wished to establish their identity. Thence he vanished like a dawn-cloud on Jakko.

Behold him, too fine-drawn to sweat, too pressed to vaunt the drugs in his little brass-bound box, ascending Shamlegh slope, a just man made perfect. Watch him, all Babudom laid aside, smoking at noon on a cot, while a woman with turquoise-studded headgear points south-easterly across the bare grass. Litters, she says, do not travel as fast as single men, but his birds should now be in the Plains. The holy man would not stay though Lispeth pressed him. The Babu groans heavily, girds up his huge loins, and is off again. He does not care to travel after dusk; but his days' marches – there is none to enter them in a book – would astonish folk who mock at his race. Kindly villagers, remembering the Dacca drug-vendor of two months ago, give him shelter against evil spirits of the wood. He dreams of Bengali Gods, University textbooks of education, and the Royal Society, London, England. Next dawn the bobbing blue-and-white umbrella goes forward.

On the edge of the Doon, Mussoorie well behind them and the Plains spread out in golden dust before, rests a worn litter in which – all the Hills know it – lies a sick lama who seeks a River for his healing. Villages have almost come to blows over the honour of bearing it, for not only has the lama given them blessings, but his disciple good money – full one-third Sahibs' prices. Twelve miles a day has the *dooli* travelled, as the greasy, rubbed pole-ends show, and by roads that few Sahibs use. Over the Nilang Pass in storm when the driven snow-dust filled every fold of the impassive lama's drapery; between the black horns of Raieng where they heard the whistle of the wild goats through the clouds; pitching and strained on the shale below; hard-held between shoulder and clenched jaw when they rounded the hideous curves of the Cut Road under Bhagirati; swinging and creaking to the steady jog-trot of the descent into the Valley of the Waters; pressed along the steamy levels of that locked valley; up, up and out again, to meet the roaring gusts off Kedarnath; set down of mid-days in the dun gloom of kindly oak-forests; passed from village to village in dawn-chill, when even devotees may be forgiven for swearing at impatient holy men; or by torchlight, when the least fearful think of ghosts – the *dooli* has reached her last stage. The little hill-folk sweat in the modified heat of the lower Siwaliks, and gather round the priests for their blessing and their wage.

'Ye have acquired merit,' says the lama. 'Merit greater than your knowing. And ye will return to the Hills,' he sighs.

'Surely. The high Hills as soon as may be.' The bearer rubs his shoulder, drinks water, spits it out again, and readjusts his grass sandal. Kim – his face is drawn and tired – pays very small silver from his belt, heaves out the food-bag, crams an oilskin packet – they are holy writings – into his bosom, and helps the lama to his feet. The peace has come again into the old man's eyes, and he does not look for the hills to fall down and crush him as he did that terrible night when they were delayed by the flooded river.

The men pick up the *dooli* and swing out of sight between the scrub clumps.

The lama raises a hand toward the rampart of the Himalayas. 'Not with you, O blessed among all hills, fell the Arrow of Our Lord! And never shall I breathe your airs again!'

'But thou art ten times the stronger man in this good air,' says Kim, for to his wearied soul appeal the well-cropped, kindly Plains. 'Here, or hereabouts, fell the Arrow, yes. We will go very softly, perhaps, a *koss* a day, for the Search is sure. But the bag weighs heavy.'

'Ay, our Search is sure. I have come out of great temptation.'

It was never more than a couple of miles a day now, and Kim's shoulders bore all the weight of it – the burden of an old man, the burden of the heavy food-bag with the locked books, the load of the writings on his heart, and the details of the daily routine. He begged in the dawn, set blankets for the lama's meditation, held the weary head on his lap through the noonday heats, fanning away the flies till his wrists ached, begged again in the evenings, and rubbed the lama's feet, who rewarded him with promise of Freedom – today, tomorrow, or, at furthest, the next day.

'Never was such a *chela*. I doubt at times whether Ananda more faithfully nursed Our Lord. And thou art a Sahib? When I was a man – a long time ago – I forgot that. Now I look upon thee often, and every time I remember that thou art a Sahib. It is strange.'

'Thou hast said there is neither black nor white. Why plague me with this talk, Holy One? Let me rub the other foot. It vexes me. I am not a Sahib. I am thy *chela*, and my head is heavy on my shoulders.'

'Patience a little! We reach Freedom together. Then thou and I, upon the far bank of the River, will look back upon our lives as in the Hills we saw our days' marches laid out behind us. Perhaps I was once a Sahib.'

'Was never a Sahib like thee, I swear it.'

'I am certain the Keeper of the Images in the Wonder House was in past life a very wise Abbot. But even his spectacles do not make my eyes see. There fall shadows when I would look steadily. No matter – we know the tricks of the poor stupid carcass – shadow changing to another shadow. I am bound by the illusion of Time and Space. How far came we today in the flesh?'

'Perhaps half a *koss*.' (Three quarters of a mile, and it was a weary march.)

'Half a koss. Ha! I went ten thousand thousand in the spirit. How we are all lapped and swathed and swaddled in these senseless things.' He looked at his thin blue-veined hand that found the beads so heavy. '*Chela*, hast thou never a wish to leave me?'

Kim thought of the oilskin packet and the books in the food-bag. If someone duly authorized would only take delivery of them the Great Game might play itself for aught he then cared. He was tired and hot in his head, and a cough that came from the stomach worried him.

'No,' he said almost sternly. 'I am not a dog or a snake to bite when I have learned to love.'

'Thou art too tender towards me.'

'Not that either. I have moved in one matter without consulting thee. I have sent a message to the Kulu woman by that woman who gave us the goat's milk this morn, saying that thou wast a little feeble and wouldst need a litter. I beat myself in my mind that I did not do it when we entered the Doon. We stay in this place till the litter returns.'

'I am content. She is a woman with a heart of gold, as thou sayest, but a talker – something of a talker.'

'She will not weary thee. I have looked to that also. Holy One, my heart is very heavy for my many carelessnesses towards thee.' An hysterical catch rose in his throat. 'I have walked thee too far: I have not picked good food always for thee; I have not considered the heat; I have talked to people on the road and left thee alone . . . I have – I have . . . *Hai mai!* But I love thee . . . and it is all too late . . . I was a child . . . Oh, why was I not a man? . . .' Overborne by strain, fatigue, and the weight beyond his years, Kim broke down and sobbed at the lama's feet.

'What a to-do is here!' said the old man gently. 'Thou hast never stepped a hair's breadth from the Way of Obedience. Neglect *me*? Child, I have lived on thy strength as an old tree lives on the lime of a new wall. Day by day, since Shamlegh down, I have stolen strength from thee. *Therefore*, not through any sin of thine, art thou weakened. It is the Body – the silly, stupid Body – that speaks now. Not the assured Soul. Be comforted! Know at least the devils that thou fightest. They are earth-born – children of illusion. We will go to the woman from Kulu. She shall acquire merit in housing us, and specially in tending me. Thou shalt run free till strength returns. I had forgotten the stupid Body. If there be any blame, I bear it. But we are too close to the Gates of Deliverance to weigh blame. I could praise thee, but what need? In a little – in a very little – we shall sit beyond all needs.'

And so he petted and comforted Kim with wise saws and grave texts on that little-understood beast, our Body, who, being but a delusion, insists on posing as the Soul, to the darkening of the Way, and the immense multiplication of unnecessary devils.

'*Hai! hai!* Let us talk of the woman from Kulu. Think you she will ask another charm for her grandsons? When I was a young man, a very long time ago, I was plagued with these vapours – and some others – and I went to an Abbot – a very holy man and a seeker after truth, though then I knew it not. Sit up and listen, child of my soul! My tale was told. Said he to me, "*Chela*, know this. There are many lies in the world, and not a few liars, but there are no liars like our bodies, except it be the sensations of our bodies." Considering this I was comforted, and of his great favour he suffered me to drink tea in his presence. Suffer me now to drink tea, for I am thirsty.'

With a laugh across his tears, Kim kissed the lama's feet, and set about the tea-making.

'Thou leanest on me in the body, Holy One, but I lean on thee for some other things. Dost know it?'

'I have guessed maybe,' and the lama's eyes twinkled. 'We must change that.'

So, when with scufflings and scrapings and a hot air of importance, paddled up nothing less than the Sahiba's pet palanquin sent twenty miles, with that same grizzled old Oorya servant in charge, and when they reached the disorderly order of the long white rambling house behind Saharunpore, the lama took his own measures.

Said the Sahiba cheerily from an upper window, after compliments: 'What is the good of an old woman's advice to an old man? I told thee – I *told* thee, Holy One, to keep an eye upon the *chela*. How didst thou do it? Never answer me! *I* know. He has been running among the women. Look at his eyes – hollow and sunk – and the Betraying Line from the nose down! He has been sifted out! Fie! Fie! And a priest, too!'

Kim looked up, over-weary to smile, shaking his head in denial.

'Do not jest,' said the lama. 'That time is done. We are here upon great matters. A sickness of soul took me in the Hills, and him a sickness of the body. Since then I have lived upon his strength – eating him.'

'Children together – young and old,' she sniffed, but forbore to make any new jokes. 'May this present hospitality restore ye! Hold awhile and I will come to gossip of the high good Hills.' At evening time – her son-in-law was returned, so she did not need to go on inspection round the farm – she won to the meat of the matter, explained low-voicedly by the lama. The two old heads nodded wisely together. Kim had reeled to a room with a cot in it, and was dozing soddenly. The lama had forbidden him to set blankets or get food.

'I know – I know. Who but I?' she cackled. 'We who go down to the burning-ghats clutch at the hands of those coming up from the River of Life with full water-jars – yes, brimming water-jars. I did the boy wrong. He lent thee his strength? It is true that the old eat the young daily. Stands now we must restore him.'

'Thou hast many times acquired merit –'

'*My* merit. What is it? Old bag of bones making curries for men who do not ask "Who cooked this?" Now if it were stored up for my grandson –'

'He that had the belly-pain?'

'To think the Holy One remembers *that*! I must tell his mother. It is most singular honour! "He that had the belly-pain" – straightway the Holy One remembered. She will be proud.'

'My *chela* is to me as is a son to the unenlightened.'

'Say grandson, rather. Mothers have not the wisdom of our years. If a child cries they say the heavens are falling. Now a grandmother is far enough separated from the pain of bearing and the pleasure of giving the breast to consider whether a cry is wickedness pure or the wind. And since thou speakest once again of wind, when last the Holy One was here, maybe I offended in pressing for charms.'

'Sister,' said the lama, using that form of address a Buddhist monk may sometimes employ towards a nun, 'if charms comfort thee –'

'They are better than ten thousand doctors.'

'I say, if they comfort thee, I who was Abbot of Such-zen, will make as many as thou mayest desire. I have never seen thy face –'

'*That* even the monkeys who steal our loquats count for a gain. Hee! hee!'

'But as he who sleeps there said,' – he nodded at the shut door of the guest-chamber across the forecourt – 'thou hast a heart of gold ... And he is in the spirit my very "grandson" to me.'

'Good! I am the Holy One's cow.' This was pure

Hinduism, but the lama never heeded. 'I am old. I have borne sons in the body. Oh, once I could please men! Now I can cure them.' He heard her armlets tinkle as though she bared arms for action. 'I will take over the boy and dose him, and stuff him, and make him all whole. *Hai! hai!* We old people know something yet.'

Wherefore when Kim, aching in every bone, opened his eyes, and would go to the cook-house to get his master's food, he found strong coercion about him, and a veiled old figure at the door, flanked by the grizzled manservant, who told him very precisely the things that he was on no account to do.

'Thou must have? Thou shalt have nothing. What? A locked box in which to keep holy books? Oh, that is another matter. Heavens forbid I should come between a priest and his prayers! It shall be brought, and thou shalt keep the key.'

They pushed the coffer under his cot, and Kim shut away Mahbub's pistol, the oilskin packet of letters, and the locked books and diaries, with a groan of relief. For some absurd reason their weight on his shoulders was nothing to their weight on his poor mind. His neck ached under it of nights.

'Thine is a sickness uncommon in youth these days: since young folk have given up tending their betters. The remedy is sleep, and certain drugs,' said the Sahiba; and he was glad to give himself up to the blankness that half menaced and half soothed him.

She brewed drinks, in some mysterious Asiatic equivalent to the still-room -- drenches that smelt pestilently and tasted worse. She stood over Kim till they went down, and inquired exhaustively after they had come up. She laid a taboo upon the forecourt, and enforced it by means of an armed man. It is true he was seventy odd, that his scabbarded sword ceased at the hilt; but he represented the authority of the Sahiba, and loaded wains, chattering servants, calves, dogs, hens, and the like, fetched a wide compass by those parts. Best of all, when the body was cleared, she cut out from the mass of poor relations that crowded the back of the buildings -- household dogs, we name them -- a cousin's widow, skilled in what

Europeans, who know nothing about it, call massage. And the two of them, laying him east and west, that the mysterious earth-currents which thrill the clay of our bodies might help and not hinder, took him to pieces all one long afternoon – bone by bone, muscle by muscle, ligament by ligament, and lastly, nerve by nerve. Kneaded to irresponsible pulp, half hypnotized by the perpetual flick and readjustment of the uneasy *chudders* that veiled their eyes, Kim slid ten thousand miles into slumber – thirty-six hours of it – sleep that soaked like rain after drought.

Then she fed him, and the house spun to her clamour. She caused fowls to be slain; she sent for vegetables, and the sober, slow-thinking gardener, nigh as old as she, sweated for it; she took spices, and milk, and onion, with little fish from the brooks – anon limes for sherbets, fat quails from the pits, then chicken-livers upon a skewer, with sliced ginger between.

'I have seen something of this world,' she said over the crowded trays, 'and there are but two sorts of women in it – those who take the strength out of a man and those who put it back. Once I was that one, and now I am this. Nay – do not play the priestling with me. Mine was but a jest. If it does not hold good now, it will when thou takest the road again. Cousin,' – this to the poor relation, never wearied of extolling her patroness's charity – 'he is getting a bloom on the skin of a new-curried horse. Our work is like polishing jewels to be thrown to a dance-girl – eh?'

Kim sat up and smiled. The terrible weakness had dropped from him like an old shoe. His tongue itched for free speech again, and but a week back the lightest word clogged it like ashes. The pain in his neck (he must have caught it from the lama) had gone with the heavy dengue-aches and the evil taste in the mouth. The two old women, a little, but not much, more careful about their veils now, clucked as merrily as the hens that had entered pecking through the open door.

'Where is my Holy One?' he demanded.

'Hear him! Thy Holy One is well,' she snapped viciously. 'Though that is none of his merit. Knew I a charm to make him wise, I'd sell my jewels and buy it. To refuse good food that I cooked myself – and go roving into the fields for two nights on an empty belly – and to tumble into a brook at the end of it – call you *that* holiness? Then, when he has nearly broken what thou hast left of my heart with anxiety, he tells me that he has acquired merit. Oh, how like are all men! No, that was not it – he tells me that he is freed from all sin. *I* could have told him that before he wetted himself all over. He is well now – this happened a week ago – but burn me such holiness! A babe of three would do better. Do not fret thyself for the Holy One. He keeps both eyes on thee when he is not wading our brooks.'

'I do not remember to have seen him. I remember that the days and nights passed like bars of white and black, opening and shutting. I was not sick: I was but tired.'

'A lethargy that comes by right some few score years later. But it is done now.'

'Maharanee,' Kim began, but led by the look in her eye, changed it to the title of plain love – 'Mother, I owe my life to thee. How shall I make thanks? Ten thousand blessings upon thy house and –'

'The house be unblessed!' (It is impossible to give exactly the old lady's word.) 'Thank the Gods as a priest if thou wilt, but thank me, if thou carest, as a son. Heavens above! Have I shifted thee and lifted thee and slapped and twisted thy ten toes to find texts flung at my head? Somewhere a mother must have borne thee to break her heart. What used thou to her – son?'

'I had no mother, my mother,' said Kim. 'She died, they tell me, when I was young.'

'*Hai mai!* Then none can say I have robbed her of any right if – when thou takest the road again and this house is but one of a thousand used for shelter and forgotten, after an easy-flung blessing. No matter. I need no blessings, but – but –'

She stamped her foot at the poor relation. 'Take up the trays to the house. What is the good of stale food in the room, O woman of ill-omen?'

'I ha – have borne a son in my time too, but he died,' whimpered the bowed sister-figure behind the *chudder*. 'Thou knowest he died! I only waited for the order to take away the tray.'

'It is I that am the woman of ill-omen,' cried the old lady penitently. 'We that go down to the *chattris* [the big umbrellas above the burning-ghats where the priests take their last dues] clutch hard at the bearers of the *chattis* [water-jars – young folk full of the pride of life, she meant; but the pun is clumsy]. When one cannot dance in the festival one must e'en look out of the window, and grandmothering takes all a woman's time. Thy master gives me all the charms I now desire for my daughter's eldest, by reason – is it? – that he is wholly free from sin. The *hakim* is brought very low these days. He goes about poisoning my servants for lack of their betters.'

'What *hakim*, mother?'

'That very Dacca man who gave me the pill which rent me in three pieces. He cast up like a strayed camel a week ago, vowing that he and thou had been blood-brothers together up Kulu-way, and feigning great anxiety for thy health. He was very thin and hungry, so I gave orders to have him stuffed too – him and his anxiety!'

'I would see him if he is here.'

'He eats five times a day, and lances boils for my hinds to save himself from an apoplexy. He is so full of anxiety for thy health that he sticks to the cook-house door and stays himself with scraps. He will keep. We shall never get rid of him.'

'Send him here, mother' – the twinkle returned to Kim's eye for a flash – 'and I will try.'

'I'll send him, but to chase him off is an ill turn. At least he had the sense to fish the Holy One out of the brook; thus, as the Holy One did *not* say, acquiring merit.'

'He is a very wise *hakim*. Send him, mother.'

'Priest praising priest? A miracle! If he is any friend of

thine (ye squabbled at your last meeting) I'll hale him here
with horse-ropes and – and give him a caste-dinner afterwards, my son ... Get up and see the world! This lying abed
is the mother of seventy devils ... my son! my son!'

She trotted forth to raise a typhoon off the cook-house, and
almost on her shadow rolled in the Babu, robed as to the
shoulders like a Roman emperor, jowled like Titus, bare-
headed, with new patent-leather shoes, in highest condition of
fat, exuding joy and salutations.

'By Jove, Mister O'Hara, but I *am* jolly-glad to see you. I
will kindly shut the door. It is a pity you are sick. Are you
very sick?'

'The papers – the papers from the *kilta*. The maps and the
murasla!' He held out the key impatiently; for the present
need on his soul was to get rid of the loot.

'You are quite right. That is correct Departmental view to
take. You have got everything?'

'All that was hand-written in the *kilta* I took. The rest I
threw down the hill.' He could hear the key's grate in the lock,
the sticky pull of the slow-rending oilskin, and a quick
shuffling of papers. He had been annoyed out of all reason by
the knowledge that they lay below him through the sick idle
days – a burden incommunicable. For that reason the blood
tingled through his body, when Hurree, skipping elephan-
tinely, shook hands again.

'This is fine! This is finest! Mister O'Hara! You have – ha!
ha! swiped the whole bag of tricks – locks, stocks, and barrels.
They told me it was eight months' work gone up the spouts!
By Jove, how they beat me! ... Look, here is the letter from
Hilás!' He intoned a line or two of Court Persian, which is the
language of authorized and unauthorized diplomacy. 'Mister
Rajah Sahib has just about put his foot in the holes. He will
have to explain offeecially how the deuce-an'-all he is writing
love-letters to the Czar. And they are very clever maps ... and
there is three or four Prime Ministers of these parts impli-
cated by the correspondence. By Gad, sar! The British
Government will change the succession in Hilás and Bunár,

and nominate new heirs to the throne. "Trea-son most base"
... but you do not understand? Eh?'

'Are they in thy hands?' said Kim. It was all he cared for.

'Just you jolly-well bet yourself they are.' He stowed the
entire trove about his body, as only Orientals can. 'They are
going up to the office, too. The old lady thinks I am
permanent fixture here, but I shall go away with these straight
off – immediately. Mr Lurgan will be proud man. You are
offeecially subordinate to me, but I shall embody your name
in my verbal report. It is a pity we are not allowed written
reports. We Bengalis excel in thee exact science.' He tossed
back the key and showed the box empty.

'Good. That is good. I was very tired. My Holy One was
sick, too. And did he fall into –'

'Oah yess. I am his good friend, I tell you. He was
behaving very strange when I came down after you, and I
thought perhaps he might have the papers. I followed him on
his meditations, and to discuss ethnological points also. You
see, I am verree small person here nowadays, in comparison
with all his charms. By Jove, O'Hara, do you know, he is
afflicted with infirmity of fits. Yess, I tell you. Cataleptic, too,
if not also epileptic. I found him in such a state under a tree *in
articulo mortem*, and he jumped up and walked into a brook
and he was nearly drowned but for me. I pulled him out.'

'Because I was not there!' said Kim. 'He might have died.'

'Yes, he might have died, but he is dry now, and asserts he
has undergone transfiguration.' The Babu tapped his forehead knowingly. 'I took notes of his statements for Royal
Society – *in posse*. You must make haste and be quite well and
come back to Simla, and I will tell you all my tale at Lurgan's.
It was splendid. The bottoms of their trousers were *quite* torn,
and old Nahan Rajah, he thought they were European
soldiers deserting.'

'Oh, the Russians? How long were they with thee?'

'One was a Frenchman. Oh, days and days and days! Now
all the hill-people believe all Russians are all beggars. By Jove!
they had not one dam'-thing that I did not get them. And I

told the common people – oah, *such* tales and anecdotes! I will tell you at old Lurgan's when you come up. We will have – ah – a night out! It is feather in both our caps! Yess, and they gave me a certificate. That is creaming joke. You should have seen them at the Alliance Bank identifying themselves! And thank Almighty God you got their papers so well! You do not laugh verree much, but you shall laugh when you are well. Now I will go straight to the railway and get out. You shall have all sorts of credits for your game. When do you come along? We are very proud of you though you gave us great frights. And especially Mahbub.'

'Ay, Mahbub. And where is he?'

'Selling horses in this vi–cinity, of course.'

'Here! Why? Speak slowly. There is a thickness in my head still.'

The Babu looked shyly down his nose. 'Well, you see, I am fearful man, and I do not like responsibility. You were sick, you see, and I did not know where deuce-an'-all the papers were, and if so, how many. So when I had come down here I slipped in private wire to Mahbub – he was at Meerut for races – and I tell him how case stands. He comes up with his men and he consorts with the lama, and then he calls me a fool, and is very rude –'

'But wherefore – wherefore?'

'That is what *I* ask. I only suggest that if anyone steals the papers I should like some good strong, brave men to rob them back again. You see, they are vitally important, and Mahbub Ali he did not know where you were.'

'Mahbub Ali to rob the Sahiba's house? Thou art mad, Babu,' said Kim with indignation.

'I wanted the papers. Suppose she had stole them? It was only practical suggestion, *I* think. You are not pleased, eh?'

A native proverb – unquotable – showed the blackness of Kim's disapproval.

'Well,' – Hurree shrugged his shoulders – 'there is no accounting for thee taste. Mahbub was angry too. He has sold horses all about here, and he says old lady is *pukka* [thorough] old lady and would not condescend to such ungentlemanly things. *I* do not care. I have got the papers, and I was very glad of moral support from Mahbub. I tell you, I am fearful man, but, somehow or other, the more fearful I am the more dam'-tight places I get into. So I was glad you came with me to Chini, and I am glad Mahbub was close by. The old lady she is sometimes very rude to me and my beautiful pills.'

'Allah be merciful!' said Kim on his elbow, rejoicing. 'What a beast of wonder is a Babu! And that man walked alone – if he did walk – with robbed and angry foreigners!'

'Oah, thatt was nothing, after they had done beating me; but if I lost the papers it was pretty-jolly serious. Mahbub he nearly beat me too, and he went and consorted with the lama no end. I shall stick to ethnological investigations hencefor-wards. Now good-bye, Mister O'Hara. I can catch 4.25 p.m. to Umballa if I am quick. It will be good times when we all tell thee tale up at Mr Lurgan's. I shall report you offeecially better. Good-bye, my dear fallow, and when next you are under thee emotions please do not use the Mohammedan terms with the Tibetan dress.'

He shook hands twice – a Babu to his boot-heels – and opened the door. With the fall of the sunlight upon his still triumphant face he returned to the humble Dacca quack.

'He robbed them,' thought Kim, forgetting his own share in the game. 'He tricked them. He lied to them like a Bengali. They give him a *chit* [a testimonial]. He makes them a mock at the risk of his life – *I* never would have gone down to them after the pistol-shots – and then he says he is a fearful man ... And he is a fearful man. I must get into the world again.'

At first his legs bent like bad pipe-stems, and the flood and rush of the sunlit air dazzled him. He squatted by the white wall, the mind rummaging among the incidents of the long *dooli* journey, the lama's weaknesses, and, now that the stimulus of talk was removed, his own self-pity, of which, like the sick, he had great store. The unnerved brain edged away from all the outside, as a raw horse, once rowelled, sidles from the spur. It was enough, amply enough, that the spoil of the *kilta* was away – off his hands – out of his possession. He tried to think of the lama – to wonder why he had tumbled into a brook – but the bigness of the world, seen between the forecourt gates, swept linked thought aside. Then he looked upon the trees and the broad fields, with the thatched huts hidden among crops – looked with strange eyes unable to take up the size and proportion and use of things – stared for a still half-hour. All that while he felt, though he could not put it into words, that his soul was out of gear with its surroundings – a cog-wheel unconnected with any machinery, just like the idle cog-wheel of a cheap Beheea sugar-crusher laid by in a corner. The breezes fanned over him, the parrots shrieked at him, the noises of the populated house behind – squabbles, orders, and reproofs – hit on dead ears.

'I am Kim. I am Kim. And what is Kim?' His soul repeated it again and again.

He did not want to cry – had never felt less like crying in his life – but of a sudden easy, stupid tears trickled down his nose, and with an almost audible click he felt the wheels of his being lock up anew on the world without. Things that rode meaningless on the eyeball an instant before slid into proper proportion. Roads were meant to be walked upon, houses to be lived in, cattle to be driven, fields to be tilled, and men and women to be talked to. They were all real and true – solidly planted upon the feet – perfectly comprehensible – clay of his clay, neither more nor less. He shook himself like a dog with a flea in his ear, and rambled out of the gate. Said the Sahiba, to whom watchful eyes reported this move: 'Let him go. I have done my share. Mother Earth must do the rest. When the Holy One comes back from meditation, tell him.'

There stood an empty bullock-cart on a little knoll half a mile away, with a young banyan tree behind – a look-out, as it were, above some new-ploughed levels; and his eyelids, bathed in soft air, grew heavy as he neared it. The ground was good clean dust – no new herbage that, living, is half-way to death already, but the hopeful dust that holds the seeds of all life. He felt it between his toes, patted it with his palms, and joint by joint, sighing luxuriously, laid him down full length along in the shadow of the wooden-pinned cart. And Mother Earth was as faithful as the Sahiba. She breathed through him to restore the poise he had lost lying so long on a cot cut off from her good currents. His head lay powerless upon her breast, and his opened hands surrendered to her strength. The many-rooted tree above him, and even the dead man-handled wood beside, knew what he sought, as he himself did not know. Hour upon hour he lay deeper than sleep.

Towards evening, when the dust of returning kine made all the horizons smoke, came the lama and Mahbub Ali, both afoot, walking cautiously, for the house had told them where he had gone.

'Allah! What a fool's trick to play in open country!' muttered the horse-dealer. 'He could be shot a hundred times – but this is not the Border.'

'And,' said the lama, repeating a many-times-told tale, 'never was such a *chela*. Temperate, kindly, wise, of ungrudging disposition, a merry heart upon the road, never forgetting, learned, truthful, courteous. Great is his reward!'

'I know the boy – as I have said.'

'And he was all those things?'

'Some of them – but I have not yet found a Red Hat's charm for making him overly truthful. He has certainly been well nursed.'

'The Sahiba is a heart of gold,' said the lama earnestly. 'She looks upon him as her son.'

'Hmph! Half Hind seems that way disposed. I only wished to see that the boy had come to no harm and was a free agent. As thou knowest, he and I were old friends in the first days of your pilgrimage together.'

'That is a bond between us.' The lama sat down. 'We are at the end of the pilgrimage.'

'No thanks to thee thine was not cut off for good and all a week back. I heard what the Sahiba said to thee when we bore thee up on the cot.' Mahbub laughed, and tugged his newly dyed beard.

'I was meditating upon other matters that tide. It was the *hakim* from Dacca broke my meditations.'

'Otherwise' – this was in Pushtu for decency's sake – 'thou wouldst have ended thy meditations upon the sultry side of Hell – being an unbeliever and an idolater for all thy child's simplicity. But now, Red Hat, what is to be done?'

'This very night,' – the words came slowly, vibrating with triumph – 'this very night he will be as free as I am from all taint of sin – assured as I am, when he quits this body, of Freedom from the Wheel of Things. I have a sign' – he laid his hand above the torn chart in his bosom – 'that my time is short; but I shall have safeguarded him throughout the years. Remember, I have reached Knowledge, as I told thee only three nights back.'

'It must be true, as the Tirah priest said when I stole his cousin's wife, that I am a *Sufi* [a free-thinker]; for here I sit,' said Mahbub to himself, 'drinking in blasphemy unthinkable ... I remember the tale. On that, then, he goes to *Jannatu l' Adn* [the Gardens of Eden]. But how? Wilt thou slay him or drown him in that wonderful river from which the Babu dragged thee?'

'I was dragged from no river,' said the lama simply. 'Thou hast forgotten what befell. I found it by Knowledge.'

'Oh, ay. True,' stammered Mahbub, divided between high indignation and enormous mirth. 'I had forgotten the exact run of what happened. Thou didst find it knowingly.'

'And to say that I would take life is – not a sin, but a madness simple. My *chela* aided me to the River. It is his right to be cleansed from sin – with me.'

'Ay, he needs cleansing. But afterwards, old man – afterwards?'

'What matter under all the Heavens? He is sure of Nibban – enlightened – as I am.'

'Well said. I had a fear he might mount Mohammed's Horse and fly away.'

'Nay – he must go forth as a teacher.'

'Aha! Now I see! That is the right gait for the colt.

Certainly he must go forth as a teacher. He is somewhat urgently needed as a scribe by the State, for instance.'

'To that end he was prepared. I acquired merit in that I gave alms for his sake. A good deed does not die. He aided me in my Search. I aided him in his. Just is the Wheel, O horse-seller from the North. Let him be a teacher; let him be a scribe – what matter? He will have attained Freedom at the end. The rest is illusion.'

'What matter? When I must have him with me beyond Balkh in six months! I come up with ten lame horses and three strong-backed men – thanks to that chicken of a Babu – to break a sick boy by force out of an old trot's house. It seems that I stand by while a young Sahib is hoisted into Allah knows what of an idolater's Heaven by means of old Red Hat. And I am reckoned something of a player of the Game myself! But the madman is fond of the boy; and I must be very reasonably mad too.'

'What is the prayer?' said the lama, as the rough Pushtu rumbled into the red beard.

'No matter at all; but now I understand that the boy, sure of Paradise, can yet enter Government service, my mind is easier. I must get to my horses. It grows dark. Do not wake him. I have no wish to hear him call thee master.'

'But he *is* my disciple. What else?'

'He has told me.' Mahbub choked down his touch of spleen and rose laughing. 'I am not altogether of thy faith, Red Hat – if so small a matter concern thee.'

'It is nothing,' said the lama.

'I thought not. Therefore it will not move thee, sinless, new-washed and three parts drowned to boot, when I call thee a good man – a very good man. We have talked together some four or five evenings now, and for all I am a horse-coper I can still, as the saying is, see holiness beyond the legs of a horse. Yea, can see, too, how our Friend of all the World put his hand in thine at the first. Use him well, and suffer him to return to the world as a teacher, when thou hast – bathed his legs, if that be the proper medicine for the colt.'

'Why not follow the Way thyself, and so accompany the boy?'

Mahbub stared stupefied at the magnificent insolence of the demand, which across the Border he would have paid with more than a blow. Then the humour of it touched his worldly soul.

'Softly – softly – one foot at a time, as the lame gelding went over the Umballa jumps. I may come to Paradise later – I have workings that way – great motions – and I owe them to thy simplicity. Thou hast never lied?'

'What need?'

'O Allah, hear him! "What need" in this Thy world! Nor ever harmed a man?'

'Once – with a pencase – before I was wise.'

'So? I think the better of thee. Thy teachings are good. Thou hast turned one man that I know from the path of strife.' He laughed immensely. 'He came here open-minded to commit a *dacoity* [a house-robbery with violence]. Yes, to cut, rob, kill, and carry off what he desired.'

'A great foolishness!'

'Oh! black shame too. So he thought after he had seen thee – and a few others, male and female. So he abandoned it; and now he goes to beat a big fat Babu man.'

'I do not understand.'

'Allah forbid it! Some men are strong in knowledge, Red Hat. Thy strength is stronger still. Keep it – I think thou wilt. If the boy be not a good servant, pull his ears off.'

With a hitch of his broad Bokhariot belt the Pathan swaggered off into the gloaming, and the lama came down from his clouds so far as to look at the broad back.

'That person lacks courtesy, and is deceived by the shadow of appearances. But he spoke well of my *chela*, who now enters upon his reward. Let me make the prayer! ... Wake, O fortunate above all born of women. Wake! It is found!'

Kim came up from those deep wells, and the lama attended his yawning pleasure; duly snapping fingers to head off evil spirits.

'I have slept a hundred years. Where –? Holy One, hast *thou* been here long? I went out to look for thee, but' – he laughed drowsily – 'I slept by the way. I am all well now. Hast thou eaten? Let us go to the house. It is many days since I tended thee. And the Sahiba fed thee well? Who shampooed thy legs? What of the weaknesses – the belly and the neck, and the beating in the ears?'

'Gone – all gone. Dost thou not know?'

'I know nothing, but that I have not seen thee in a monkey's age. Know what?'

'Strange the knowledge did not reach out to thee, when all my thoughts were theeward.'

'I cannot see the face, but the voice is like a gong. Has the Sahiba made a young man of thee by her cookery?'

He peered at the cross-legged figure, outlined jet-black against the lemon-coloured drift of light. So does the stone Bodhisat sit who looks down upon the patent self-registering turnstiles of the Lahore Museum.

The lama held his peace. Except for the click of the rosary and a faint *clop-clop* of Mahbub's retreating feet, the soft, smoky silence of evening in India wrapped them close.

'Hear me! I bring news.'

'But let us –'

Out shot the long yellow hand compelling silence. Kim tucked his feet under his robe-edge obediently.

'Hear me! I bring news! The Search is finished. Comes now the Reward ... Thus. When we were among the Hills, I lived on thy strength till the young branch bowed and nigh broke. When we came out of the Hills, I was troubled for thee and for other matters which I held in my heart. The boat of my soul lacked direction; I could not see into the Cause of Things. So I gave thee over to the virtuous woman altogether. I took no food. I drank no water. Still I saw not the Way. They pressed food upon me and cried at my shut door. So I removed myself to a hollow under a tree. I took no food. I took no water. I sat in meditation two days and two nights, abstracting my mind; inbreathing and outbreathing in the required manner . . . Upon the second night – so great was my reward – the wise Soul loosed itself from the silly Body and went free. This I have never before attained, though I have stood on the threshold of it. Consider, for it is a marvel!'

'A marvel indeed. Two days and two nights without food! Where was the Sahiba?' said Kim under his breath.

'Yea, my Soul went free, and, wheeling like an eagle, saw indeed that there was no Teshoo Lama nor any other soul. As a drop draws to water, so my Soul drew near to the Great Soul which is beyond all things. At that point, exalted in contemplation, I saw all Hind, from Ceylon in the sea to the Hills, and my own Painted Rocks at Such-zen; I saw every camp and village, to the least, where we have ever rested. I saw them at one time and in one place; for they were within the Soul. By this I knew the Soul had passed beyond the illusion of Time and Space and of Things. By this I knew that I was free. I saw thee lying in thy cot, and I saw thee falling downhill under the idolater – at one time, in one place, in my Soul, which, as I say, had touched the Great Soul. Also I saw the stupid body of Teshoo Lama lying down, and the *hakim* from Dacca kneeled beside, shouting in its ear. Then my Soul was all alone, and I saw nothing, for I was all things, having reached the Great Soul. And I meditated a thousand thousand years, passionless, well aware of the Causes of all Things. Then a voice cried: "What shall come to the boy if thou art dead?" and I was shaken back and forth in myself with pity for thee; and I said: "I will return to my *chela*, lest he miss the Way." Upon this my Soul, which is the Soul of Teshoo Lama, withdrew itself from the Great Soul with strivings and yearnings and retchings and agonies not to be told. As the egg from the fish, as the fish from the water, as the water from the cloud, as the cloud from the thick air, so put forth, so leaped out, so drew away, so fumed up the Soul of Teshoo Lama from the Great Soul. Then a voice cried: "The River! Take heed to the River!" and I looked down upon all the world, which was as I had seen it before – one in time, one in place – and I saw plainly the River of the Arrow at my feet. At that hour my Soul was hampered by some evil or other whereof I was not wholly cleansed, and it lay upon my arms and coiled round my waist; but I put it aside, and I cast forth as an eagle in my flight for the very place of the River. I pushed aside world upon world for thy sake. I saw the River below me – the River of the Arrow – and, descending, the waters of it closed over me; and behold I was again in the body of Teshoo Lama, but free from sin, and the *hakim* from Dacca bore up my head in the waters of the River. It is here! It is behind the mango-tope here – even here!'

'*Allah kerim!* Oh, well that the Babu was by! Wast thou very wet?'

'Why should I regard? I remember the *hakim* was concerned for the body of Teshoo Lama. He haled it out of the holy water in his hands, and there came afterwards thy horse-seller from the North with a cot and men, and they put the body on the cot and bore it up to the Sahiba's house.'

'What said the Sahiba?'

'I was meditating in that body, and did not hear. So thus the Search is ended. For the merit that I have acquired, the River of the Arrow is here. It broke forth at our feet, as I have said. I have found it. Son of my Soul, I have wrenched my Soul back from the Threshold of Freedom to free thee from all sin – as I am free, and sinless! Just is the Wheel! Certain is our deliverance! Come!'

He crossed his hands on his lap and smiled, as a man may who has won salvation for himself and his beloved.

TITLES IN EVERYMAN'S LIBRARY

This book is set in EHRHARDT. The precise origin
of the typeface is unclear. Most of the founts were
probably cut by the Hungarian punch-cutter
Nicholas Kis for the Ehrhardt foundry
in Leipzig, where they were left
for sale in 1689. In 1938 the
Monotype foundry pro-
duced the modern
version.